She could not hunt and dared not sleep. A raw wind blew from the north. It dusted the grass with frost and snow. Red-eyed and shivering, Cat came to bay far downstream. She loosened her wet hair and slipped into a death-trance as the dawn light touched her back.

Wild creatures did not bargain with death. When the now was over, they simply stopped. The tension of the long chase drained down Cat's spine. She was at peace, waiting for teeth and claws she would not feel. She stopped shivering. Her hair dried into a brilliant red curtain.

Sunlight fell directly on Cat's face. The bright light made her eyes water. She closed her eyes because she could no longer keep them open.

It will be over soon, Cat thought . . .

Other Elfquest titles
published by Tor Books

ELFQUEST
Against the Wind

The Blood of Ten Chiefs Vol. 4

Edited by
Richard Pini

TOR
fantasy

A TOM DOHERTY ASSOCIATES BOOK
NEW YORK

AGAINST THE WIND

Copyright © 1990 by WaRP Graphics, Inc.

Elfquest ® is a registered trademark of WaRP Graphics, Inc.

A Tor Book
Published by Tom Doherty Associates, Inc.
175 Fifth Avenue
New York, N.Y. 10010

Tor ® is a registered trademark of Tom Doherty Associates, Inc.

Cover art by Wendy Pini

ISBN: 0-812-52274-5

First edition: October 1990
First mass market printing: October 1992

Printed in the United States of America

0 9 8 7 6 5 4 3 2 1

To Murrel and Seilein

ACKNOWLEDGMENTS

CONTENTS

Timmain —┬— true wolf

    TIMMORN —┬— Valloa / Murrel

        RAHNEE —┬— Zarhan Fastfire

          Prunepit / PREY-PACER

Wreath —┬— PREY-PACER —┬— Softfoot

   SKYFIRE   Swift-Spear / TWO-SPEAR

SKYFIRE —┬— Dreamsinger

   FREEFOOT —┬— Starflower

      TANNER —┬— Stormlight

        GOODTREE —┬— Lionleaper

          MANTRICKER

MANTRICKER —┬— THORNFLOWER

   BEARCLAW —┬— Joyleaf

      CUTTER, Blood of Ten Chiefs

Prologue

by Richard Pini

The young chief rose to complete the tale that others had begun earlier in the howl. As he did, the tribe's storyteller leaned forward just a bit more, to make certain he did not miss a single word. Some of the events he knew because he'd been there when they'd happened, but there were other things he'd not witnessed. Anyone paying particular attention to him would not have thought he carried within his mind—and his love of dreamberries—a wealth of stories and fragments of stories that had been passed on to him. Truth to tell, he did not himself fully realize the legacy he guarded—no one in the tribe did, yet—but it was there. Someday, perhaps, he would feel the urge to dig deep through the images and weave his own tapestries of legend; for now, he was content to listen to his chief.

"The humans say there's magic left in the woods from the time of the High Ones' coming," Cutter began.

The storyteller, despite his resolve—never that strong anyway—to pay attention to his chief, began to let his mind wander over the tales he'd heard since the time he was little, many turns of the seasons ago. Tales of those selfsame High Ones, and of the ones who came after, generation after generation after . . . He blinked and came back to the present.

"Small magic that went bad, like pools of stagnant water," Cutter went on, "because the High Ones couldn't control their powers here at first. If that's true, then I guess we've paid for it in a way we'll never forget."

The storyteller knew what was coming, at least in part. This howl, he knew as did all the gathered Wolfriders, was for Cutter's parents, Bearclaw and Joyleaf, gone these six turns. He could still conjure them in his mind's eye, clear as moonlight. Bearclaw was taller than his young son, sharp-boned, sly-featured, bewhiskered, and ragged—one who stabbed through life ungently. Joyleaf's hair was spun from sunbeams. Her eyes were her son's eyes, and she bore a bow as capably as she'd borne that son seventeen turns before.

Now, as Cutter spoke, the storyteller narrowed his eyes, which gave his usually jolly, cheeky face a rare and serious cast. He'd not gone on the hunt with the others, that night, and as much as he could now he wanted to put himself with the party as it rode through the dark wood in search of game, riding toward a fate as yet unsuspected.

Something was in the woods. Something unnatural waited there in the darkness. It was that which had made all the tribe restless and irritable for many days. Cutter described it as a scent like nothing the Wolfriders had known before. They felt its eyes fixed upon them, gagged on its stench; but no matter how they searched, they could not uncover the terrible presence that had invaded their domain. It was there, watching them, shadowing their trail, but always just beyond arrow range, always just quiet enough to make them doubt their senses. It seemed to possess a malevolent kind of intelligence, yet it smelled of beast . . . and something else, all twisted together.

The hunt for the intruder went on all night, fruitlessly, until toward dawn they discovered a young wolf lying dead in a clearing. Its stomach was torn out and its ribs exposed, and it weltered in a puddle of its own gore. The stench of the killer hung so thickly in the air that it had no source, no direction. It was all around them.

Death came suddenly, without warning. From the bushes a great curved claw struck out, slitting the throat of its first elfin victim. He was called Rain the Healer, and he was the first to die, as if by design. His powers would not help the next ones to fall.

Cutter's words began to fail him here as he attempted to relate from memory what had happened. Skywise remembered, and One-Eye, and Treestump, for they had been among the ill-fated hunting party. Only an open sending to the others at the howl could convey, now, the jumble of nightmare images that defied description, and Cutter refused to do this, knowing that such agony relived would do no one any good. But the storyteller felt his own personal anguish at his chief's compassion, for he desperately wished to possess the living memory of the carnage that had taken his father . . .

Cutter continued, finding his voice, but it was difficult. To have senses was to be witness to chaos: a monstrous, black shape rearing up in the half-light before dawn, the glint of sword-sharp fangs, the pain of cruel talons raking unprotected skin, wolves and riders flung back, broken, a serpentine body as big around as a tree, thrashing and coiling with unassailable power. And most horrible of all, the monster was sending! It had the power to attack the mind as well as the body!

The storyteller closed his eyes and let Cutter's words run with his imagination. Lightning and fire, a longtooth cat and a huge black serpent locked in mortal combat, a pocket of the High Ones' forgotten magic rekindled by the sky-borne flames and charged with the blood madness of the struggling beasts.

The magic! An ancient spell, asleep for untold time. A fire-spell, perhaps, from as far back as the time of Zarhan or Renn. Fire was the great changer, the transformer of all things: metal to molten liquid, water to steam, wood to ash. Perhaps a group of High Ones, cold, desperate, had sought to warm themselves with a fire-spell. The magic had failed, but the seed of the magic had remained, asleep, for countless years until lightning struck the spot and brought the seed to life. Two mighty creatures—the longtooth and its enemy, the serpent—battling to slay each other, had unwittingly rolled into the pool of fire-magic. Like metal or water or wood they had been transformed.

Change . . . joining—a twisted, newborn brain ablaze with the joy of slaughter. And the monster had a name! The Wolfriders named it even as they died in its jaws. It was Madcoil, and it was death! A snake with the head and claws of a lion, all black and scaly. The glowing red slits that were eyes; the poisonous fangs; the jaws that nearly folded back on themselves, so wide did they gape! So huge that head and those rending fangs, so swift and silent that rushing, gliding body slithering about the wood to kill because that was all it knew to do.

The battle between Cutter and his fellow hunters and the ravening monster became a rout. Nearly mindless from the pain of the creature's distorted sending, half blinded by their own blood, the elves gave up and scattered, somehow ending up high in the trees as Madcoil's howls of fury died behind them. The survivors began to call for friends and kin; a sick fear washed over them as they realized that half the hunting party—including Joyleaf—was missing. Ignoring the danger, for the monster might still lurk in the shadows below, Bearclaw leaped down to the forest floor and stood still as a stone, sending. It was a special call, meant only for his lifemate, but he was silent too long . . . too long.

"The hunting party had been ten," Cutter said. "Madcoil made it five." Yes, the storyteller thought, five gone: Joyleaf, and Foxfur, and Brownberry and Rain and Longbranch . . . who had so very recently decided to change his name from Longreach. I will miss you most.

"Treestump, Skywise, and One-Eye went back to the holt; Bearclaw sent them away," Cutter continued. "He tried to make me go too, but I wouldn't. Madcoil had taken his lifemate—but it had taken my mother too. I defied my chief-father." Cutter paused. "It was the first time I ever did that. I didn't know it would be the last . . ."

Something tugged at the storyteller's memory. Cutter probably still thought that he had done the unthinkable by standing up to his grief-maddened father. But there had been others, Pike realized even as he listened, as bits and pieces of tales that Longreach had shared with him bubbled to the surface of his mind. Perhaps someday he should share some of them with Cutter; maybe it might make his chief feel a little better . . .

The Good Summer

by Lynn Abbey

Time came.

Time passed.

Flowing with the seasons, Rahnee She-Wolf led her tribe in a great circle from the taiga forests to the open tundra, and back again. Everyone and everything changed as the circles became spirals, but only a few noticed the changes.

The previous winter was harsh; among the harshest the tribe had endured. Or so said the old elf, Talen, who was obsessed about such things. No one—not wolf, nor elf, nor mixed-blood hunter—gainsaid him. The winds howled early and without warning. The snows, which should have made a protective blanket on the land, came late and sparse. The chieftess hustled her tribe to a deep cave. The frail elves and cubs were safe there, but hunters braved the fierce weather for food.

Sometimes they came back empty-handed, and twice they did not come back at all.

Thaw brought no relief. The moisture that had not come as snow came as torrential rain. Streams jumped their banks. Lakes rose across the land. The mud could swallow a bull branch-horn in a single gulp. An innate sensibility warned the elf-blooded away from the carrion, but they could not compel their wolf-friends from the easy feast.

A bloody flux raced through the pack as the leaf-trees turned green. Ten wolves died, including Silvershine—the pack-leader and Rahnee's wolf-friend. That howl was long and heartrending. When it ended there was not a wolf-blooded elf who resisted the healing timelessness of wolfsong.

Now it was summer. Winter was a lost memory within the wolfsong. The dozen-odd elves without wolf-blood were exiled to their cook fire. They needed the tribe far more than the tribe needed them.

"I simply can't stand it any longer," Rellah complained— as she usually did—when Zarhan Fastfire brought their share of the kill.

"You can, and you will," Fastfire chided as he dropped the bloody meat. He stoked the fire with his magic.

Rellah scowled at the dark droplet on her forearm. She wiped it away with a handful of grass, then threw the grass toward the noisy circle of wolves, hunters, and cubs. "That's easy for you to say. You and Willowgreen, your feet never get sore. You can walk all day and all night. And you *like* the taste of raw meat."

A handful of biting replies lurked under Zarhan's tongue. He kept them there with considerable difficulty. He did not *like* bloody meat. He didn't like grubs or worms either, but he preferred them to starving, which was what he and the other elves would do without the youngsters to hunt for them. And as for walking, Rellah and the rest were tougher than he was; they had the strength to walk *and* complain. The only elf who truly suffered when the chieftess and the hunters were listening to wolfsong was Samael Dream-keeper, and he never complained. He never asked anyone to carry his basket of dreamberries, but trudged along, thin-lipped and pale, until someone remembered to take it from him.

Besides, they hadn't walked much this summer. The click-toe deer came to this place while there was still ice in the shadows. The herd hadn't left, and neither had the tribe. Not like other summers when the hunting circuit stretched south and they verged into territory where the tribe was judged prey by five-fingered hunters.

The fire rose into the lavender night. Zarhan set the spitted meat on a frame of broken spears. Complaining, he suddenly realized, was the elfin version of wolfsong—without wolfsong's rhythm or harmony.

Zarhan no longer shared such unwelcome observations with the elves. In many ways he was the greatest exile of them all. For most of his long life, he'd been the youngest of the elves; they still thought of him as a child. Yet he was a hundred turns older than his lifemate, Rahnee She-Wolf. As far as the hunters were concerned, he was as old as the trees and rocks—just like the rest of the full-blooded elves.

He wasn't the youngest elf now. Rellah's daughter, Willowgreen, was. But Willowgreen scorned her elfness. She tried to howl and she tried to hunt; she even tried to share her thoughts with the wolves. She did none of it well, but the hunters tolerated her and Zarhan Fastfire found himself more on the outside than ever.

The daystar danced with the moons. The sky family danced together in high summer, as Fastfire's family did not. He ate with the elves and slept alone while his lifemate prowled the silver-green plains. When he wasn't eating or sleeping, he worked alone with his magic.

"Have you found anything interesting?" Talen inquired as he made himself comfortable in the shade.

Zarhan's eyes were closed. A tenuous finger of steam rose through a reed poking out of a carefully smoothed clay mound. When the steam stopped the red-haired elf relaxed.

"There are as many ways to make glass as there are grains of sand. I guess some of them are interesting," he replied with a weary shrug. He turned his attention to a similar mound where the clay was dry and cracked. Taking up a shaped stone hammer and length of fire-hardened bone, he began chipping at the mound. He hoped Talen would get the message and go away. When the old elf didn't, Zarhan leaned on his elbows and stared at the bright blue sky.

Talen took this as an expression of interest. "Rellah's

found an old song. She'll sing it at the fire tonight. She calls it 'Arrien's Lament'; it's about the stars. *They* won't like it."

Fastfire sat up again. He didn't care much for laments, sung or howled. He didn't care much about the stars, either, though like the other elves he could follow memory's path away from this worldly prison, if he chose. He didn't choose to dwell on what they'd lost—but that was something else to set him apart.

Rellah searched her memories whenever they had a day's peace, always finding songs that perfectly expressed her frustration. Willowgreen, who couldn't help being full-blooded, and Samael collected plants, then argued over what to do with them. New-Wolf found intricate patterns to weave into her baskets. Changefur made wondrous things from pebbles, seeds, feathers, and her honey-gold hair. When Zarhan searched his own memories he found his father's fire-magic—and the urge to experiment with it.

Talen didn't do anything but count or complain.

"It's not that the hunters won't like it, Talen, they simply won't notice it. The stars don't mean anything to them." Fastfire wedged the bone into a crack, then struck it with the hammer. The mound split apart, revealing its carefully constructed layers of mud, grass, and—at its heart—the disk of colored glass. "None of this means anything to them. They're content with what they've got, and we should be grateful."

Talen wrestled with the notion that he should be grateful to the wolfsong that protected the youngsters from an aching boredom he could not escape. He'd been born on this world, but unlike Zarhan, he didn't have to dig in his ancestor's memories to see Timmain's face. He remembered her and the others who had roamed the stars before the disaster. If he'd dared, Talen could have reckoned the exact sum of his seasons on this world of two moons and a single, unremarkable star. He did not dare. To know that would be to know how much of his life had been spent trudging behind wolves and wolf-blooded elves whose thoughts began at yesterday and stopped at tomorrow.

"Grateful." He spat the word out. "Grateful to live like an animal? Grateful to pass each day listening to my stomach digest yesterday's meal? *They* don't need a purpose—just hunt, sleep, eat, and frolic. I remember hunger, yes; I remember freezing, too . . . *and* building a home with four sturdy walls and a roof." He studied Zarhan's glass. "I remember windows that glowed in the sunlight. We were individuals full of purpose and direction. It was better then."

Fastfire took back his handiwork. "Do you remember *men*?" he asked in a whisper and Talen turned away. Zarhan Fastfire did not, himself, remember houses, walls, roofs, or windows, but he remembered men—five-fingered hunters who preyed on elves. Unlike the wolves, or the bears, or the great cats, men would not make room for another predator. Perhaps men did not see themselves as predators. Men believed in magic, but men had no magic—not even the simple elfin magic that survived their disastrous arrival on this world.

"We could have fought back," Talen whispered.

"We did. Their spears were stronger than our magic, and we could not endure their death-agonies when we *did* kill them."

"We could fight them now. The youngsters could. Death doesn't bother them. It's . . . it's part of them, part of their lives. They could lead us back to the place where it all began . . ." Talen's eyes misted. His yearning was as tangible as the tundra, then it was gone. "How do you stand it, Zarhan?" he snarled at the younger elf. "Turns upon turns, and there's no sign of us in her, just the wolf. No way to reach her, to show her what might be."

Talen snatched the glass from Zarhan. He tried to rub away the remaining clay, but the clay concealed a crack, and the disk shattered. It seemed, for a heartbeat, that he was embarrassed and might apologize, but Talen had evaded much larger guilt. "If she cared, she'd let you practice until you mastered it. But she won't let you master it . . . won't ever let you master it. Won't let any of us *do* what *we* can do, be what we can be. The youngsters don't want to be anyone . . . any *one*."

Zarhan retrieved the sharp fragments. Rahnee thought he *had* mastered the process. Broken glass was far more useful than the smooth, clear stuff he longed to make. Once the glass was broken, it was no longer fragile. There were no better spear-tips than the ruins of his magic.

His concentration broke, and a bright red line appeared on his thumb. The cut was as painless as it was deep.

"They're happier than we are. They don't fight with each other. They love, they share. What makes you so certain that they're wrong to submerge themselves in the tribe and we're right to insist on being ourselves?"

Fastfire closed his eyes. Steam rose again from the mound of wet clay. Talen's stinging retort went unheard.

Rellah sang her song that night. It was intricate and filled with shaded meanings the tribe had no need to know. Long before the story reached its climax the wolves challenged her right to sing alone. The youngsters sang with their wolf-friends, and Rellah fled in tears. Zarhan turned to the silver-haired chieftess, but Rahnee was with the wolves. She did not react when he left the circle.

Wolfsong was not blindness or ignorance. Rahnee had noticed the disruption within her tribe. Her solution was simple and direct: time to move the tribe to a new place. Zarhan abandoned another colony of clay mounds.

"Did I not say this would happen?" Talen said as he fell into step. "Not that your lifemate knows where she is taking us. Would it ever occur to her to apologize to Rellah? Would it ever occur to her to send those wolves away for just one night—as a favor to us? Suns, moons, and bright, bountiful stars, just once I'd like her to act like an elf not a wolf."

Zarhan shifted his pack. He gave Talen his best enigmatic smile. "What if Rahnee started acting like you?"

Talen surged ahead to share his angst with Rellah and New-Wolf, who were more likely to agree with him. Zarhan's shoulders shook with silent laughter.

Something was happening to the tribe. The hunters had noticed Rellah's song and responded to its mournful phrases. Talen was right, the chieftess had not responded the way any of the elves would have, but she hadn't responded like a wolf, either. Wolves needed a better reason than Rellah to abandon a hunting ground.

Rahnee made a new camp downwind of a marshy stream where the click-toes came for water. Reeds grew higher than Samael's head. They provided cover for the tribe's hunters and raw materials for the elves' hobbies. Zarhan found himself a suitable hummock, then set about making a rash of muddy mounds.

He did not notice when his lifemate sat down beside him. The chieftess waited patiently while he changed the mud to steam and clay. She counted the mounds with her fingers, then with her toes. When she ran out of toes, she ran out of patience.

"Why do you do this?"

A mound exploded, spewing warm globs over both of them. Zarhan leaped up without considering the sloppy ground beneath his feet. He flailed for balance and propelled himself onto his rump in the cold muck. The chieftess laughed so hard she had to grab the reeds to keep from joining him. Fastfire's anger ran down his back with the water. Each time Rahnee became herself—her elfin self—was like the first time the bolt of Recognition had passed between them. Knowing it was coming was never sufficient preparation for the moment itself.

He crawled onto the hummock beside her. "You could have warned me you were here," he said as he squeezed a damp, red braid with a very dirty hand.

Rahnee was still laughing. She whooped then coughed and gradually got herself under control. "You should have heard me. *I* never get so lost that I can't hear *you*."

"I'm not a wolf when I get lost in my thoughts."

There was no bitterness in his voice, nor denial in

Rahnee's shrug. She lunged for his shoulders and held him tightly, filling herself with his scent and taste. Fastfire was always careful of her strength and energy. Frolicking with her was very much like wrestling with the wolves, but he'd learned a thing or two about wolves as the seasons turned.

He slipped through her arms and rolled away into a panting crouch. Her eyes were bright and her teeth shone through her smile. Then, without warning, wrestling and frolicking were forgotten. The chieftess was on her feet with her back toward him and her arms spread wide enough to hold the horizon-hugging daystar.

"Have you ever seen such a beautiful summer? I wonder what's going to happen next."

Zarhan relaxed on one knee. He shook his head and marveled that she always knew exactly why she'd come back.

"No one's hungry. Everyone's healthy. The hunting's warm in my belly and the light is warm on my back. It's *made* for us. It's a time for running into the wind and plunging into the deepest water. There'll never be another summer like this . . ." Her arms dropped to her sides. She turned and her eyes bore into her lifemate's. "Will there?"

"It would be hard to imagine a better one," he replied cautiously.

The She-Wolf looked at the daystar. That was the answer she expected; the answer she'd found herself but would not trust until he confirmed it. "Perfect," she whispered. The absence of everything that was difficult. She said it again, lingering over each syllable of the unfamiliar word. The abundance of all that was good and pleasurable.

Perfect. She'd never felt it before. Something said this was everything she had ever wanted from life, and that she should get back to being excited. She lifted her arms, but the gesture no longer fit. She wrapped her arms over her breasts instead, as if she were suddenly very cold.

Zarhan tensed in a heartbeat. Rahnee was not sharing her turmoil but he could guess her thoughts. He knew that feeling—the feeling that life could get no better—and its underside echo: it can't last, won't last, wouldn't be worth having if it did. He had no idea how Timmorn's daughter would react.

He stopped breathing when she turned away from the daystar to study his mounds. She knelt down to examine the clay with her fingers and thoughts. They had traveled far together; he'd helped her find her inner name in a place that was not part of this world at all. Between them they had birthed two cubs, and mourned together when the eldest died. There were no secrets between them.

The chieftess ran her fingers through her hair, lifting it so she looked far more lupine than elfin, and just a little bit overwhelmed.

"I could never do this, beloved," she sighed. "Even if every tomorrow were just like every yesterday, I could not lose myself making poor copies of that which lives in my mind."

Zarhan looked down at his toes. Rahnee's innocence and honesty was a fearsome thing. He felt his dreams wither.

She gathered him in her arms. "I'm sorry, beloved." She rubbed his forehead as if he were a wolf-friend. Fastfire did not resist; did not relax. **I didn't mean what I said—not the way that I said it.** The daystar touched the horizon. **I'm not good at perfect, Zarhan. When there's nothing to do, I do the wrong thing.**

Twilight revealed the moons and the pattern of the brightest stars. Rahnee sought the emptiness of wolfsong, but the night was as beautiful as a warm summer night could be; nothingness was beyond her reach. They remained together, and alone. Vitality returned slowly to Fastfire's limbs. He accepted the comfort she wanted to give, but he had nothing to give in return.

The wolves began to howl. To Zarhan, despite his many turns with the tribe, the chorus set his teeth on edge when it didn't send shivers down his back. He knew it was different for his lifemate, but he was trying not to think about the gulf between them at the moment. The chieftess tasted the still air. The muscles in her face tightened as she strained to separate one wolf-voice from another. Zarhan knew she was trying to find her wolf-friend. He crawled away lest his elfness interfere.

Rahnee had searched for her father, Timmorn Yellow-Eyes, in the second winter of his exile, and from her father she had received the first wolves. It was, so far as anyone knew, Timmorn's last gift to his mother's kindred and it fixed the shape of Timmain's magic for all time. They would become Wolfriders—small, strong, and hardy, yet essentially elfin; and these were *their* wolves—outwardly no different from other wolves but who carried a trace of elfness hidden within them.

Naturally the chieftess bonded with the dominant wolf, Silverice, but the tribe heeded a life rhythm different from the wolves'. Silverice lived longer than any native wolf. She outlived her mate and took another from the unbonded bachelors, but in time her eyes clouded over and pain was her closest companion. One day Rahnee, Silverice, and the young male went into the forest. Only the She-Wolf and the young wolf returned. Rahnee, who was never her best with names, called him Icesilver. The seasons cycled, Silver followed Icesilver, Silvershine followed Silver. Silvershine died of the flux in her prime.

Now there was Prickle, a rambunctious yearling with huge paws and a penchant for gnawing holes in any untended boot. He loved Rahnee as only a wolf-friend could, but he was seldom where she needed him when she needed him to be there. He couldn't be. Pack-law was immutable, and Prickle was at the age when his status in the pack was most precarious. It was likely that he'd mature into a powerful, dominant wolf—and it was just possible that he'd get himself driven off first. Fastfire hoped with warm fervor that the pack wasn't singing Prickle's exile.

Long moments passed; the chieftess trembled from the strain. She reached behind her back, her fingers weaving toward her lifemate.

We must go, an imperative sending flowed into Zarhan as they touched. **It's Cat.**

Fastfire could not feel what she had gleaned from Prickle; but he felt everything else. He trusted her to guide him while his mind quested to the elders. His eyes were closed and his feet fell in her footsteps as they raced across the marsh.

Talen, always the easiest elf to find when the wolves were howling, had all the answers. **Your daughter and her suitors have found something that can be neither eaten nor shared, and they won't rest until they've destroyed it.**

Under better circumstances, Fastfire's curiosity would have been roused by such a description, but this was not the tribe, this was his daughter who bore the weight of Talen's scorn. He severed the contact and urged Rahnee to reckless speed.

Zarhan would have avoided his elders, but they'd gathered on one hillock with a clear view of the fracas. Rahnee was breathing hard and showing her teeth as they came up the far side. The elves needed no urging to make a path for her, but neither did they trouble to hide their amused, expectant expressions.

The sky overhead was rich violet. It was the middle of the night. A double hand of hunters and cubs crowded around a click-toe carcass. They weren't part of the brawl. Purple shadows turned the rest of the tribe into a single beast writhing in the stream. It was impossible to tell who was who—with one exception. Cat had her father's flaming hair and her mother's powerful voice. Both were unmistakable at the middle of the fray.

The chieftess's eyes were wide and black. An aura of rage grew around her.

"They're acting like they used to when Three-Toe led them. Brutal as wild wolves," Changefur said under her breath.

Rahnee's shoulders rose and her neck shortened. When she glanced behind her, there was murder in her eyes.

"They're acting like *elves*," Zarhan Fastfire corrected as he hurried to her side before the situation got worse.

The She-Wolf was not the largest or the strongest of the hunters, but she was the chieftess. When she waded into the seething mass, it gave ground. Indeed, once they realized the She-Wolf was among them, and the temper she brought with her, a good many hunters sought high ground beside the elves. Those who didn't found themselves cuffed and booted until there were only three brawlers left. Talen had it right: Cat and the hunters who were her constant and smitten companions, Slowthrower and Lightfeet.

"I said . . ." The chieftess took a neck in each hand and cracked the heads together. "I *said*: enough is enough!"

The sound compared favorably with stag clashes during the click-toe rut. Both hunters were stunned. Lightfeet fell on his face as soon as Rahnee let go. Slowthrower, true to his name, sank to his hands and knees, then crawled slowly away from his chieftess's displeasure. Mother and daughter were left in eyes-locked confrontation.

The chieftess twitched her hand forward.

"It's *mine*," Cat shrieked without revealing what was so precious.

Rahnee didn't move and everyone thought of challenge. Challenge was a lupine legacy. Wolves challenged because their identity was bounded by their place in the pack. The wolf-blooded could stumble into a challenge anytime the chieftess didn't get her way. Either the challenger backed down, or the tribe became two tribes. There was no third way. Zarhan felt his knees loosen and his tongue grow pasty.

After a long moment while her heart beat wildly, Rahnee let her arm drop to her side. If this was challenge, she did not know how to meet it.

You find out what's bothering her, she sent and turned her back to Cat.

Obligingly Zarhan squatted down beside his daughter. He kept his empty, relaxed hands in clear view between them.

"What did you find?" he asked, in no way disputing her right, or need, to possess it.

"It's pretty. It sparkles in the light."

"Pretty enough to show me?"

The young huntress wrinkled her nose, considering the question. Her eyes were slanted; her nose was tilted upward ever so slightly as if her great-grandmother, Timmain, had gone shape-shifting among the snow-cats rather than the wolves. Beauty was in the elf-blood, but Cat was special. It was no wonder that the young men got rowdy in her presence.

"It's mine," Cat reiterated as her fingers unfolded.

Perhaps the pebble had sparkled in the daylight. It was just a dark lump now. Cat shuddered slightly when she looked at it and cast it far away before Zarhan could ask to hold it.

"It was pretty," she whispered, sounding like a cub again, looking to her elfin father for wisdom and assurance. "It was like nothing else I'd ever seen. I wanted to keep it and give it a name of its own."

Fastfire wrapped his arms around her. He tucked her head into his shoulder with his chin. **You can look for more tomorrow, but you shouldn't take stream-stones from their water.**

Cat dissolved into tears and thoughts only her father could understand. The tribe lost interest and wandered. Only the chieftess, and mother, lingered with them. Zarhan tried to make room on one shoulder for his lifemate, but Cat dug in with eight strong fingers. There'd be no sharing her father tonight.

Was it worth the fighting? the She-Wolf demanded of her lifemate.

No.

Then why did they fight over it?

Fastfire sent nothing and the chieftess stalked away.

The bountiful summer continued, and so did the brawls. The chieftess kept the tribe moving, hoping they would be too tired to find the contentious treasures. It was a hope as reasonable as it was futile. The wider the She-Wolf ranged, the more her tribe found, and the more they squabbled. She exhausted herself separating the fighters and confiscated every one of their treasures. In no time at all she became the guardian of a large trove of pebbles, feathers, antlers, bones, and odd-shaped twigs. It outgrew her belt-pouch. It left a nasty bruise on her hip. It rooted her to the camp while the hunters searched for more. And her lifemate—might worms make a den in his gut—withheld the answers she so desperately needed.

Tell me what I'm supposed to do! the She-Wolf bellyached one short night when the moons were dark. Her shoulder burned like wildfire; she'd wrenched it ending another brawl, but she was too proud to seek Willowgreen for help. The treasure in her fist was the color of honey; it was warm to her touch, and she had absolutely no use for it. She studied her swollen belt-pouch. **Tell me!**

Ask New-Wolf to make you a basket, he helpfully suggested from well beyond her reach.

She shook the bulging sack at him. The knots slipped and the entire collection rained into the grass between them. Zarhan guessed he'd gone too far. He braced himself for her wrath, but Rahnee just stood there. He realized he was many nights past too far. She sank to her knees and groped through the grass. Her tears joined the little treasures.

An elf's eyes were good, a wolf's eyes were better, but no eyes could find treasure on a moonless night. Fastfire reaped a handful of grass then set his magic into it. Rahnee was shamed by her frustration and turned away from him.

We . . . I do not *need* any of this. I took these things away, so they could not start brawls. And now I cannot escape from them. They call my name!

The fire swallowed itself.

You are not a wolf, beloved, he sent with more gentleness than he'd used of late. **Timmain became a wolf so we could all survive, but when survival is not in doubt the elf within you needs something different . . . You have a self, beloved. A self that is more than a name, even an inner name. As much as you need to be part of the tribe, to be a part of the wolf, you have just as strong a need to be your own self, but it is not as simple as being a wolf.**

Rahnee blinked away her tears. She knew her lifemate by sight and scent, by the texture of his thoughts, and the sound of his voice—but he made himself in other ways. There was a thong of green glass beads woven in his braids; there had always been a thong of green beads, though she never noticed them. His knife, which he had tried unsuccessfully to give her, bore a likeness of Silverice on its hilt.

She turned her mind's eye toward the other elves, and saw that they, too, had these peculiarities. So did Glowstone, a firstborn child of Timmorn like herself, who became a shadow when he lost his cat's-eye talisman. Rahnee herself carried the metal knife that had come from the sky with her grandmother.

Why do I need Timmain's knife?

Fastfire caught the thought as it shot past him. The time had come for answers, but he was not sure the question had been meant for him.

Why do I need more than I needed? Her fists squeezed over his wrists.

"You don't," he said, because pain would poison his thoughts. He tried to twist free and her grip hardened. "Needs change. A cub needs milk; a wolf needs meat."

Nails as hard as any wolf's pressed nerves into bone. **Are we all cubs to you, still?**

Cold sweat broke out on Zarhan's forehead. He tried to block the agony. "No," he gasped. "You're hurting me."

Rahnee released him so suddenly that he might have used his fire-magic on her, but he hadn't. She stared at her stiff fingers as if they could not be a part of her. She hadn't meant to cause pain. She was a hunter; they were all hunters. Hunting was killing, but killing wasn't hurting.

I did not do that, she thought, *I would not do that*. Rahnee turned dark and bitter. Zarhan Fastfire spoke of the self as if it were some precious thing; she saw it as more worthless than the treasures she had lost in the grass. If this were self, there was no mercy in it.

Fastfire felt his lifemate's thoughts retreat. He knew Rahnee was no half-blooded creature like the mongrel dog-wolves that men kept. Both wolf and elf were pure within her, without becoming one. He couldn't imagine what happened when wolf and elf confronted each other, but watching Rahnee tremble, he knew it couldn't be pleasant. He reached out for her. She shuddered free of him.

I do not like myself. I do not want to be myself. Her thoughts bit like ice crystals. **My self is dark.**

Fastfire reached again. She eluded him.

Stay away! It has all gone wrong. I would not collect bright pebbles or disks of hard water. I would make more of me by making less of you. I would take your name, your self. It is worse than darkness. I cannot be chieftess. I can't feel the tribe, only this *self*. This self is a bad thing.

She spoke nonsense, and with all his heart Zarhan wanted to tell her so. Except Rahnee never indulged in nonsense—he'd learned that as the seasons spun away if he'd learned nothing else. He hammered through his own consciousness, seeking the place from which he would anchor a bridge of empathy.

This self would not have a lifemate of darkness. He used her thoughts, her images, and he laid them on thick. **This self knows you better than you know yourself.**

Too thick for an elf or a wolf, and not entirely truthful, either. Rahnee assaulted Zarhan with sendings that exquisitely conveyed all she found unacceptable within herself. Once again he had underestimated her. Ancient words crystallized before him: tyrant, oppressor, slavemaker. He felt his flesh grow warm in reflexive self-defense.

Zarhan's anger didn't flare at Rahnee, but at the High Ones who had been foolish enough to strand themselves here in the first place. And at Timmain who had reshaped herself with the same impulsiveness. He found his thoughts drawn back to Timmorn's disappearance. No one had expected that a nameless, mateless child would become their chieftess. Three-toe was Timmorn's heir. Three-toe who used fist and fang to make certain he had the best of everything.

Even now when a cub was born they looked at its hands and feet. Five was the natural number of this world. They feared five because it reminded them of man. A cub born with five fingers or five toes always sickened. Four was their number. Elves had four, so did their wolves—until Willowgreen came along to say their wolves had *five*. That hard, scaly lump midway up their lower leg was the fifth.

Three-toe was born with misshaped feet. No one worried; it wasn't as if he had five toes. Zarhan and the other elves feared Three-toe, but until this moment he'd never really understood why.

Three-toe was the wolf and elf together. There was no conflict. The thought escaped and Fastfire could not call it back. He hoped Rahnee hadn't caught it, but the startled, frightened look in her eyes stripped that hope away.

"Oh, my father . . ."

Pain grew force between them. Rahnee seemed to shrivel with shame. Zarhan had the thought to reach out to her, but he had lost a large measure of innocence as well. His will was divided, and his arms did not move.

"The good summer. The perfect summer." Rahnee turned the words into a curse. "We were better off when winter was our enemy."

Fastfire had nothing to say. His thoughts were a stream that jumped its banks to find a steeper course; there was no going back to the old. He would not seek out the other elves, but they would see what he had seen the next time Samael gathered the whole tribe around the dreamberry bowl.

"I'm sorry, Rahnee," he whispered. Regret was not something she appreciated under the best of circumstances. "I'll be leaving . . ." She didn't ask if he meant for now or forever. He wouldn't have had an answer if she had. His inner voice insisted nothing had changed. The voice wasn't strong enough to move him closer to his lifemate, but it was strong enough to keep him from leaving.

He didn't hear the first scream. The sound was such a complement to his mood, he didn't grasp that it wasn't his until it was repeated. At sunset Fastfire could have sworn he'd never heard its like before. Now he had heard it twice. The first time it could have been his own. The second time he knew it came from his daughter, Cat. Zarhan's head echoed with anger, outrage, and pain: his and hers; identical, yet separate. The elf was repelled by his own urge to violence— thinking for a heartbeat that wolf-blood was contagious. He eluded that distasteful conclusion, but not the next: Timmain's shape-shifting served to awaken a darker nature in her kin.

It was easier to turn away from his daughter than to examine himself.

Zarhan closed his ears and his heart. The world became quiet. He was alone, serene.

The sound touched Rahnee as well. There was nothing at all familiar about it, much less something she would have recognized as her own. Her first reaction was to get rid of it, but a mindful of bad thought was unlike a mouthful of bad meat. It could not be disgorged. She shook herself all over and got to her feet.

The elves made much of the endless now of wolfsong that joined past, present, and future into a seamless whole. But there was another mode to wolfsong, a NOW that was fire and ice together, a NOW that made every hair stand on end. Rahnee would have neither peace nor freedom so long as it was present in her mind.

Cat tried to get up but a searing pain paralyzed her. Even if there hadn't been physical pain, she might not have been able to move. What had happened, what still happened an arm's length away was so far beyond her understanding of the world as to be paralyzing by itself.

Slowthrower and Lightfeet were her lovemates. They were her friends and they were friends to each other. From beginning to end, they were a laughing, frolicking, inseparable trio. They did not need to speak to each other; they rarely needed to send. Their instincts had always been in harmony.

Today they had hunted and feasted with the rest of the tribe, then they had hunted alone for treasure, as had become their custom this summer. Each went in a separate direction, but they'd returned at almost the same moment. Slowthrower had a red feather, unarguably the treasure of the night. He'd given it to her to weave in her braid. There was nothing unusual about that; there was nothing they did not exchange.

Lightfeet had nothing, but yesterday he'd found a banded pebble, and who knew what he might find tomorrow?

Tonight, yesterday, tomorrow, and only tonight was truly now.

She rubbed her cheek against Slowthrower's hand. His empty hand strayed down her back. She teased the laces of his tunic. He got a finger through her knotted belt. Cat never chose between them, couldn't imagine choosing, but there was only one of her.

Lightfeet grabbed her arm with enough force to wrench her away from Slowthrower's loose embrace.

You have the red feather. Cat's mine.

Slowthrower belied his name. He latched onto Cat's other arm and pulled.

I found the red feather. I gave it to her, now they're both mine!

The argument was uglier in sending than it could ever be in words.

No! Cat's denial exploded between them. **You're hurting me.** She pulled with all her might, and succeeded in dislocating both shoulders. That produced the first scream to reach her parents' ears. **I'll have neither of you! Do you hear me? I *hate* you!**

Cat had never used the word "hate" before. Within the tribe hate had meaning only in the sense that men hated elves. Cat had never seen a man. Yet it fell easily into her mind and off her tongue.

I hate you both. Now leave me alone!

Time congealed as Slowthrower raised his free arm, made a fist, threw a punch. Suspended between them, Cat was vulnerable, but the sight of her lovemate's fist was so horrible she could not have defended herself. They still thought as one, or Slowthrower and Lightfeet did. They released her wrists the instant before the punch landed. That was the second scream.

Without Cat to hinder them, Slowthrower and Lightfeet fought in earnest. The screams had been enough to get everyone's attention, but it was the blood scent that brought elves, wolves, hunters, and cubs running.

Cat was beyond pride. Acid tears covered her cheek and she wished she were dead. Tailchaser reached out to her stricken elf-friend. The wolf licked the salty tears and made cub-comfort noises deep in her throat, but Cat remained numb.

Wolves sent, but their sendings were not words, nor even thoughts. A notion would crystallize in a hunter's mind, and the friends would understand each other. Tailchaser conveyed no need for anguish. This was solution, not problem. They had been three-in-one-place—not secure in the pack. When the fight ended, they would know the order that named them.

There should have been a third scream, but it could not rise above the weights on Cat's heart. Pain spread through her the way it spread through a fish that swallowed the bait, the hook, and the line. There was so much pain, both physical and emotional, that pain almost replaced outrage in the forefront of her mind. Cat was her mother's cub, and ultimately nothing could replace outrage.

Tailchaser stretched her neck as growls rumbled out of

her elf-friend's throat. She tucked her tail beneath her legs and crept away on her belly. A wolf knew what those sounds meant.

With spine and will, Cat prepared to stop the fight. Her arms were deadweight, but that wasn't what stopped her. She stopped because Tailchaser had been right. The fight between Slowthrower and Lightfeet was challenge and she was the prize. The tribe was forbidden to stop a chief's challenge, and Cat could not interrupt her erstwhile lovemates.

Rahnee appeared just as Cat's esteem sank lowest. The chieftess rested her fists on her hips and studied the fighters with the unconscious majesty only she possessed. Everyone, including the full-blooded elves and wolves, had the explicit right to challenge her, but they were implicitly forbidden to challenge each other.

Spear, the chieftess sent to her tribe.

It didn't matter whose spear; this was not going to be delicate work. A youngster named Flint offered his with a trembling arm. The chieftess had killed within the tribe before, but her victims had suffered froth-madness, and the slaying was more mercy than murder. None wished to witness another death, though it seemed they would, for Slowthrower had gotten his arm against Lightfeet's throat. No one breathed while Lightfeet's struggles ebbed. The chieftess reversed her grip on the spear.

She rammed the butt into Slowthrower's side. He collapsed and found her foot planted on his chest.

"You are lone and outcast!" she bellowed. "Your thoughts are empty and unheard. We do not see you or scent you. Our paths shall not cross while the season lives." The words echoed and when the echo died, Slowthrower was exiled.

Rahnee lifted her foot. Without hesitation, she put her back to Slowthrower. Lightfeet tried to meet her eyes but couldn't.

"You are lone and outcast. Your thoughts are empty and unheard. We do not see you or scent you. Our paths shall not cross while the season lives."

Slowthrower was on his feet. He did not look at the chieftess or Cat, but he did offer his hand to Lightfeet. They leaned on each other and hobbled into the darkness. Rahnee felt nothing when they disappeared; she did not allow herself to know what anyone else felt.

How did this come to happen? she demanded of her helpless daughter.

Cat hung her head. She would have taken exile, had that been offered. Instead, she tried to swallow what was foremost in her memory. But sending could not lie, and confronted with her mother's sharp inquiry, her resistance was a sufficient answer.

Is this what comes of treasure-seeking?

The question was meant for her lifemate, but Zarhan was not nearby. She sent further. Her thoughts passed over the hollow shells of Slowthrower and Lightfeet. Her anger was gone. Had they turned around, she would not have driven them away. But the pair did not sense her passing, could not feel the absence of her anger, and did not turn around. If they lived when the frost came, if the tribe lived, then they would return. Rahnee's question spiraled outward until she found her lifemate.

They go beyond lifemating. They seek dominance beyond challenge and pack-law. There must be some other way, beloved. This is not the good way of the elf or the wolf. Come to me, beloved. Share your wisdom . . . ?

A dark sphere slid between them as Zarhan withheld his thoughts.

Zarhan! She railed against him. No one could stand against the chieftess's will; Zarhan Fastfire knew that better than anyone. The only way to deny her was not to stand at all. The obsidian presence faded. Rahnee knew he remained as he was, but she could no longer focus her will on him. "Worms in your gut, beloved. Blind, white worms eating to your skin . . ."

This daughter of Timmorn Yellow-Eyes had an instinct for

vengeance, but no patience. Her thoughts flowed back to the question: How did treasure-seeking become lawless brutality?

Is this what you wanted, Cat? Rahnee turned her attention once again to her cub. Cat's mind was empty, her flesh was warm, and her joints had begun to swell. **Willowgreen!** The elfin healer did not respond. Rahnee honed her thoughts. **Darrel!**

The elves all had an inner name, or soulname, that appeared to everyone when the unborn quickened. Most of the full-blooded elves, for privacy or camouflage, took a second name from the world around them: Zarhan Fastfire, Samael Dreamkeeper. The firstborn, like Rahnee herself, had two names, though each had journeyed to death's door before finding the inner name the elves heard when they quickened. The youngsters, the hunters who were three generations or more removed from Timmain, recognized only the names they chose for themselves.

Willowgreen would have preferred to forget her inner name, but then, Willowgreen would have preferred to be a huntress. She was elfin, though, and her inner name belonged to her chieftess. Like Fastfire, she denied Rahnee's sending.

A huntress needs you! The She-Wolf knew she could be heard.

Willowgreen appeared. The healer pressed the edge of her hand against Cat's shoulder. She lifted Cat's arm and the bones snapped loudly into place. She repeated the process, then laid her hands over Cat's eyes to take away the pain.

You should not have interfered, the healer chided while she worked.

????

You took away what they found. If you left them alone, they would not have needed to claim something you could not take away. Although you took that too, didn't you? Sending her lovemates away and keeping her here.

The tribe needed a healer. Herb lore couldn't do everything. Willowgreen said things that would have balked Zarhan Fastfire, and she got away with them.

They were not lovemates when they hurt Cat, nor when they fought each other. Theirs was not the Way.

What Way? Willowgreen stood up, and was grateful for the elfin height that let her stare down into the chieftess's face. **You're not part of the tribe's future, Rahnee. You're a part of its past, you and the rest of the firstborn, and the elves. What the Wolfriders do is the Way. Your father knew when it was time to leave.**

The chieftess could have called the healer's elfin insolence a hunter's challenge and crushed it like a maggot. But there was the chance that Willowgreen spoke the truth. Rahnee walked away chewing on a snarl in her hair.

She bit through the snarl and spat the tangled hair to the ground.

Wolves did not need treasures, and elves made theirs. Wolves didn't need treasure because the pack was everything for them. Elves made treasures because, or so her lifemate implied, they had *selves*. Did a self make treasure the way a cloud made lightning, or was a self already a treasure? Did wolves have selves? Wolves didn't have names until an elf-friend gave them one. She hadn't had a name until she became chieftess—if She-Wolf could be called a name. She hadn't had a real name until she Recognized Zarhan Fastfire.

Were treasures causing all the tribe's problems? Or selves? Or names?

Laststar?

Rahnee's sending shattered her sister's sleep, and reaped a bolt of anger for a reply. The She-Wolf seldom sought any of her half-siblings. What the firstborn shared was nothing they wished to dwell upon. Outnumbered by their descendants and by the full-blooded elves, except for Rahnee, they made themselves inconspicuous.

May I speak with you?

I'm awake now, aren't I?

The sisters were as similar as snowflakes: the same brindled silver hair; the same violet eyes, narrow chin, and sharp-nailed fingers. It was as if Timmorn and Murrel had produced two versions of the same daughter—and therein lay the cause for Laststar's smoldering resentment.

Why haven't you gone questing for treasures with the rest of the tribe?

Aren't you gathering enough from the rest?

Whether they wanted to or not, full siblings shared a rapport that was somewhat more than sending but less than Recognition. Rahnee used it to garner Laststar's cooperation. **Surlin—that's not good enough.**

I don't know, Rahnee. The same reason you don't, I suppose, Laststar sent with a shrug. **I already know who I am.**

"That's it?" Rahnee squatted on her sister's sleeping fur.

"Sometimes Surlin, sometimes Laststar. Not an elf, not a Wolfrider, either. My father vanished. My mother never heard my inner name; I hear my cubs' inner names when they quicken and again when they're born, but never again. You know—firstborn, we don't quite fit anywhere, so you've got to be yourself. Or is it different for you because you're Timmorn's heir?"

Bright, beautiful light dawned in the chieftess's mind. "That *is* it!" She gave her sister an exuberant embrace that left both of them a little shaken. "I mean, I thought I *was* different . . ."

"Well, aren't you? You're chieftess. Zarhan Fastfire is your lifemate. You know everybody's inner name . . . and you use it."

Rahnee nodded. She was the only chief. She was the only firstborn who had lifemated with a full-blooded elf; for that matter she was the only firstborn who was lifemated with anyone. But she didn't know everyone's inner name. **I thought it was just me, and my cubs . . . They must lose their names as they're born. They don't feel the emptiness in wolfsong, but that's why they're looking for treasures, and fighting each other. I understand everything now."

Laststar wrinkled her eyebrows. The only thing she understood was that she didn't understand her sister, and that wasn't worth losing sleep over. "I suppose if you can make them stop fighting with each other . . ."

Rahnee's face mirrored Laststar's. "I didn't say I could stop them, I said I knew why they were doing it. They should be looking for their inner names, not pebbles and feathers. I'll tell them."

"Why don't we just tell them their names and get it over with?"

The suggestion was so simple, and so very wrong. Rahnee shook her head heavily trying to get rid of it. She took a step backward, then another. "No. No. Can't do that. Can't tell them."

"Why not? It's not as if there's some *mystery* to an inner name." Laststar didn't know herself where she'd found that old, elfin word "mystery," but as soon as she said it, both firstborn knew that "mystery" was the only word. Her shoulders gave an unconscious shudder as she remembered the moment she knew she was Surlin. "If it's going to be harder for the young ones . . ." But she didn't repeat her suggestion that Rahnee spare them the quest.

Cat heard the excitement in her mother's call. She turned, and even took a few steps, then stopped. A great hunt? A dreamberry feast? A journey to the other side of the horizon? The chieftess had nothing to offer except what she had offered many times before. But the tribe was not like before, not with Slowthrower and Lightfeet gone. She was leaving, as others had left before her, but for reasons she didn't fully understand herself, she wasn't trailing her lovemates.

"Are you leaving, too?" Cat asked when she came upon her father who also ignored Rahnee's summons.

He was startled like a stunned ravvit. Elves. They could hear as well as anyone, but they never seemed to be listening.

"I'm leaving," she said when a shadow of intelligence reappeared in his eyes.

Her father nodded as if he'd been waiting for her to come out of nowhere with that exact statement. "Have you made peace with her . . . your . . . the chieftess?"

Cat shook her head. "No use in it. There's emptiness here now."

"I'll tell her, then." Fastfire smiled as he touched her cheek. "You'll live in my thoughts so long as you live under two moons."

Their eyes met; Cat looked away first. She hurried away from her father. Live in his thoughts, he said in that elfin way that left one wondering what, exactly, was meant. Who knew what went on in an elf's mind? Elves spent so much time in the past, maybe they did know the future as well.

Past was past and useless. Future was future and just as useless.

Cat told herself that her way—the way she and the others of her generation learned from their wolf-friends—was the best way. If past and future were useless, then live in the now. A hunter had to be more concerned about the ground beneath her feet than the clouds along the horizon.

Cat wasn't quite sure where she was going, but that didn't stop her from putting a substantial distance between herself and the tribe before weariness called a halt. There wasn't a hunter in the tribe who hadn't laired alone for a night or two, especially in the light nights of summer. Clear away the worst of the rocks, weave the tall grass into a windbreak, weave more of it into pillow, then curl up and close your eyes. Cat did it all, thoughtless and sure-fingered, but sleep eluded her.

This was a new kind of alone. Not the hunkered-down alone when you didn't want to share your meat or your dreams, but a huge alone. There wasn't a living scent in the air, nor a familiar thought to echo her dream sendings, not even Tailchaser. Cat sat up. She rubbed her aching shoulders. She sang to the stars, but her song died quickly. A lump jelled her throat. She swallowed; it would not go down. She coughed; it would not come up. She lay down to stare at the night and did not notice when sleep joined her.

When she opened her eyes again the lump was gone and the only emptiness was in her belly. Unlike the wolves, who were carnivores, and the elves, who were hopelessly fastidious, Cat ate just about anything when she was hungry. She rummaged around her makeshift den and by the time the daystar was four hands above the horizon the emptiness was gone.

Cat was alone. She had not forgotten the tribe, but she didn't remember them, either. They were no longer part of her now-content mind. When hunters came near, Cat slipped away without thinking of what she did or the why of it. She wandered south, toward the winter forests, but it was instinct, not self, that guided her.

An eight-of-days passed. The moons completed a dance and began another. Cat flowed with daily and seasonal rhythms, but did not notice them. Then, as she stretched and yawned her way out of an afternoon's nap, she realized she was no longer alone. She hefted her spear and made herself wary. She scanned the horizon, tasting the air in every quarter. She named everything she sensed; she emptied herself of what she named, and was still not alone.

Her neck hairs stiffened. In her own life Cat had never seen a predator become prey, but she knew the tales of men. She gave a call that was both warning and apology, then surrendered the ground where she had napped. That signal would have satisfied any predator she knew, but it did not satisfy the one who followed her.

Cat made tracks as she had not done since leaving the tribe. She came to a stream and hurled herself across it. She didn't know a predator who would risk swift-flowing water for a meal. With her breath still ragged, she flattened herself in the grass, hoping to catch sight of her pursuer so she might know and avoid its kind forevermore. There was no sound above the sound of the stream itself. Nothing moved, until a cool shadow fell on her back.

Cat threw badly. Her spear glanced off a rock; it fell empty in the grass. No other movement. No sound or scent. No bent grass to show where it had stood. Cat wanted the comfort of her spear. She would have braved death itself to retrieve it, but the place where her spear lay was worse than death.

The shadow was never far away after that. She rode the stream until her lungs were half filled with water, and came to understand that it did not hunt by scent. As the pack harried the click-toe, driving them past fear to exhaustion, the shadow-hunter harried Cat a day and a night.

She could not hunt and dared not sleep. A raw wind blew from the north. It dusted the grass with frost and snow. Red-eyed and shivering, Cat came to bay far downstream. She loosened her wet hair and slipped into a death-trance as the dawn light touched her back.

Wild creatures did not bargain with death. When the now was over, they simply stopped. The tension of the long chase drained down Cat's spine. She was at peace, waiting for teeth and claws she would not feel. She stopped shivering. Her hair dried into a brilliant red curtain.

A ravvit broke cover. It reared up, flicking its ears at this strange, staring creature suspended between death and life. It thumped the ground, for good measure, but there was no danger and it continued down the bank to the water. Raptors congregated in lazy circles far above the stream. The ravvit found danger in the echo of their shrill call; it vanished into the grass. But the birds were waiting, not hunting.

Sunlight fell directly on Cat's face. The bright light made her eyes water. She closed her eyes because she could no longer keep them open.

It will be over soon, Cat thought, but soon dragged on. Her shoulders twitched. A cramp exploded in the calf of her right leg. She could no longer wait for soon. With a soft cry, Cat slumped forward. She was weak beyond one night's running; she had been to death's door, and been turned away. Many moments passed before she had the strength to raise her head.

The world had turned a shifty, iridescent green. She ground her fists into her eyes; the greens were only brighter. Cat was sun-blind. She panicked, forgetting everything she knew about survival. She stumbled headlong into the stream and was half drowned before she remembered how to swim.

The stream plunged into a gorge. Twice she lost up from down and took a breath of water by mistake. Both times she righted herself. She was battered and bleeding, but the huntress who had resigned herself to death now fought tenaciously for her life.

Luck caught up with her and Cat found herself spun out of the mainstream into a shallow pool. Her weight kept her out of the current while she coughed water from her lungs and stomach. Everything ached, but nothing was broken. Cat hauled herself onto a dry rock that was warmer than she was. She lay there a bit before raking her hair away from her face.

The world was still a sick, seething green.

Father! Father, help me! I'm cold and I'm hurt and I'm scared. Mother. Rahnee She-Wolf. Chieftess. It's me . . . Cat . . . your daughter.

Nothing—though the sendings flowed from her until the warmth began to fade from the rock. Cat had been beyond her parents' reach from the beginning. Comfort came from the echo of her own thoughts.

It's me . . . It's Cat . . . I'm here.

Cat's rock lost its heat quickly. The breeze promised a heavy, lasting frost. On her hands and knees, Cat explored the bank. She moved slowly because she had to, and more wisely because she wanted to live. She searched for safety and found it in an abandoned den. It was rank, musky, and littered with bones, but it was also dry and facing away from the frost wind. She pushed the midden out with her feet and settled against the curve of the back wall.

I'm here now. Me. Cat. I'm here.

Her body relived the day as she slept. The light was pleasant on her back, then it circled until it was on her face and no longer pleasant. Cat cried out in her sleep. Her eyes watered and she covered them with her hands. Then she was in the water. It carried her more gently this time, playing with her as she played with the cubs. It whirled her around and tossed her in the air. The corners of Cat's mouth turned up; her tears ceased. She sang to the water and it sang a one-word song back to her: Mar.

The dreams were more pleasant than the waking. Cat's bruises and cuts throbbed; her throat was raw from retching. She didn't need Willowgreen to know she was gut-sick as well. The world was less green than it had been. She could distinguish dark from light, motion from stillness. A shadow quivered over the mouth of the den.

The shadow-hunter did not come in after her, neither did it leave. Cat tried to hear its breathing, but there was only the stream and the song she heard in her dreams. She slipped into a stupor. Day became night, night became day, Cat neither noticed nor cared. She lost all awareness of the world beyond her aching body, the den, and the shadowy presence.

Come for me. I'm ready. Make me a part of you.

Rahnee fussed with the lacing of her winter tunic. The white and lavender nights of summer were over. The click-toe stags had finished their rut and shed their antlers. There was a raw edge on the wind; ice would lock the marshes within a moon-dance. Now was time to flay their kills and scrape the hides for winter clothing. **It's now-time for leaving,** she sent to her lifemate who stood only a few paces away.

Zarhan affected not to hear her. His mud mounds had gotten bigger as the days grew shorter. This one was shoulder-high. He'd kept its fires burning for a day, then waited another day while it cooled. A deep crack spiraled down from the crest.

Open it now. It's now-time for winter-coming. Now-time for leaving. The chieftess resisted wolfsong, but every day thoughts had fewer words and more images.

"Not yet."

Now. She butted her spear into the baked mud. The mound collapsed.

Zarhan said something he hoped she'd neither hear nor understand. He retrieved a skull-sized lump from the wreckage. A hollow turquoise ball emerged from the casting. He placed it gently in his lifemate's hands.

"It's a bowl, a basket for water. You can drink from it."

She gave him a sidelong glance but raised the object to her lips.

"You have to fill it first," he explained, taking it from her. Wolfsong inhibited imagination.

Now-time for leaving.

A streak of mud clung to the bowl. Zarhan chipped at it with his fingernail and found it went through the glaze to the fused sand core. His hands tensed and the bowl crumbled.

No more mud, fire, baskets-for-water. Now-time for leaving. Now-time. Rahnee took his wrist to lead him away.

He escaped. "We don't have to leave yet. The days are cool, but there's no ice. There's still time. She might be coming back."

The chieftess shuddered. She hadn't forgotten Cat—yet. Her cub's departure brought peace back to the tribe. The restless treasure-seeking stopped, and so did the brawls. None of the youngsters had been stirred to seek their inner name, but who needed a solution once the problem was gone?

Wolfsong came out of hiding. Slowthrower and Lightfeet rejoined the tribe without incident. The problem, most definitely, had been Cat.

Rahnee took Zarhan's wrist again. **Her leave-time is no more. Ours is now.**

"You can't just abandon her, beloved . . ."

Rahnee cocked her head to one side. **Abandon? What abandon? Where? All this happens before and again, but no abandoning.**

"This has *not* happened before, Rahnee. Cat is *our* daughter. Doesn't that mean something to you? Cat . . . Mara. Don't you hear her name calling?"

The She-Wolf bared her teeth. What the wolves did not understand, they drove away. **Cat was not one within the tribe. I do not hear her now or ever. She is emptiness in your mind. That is the *Way*, beloved.**

"You've changed the Way before."

She is emptiness.

"Search for her. Yellow-Eyes chose you over the rest of his children. You're the chieftess; you make the way. Have you even tried?"

"No. She left. She's gone. My mind is empty of her."

"She isn't dead, beloved. I can hear her, but I can't find her. Try to find her, for me if not yourself."

The chieftess's gut heaved with indigestible notions. She did not want to think about the Way. She did not want to think about Cat. She did not want to think about the emptiness that wasn't quite empty. She did not want to think at all. Rahnee stole a glance at Zarhan. He wore his implacable face.

"While we travel?" she bargained.

Zarhan relaxed. **Yes,** he sent, and allowed her hand to slip around his wrist.

Rahnee started the tribe on its autumn migration that very

afternoon. She drove them hard until the moons set. The chieftess didn't need Talen's memory of other migrations to know that they'd travel farther the first day, before their muscles cramped up, than they would in the hand-of-days after; she needed nothing more than the stone-tiredness in her own legs.

Here. Now.

Her traveling bundle of furs, spears, knives, and knapping stones was the first of many to thump on the ground. Zarhan was in the rear with the elves. By the time he trudged forward, Rahnee was sound asleep. He'd sooner provoke a longtooth cat than awaken the She-Wolf. He shook out his sleeping furs and stretched out beside her. There'd be no searching for Cat until the daystar was well above the horizon.

The night was cold. They wriggled toward each other without waking. Their dreams merged. *Penda*, their first-born, shapeless and cool; *Tirak, Kreanne, Genrow, Fowler* shining like stars, waiting for the moment of their quickening; *Mara*, the emptiness that could not, would not, be filled. *Mara. Mara. Mara.*

Rahnee sought freedom. She struck something with all her might. Her lifemate vanished.

Zarhan barely avoided a second spear-thrower's thrust. **Beloved!** He scrambled out of reach. **Beloved!** He couldn't rouse her, and he couldn't remember anything of the dream they shared. The worst dreams were also the shortest ones, he assured himself as he tightened his tunic against the winds.

The nightmare did not abate. Rahnee moaned as she thrashed, and the wolves howled with her. Unwilling and ill-tempered, the tribe abandoned their rest.

"What did she eat?" Willowgreen groused from a safe distance.

"It's nothing she ate. It's an overripe dream."

The healer dismissed Zarhan's concerns with a sniff.

"Overripe dreams. I saw her eating berries as we walked. Probably frost-touched: sweet and strong." She waited for a lull then placed her hands on the chieftess's forehead. She searched for gut spasms and found something quite different.

"It's me. I'm here! Come for me!"

The dream—if it was a dream—was strong enough to hold Willowgreen. She and the chieftess spoke as one, but neither was the source of the words.

"Mar!"

Rahnee shuddered as she screamed the final syllable. Willowgreen's hands moved and she was free. The chieftess went limp.

"Mar," Willowgreen repeated. The look she threw toward Zarhan was deadly with contempt. "She has found Mar . . . or Mar has found her."

"Mara," Zarhan corrected.

"No, Mar." The healer got to her feet and made a show of cleaning her hands. "Cat was a hunter. She was everything she needed to be, then she went looking for more. Now what is she? Half an elf? Why couldn't you leave well enough alone, Fastfire? Don't the flaws in your glass tell you anything?"

Zarhan had no ready answer, so Willowgreen enlightened him. "Elves have nothing to give to the hunters. Anything we give them diminishes them. They have the Way, and we do not. It is bad enough that you tamed the She-Wolf, but now she has destroyed her daughter. They're both gone where I cannot reach them."

Zarhan turned away. His breath came in short gasps and his fingers stiffened. Willowgreen smirked with satisfaction, not guessing how close she stood to the fury of his fire-magic. Fastfire had killed just once—a wattleneck with a conscious mind smaller than its fingernail brain—but he still remembered the instant of its death and so the healer was spared.

He was calm when he faced Willowgreen again. "You are the one who knows nothing. You will not understand yourself, so you cannot understand anyone or anything else. Perhaps I do put my flaws in my glass; maybe because I am an elf everything I do is doomed to flaws, but hear me clearly, Darrel, *this* elf does not give up. *This* elf will not abandon what he loves because he or they are less than perfect."

Willowgreen opened her mouth, then reconsidered and escaped into the night. Fastfire dropped to his knees beside his lifemate.

Rahnee, beloved, are you there? Can you feel me?

He was no healer, nor did he have any measure of the rapport Samael brought to the dreamberry bowl, nothing at all to guide him as he surged into the maelstrom. He was lost in a heartbeat. Wolf-cubs and his own children did not cry out when they were alone or afraid, but elves were not attuned to the dangers of the unknown. Like a lightning bug, Zarhan broadcast his lifemate's name.

You found me, Rahnee assured him, though the opposite was closer to the truth. Her presence crystallized the maelstrom, but her thoughts were tinted with sadness. **Can you feel her?**

Fastfire molded his thoughts to hers and found his daughter. Cat had been battered by her ordeal. There was an undercurrent of ache and exhaustion to her sendings, but only an undercurrent. The main current was an impenetrable ecstasy. Cat had found Mar or Mar had found Cat, either way their joining was complete.

Why are you sad? Zarhan asked Rahnee. **She's found her name. Isn't that what you wanted?**

The chieftess tumbled back to her body. She shivered in her lifemate's arms. **Mara. Her name is Mara. I do not know who she is. I . . . I thought that they were apart because they didn't know their names. I thought if they found their names . . . like I did . . . then they'd belong again. But this is worse. She's found only part of her name, and it's pulled her further away. She's so far away she can't share.**

We know where she is. The tribe can go to her. We can meet halfway . . .

Our feet can, but not our thoughts. She called me . . . Cat called me; I was with her at the finding, and then I was shut out.

Rahnee pressed her head against Zarhan's shoulder. Her tears were warm, then icy against his skin. "I have failed them. This cannot be what my father wanted, or what my grandmother meant. I hear her, beloved. I heard Willowgreen; I've destroyed my cub. I've destroyed the Way."

Fastfire got his fingers under her arms. He pushed her away. Dawn was coming and he could tell when she looked at him. "That, beloved, is nonsense. I don't know what Timmain was like, but the Way you've found is better than Timmorn's. Do you think our daughter could have found even *half* a name in your father's time? You certainly couldn't."

The chieftess sniffed up a stream of tears and nodded slowly. "I was always too hungry to worry about a name."

"There, what more do you need? All this has happened because no one was hungry this summer. If Cat had been fatter when she left, she'd have found Mara, not Mar. It's as simple as that."

She shook her head, but her eyes were dry and there was a faint smile at the corners of her mouth. "I think not," she said gently as she got to her feet. "But I do not think I could understand more, and I know I cannot change it, so I will believe you anyway."

Cat rejoined the tribe when the moons were new. She was eager to tell the other young hunters what had happened, but she did not tell anyone her shadow-self's name. A new mark was placed on the path of the Way. Lightfeet and Slow-thrower were among the first hunters to deliberately seek their names: Bur and Orn. They each had a secret, but the secrets were equal and they were a threesome again. Life seemed to be just as it had been before, then, in the spring, they Recognized each other. There were no more secrets, and life was definitely better.

Court and Chase

by Katharine Eliska Kimbriel

It took a long time for an elf to be born. A flare of Recognition, that genetic imperative which triggered fertility and conception, and the slow, secret cycle began again. Recognition was rare; a love child, born without it, even rarer.

With the wolves, it was simple; the frenzy of mating season, coinciding with snowmelt and the first clear days of spring, and then the pack returned to normal. Only the digging of pregnant she-wolves excavating dens gave any indication of what had happened.

But the mind and soul of an elf was a complex thing, and it took time to create a creature born both of two moons and the stars. Twice the seasons would run their course; twice the winds of winter howl like lonely wolves, and twice the golden leaves of the dying time carpet the ground like lion skin. A silent and secret thing, the creation of an elf; silent because there was little discomfort until the last third of the pregnancy, and secret because two thirds of the time passed before anyone save the parents knew what was going to happen.

It should be as simple for us as for the wolves. The thought was colored with irony, but Windwhisper fought to keep herself from bitterness. She carried new life—a life needed by the tribe—and the results of this joining would be a healthy cub. How could she have predicted what had followed? Perhaps she should speak, and end it. No . . . there was no guarantee that would end it. Surely the chief would have asked her to speak, if he had thought it would ease tensions.

"Hungry?" came a voice, and she glanced up from her nest of furs to see Dove, firstborn of their chief Prey-Pacer and his lifemate Softfoot. The elf-woman was offering a scrap of dried deer, almost the last of their store.

How could she deny hunger? It alternated within her, this new nausea and the aching need for food. Rellah had told her it often happened that way, but knowing it was normal did not make it easier. "Yes. Thanks."

Handing her the strip of flesh, Dove settled in the hollow Windwhisper had formed for visitors. The silver-haired elf was one of the few among the Wolfriders who would sit in so obvious an example of rock-shifting. Although Rellah had been pleased to accept a lair similar to Windwhisper's own, young Merewood had refused to come near the smooth, undulating stone, despite visual evidence that it eased the discomforts of pregnancy.

But then Dove is a chief's daughter, and little frightens her, Windwhisper thought, chewing on the scrap of meat. To be fair, if she was in Merewood's position, she would be anxious, too. To be carrying Graywolf's cub! Would it be elf-cub, or "hunt," as the old ones called those born with too much wolf in them? Many privately thought Graywolf was himself too much wolf, as opposite from his twin brother Owl as could be imagined. And now both would become fathers, although Rellah did not seem to have Merewood's fears. At least Owl and Rellah weren't at each other's throats, like Merewood and Graywolf. *Will my cub be too much elf?*

"I thought you might need a bit of food to sustain you," Dove went on, her tone casual and yet somehow studied.

Windwhisper heard the silent warning. *Oh, no.* She listened carefully . . . not close, yet. There was little even to sense—her wolf Nightshadow was still out of reach, and Windwhisper knew the alpha female would be at the head of the day's hunting party. **Wasp and Sundown?** she sent tentatively.

"Who else?" Like her chieftain father in his youth, Dove did not send very well, although she had no trouble understanding. "And I think they've finally pushed Starfall too far. They're coming back the stream trail," she added, as if she had read Windwhisper's thoughts.

"High Ones give me strength," Windwhisper murmured, burrowing deeper into her furs. That meant they were still around the bend—just barely within sending range, but visible from the peak above. Dove enjoyed look-out duty, and had served as the eyes of the tribe since a hunting accident had made her unable to grasp with her spear hand. Glancing over as the thought came to her, Windwhisper saw that Dove was dutifully squeezing the many-layered leather "fake fruit" that Willowgreen had had made up for her. The roundish body gave slightly when she gripped it, and was clearly helping her hand regain its old strength.

"You'll be able to hunt soon," Windwhisper offered, trying to change the subject.

"Yes, Windwhisper," Dove said abruptly, "don't let them worry you. If I were you, I'd tell all three of them to keep their distance. It's no one's business who the father of that cub is . . . all the tribe sees to its cubs. And I don't think naming the father would calm them in the slightest." Frowning slightly, her dove-gray eyes white in the glare of Talen's fire, she added: "They'll just have to work it out for themselves. Unless you want to lie to them, and tell all of them that they are the father!"

This was clearly a joke, and Windwhisper managed a smile of appreciation. Dove knew as well as she that it was almost impossible for a Wolfrider to lie to one of the tribe—if body language did not give the secret away, then shadings within their sending surely would. Besides, Windwhisper had kept her secret *too* well. This was no love child she carried—all three of the cubs-to-be were seeds of Recognition . . . and none of her three would-be suitors was the father of hers. To say it had been Recognition might end one type of tension, but it would surely breed another.

Chewing her own strip of deer meat, Dove curled languidly into the stone hollow, keeping her distance from the fire. Envying the Wolfrider's calm, Windwhisper let her thoughts trail back . . . back. . . . It had all begun when the day of the long sun neared, and the nights were short and sultry . . .

The Wolfriders had been preparing to leave on one of their extended journeys. Windwhisper had controlled her usual disappointment—Prey-Pacer had still been against her going—and had done her best to help with preparations. A veiled suggestion to her chief that she hang back during the hunt and carry some of Willowgreen's potions against illness and injury had met with no more success than any other strategy she had tried. Instinctively she had known better than to remind him about her new talent for shaping rock. Prey-Pacer was fairly relaxed about his chieftainship, but anything varying too far from the norm troubled him. He had accepted her abilities and appreciated their usefulness —but they did not compare to honed hunting skill. And it was still elf-magic; something not quite to be trusted.

Restless, Windwhisper had fled into the forest at dawn, drowning her thoughts in elvish handwork since wolfsong spoke only of the coming trip. Sensing her unease, the older elves had been kind, directing her to reeds that needed cutting, or places to find deadwood for their fires. Nothing had helped the pain of pending separation, and so Windwhisper had wandered down the stream path, to watch the sun rise over flowing water and through sparse trees that framed grassland east and south and shadowy mountains beyond. A few steps farther, just out of sight, she had heard one of the elves splashing in the shallows of the stream.

Curiosity had sealed her doom. Peering through pine boughs, she had seen Talen, one of the true elves, digging out wet clay and placing it on a deerskin for transport to their cave. Finally hearing her movements as her toes touched the water, Talen had glanced up, his mouth opening to give a greeting that never came. A peculiar feeling had swept through Windwhisper, as if the wind had caught her up and tossed her like a leaf. Normally she had been shy of the elder elves, but that time Talen's pale blue eyes had not frightened, they had drawn her in—drawn her down, much like the strength that once had pulled her into the mountain's heart. Something in his expression had suggested the same strange sensation was flowing in his veins.

Then a startled sending had whispered in her mind, questioning her very name . . . and the name it had murmured was her soul's. Almost as startling had been the knowledge of Talen's soulname, dancing on the tip of her tongue, begging to be spoken.

Windwhisper had recoiled in shock. Terrified, she had slipped away, no more than a shiver in the leaves, leaving Talen kneeling in the water with clay dripping from his hands. How far had she run? She had had no way of knowing—only that sense had finally taken over, and stilled her frantic feet. Dropping down on a nearby stone, unconsciously shaping a depression for her comfort, Windwhisper had tried to control her ragged breathing.

Although her breathing had slowed, her heart had refused to respond, racing like a ravvit in fear for its life. A flush of body heat had made her tingle, as if she were splashing in spring water on a sunny day. Recognition. It *had* to have been Recognition—how else could anyone have known her soulname? No one, no one had known; she had shared it with no one. No one else could have called to her—it had to have been Talen. Which meant . . .

Seeking common sense within her fears, Windwhisper had found a pool of calm. Silly child, she had scolded herself. You knew your turn would come. But she had always hoped it would be Starfall. . . . Talen, of all people! He was *ancient*. Without intending to, Windwhisper had smiled at her own outburst, for in that fragile moment all had changed. Her elder Talen might have been, but the adult female within named *Chat* had seen him differently than the young

Wolfrider Windwhisper had . . . she had seen him anew. Talen was no elder, not in that sense—he was a staggeringly attractive elf in the prime of his life.

In hesitancy and embarrassment, it had seemed like days before she had made up her mind to find Talen. In truth the sun had been barely above the young pines which rimmed their cavern nests. Windwhisper had found him with Rellah and New-Wolf, slamming water from his clay with unusual enthusiasm. Instantly aware of her presence, Talen had glanced at her from the corner of an eye, oblivious to the elf-women's conversation.

That glint of blue eye had given her boldness; she had already loosened her thick braid of black hair. A long tendril had fallen forward over her shoulder . . . it had draped as she bent toward him, its coiling satin finger a private invitation. Narrowly, privately, as Talen and Rellah had taught those who wished to learn, Windwhisper had sent his soulname to him. Since that moment she had often wondered how long it took Rellah and New-Wolf to notice that Talen had disappeared.

It had been a long, luxurious day of private reflections and promise fulfilled . . . passion and relaxation, and then passion again. Wolfrider had learned much about the elders, things that the youngsters had never bothered to discover, while elf had added to a vast storehouse of knowledge. Relief, acceptance—even pleasure, for no one said duty had to be a burden. They had never *disliked* each other, certainly, although Windwhisper had had her lovemates and Talen had stayed mostly with Rellah and New-Wolf. In Recognition they had found they liked each other. If Recognition came again, it would come . . . and it would pass.

Sooner than anyone could expect. That evening they had slipped back into the camp, to see the major portion of the Wolfriders off to the great hunt. No one had seemed to notice either their absence or their reappearance. One day of Recognition . . . one day had been enough. Who would have thought that the timing could be so perfect?

Hunters hunting, the core group gathering and storing food while the forest was generous—why bother to mention it? Rellah had Recognized Owl earlier, so there would be two cubs at least when the time came. Talen had returned to Rellah, and her own arrangements with Starfall and Sundown had been fine (or as good as they could be with a rivalry brewing . . .) so Windwhisper had kept silent.

Then Merewood and Graywolf had Recognized. A full eight-of-days and more had passed before they had answered the call, and it had been hard on them. In the tension and chaos that followed, Windwhisper had kept silent.

Seasons flowed one into another—long sun, dying time, deep cold, snowmelt, new buds—and the Long Day came again. Gathering time arrived, and once more the hunters headed south to find the game that had not returned. Through it all, Windwhisper kept silent.

Three dances of the moon the hunters were gone, that time. They brought back a variety of game to those who did not hunt . . . they also brought back tension, for three elves were obviously pregnant, not two, and that meant—

"Here you are!" The cheerful tenor voice mercifully shook Windwhisper from her memories just before her problem had begun. Of course the problem still continued —and had just returned home.

An arm of corded muscle extended into her line of sight, holding a prime slice of fresh prong-horn. Smiling faintly, Windwhisper reached for it before realizing that even this simple offering could cause trouble.

Dropping down at her feet, his brilliant red hair molten gold by the fitful firelight, Sundown gave her a sharp look. "They're outside dividing the catch and giving the wolves their share. Go ahead and eat."

Windwhisper started chewing. No point in angering him by refusing his gift. Off to one side, just beyond the fire's gleam, she saw Willowgreen toss her head and settle on her stuffed skin. *Ouch.* Simple dislike had grown into active hostility, there. Well, Windwhisper did not feel a great deal of guilt over it. If Willowgreen had not blown first hot, then cold, as pliant as her name, Sundown would not have grown angry and started chasing other females. Still, the antagonism from the healer was not a comfortable feeling.

One could not bolt down raw prong-horn—it had to be thoroughly chewed, or it sat in the belly like accidental stone. So she was still chewing when Wasp arrived, a thick slice of deer in his hands. To her right, Windwhisper heard Dove stifle a queer sound and fought the urge to snap at her like a wolf. *It's not funny!*

Black eyes met black, and she saw hurt reflected in Wasp's eyes. How could she help but hurt them, each of them, over and over, if they persisted at this game? To compensate for his late arrival, she gave him a dazzling smile. Slightly mollified (more so, after Sundown threw him a suspicious glance, trying to figure out what he had done to earn such a response), Wasp sat down near his mother, Rellah, and offered her some deer.

Long years of experience might have sharpened Rellah's tongue, but they had also sharpened her humor. Instead of giving him the satisfaction of making a face and turning away, Rellah promptly reached for a pointed stick and presented the tip to him. Pretending to pout, Wasp impaled the flesh on the branch.

"Are you sure you want to burn this?" he asked, reeking of solicitude.

"Cook it," she ordered, "or I'll throw up on you."

This was no idle threat from a pregnant elf, and Wasp hastily stuck the polished rod into a crevice to suspend it above the flames. Windwhisper could not help but laugh, and reached out with gentle fingers to touch his face in appreciation of the jest. Sundown's response was to take a deep breath, as if trying to keep from speaking, but before Windwhisper could think of what to say or do, mingled new scents reached her nose.

Easily removing her hand from Wasp's cheek, she turned her head to where she knew Starfall's impassive visage towered above them all. He was carrying something in a bowl—this was what was overpowering the wolf-scent brought in by the hunters. Her nose recognized the wild rice which grew in the marshy part of the stream. It was one of the few cooked dishes made by their elders that the Wolfriders not only tolerated, but actually liked. Windwhisper adored it.

This was one-upmanship of impressive proportions, and as Windwhisper's eyes lit up, Wasp and Sundown both stiffened in response.

A familiar cold nose trimmed in feathers touched her neck. Wiggling up from her furs, Windwhisper reached to scratch the ears of her wolf, Nightshadow, who had left her to join the hunt this day. A nice suntail, barely warm, dangled from her jaws. It must have been caught on the return, after her group had filled their bellies—

Now don't you start, too! she sent privately to the wolf. Dropping the bird on her arm and grinning hugely, the big female walked around and actually sat on her feet. Windwhisper controlled a sigh and briefly contemplated hysterics. *Death by affection.* She threw Dove a desperate look.

"So, how did it go?" Dove suddenly asked, leaning forward for details of the hunt. In doing so she vacated the seat Windwhisper had hollowed out two moons ago. Starfall promptly dropped into it and offered the bowl of rice.

"Careful, it's still hot," he warned, as she gave him a smile of gratitude. Over his shoulder Windwhisper could see their chief enter the cave, his youngest cub, a ten-turns son who had recently picked up the name Spear, in close pursuit. Prey-Pacer's eye quickly took in the tableau, and a tight smile crept across his face. He actually nodded his approval at her handling of the situation, and then moved to greet the others within the cave. Although he did not comment on the fire Talen had lit for Rellah, Windwhisper noticed that he carefully positioned himself so that his legs could gather some reflected heat while most of his body kept its distance from the flames.

What could she say? Prey-Pacer was right—this was as calm as it had been since the hunters had returned at the end of summer. Merewood and Graywolf Recognizing had been bad enough; since then fighting had often erupted without warning. The evidence of her own condition merely had added to the excitement and tension. Three more mouths to feed in the spring, and game had been falling off in these parts.

Then she had sensed it—the smoldering antagonism between Sundown and Wasp. It had quickly become apparent that *she* was the bone of contention. Those who wondered aloud why Starfall was not involved quickly held their tongues after a series of private fistfights caused all three elves to appear with a variety of minor injuries. The fights had ended once the leaves began falling in earnest— because food was getting harder to find, or because of Windwhisper's own distress over their active quarrel?—but the competition had continued.

Talen had been gracious enough to let her keep her own counsel. Perhaps she should have spoken before, at the beginning—but this season of Recognition was not like any in recent memory. Before, the curse seemed to fall on the same pairs, over and over, causing them to end up lifemates even if they kept lovers elsewhere. Not since the very beginning of the She-Wolf's chieftainship had so much anger accompanied the event.

So far Windwhisper saw no indication that she and Talen had formed a permanent bond. Remembering a fragment of a story, Windwhisper had questioned Owl about a tale of Rahnee She-Wolf and Zarhan Fastfire, one that mentioned "the many names they heard between them." In that long, lazy afternoon, she had heard only Talen's true name, until finally a third name, many-syllabled and melodious, seemed to shape itself from their longing. Only one name; a name that still resonated in the air, at least for Windwhisper. What did it mean?

Would she bear only one cub in her life? Only one with Talen? Or was that sensitivity something that faded as the generations marched on? Even as she willfully demanded the latter choices, she feared the foremost, and so her decision was made. Nothing would interfere with this cub—nothing. Not even her own desires. It would have the best chance she could give it. But the big game animals had left this part of the woods . . . how would they eat, come spring? Were there enough animals for them to make it until spring?

Her eyes remained on her chief. Behind his impassive face, he was thinking of moving—she could almost taste it, she was so sure. Moving with a double handful of cubs under ten turns and three pregnant females. . . . The thought was horrifying. Windwhisper knew she would fear it even if she wasn't pregnant . . . and this time, she was one of the true liabilities.

Seizing a handful of feathers, Windwhisper ripped at the bird, letting the blood sizzle into the fire pit.

"Save it," Starfall ordered, sliding another bowl before her. Surprised, Windwhisper did as he asked. True, blood was nourishing when added to stew, but the elders did not use it until meat was scarce . . .

"How went the hunt?" she said softly, trying to hide her uneasiness.

Starfall shrugged slightly. "Wreath's group ran down a prong-horn, and the chief got a deer. We cleaned up some small stuff."

Windwhisper stared, her grip on the bird loosening. "The wolves?"

"We gave them most of the prong-horn," Sundown said quickly. "We have to keep their strength up—they weaken quickly if they don't get enough to eat." He took the bird from her hands as he spoke, slitting it up the breastbone with a sharp flint knife and dumping the entrails in the bowl.

Feathers floated in the air as he swiftly began plucking out quills.

There were no more questions to ask. The wolves hovered at about three times the size of a true-wolf pack—thirty-three had lived at first snow, the last time Windwhisper had gone hunting. To keep up full strength, the entire pack needed at least three prong-horns every five days . . . and there were currently fifty adult elves and eight children besides. The dried meat was almost gone. . . . Extending her hand, she scooped up the entrails of the bird and offered them to Nightshadow, who graciously took the offering. Not as if she were extremely hungry . . . she had not gorged, then. Perhaps the low-status wolves had gotten food, too.

"Can we last until spring?" she finally said.

"Of course. Don't worry about it." This terse remark was from Wasp. She slid her gaze in his direction, and saw the lines pulling at his mouth. Too young to hide his own unease, yet trying to keep others free of worry—

Windwhisper shook her head slightly, the wonder in her renewed. Why was Wasp in this competition? Their involvement was recent, actually after Recognition had taken place. Perhaps wishful thinking, or staking a future claim? *Did you hope to change the laws of nature, to speed up your own maturity and hold back mine?* But she could not ask him that. Without comment she watched as Starfall passed the bowl of blood to New-Wolf, who soberly added it to the big cooking pot full of water she had wedged among the stones. Dropping in the tatos she had peeled, New-Wolf began to add the pieces of bird as Sundown handed them to her.

That cold nose was against her neck once again. Nightshadow was restless; she did not like being in the cave, but since her wolf-friend's condition had become obvious, she had been staying close. Sometimes Windwhisper was sure she heard an echo in her mind, the crooning of her wolf—winter was a foolish time to bear cubs, why was she carrying cubs now? There was no way to explain, so

Windwhisper merely scratched her ears and let her slip back out to her mate's side.

"This is going to get cold," Starfall's voice reminded her, the rice entering her field of view.

No stomach for food, none at all—but she took the bowl and started to eat. While there was food, she was going to eat. Nothing would interfere with this cub—nothing.

Rising wind curled through the cave, causing the fire to leap and the elves to shiver. Sundown cautiously pushed on the end of a log, sliding it deeper into the pit. Around the fire sleepers stirred restlessly, unable to find a spot sheltered from the wind. It held risks, keeping the fire burning at night, but they dared not let it die. Snow was falling once again, even as the temperature continued to drop. Wolves could pile together for warmth, their thick winter fur keeping them safe. Wolfriders made do with borrowed heat—from sleeping furs, from fire, from each other.

Bitterly cold—for once there had been no staring match over who would sleep beside her. Windwhisper had ignored all of it, curling in her little stone nest lined with furs, Starfall on one side and Wasp on the other. Sundown had alternated between lying across everyone's feet and tending the fire.

"My turn," Windwhisper heard Talen say.

"It's all right. I can't sleep," Sundown replied.

"You must try. I can sleep during the day, but in snow you must hunt by day, and every day," Talen said patiently.

"Are you ready for mouse stew?" Light, but not bantering . . . Windwhisper heard the slightest touch of sarcasm.

"It was that bad?"

"Even during successful hunts, we miss eight times for every kill. There is no longer any margin for error . . . none at all." This was very soft, and Windwhisper quailed inwardly to hear Sundown reduced to such despair.

He is a better actor than Wasp. Even as the thought flitted across her mind, Starfall's arms tightened around her fiercely, and she knew he had heard those words, too.

"We are strong," came Prey-Pacer's voice. "We will make it. But we may have to travel again."

"How can we leave when there's no food for those who wait?" This was still respectful, but just barely.

Prey-Pacer did not take offense; their chief's reply was tranquil. "There is enough to leave them for a dance of the child moon. Then we shall see."

Windwhisper did not remember any more speech, but when she woke her hands were clutching an imaginary spear.

It was like the wearing away of stone . . . not as elvish magic molded stone, but as wind or water carved it. Each day the hunt left camp, seeking nourishment—sometimes they returned with meat, but usually they returned empty-handed, their forays accomplishing little beyond lining the wolves' stomachs. A longer trip was taken, before the dried stores completely ran out. It brought fruitful results, and gathered enough deer to smoke supplies against the continuing cold. A second trip was planned . . . and then the luck changed with the weather.

Day hunts were yielding almost nothing. It was vermin stew all the time, now, and that was good for maintenance only. Slowly the elves were losing ground . . . and it was the cubs and pregnant females who were showing it first.

Merewood had always had trouble eating mice—now she could not stomach them. She grew gaunt in the face, drawing herself into wolfsong to block out the hunger pangs even as Willowgreen tried to force her to eat the tatos and punkins the true elves had harvested during the dying time of the year.

"The baby will take what it needs," Willowgreen said impatiently. "You must eat! If you weaken, it will begin to weaken, because it takes its strength from you."

"Perhaps it should not be born," Merewood whispered. "Perhaps it is better this way."

"That is not our choice," Windwhisper snapped, infuriated by her attitude. "Recognition always knows, and it wants this little one. You are trying to cheat Recognition."

"It's not a living thing," Willowgreen pointed out. "If the baby is damaged from not enough food, Recognition won't know that. Once it's conceived, the survival is up to us."

"What would you know about it?" Merewood gasped out, dragging herself from the wolfsong. "What would either of you know about it? Recognition might as well be alive—it is no more to be denied than a pack challenge, or a charging stag."

Her look was defiant, and Windwhisper decided it was time for partial truth, at least. "I know," she answered simply. "Recognition cannot be denied, no matter what your own feelings are."

Merewood, already sinking back into wolfsong, did not seem to understand. The healer, however, gave her a sharp look. Windwhisper returned the glance, her face intent, her expression saying as clearly as words: *Keep this to yourself*.

Too much to hope for . . . either Willowgreen had talked, or someone had overheard. Waiting on sharp pebbles for the reaction of her would-be swains, Windwhisper prepared herself for confrontation.

Of course they did not confront the object of the entire conflict.

Windwhisper! The shriek was momentarily unfamiliar—Yarrow, who did not like to send. It was clearly an alarm. Pulling herself out of her usual nest, Windwhisper made her way to the entrance of the cave as quickly as she could move.

There was a snarling fury of snow and mud wrestling in the clearing below; something dark waved in the air like a chief's lock, and Windwhisper realized it was a flint knife. "Stop it!" she yelled, starting to slog down the path. "Are you crazy? Stop it!" Nearing the bottom, it suddenly occurred to her that she was in no condition to be breaking up a fight.

Throwing back her head, she let loose a spine-tingling howl.

Yarrow and Wasp were on the fringes of the battle, and they both lent their voices to the cry, calling to those who were still out hunting.

They won't get here in time, they can't get here—

Like a dark bolt of skyfire, something streaked from the trees, barreling into the fighters like a wolf-cub playing pounce. The offense startled the combatants enough that they loosened their grips upon each other. Seizing the opportunity, Prey-Pacer grabbed what he could see of red hair and hauled Sundown off Starfall. Noticing the flint knife, he contemptuously kicked it out of the youth's hand and sent him spinning after it.

Starfall was already on his feet. The knife had barely broken the skin; a thin trickle of blood oozed over one collarbone and stained his tunic. Only now could Windwhisper see that he was unarmed.

Have you lost what little wits you were born with?

The tribe cringed as one from this sending—Prey-Pacer had never been particularly adept at it, and had avoided using it in conversation, but they would never have known it from this demonstration. From the sounds behind her, Windwhisper knew he had roused the elves within the cave with its strength.

"We have two moons until snowmelt," he started, moving toward Sundown like an avenging windstalker. "The deer have vanished, we are hanging on by our nails, and *you* just tried to stick a knife into one of our best hunters!" The chief's voice had lowered to little more than a snarl, and Sundown had averted his face from those glowing eyes. Cuffing the elf enough to stagger him, Prey-Pacer turned his back upon the youth and faced the half-circle of elves. "You." He pointed at Starfall. "And you." A jerk of his finger brought Wasp running. "And *you*—" He did not have to turn for Sundown to know he was being addressed. "I don't care who started it this time. I don't want to hear about it again.

Until the game returns, I don't want any of you within ten paces of each other! *You* stay with my group—Wasp, you hunt with Wreath's group from now on. And it will stay this way until I say differently!"

Straightening from his menacing crouch, Prey-Pacer raked the young Wolfriders with his hard eyes. "Have you no sense at all? From the wolves I expect this, but from the tribe! Don't you understand? The cub exists! You cannot change that fact without destroying what you are fighting about . . . or isn't she what you're fighting about?" Shaking his head in disbelief, his anger dissipating, Prey-Pacer walked back to his wolf and started into the trees.

Silence. The gathering began to slip away . . . no one wished to attract the chief's attention. Windwhisper realized she was shaking. Forcing herself once again to breathe, she leaned against the rocky wall of the trail for strength. What was she to do? She wanted to go to them both—High Ones, they could have killed each other—why had they started fighting—

"Wasp wouldn't stop it." It was tiny Yarrow, her voice raspy and hard. "He thought it would settle something. Idiot!" Grabbing Windwhisper's arm, she offered herself as a staff for walking. "You look pretty white, come on." Shivering despite her fur jacket, Yarrow started pulling her friend up the cave path. "Whee! Sometimes I forget we have a chief, with Prey-Pacer so easygoing about things. Then he gets his back up and POW! Rules are rules, and if anyone breaks 'em, they get a broken head!"

"If his wolf wasn't the fastest in the pack—" Windwhisper started softly.

Yarrow shook her arm. "Don't think about it. Come on."

"But the hunt—"

"Your worrying won't make the deer return. Now *come!*" Yarrow was not to be denied, and Windwhisper accompanied her back into the dark cave.

Mother moon traced her path once again, and it was the

worst time Windwhisper could remember. If she had had the strength to ask the elders, they could have told her of one or two winters that were worse . . . but only one or two. The tribe was reduced to rationing the marrow from the bones of any creature they were fortunate enough to catch, and one day Windwhisper realized that New-Wolf was boiling a deerskin in her cooking pot.

Magic had its limits. Rock held mysteries and secrets, but it could not tell her where to find game. Wolfsong carried her further than she had ever gone, all the way back into memory once again. She kept hearing water calling to her, and wondering why a stream in the heart of the mountain should bother to call out its name. *We have plenty of water—*

DEER. The image was blurry, but Windwhisper caught it, hung on to it—forced it to grow solid. More than one deer . . . a deer yard, hollowed out so they could reach overhanging branches for greens, but a death trap, when snow came again—

"Deer!" she shrieked aloud, pulling herself upright. It was still daylight—was anyone close by? Nightshadow's image was so clear—

"They've found deer!" It was Rellah, her beautiful silver eyes gleaming with undisguised pleasure. "The Wolfriders have already left to follow the pack."

"Yes." The pang at not running with them was lulled by the knowledge of food. "Deer. Merewood won't starve." She glanced over as she spoke, to where the maiden lay dreaming, wrapped in the depths of the wolfsong. "Soon we'll have food."

It was a mixed blessing. A yard full of deer, mostly young who had not known the danger, and had failed to leave themselves a way out of their sheltered area. Snowdrifts had trapped them, leaving them to slow starvation. After a brief survey of the group, Prey-Pacer decided that none of them had enough strength left to make it to another yard, much less survive until spring, and so there was a great kill. The wolves gorged themselves, their bellies actually brushing the snow as they wandered back to the camp. Following their trail were the hunters, bowed under their burdens, leaving nothing to chance, leaving nothing for any scavengers.

Knowing better than to eat like the wolves had, the tribe ate what would not keep and furiously cured the rest. Prey-Pacer usually did not push his people to smoke their supplies, but now he was practically supervising the fires. Windwhisper watched him from her stony nest and knew what was coming.

"We will leave before snowmelt?" she asked quietly, once when he was near. Lifting his head, her chief shot her a keen glance, but did not answer.

That night he told them all.

"Berries, Owl," he requested, and the precious dreamberries were passed about, only one apiece this time, because the harvest was thin there, too. This could bring them together in a way nothing else could—only during the dreaming were they truly one tribe. Prey-Pacer asked for tales of travel, and, as always, got more than he'd asked for—travel had never been easy for their people. But there it was, the reason for this sharing . . . always at the end it was better. Each migration ultimately had proved to be a good move. Sometimes it soured quickly—weather, or five-fingered humans drove them along—but for a time there was food in plenty and a place to rest. They had lived without caves before . . . during Rahnee She-Wolf's time, at the very beginning, they had lived under tarps while traveling. Not pleasant, perhaps—the old ones stirred, remembering the cold, the damp—but adequate.

"We must go, and go now, before another snow can block us in," Prey-Pacer said heavily. "I have thought on this a long time, and I do not see another way. We have been at this base too long; it takes a dance of the child moon for the hunters to return from the killing fields. Last trip we had to smoke the meat before returning! And then turn right around, to get fresh meat for the wolves. Two seasons the herds have not returned . . . we cannot last another year without them." He shook his head. "If the hunters left now, taking what food they needed, the rest of you would be on the edge again before we could comfortably return . . . and there is no guarantee we will find game. If we remain together, there is a chance." He straightened, then, his sharp eyes touching each of them in turn.

Feeling eyes upon her, Windwhisper was afraid to look up. Too heavy to ride her wolf . . . it would be a long walk south.

"Three days from now, weather permitting, we will start over the stream and through the pine forest toward the plains. Scouting and hunting parties will be decided tomorrow. Pack light," he added, and Windwhisper remembered how much was left each day as Rahnee had led the elves south. Could Nightshadow carry? Now was not the time to worry about it.

The image of warm greenery and plentiful food faded as the single berries quickly lost their effect. Trying not to think about the cold, Windwhisper piled on her warmest furs and snuggled beneath them. One good thing had come of Prey-Pacer's earlier explosion . . . the hovering sense of tension was gone. But the three young men had taken his words to heart, and it was going to be another cold, lonely night.

Sleep came while she watched Talen put his fire pit to sleep.

They had all forgotten one thing, in their desperate drive for food—winter was winding down. And that meant mating season was drawing near. It began slowly, almost imperceptibly, as the days began to lengthen and the sun stayed with them. Where once friendly comradery was the order of the wolf-pack, tension now reigned. Nudges became bumps, and quick licks became nips. The pack-leader, Prey-Pacer's Stormcloud, exerted his dominance much more frequently than usual, and with a shade more strength.

It was just the beginning. Now, the pack was still confused, uncertain about what was happening to their strictly defined order. Soon, instinct would remind them why they felt twitchy and irritable . . . then the Wolfriders would have their hands full. Hard enough to endure the pack's internal breakdown when other facets of life were polished smooth and bright. In the wake of relocating before the thaw, mating season promised to be agonizing for everyone.

There was not a great deal Windwhisper wanted to take. Only the fur cloak made for her from the mink she and Starfall had trapped, and the clothes she wore when she was not bloated with child. Her spear and extra points were light enough; Windwhisper began to feel a bit better about the trip. There were enough worries over Merewood and the elf-cubs—she vowed not to be a burden.

Words were easier said than fulfilled. What little she carried was not what slowed her down. Even the awkward tilt of her body was not so bad—she managed to walk the log across the stream without mishap. It was the hours and hours spent on foot that began to defeat her. The first day traveling was always a time for nerves and restless feet to run riot. Pain and silence usually came later. But the elves could not remember trying to travel during winter, much less traveling with pregnant Wolfriders.

They halted long before sunset, much to the hunters' disgust. Prey-Pacer immediately sent out two of the hunting groups, Wreath's and Starfall's, both to silence Wolfrider-grumbling and to forestall the terse concern radiating from Windwhisper's swains. Sundown he set to rigging snares for ravvits, much to the youth's dismay. As always, however, they all obeyed. Foolish enough to cross the chief during quiet times; it might actually be dangerous when food was scarce and a third of their tribe footsore.

"Dove, scout around for signs of five-fingers," Prey-Pacer said briskly, striding through the camp like a bull elk.

"This far north?" she asked, picking up her spear.

"We saw signs of them this far north during one hunting trip," was the even reply. "We need no surprises this time. Talen, a fire, please—a small one," he added. "Wait on Dove's word before building it up." Turning to where Windwhisper and Rellah sat upon a fallen log, Prey-Pacer said: "Just sit quietly and keep your feet up off the ground."

"But—" Windwhisper started.

"Hush," Rellah told her, reaching to hook her pack. Pulling it closer, she lifted first one foot and then the other, placing them on the bundle. "Prop up your feet."

"My legs are so heavy I can scarcely move them," Windwhisper admitted softly.

"I know—mine are swollen like logs in a pond. Put them up and rest them, or it will get worse." Her elder gave her a fierce look. "It will get worse, not better, Wolfrider. If we expect to walk at all tomorrow, we *must* rest now. Do you understand me?"

Ominous, those words, but Windwhisper was in no mood to pursue the subject. Gingerly she lifted her feet, balancing them on the edge of Rellah's large pack. Guilt pricked at her as Talen started the fire near their perch, but he shook his head at them both when Windwhisper leaned over to gather what kindling was in reach.

"Don't even try," he said gently. "You must let us help for now, or you will be unable to travel. We cannot dawdle here—anywhere—long, not until we catch up to the deer. Do not force the chief to leave you behind."

Windwhisper privately doubted that would happen; Prey-Pacer would construct dragging litters before he left any of them behind. But that would slow them still further, so she took Talen's words to heart and remained still.

"Where is Merewood?" she asked after a time, craning her neck around to see what the others were up to.

"Sleeping," Talen said briefly. "Willowgreen is with her," he added.

"Willowgreen is here," came a voice. It was the tall,

graceful healer, carrying one of the precious clay pots. "Here, melt some snow in this thing. We need to make willow tea now, before we all start to get sick from the cold."

"You'll have to start it yourself," he said gently, giving the fire one last stick and then standing. "I need to start cutting snow blocks."

"So soon?" Windwhisper asked, peering up at the sun, low in the sky.

"Enough snow walls three blocks high for all of us will take several hours, plus we must spread the tarps above and below. There will be scarcely enough time as it is." Giving the two pregnant elves another stern look of warning, Talen turned and moved off from the fire.

Watching fair Willowgreen scraping clean snow into her pot, Windwhisper recognized her own symptoms: *This must be what Willowgreen feels like when there is no one sick to care for. . . .* It couldn't get much worse than feeling useless.

Wind whipped up again after sundown, leaving them clumped and shivering within their snow caves. Clutching the dregs of her willowbark tea, Windwhisper wished *someone* would start talking to her again. Sleeping alone was very cold. All three of her suitors had kept their distance from her and from each other since Prey-Pacer had let them know his feelings about the situation. Between her aching heart and her aching legs, Windwhisper could not remember feeling so miserable.

Windwhisper? It was a private, narrow sending, the concentration great.

Windwhisper tried to mask her surprise. It was her chief. **I am awake.**

His thought crept through her mind like Nightshadow's . . . a rustle of leaves, scarcely audible over her own busy thoughts. **Which one of them is the father?**

None of them. Why ask now? Unless their agitation was causing the hunt to go sour . . .

The pause was very long. Windwhisper knew he was

weighing all the possibilities woven in her response. **Recognition, then.**

Her mote was affirmative. Gratitude that he did not ask why she had kept the secret leaked from her.

It was no one else's business. Prey-Pacer was almost brisk in his answer. Images touched her mind, the visions her chief examined within. He knew only that this child was of Recognition, and so did not press on that point. **It was well done, I think, but at the last it has failed.** A strong hand reached out of the darkness and gripped her lower arm. **Perhaps they are younger than I thought. Perhaps elf and wolf war within them . . . I cannot guess. But now your silence hurts them more.**

Must I choose? Her anguish was such that, at her back, Rellah stirred uneasily.

I suspect you have already chosen . . . and you cannot avoid wounding the others. It has gone farther than lovemates, then?

Windwhisper had no answer. This was something she had avoided since the beginning. If she had Recognized one of them, it would have been so simple! The bond overcame everything. But now, to choose among them, to hurt valued friends . . . And he had never said anything, made any sign that she was special to him—*Help me, mother of us all. Help me, Timmain. You knew when it was Recognition—you knew when it was time to be a wolf. How can I know, without a crisis demanding answers?*

Rest, now. Prey-Pacer's sending was scarcely an echo in her mind—it still tired him to expend energy in such a manner.

Exhaustion stole over her, as well as a bitterness she could no longer keep at bay. *Do they think it's a game, with me as the prize? Do they think I find it amusing?*

Suddenly Windwhisper wanted desperately to weep, but she found no tears within.

* * *

The days on the trail blended for Windwhisper. Ignoring
her aching legs, she measured time from fight to fight among
the pack. Things were moving to a fever pitch—if the wolves
were not moving, they were milling, their unease almost
palpable. Others were affected by the wolves' behavior—
Graywolf's high-status male was competing for her Nightshadow, who would have none of him, preferring Prey-
Pacer's Stormcloud, the dominant wolf of the pack. This
made Graywolf nervous and surly, prone to snapping verbal-
ly without provocation. Merewood's wolf was in the midst of
a quadrangle of unrequited lust, and she spent most of her
waking hours near hysteria, as watchful as her wolf for
attacks or an opening *to* attack. Most of the Wolfriders found
that constant proximity to their wolves was making them
irritable.

Fortunately Stormcloud wanted Nightshadow—at least
there was no confusion of desires at the top. Still,
Stormcloud had the worst of it; not only driving off
Nightshadow's other suitors, but keeping the peace among
his increasingly unruly troop. Nightshadow, as alpha female,
was busy running off hopeful bitches trailing after
Stormcloud and cuffing yearling cubs who didn't understand what was going on but wanted in on it. It was a mess,
both figuratively and literally. Those who had tried to tie
bundles on their wolves soon gave it up . . . it was the wrong
season to expect cooperation.

Windwhisper stayed close to Rellah. The elder elf-woman
was occasionally cross, due to her swollen legs, but her
temper was even compared to the others in the group. The
true elves were carrying most of the camp burdens, except
for the skins used as tarps—the hunters carried those, when
they were not tracking game. Everyone had reason to be
irritable.

Game . . . the very word made Windwhisper's mouth water. The pines were beginning to thin out; the plains now
filled their sight. So far that meant little improvement in

their situation—an aged prong-horn had filled the wolves' bellies two days ago, and Sundown's ravvit snares occasionally brought results, but they had yet to find deer.

No one ever spoke about their destination . . . the swelling, rolling land of the plains called to them, and they kept walking. Two days past the last copse of trees, surrounded by dirty clumps of snow and whistling dry grasses, they found their first deer.

"Is it a deer?" someone asked in a low tone when the hunters brought the creature back to their makeshift camp. It was small and round, with dainty legs and horns . . . not much larger than the wolves. In response Prey-Pacer shook the beast down from the pole they had carried it on, and swiftly slit open the belly. Sniffing carefully, he made a few preliminary explorations, and sliced himself a piece of flank.

Several moments later, he announced: "Different from our deer, not just smaller—but flavorful and tender. Healthy, this one. We'll use all of it." As he spoke, heads shot up into the air as Starfall's sending reached them. His group had brought down another little deer!

That night they ate fresh meat for the first time in moons, and it was difficult not to overeat. Windwhisper cut tiny chunks and forced herself to chew slowly, relishing the tangy game. She could come to prefer this type of deer. "Strange that the hunters never saw them before—"

"At a distance," came a soft voice. Growing still, Windwhisper recognized Starfall's tones. "We have seen them at a distance, but they have incredible senses—they usually know we're coming. The big deer are easier to catch, especially among trees."

"Then you've been this way before?" she heard herself say.

"Yes, during new leaves and dying time both." His voice sounded different, somehow.

"What is it you fear?" she asked.

Silence. "Sometimes I think you read minds," he said finally. "It's . . . there isn't much water out here, except in new leaves, when the snow has melted in the mountains. We're getting to the end of the snow, and we haven't found any streams yet. Except during new leaves, the hunt always went to sun-goes-down or sun-return." His frosty eyes flicked a glance in her direction. "A few deer is fine, a good sign . . . but we need a place for a permanent camp, and that means trees or a rocky area. And we haven't seen a lot of these little creatures—they're rarer, and harder to catch. We're going to have to work hard for what we do find."

Nodding, Windwhisper offered him a chunk of meat. Reaching for it, he hesitated, glancing quickly around to see who was nearby. As exasperation rose within her breast, Windwhisper bit back the words which threatened as she saw the look on his face. Pensive, even sad . . .

"It won't happen again," he said simply. "I won't fight. But it's better not to aggravate each other."

"Has anyone contemplated asking my opinion?" *I can't believe I said that!*

"We might not like what you have to say," was the wry answer. His expression now was unfocused, remote. "But that we came close to *killing* each other—" The shudder that ran through him was very real. "I like to think that . . . we would have stopped even if Prey-Pacer hadn't arrived when he did. But maybe we wouldn't have." His silver-gray eyes flicked back in her direction. "I still don't understand what came over us."

"I'm not a wolf bitch to snarl over," she announced tartly.

"No—the wolves would have broken off sooner," was the quick reply. He paused in his chewing, and then continued, but more slowly. "I hadn't really thought about that. That the wolves would have handled it better, yes, I remember thinking *that*." His self-contempt was acid. "But they would have broken off sooner—one of them would have backed down to the strength of the other. Wolves so rarely fight to the death . . ."

"Life is worth more than status, perhaps?"

Starfall stopped eating and turned his body toward her. "It wasn't the wolf in us that made us fight. Compete and snarl, maybe, but not fight. It . . . was the elf?" He looked both lost and confused.

Did she have any words to comfort him? "Talen told me once that humans sometimes fight over mates. But they rarely kill each other. They have all kinds of rituals for setting up new family groupings—sometimes there is a schism, and a new tribe is formed. Sometimes one of the men actually leaves the camp. Talen wasn't sure if it was a status battle, or something else."

"Maybe the personal status within." Scarcely a whisper.

She looked long at him, wondering what he was thinking, but Starfall kept his thoughts to himself. Finally, she said: "I think that's how Zarhan Fastfire won Rahnee, by refusing to challenge. Only he wasn't really competing with another suitor, not as I remember it . . . it was Rahnee he battled."

"That was before we learned that to be chief wasn't like being pack-leader," he pointed out. "That the chief isn't always the strongest male. The Wolfriders have much in common with the pack . . . but we are not true wolves."

Fascinated, Windwhisper continued to watch his face as he quietly chewed on a strip of deer. Often the Wolfriders—those who were descendants of Timmain's sacrifice, not the true elves—seemed suspicious of anything that seemed too elvish. Given a choice, they saw their elfin heritage as weak and the wolf within as strong. On the surface, this seemed the same case; the wolves were smart enough not to kill each other over mating season. *But wolves do not have Recognition. Humans don't seem to, either. So elves must find their own way . . . and we are still more elf than wolf.* That Starfall could admit to thinking such a thing. . . . It was time to deal with her own troubled heart.

"Time to drape tarps," came a brisk call out of the twilight, and Starfall obediently rose to his feet. Windwhisper ground her teeth in frustration.

"Stay close to the others," he told her, moving away before she could accuse him of being overprotective.

Without snow or cloud cover, the nights were bitterly cold. Daylight brought slowly warming temperatures, but it was still cold behind them to the north, and Starfall's words proved true—they were finding very little water.

Why can't I hear the water anymore? Windwhisper thought as they continued the weary trek southward. Surely the water within the mountains could be found under the plains. How far down—? She could check when they halted, but it was so frantic when they stopped, the wolves snarling and snapping, elves keeping their distance—and at night, she was so exhausted she often fell asleep still clutching her dinner . . .

They were watching her. Exhaustion took her past preoccupation with her body's betrayal into new awareness. Although Starfall mostly kept his distance, and neither Wasp nor Sundown had spoken to her in days, they all watched her. Unease, even worry followed her like the underdog trailing the pack. Concern washed over her in a wave of emotion, and she had no strength to block them out.

It took stumbling to signal verbal communication.

Using her spear butt as a walking stick, Windwhisper had fared better than some of the frailer members of the party—until she misjudged the ground beneath them. Striking mud, the pole slid away just as she settled her full weight upon it. The jolt brought her to her hands and knees.

Are you all right? Repressed panic laced the sending, and it was Wasp who was suddenly at her elbow.

Yes. She did not trust herself to speak aloud—saving herself from landing on her face had hurt, and she knew her voice would reveal it.

"It didn't—hurt the—" he started tentatively, helping her to her feet.

"No." The spear was now slimy from the mud, and would be, until the wind dried it. Owl pellets.

"Lean on me." It was not issued like an order, nor was there that pleading tone she had sensed through many days. A simple offer of help . . .

Windwhisper took hold of his lower arm, and they started off again.

"You're doing just fine," Wasp went on, trying to sound reassuring. "Once we get settled, you'll be dancing in no time."

"Hummph." This was very quiet, scarcely a clearing of the throat, but Wasp knew it was intentional.

"Few of us are as light on our feet as you—" Feeling her tighten, he rushed on: "Seriously! Rellah and Merewood can barely walk, and you keep going." Softly, he added: "It *will* end sometime, you know. And then maybe we can be easy again."

The trek or the pregnancy? Both? "Soon. Or we may have to stop for a time." At his puzzled look, she said: "Your mother was pregnant before I was—if we don't settle soon, we may have to pause for a birth."

Smiling tightly, Wasp said: "Owl is oblivious to his first child's coming, and Graywolf—"

Finds Merewood an unsatisfactory choice in a mate. I know. She is not happy about him, either. This was as wry as a sending could be, and Wasp actually chuckled. Then his young face smoothed, and something in the tilt of his head promised a pronouncement.

"I . . . I know the cub is not mine." Quiet words falling like the first drops of a winter shower. "I heard . . . that it was Recognition. I understand it's unmistakable."

This was new; that his dry, biting wit should be turned on himself. Windwhisper was uncertain how to respond, and finally said: "Yes."

"I'm sorry we made things so hard for you." His voice had tightened, and Windwhisper carefully did not look at him, concentrating on the rough path beneath their feet. "It's just . . . I thought of us as close in age. Only elders have cubs, not we children. Now . . . everything is different. When I think of the chief and Softfoot, or Dove and Long Walk, well . . ." He sighed. "It will never be the same again."

"I have formed no bonds with the father of this cub, Wasp," she replied gently. "Other than the cub itself, of course. And even if I had . . . you know how it is, after a great kill, or a celebration. Some stay with their heart's desire, and others embrace many friends. Did you think I would turn from you forever?"

The arm she gripped pressed close, pinning her hand against furred vest. "I did not know. Sundown and Starfall were acting so strange, so hostile—I didn't understand why. Recognition is Recognition—who would try to argue with it?"

Ah, Wasp. The tenderness in her sending startled him. **In some ways you are a second-year wolfling, knowing why your elders argue yet aware you cannot yet compete. Then there are other ways . . . and you are much older than Sundown, or even Starfall.**

Relaxation threaded the arm she hung from, and Windwhisper decided he took her words as a compliment.

"I didn't want to lose you . . . but I knew that—that what Prey-Pacer and Softfoot have is not what is between us." This was very slow and spaced.

Did you want that? Really? Right now there were few lifemate pairings among the Wolfriders. So many had died— from the allo attack which decimated their hunters and brought Prey-Pacer the chief's lock, long before she was born, to recent illness and hard living. Only ragged halves of pairs, even to this day. Their chief and his mate were a source of wonder and inspiration to most of them. An easy, wordless companionship by day, and at night soft words and long, thoughtful silences, as they shared the burden and responsibility of the tribe's safety. *Yet such a bond can be so important, we cannot survive if we lose it . . .*

"No, it is not," she said honestly in answer to his almost-question. "But as much as they adore each other, Wasp, there are times they seek comfort elsewhere, in the frenzy of a spring night. Even our chief! If you mean not intruding on a pair, well, yes . . . but it is no loss of face to ask and be refused." Finally she turned her head toward him, and her dark gaze was candid. "It is one of our few pleasures in these fragile bodies, Wasp. Must we possess, not merely love? When Recognition finally rips through your soul, you will understand possession. Why do you think Rellah never complains about the many Wolfriders who have fathered her children? She returns to Talen as soon as it is done. We are not wolves, who choose a mate and then lose status or even life at its loss. We are not humans, to choose and discard, or to trade our children among different camps. We are not even elves." This brought a tiny sigh from within. "Elves were not trapped in these bodies, or so the dreamberries tell us. Our ancestors knew each others' soulnames from the very beginning, from each birth. Somehow they knew each other, even in other form . . . did they not know Timmain, even as a wolf?"

"We do not know each other that way." There was yearning in those words, and her grip on his arm tightened. Out of the corner of her eye, she saw that Sundown had grown closer to the pair of them. Just as she considered whether this might be a problem, Prey-Pacer and Storm-cloud dropped back, edging between Sundown and Wind-whisper's wolf Nightshadow.

Confident that her chief had things under control, she said: "No. In Recognition, there is nothing except the echo of your own soul, and that of your mate. Then another name joins the dance . . . but it fades, after a time. The world was no larger than those three names, but now that new mote is fragmented, fading . . . I do not know if I will remember my child's soulname, when it is finally born. We must reach for each other, always reach for each other, because our lives depend on each other, and we join only briefly, whether physically or mentally. We are not like wolves, or humans, or even elves. We are Wolfriders, and we are something new. We cannot have the effortless freedom of the skies."

Her last words roused a memory, feebly, but Windwhisper did not have time to analyze what she had said. "We must not fall prey to the High Ones' fate—what they passed on to their children."

"Their fate?" This puzzled Wasp so much that he slowed his walking.

"I just realized something important," she said clearly, not caring if anyone else heard her speak. "The High Ones always alternated between elation and despair. One moment they felt superior to this harsh and frozen world, trapped like ravvits in a snare; they wanted freedom, with no bonds to hold them. Then our world showed them that it would not forgive carelessness and arrogance . . . it was nearly their deaths. Without Timmain's sacrifice, we would be no more."

"The wolf within knows—" Wasp started.

"No! Just because it is right for wolves does not mean it is our way as well!" Perhaps the child was making her irritable —perhaps it was fever. But this thought was swirling about within her, and demanded escape. "Sometimes we give in to despair, when the world becomes too much for us, or to arrogance—pride in the gifts our elders brought with them to this place. Sometimes we become more like the wolves, and the hunt and howl are all we know. But we are the Wolfriders, and we are something else! We must control our heritage—we must lay out our own path."

"How?" This was so full of his usual curiosity, Windwhisper wondered if he had forgotten how they started on this conversation.

"I don't know!" She felt cross, and wondered how these words had fallen to her. "We cannot be too proud of the gifts of the High Ones. It is something we are born with, not a skill acquired, like what Softfoot can do with a spear. We cannot use those talents to try and gain status—we cannot act as if shaping or healing or what the elders do to the skins to make them soft are more valuable traits to our people than . . . than finding herbs when we are sick, or hunting, or making flint tips for our spears!"

"Hunting is most important," Wasp told her, a martial look in his eye.

"Not when we have spring fever," she said firmly. That silenced him. "Not when we are so sick that Willowgreen cannot hope to heal us all, and must turn to those smelly plants to keep us strong. Hunting is not first when we have no flints left. Will you bring down game in your teeth like your wolf?" He half nodded, admitting the reasoning behind that, knowing that when he chose to leave his dream world, Owl made flint blades as perfect as jewels.

"You mean . . . nothing . . . is more important?" he asked tentatively.

"Nothing is more important than the health and well-being of the tribe." It was the only summing up she could find that she felt he would understand. "All our gifts—good hunters, healers, tanners, shapers, even cooks! All our gifts have value, because all make us what we are. We are the Wolfriders. It is time we stop pretending to be something else. It is when we try to be too much elf or wolf that we fail. We are elves, but we are Wolfrider elves. We must take the lessons of the wolves to heart . . . and be better elves."

"How can we be better than the High Ones?" This was as close to scorn as Sundown had ever directed toward her, startling her out of intense thought. "How can we be stronger than those who shaped themselves to this world's dance, who made water burn and carved hollows from solid rock?" His last words faded, as he remembered what Windwhisper could do with stone.

"We can belong here," she said simply. "The High Ones did not belong here. Our elders probably could not survive without us . . . but we, we belong here. And we must make it our home. Someday we will not have to fight for every meal we put into our stomachs . . . we must remember where we came from, against that day."

Both Wasp and Sundown studied her as if she were an exotic plant that had suddenly burst into bloom before their very eyes. Others had drawn close; Starfall was nodding his head, that thoughtful look on his face. It was her chief's shrewd, intense gaze, however, that held her attention. He moved along the path like a part of his wolf, a gliding shadow against the dry, rustling grass that whipped in a constant north wind.

I am not totally convinced, his sending murmured privately to her. **But I find myself sorry that you are so far ahead of my son. Still, I think *he* is good enough for you.** Lifting his spear in a purposeful gesture, Prey-Pacer indicated that the hunters of his group should spread out.

Sundown hesitated before jumping upon his wolf, his expression tense, his dark brown eyes troubled.

Windwhisper smiled at him. "I'm not going anywhere. Take care." As she watched him race off, following his chief, and felt Wasp squeeze her arm in farewell as his group took the right side of the area, she caught herself wondering: *Just who is he? Does my chief know more than I do?*

For the first time in many long moons, her heart felt lighter within.

That night they began rationing water.

Sundown maneuvered his own position near the fire pit so that he was able to bring Windwhisper her share of food and drink. For once Windwhisper hung back from the heat of the flames; despite the huge circle Talen had turned over, completely burying the dry grass, she found herself fearful of wildfire. Sundown also seemed nervous, although she doubted the fire pit was causing his unease. They sat in silence for a time, chewing quietly, sharing snippets of dried deer with their wolves, who found the smoked strips of meat poor fare indeed.

After a time Nightshadow's sending filtered into her mind.

Hunger. She nosed her chosen Wolfrider purposefully, and visions of the hunt danced through her thoughts.

"What are you going to find here at night?" Windwhisper asked, pulling playfully at her wolf's ears. "Especially in this high wind."

The image of a mouse flickered through the wolf's sending.

Laughing, Windwhisper was about to send her off, when Nightshadow spotted a wolf bitch flirting with Stormcloud and raced to run her off.

"When do they have time to mate?" Sundown asked aloud.

Windwhisper glanced sidelong at him. "They don't. That's one of the reasons only the lead pair usually breeds. Occasionally a second pair also has cubs, but Mother told me once that's mostly when the dominant female prefers a male other than the pack-leader. She cooperates while the leader is breaking up another fight. In those years, sometimes the lead wolf doesn't breed at all."

"Huh." He studied his slender hands, stained with dirt from many days of setting snares. "I'll be glad when it's over."

Nodding, Windwhisper wondered exactly how this conversation would fall out.

Sundown was full of surprises; he was even blunter than Wasp. "I wouldn't have killed him." The look he gave her was both scared and defiant. "I couldn't have . . . we've been almost like brothers all these years. But—" Controlling the keening whine that threatened to burst from him, he hissed: "When I found out it was Recognition, all I could see was blackness. It seemed so *unfair*! I wanted to tear him apart with my bare hands . . . I don't know how the knife got into it." His tenor voice was very low as he added: "I could bear it, before. Sharing your time with him. But now that Recognition is part of it, I—"

"Starfall is not the father," she said simply, the words rising up in her.

Sundown stared at her a long moment. His expression grew incredulous, and he turned to look at Wasp, who was settled by Yarrow and trying to amuse her with a funny story about the wolves.

At least he doesn't think Recognition slipped by us, she thought. "No," Windwhisper said aloud. "Not Wasp."

"Then . . . none of us?" She shook her head negatively. "Then why—"

"First because it happened so fast. It didn't seem like it mattered much; after all, the cub was two turns away. Then because the business with Merewood and Graywolf was so bad. Finally because I became convinced that mentioning it would only make things worse."

"But if you had told us—"

"What? You would have gracefully accepted the situation?" He did not attempt to answer her. "You heard someone mention a *rumor* of Recognition and nearly stabbed Starfall in the throat! What if you'd gone after the father? If all three of you had decided to show him you weren't giving up? Before he could even declare he wasn't interested in me? Would you have believed anything we said?"

"I don't believe he doesn't want you." This was so definite Windwhisper started laughing.

"Sweet friend, you are a boon to my pride, especially since I look like a she-bear entering hibernation!" Controlling her laughter, Windwhisper considered whether he was ready for the entire story. *Have you grown enough for this tale*? "Recognition cares nothing for the parents, Sundown. Only for the children. It will creep up on you someday . . . maybe on us. Talen is the father."

He blinked several times at her, his expression owllike. Silence . . . it went on for so long Windwhisper started to worry. At last he said: "*Talen*?" It came out as a squeak, his usual rolling tones nonexistent. "He's so *old*."

"Not at all. He *has* lived a very long time, but old he is

not!" Smiling faintly, she added: "He may have seen me differently in the haze of Recognition, but now I am simply a spindly child to him, a child carrying a child. Rellah is the one he seeks when he needs comfort, or conversation, or merely companionship. I was merely a flicker of an eye."

"I guess I am, too." Shivering in the wind, Sundown lay down in the dried grass, seeking shelter from the chill breeze. When he gestured for her to join him, it was slow and gentle, an invitation studied yet casual.

Could she do anything about the wind? No . . . she was tired, and shaping rock would only make it worse. There was nothing to be done for water, either. Sundown had nested behind the only rise for miles . . . in a few moments she joined him.

The child moon waxed and waned, and the journey went on. The truce among her lovers might have been inspiration to the wolves. Suddenly their quarrel ceased, as if by mutual consent. Now the nervousness among them was limited to Nightshadow, who alternated between her Wolfrider's side and sniffing inquisitively at every bush and tussock. Soon it would be time for digging a den. Three times Mother moon had run her course, and still they walked. The snow was completely gone, but the grasses had yet to sprout. Now the water was dwindling, even as the mountains to the south rose higher. Surely there would be water in those hills . . . surely new life was stirring here. Somewhere, it had to be spring.

Game still appeared occasionally. It was a battle to keep the wolves full, and what food remained Prey-Pacer rationed among the children and pregnant females. Windwhisper knew better than to argue; thirst was beginning to prey on her mind, and fresh meat helped keep her need at bay. She was so tired of eating field mice!

Mountains began to hang over her dreams. Weariness and lack of food and water bred a strange form of delirium . . . at least Windwhisper thought it was delirium. Surely stone could not speak? Not even to a rock shaper. Yet she heard voices calling to her, insistent voices that promised rest, shade—water . . .

"Windwhisper?" It was Starfall; he had taken hold of her arm. "You were starting to sway."

Staring at him, trying to absorb his meaning, she realized she was farther to the right than the others. Why—Oh. Swaying off the straight path. Yes . . . Her head turned back toward the south, to the mountains that now blotted out the very sky. Already the path was slowly rising . . .

"There is water in the hills," she said slowly, clearly. "We must keep going."

"Of course. Hang on to me." Starfall still had hold of her arm; he would not continue until she slipped her hand into the crook of his elbow.

"I can call the water, you know," she said seriously, watching the path before her begin to shimmer.

"I'm sure you can." It was neither soothing nor skeptical, but then, Starfall always believed her when she told him of her little discoveries. Was always interested . . .

If only you had loved me. I never wanted anyone else, but I would not beg you to stay. Starfall's arm was rigid beneath her touch . . . that could be caused by many things. *Did I speak aloud?* she wondered. And you accuse them of pride, foolish Wolfrider. You wanted him to yourself, and when he seemed to prefer others to you, you found Sundown. *You did not want me until Sundown did, but I always wanted you.*

His concern beat upon her, more draining than the sun, and she could not block it out. Or maybe it was all of them, together, not just Starfall and Wasp and Sundown but the rest as well. Merewood's agony spun like a flaming stick in her mind. *She must be very bad,* Windwhisper thought idly, realizing Graywolf had tossed the elf-woman up onto his wolf. *So, at the last, you will protect the cubs, whether you want them or no . . .*

They were well up into the hills by the time the sun grew low. It vanished into the mountains, which curved back north at their western edge, far, far in the misty distance. Still no water . . . still only ravvits for game.

Where are the deer? The enraged sending came from their chief, who gestured for the group to make camp even as he continued onward, his eyes searching the ground for any trace of game. **They have been here, and recently!** He stalked off into the scraggly pines, up and inward in his anger. A pause, as Softfoot considered following him . . . then she slipped off her wolf's back to the ground.

"Just leave him be," she said shortly. "Talen, would you make a fire?"

The astonished elder did not comment on her unique request—Softfoot feared fire. He merely went in search of dry deadwood. After a few moments of indecision, several Wolfriders actually bent to help him.

More than warmth, the fire was comfort in a strange land. What if there were humans here, or other predators? Did they have the strength to protect themselves—

Prey-Pacer's howl of triumph rang through their hollow, and several hunters leaped to the backs of their wolves as the animals sped by. It was a while before the group returned, a deer carcass strung across several spears. A real deer, not one of the tiny plains creatures. Deer!

Food pushed thirst to one side, but only temporarily. A bit of blood could not replenish the moisture they had lost over many days. But it was life, this gift from their finest hunter, and tomorrow they would find the strength to hunt again.

Windwhisper's private worry became fact late that night. After tossing restlessly for hours on end, Rellah finally woke her neighbor with a gasp of pain. Talen had already gone to rouse Willowgreen.

"What can we do?" It was Wasp, right by her ear. Groaning herself, Windwhisper pulled herself up on his arm.

As if I've been through this before, she thought dryly. "Stay out of the way. Willowgreen might appreciate a shelter, in case the wind picks up again . . . and find water. She will need water badly." *High Ones, giving birth without even water to cleanse the blood away!* Surely they did not deserve that . . .

The elder elves rigged a tent with surprising promptness, while the hunters took to the trails once again. Deer trails meant deer—and, more importantly right now, they meant a path to water. Somewhere up here there had to be water—

"What if it's a day's journey?" Yarrow whispered, her eyes following her chief in the early-morning gloom.

"The sooner we leave, the sooner we return," was Sundown's terse statement. "Coming, Starfall?"

Nodding, the other elf stood and looked for his wolf.

Still dizzy from her rising, Windwhisper watched them first shrink, and then finally disappear into the pines. Rellah's discomfort gnawed at her, and she moved to grip the elf-woman's hands. If it was all she could do—

It did not seem like enough. Light brought them day, and gave definition to the hours, but the baby did not come. Talen finally came to offer Rellah what support he could, and she literally leaned against him, drawing on his strength, his very presence, willing the child to be born. The hunt had not returned.

Delirium rose again, and Windwhisper began to fear she was losing her mind. *Silly child, didn't you think that once before, when the shaping came upon you?* Awareness finally trickled through the pain, the exhaustion, the horrible dryness of her mouth . . . she forced herself to concentrate. *Trust your instincts.* Raising her head, Windwhisper looked for Nightshadow, who was never far away these days.

A soft whine, and pawing . . . had she started her den? Owl pellets, that meant the pack would not budge from this place for four Mother moons, at least—Rising slowly to her feet, Windwhisper went over to her she-wolf. A stone outcropping . . . "Do you want me to help you dig?" she asked, feeling stupid and slow in the morning heat. She'd been so dreamy lately . . .

A quick yap of impatience, and Nightshadow pawed at the stone. Bending over as well as she could, Windwhisper sniffed. A ravvit, perhaps?

Water. The smell almost made her ill, her need was so great. Not close, but not far, if the wolf could smell it. Water beneath the mountain . . . *I know your name*, she silently told the stream. *You are kin to that which runs beneath our longtime home. Will you be a friend to us, too?* Without planning to, Windwhisper pushed gently at the outcrop, smoothing it, creating a curve like the arch of a water mussel. *Come to me, friend. Come, Stars Dancing. It is time to tread the pathway to the sky.* She reached into the crevice, molding the rough sides into tiny bowls, letting her strength trickle down the bones of the mountain like rainwater seeking a puddle.

"Should you be doing that?" Yarrow's voice came from somewhere behind her, and it was worried. "Doesn't that take a lot of energy?"

Didn't Yarrow go with the pack? How long had she been away from the little tent? "I'm calling the water," Windwhisper said confidently. A snap, like a twig breaking, told her Yarrow had gone away. *Come to me, Stars Dancing. I know your name, I have dreamt of you—*

It exploded like a beaver dam swollen past endurance, the column of water rising like the geyser she had seen in a dreamberry vision. Only for a moment, bathing her like a waterfall, its touch cold and clear and tasting of minerals— She remembered sliding down next to her wolf, throwing her arms around—

Waking brought no clearer vision. Where was—? A cool breeze caressed her face, and she realized the sky was hidden. Raising a hand—

It's all right. Starfall. Then the hunters *had* returned.

"Where is the sky?" she asked softly.

"You're under the tarp, silly child," Starfall said sternly.
His arms tightened, and she realized she was lying in his lap.
"Can't I leave you alone for half a day without you getting
into trouble?"

"I had the strangest dream," she murmured, trying to
remember what was real and what a part of her delirium. "I
called to the stream, and it answered me . . ."

"It certainly did." His snort of mirth was tight, and his
worry brushed against her.

"It did?" *Sometimes I'm so stupid.*

Fingertips swept loose hair away from her face. "I love
you, you crazy rock shaper," he whispered, his slight smile
for her alone.

"You do?" She frowned at him. "Then why didn't you ever
say so before?"

"At first I was arrogant enough to think you already knew.
Then Sundown started showing up all the time, and I
thought I wasn't anything special to you . . . just all right for
fun and games." He shushed her squeak of indignation.
"The rock shaping scared me . . . and then you were pregnant, and I knew I wasn't the father—"

"It was Recogni—" she started.

"I know. Sundown told me. It doesn't matter . . . you're
all that matters." After a pause, he continued. "Anyway, I
had to do a lot of thinking. It was hard on you . . . as hard for
you as for me, I guess. I'll need to make it up to you."

"Isn't anyone going to ask my opinion?" Windwhisper said
weakly, her arm flopping to her flat belly. Stiffening, her
fingers began walking down her stomach. "I'm missing
something."

Starfall started laughing, his dirty face alight with joy.
"You're not thirsty anymore, either. Do you remember
drinking the water we brought you?"

"No . . ." A thin wail interrupted her thoughts, and she
said: "Rellah had her baby? *I* had my baby?"

"It all happened so quickly! You were kind enough to wait

until Rellah was finished. Willowgreen was tearing her hair out—"

"She likes to feel needed." Windwhisper dismissed his words with an airy wave of her hand. "Idiot! What was it? What were they? Where—"

"Right here," came Willowgreen's voice. "You have already nursed once. They know who *you* are." Smiling broadly, the healer came up with a bundle in her arms.

They . . . A sick feeling ran through her. Had Rellah . . . "Did Rellah—"

Bewildered looks met her expression.

"Idiots, indeed," came Rellah's voice from somewhere behind her. "You're frightening her, fools. I live, Wolfrider, and I have a son. *You* have two daughters."

"Two?" The word didn't really come out, although her lips shaped it. More than one? No wonder she had been so huge; no wonder the name she had heard had fragmented into pieces . . .

"It seems Owl and Graywolf were not an aberration, but something new which will come again," Willowgreen said loftily, settling the tiny bundle against Windwhisper's side. "This one is always hungry, you might as well start with her."

"You must get strong," Starfall said firmly. "There is water flooding down the hillside, and you need to narrow the opening—no, not yet!" He pushed to keep her from sitting up. "You actually dropped the water level at the spring we found. We need another spring, not a waterfall."

"Maybe I can do both." She considered the problem, and then all problems were lost in the glowing blue eyes of the black-haired infant she held. "She is so tiny . . ."

"We'll take care of her, don't worry." Before she could speak, he added: "Do you really plan to take care of *two* this size by yourself?" His grin was infectious. "Two miniature Windwhispers! I can't wait until they start mashing pebbles onto boulders like clay."

A crooked grin bloomed in response. *There is nothing to worry about in Wasp . . . Sundown needs time to deal with things. But I think we were meant for each other all along, no matter what else crosses our paths.* **I love you, too.**

It is hard to nuzzle an elf who is nursing . . . The rightness of it swept away all fears—food, shelter, water, Merewood's unborn cub—all would be well. It was not elf or wolf who knew this fact.

It was Wolfrider.

Ties That Bind

by Mercedes Lackey

Graywolf lay belly-down on the pungent pine needles of the thick grove of trees above the holt. The drooping branches above him cast blue shadows that hid him from any eyes but the sharpest. Late summer sunlight fell on his ankle; *hot* sunlight, for this time of year. He rested his chin on his crossed arms and glowered down at the three tiny, russet-clad figures in the central clearing below him. Talen, silver and russet, tallest of the three; sitting off by himself, dreaming, probably. Then two together, bent over some mysterious task: Rellah, graceful, golden hair pouring over her shoulders and pooling at her feet—

—and smaller, paler copy—Willowgreen.

He narrowed his eyes, and his thoughts smoldered with resentment and an alarm that no other elf *or* wolf seemed to feel. And the cause of that alarm was the third of those figures below.

He scowled as a bright peal of laughter carried up to his perch on the height above the holt. Willowgreen moved about her tasks with more smiles than tears, these days. And *that* was different. Profoundly different.

She had changed, changed to a creature Graywolf hardly knew. She troubled him, haunted his dreams, occupied his thoughts constantly, so that he worried at the problem she posed like a wolf with a piece of tough old jerky. And still he could not fathom the "new" Willowgreen. The old, coward, weak, weeper, he knew. *This* was not she.

One of the cubs toddled up to investigate. Rellah pointedly ignored it. Willowgreen laughed at its curiosity, bestowed a caress, and sent it away. She, who had once feared the wolves of the pack and winced away from even a friendly sniff.

Willowgreen now welcomed the four-footed with the two-footed on return from the hunt, and cheerfully tended their hurts and ills on an equal basis with their bonded elves.

This alone would have been enough to raise the hair on the back of his neck, but there was more, much more. She was woodswise, now; she accomplished tasks she would have fumbled and failed at, not that long ago. She had somehow acquired a strange familiarity with new herbs and the food value of unlikely plants in the time she had been gone, lost out of the ken of the tribe. Too much to have learned in a scant three moon-dances, or so Graywolf reckoned. This incredible fund of wisdom extended to many things that had been out of their season in the time she had been absent— and no one but Graywolf seemed to find this odd. She had been careful about displaying this newfound wisdom, at least at first: "Healer-sense told me," or, "I saw a ravvit, a treewee, a squirrel eating it," she would say. But why so many revelations now, when healer-sense and ravvits had not availed her in the past and the case had been more desperate?

A hand of turns of the seasons had come and gone since the flood and the disappearance; moon-dance after moon-dance passed as Graywolf watched her covertly, and *still* Willowgreen remained an enigma.

Moonfinder whined and nuzzled his arm, his nose leaving a cold, wet spot in the crook of his elbow. Graywolf ignored his wolf-friend, concentrating on his own dark thoughts.

I don't trust her. Something *happened to her, and she won't talk about it.*

Good, Moonfinder sent, whining. **Willowgreen good. Finds sourgrass, pulls thorns.**

Graywolf snarled, and shoved his wolf-friend's nose away. *A few thorns pulled out of his paw, a couple of burrs taken out of his tail, and she even has* Moonfinder *telling me I'm a fool! She turns my own wolf-friend against me!* He scrambled to his feet, and set off away from the holt, leaving Moonfinder to follow after as best he could.

The wolf yipped in puzzled surprise, and loped around through the brush to take his accustomed place on the game trail ahead of Graywolf.

Hunt now? he asked hopefully.

Graywolf didn't answer him. He stormed down the trail to the river, taking no care about how much noise he made, frightening the birds into silence as he passed. *She even has Two-Spear fooled . . .*

The way Two-Spear *depended* on the softhearted elf-woman enraged him. The chief turned to *her* for the support he *should* have been seeking from his cousin and the tribe. Even when Two-Spear was angered, caught up in one of his half-mad rages that only Graywolf had been able to calm—before—*she* placed herself fearlessly in his path and tried—

Then Graywolf stopped dead in his tracks as a memory of a peculiar look on the chief's face passed through his mind. That expression—compounded of equal parts of bewilderment, unhappiness, and arrogant anger, had shadowed Two-Spear's face more than once lately. And always when Willowgreen crossed his will.

. . . Or does she? She never used to even stand in his way. Now she defies him. Not often, but . . .

Huh. When she does, it's to take the same position Skyfire would, the very same—only without the challenges and shouting.

It catches him by surprise. He doesn't know what to make of her, either.

I wonder if Skyfire has anything to do with this? When she went away—was she off with Skyfire? That would explain a lot.

Graywolf tangled his bony fingers in his long, coarse hair and thought, a frown of concentration making his forehead ache. *I'll have to watch her, more closely than I ever did before,* he decided. *Something she says or does will give her away. If she's gone over to Skyfire's camp, and I can prove it . . . Two-Spear will have to do something about her.*

He smiled in satisfaction, and reversed his course, moving silently back up the trail.

I'll watch her every movement. She'll slip. And I'll have her.

". . . then make a poultice of the pounded leaves with the bark," Willowgreen directed, feeling *very* strange about instructing a High One who had seen so many more turns of the seasons than she had.

Still, she asked. She's the only one ever to be interested. And if anything ever happens to me, Rellah will be the only healer the tribe has.

The High One bent over her task with a frown, bruising the flat leaves between two stones until the juice stained her fingers a pale and streaky green. She laid the pulped leaves on the strip of soft, inner bark of the birch tree, and looked up through the curtain of her hair. "Now bind it on the wound, right?"

"Right. But since no one is wounded right now"— Willowgreen chuckled, took up the finished poultice, rolled it into a packet, and tossed it into the cold and seldom-used fire pit—"and since plantain would take over the forest at this season, given half a chance, I don't think we need to dry the leaves for later. I already have enough dried to see us through next white-cold season. Now, dried, it's *also* good for—"

"The sour belly of jealousy?" Rellah interrupted.

Willowgreen looked back at her in surprise, and saw that Rellah regarded her sardonically. "Don't tell me that you hadn't noticed," the High One continued. "Graywolf is as green as grass whenever he looks at you. There's going to be trouble there. I feel it coming. Trouble for *you*, Healer."

Willowgreen shook her head and sat back on her heels, all

pretense of instruction forgotten. She searched her mind for words that would be neutral. "I can't imagine what he's jealous of," she said finally.

"Two-Spear," the High One replied. "Even a child could see that. They were inseparable until *you* became Two-Spear's lovemate. Before you vanished in that storm, Graywolf was the only one who could keep Two-Spear's forays against the humans within bounds. Now, since you returned—when the chief listens at all, he listens to you."

"Which is seldom," Willowgreen whispered, more saddened than bitter, and she clenched her leaf-stained hands in her lap. "And growing more seldom."

"Even so," Rellah said flatly. "There is enough there for the wolfling to be jealous of. You have taken his position as second in the pack; that is what he sees. He will challenge you for it, one day."

Willowgreen shook her head. "No," she said firmly. "He won't. Male won't challenge mate for second position. That isn't the Way."

"And what do *you* know of the Way?" the High One scoffed.

Willowgreen raised her head and stared into Rellah's eyes—and the High One was the first to blink and look away. "I know enough," she said with conviction.

I know more than I can tell you, teacher, friend, she mourned, somewhere deep in her soul. *I know that you are the last of your kind, doomed. I know that you, Talen, and every High One are outside the web of this world's weaving, and that the web itself will act to remove you. That is what Timmain worked for us halflings; trading stature and immortality for lives that fit in the web of life here. I cannot bear to tell you that—and even if I did, I do not think you would believe me.*

So she let not a particle of her thought show on her face, or trickle over into her surface thoughts.

Halfling though she was, she was more elf than wolf, and sending came easier to her than speech. And that was the problem in hiding this knowledge she had gained from the High Ones—for they had even more skill than she at penetrating thoughts, and would hear what she was really thinking if she did not guard herself.

"I know enough," she repeated, gently. "I hear the wolfsong as clearly as any of the tribe, now."

Rellah brought her eyes back up to meet Willowgreen's. "Indeed," the High One said thoughtfully. "Now. I would give a great deal to know what it was that changed you so, when you were apart from the tribe. I find it hard to believe that it was only injury and solitude."

Willowgreen kept her gaze level and her thoughts to herself, something that, before the disciplinary training she'd had with Shayana, would have been impossible.

"Well," Rellah said with a sigh, when several moments of waiting brought no response, "I suppose it doesn't matter—"

The healer was saved from answering by the arrival of a lean, gray-brown she-wolf, who loped into the clearing, and flopped down beside her. Rellah flinched away from the wolf, Mist's Cloudchaser (who had bonded to the Wolfrider when Darkwater died), a lively, playful bitch with a litter of half-grown cubs. Three had bonded already; one, the biggest of the lot, seemed inclined to run his mischief alone. Willowgreen gladly turned her attention away from the High One to the wolf.

Cloudchaser? she sent.

***Cub*chaser,** the wolf replied, panting, her thoughts sharp with disgust. **Cub in pricklepatch, prickles in cub-fur. Mist fishing. Willowgreen help?**

Cloudchaser was one of the brightest of the pack, her sendings the most complex. The image that came with the sending was of a woebegone and uncomfortable cub liberally covered with the tiny, prickly seeds produced by a scrubby weed that grew in the sandy soil near the river. The little barbs were tenacious—and much inclined to hook into the tongue and gums of any wolf trying to chew them out of fur herself. The elf didn't blame Cloudchaser for looking for help.

Willowgreen sighed, shook her head, and sent a wordless assent.

"Cloudchaser's cub got himself into trouble again," she told Rellah. "Prickleseeds. If I don't get them out now, he'll get them worked into his fur so badly we'll have to shave him."

Rellah shook her head, her lips pursed. "Strange to see *you* running off at the behest of animals."

Willowgreen repressed a flush of anger at the scorn in Rellah's voice. "Someday that cub may help keep *you* fed in the dead of white-cold," she snapped. "Will you call him 'animal' then?"

She strode off down to the river before Rellah could answer.

The half-grown cub had done an incredibly thorough job of working prickles into his fur.

"What did you *do*?" Willowgreen sighed when she saw him. "Roll in them?"

The cub cringed submissively before his disgusted mother, and feebly wagged his tail, looking up at Willowgreen in the pathetic hope that she would take his side.

"Oh, I'm a fool," she sighed, unable to resist those sad, liquid eyes. She found a bare spot and folded her long legs under her, then patted the sandy ground in front of her. The cub inched over to her on his belly.

Hurt, he sent plaintively, both to her and his mother. **Prickles hurt.**

Stupid, Cloudchaser sent in return.

Not stupid, just a cub, Willowgreen replied to both of them. **Now he knows better, right?**

Hurt, the cub affirmed, closing his eyes in misery. **Never go in prickles again.**

You see? Willowgreen told the she-wolf, patiently untangling fingernail-sized burrs from the fur of the cub's ruff.

Cloudchaser sighed, and flopped down beside the elf in the dust.

"Tedious" was not an adequate description for the task Willowgreen was faced with. She had plenty of time for her thoughts to roam; and they wandered back to Rellah's warning about Graywolf.

He's always hated me, I think. I can't remember a time when he didn't hate me. She shivered, remembering his strange yellow eyes glaring at her from across the heads of those surrounding her on far too many nights, of late.

He suspects something. He must. And if he ever finds out that I was with a human—

But Shayana wasn't just any human—she was my friend.

She saved my life. She taught me so much—

She taught me how to stand up for myself. How to be myself. And that was the greatest lesson of all.

Willowgreen's hands worked burrs out of fine, soft fur, while her thoughts continued to wander in the past.

Her first glimpse of Shayana was etched into her memory with pain and fear—the pain of her broken arm and leg, the throbbing of her head; the fear of the horrible monster that had caught her and would surely kill her. Slender, wiry, leather-clad body; long, gray-threaded hair in coiled braids —and that alien face with its narrow eyes and tiny, round ears. Uncanny, five-fingered hands. Voice pitched lower than *any* elf could reach. So strange, so like and yet unlike an elf.

It had been the first time she'd ever seen a human up close. She'd been certain it would be her last.

I was so wrong. She healed my hurts, she tended me like one of her hurt animals, then she made me grow up whether I liked it or not. She taught me to heal with my hands when I thought the blow on the head had taken my healing power from me. She made me see her kind as something other than an enemy.

She who saw her own kind as an enemy, who hated them as much as any elf.

What was it she said? "Humans fear the different"? Something like that. But are we any better? She seemed to think we were. I don't know. Both our kinds seem to follow the same pathways, to the same dead ends. Two-Spear is afraid of the High Ones because they are so different from him. The High Ones are afraid of Graywolf because he is so different from them. Skyfire is constantly at her brother's throat, and is it for the good of the tribe, or for the sake of her own ambition? I just don't know. It all seems as stupid as anything any human could do.

The last of the burrs were gone, and Willowgreen stroked the cub's neck and scratched his ears absently. The cub sighed and closed his eyes, resting his chin on Willowgreen's ankle. His mother grunted a bit jealously and nudged the elf-woman's elbow with her cold, damp nose. Still lost in her own thoughts, she transferred her right hand to Cloudchaser's head and the she-wolf curled a little closer to the elf's leg, then relaxed, her mind humming with bliss, becoming one with the "now" of wolfsong. Willowgreen "heard" the song, "heard" Cloudchaser join it, and bit her lip.

Wolfsong—the wolfsong I couldn't hear before Shayana gave me that mushroom, hoping it would reawaken my powers of healing. It did—and gave me so much more.

Sometimes—sometimes more than I wanted. I'm not sure I like being able to feel what the others feel, hear what they think, without them knowing I am. I'm glad it only happens once in a while.

I wonder if Shayana knew that might happen? I wish I could talk to her. She was so—steady. When she wasn't thinking about what her own kind had done to her, anyway. She could help me think things out if she was here.

Willowgreen sighed, filled suddenly with the longing to see her odd friend again.

If nothing else, it was always so peaceful around her. I'm so tired of Two-Spear's tempers—

Her eyes filled with tears, and she blinked to clear them. Two tears fell on the cub's ruff, and her long, slim fingers smoothed them away.

I love him. I do. But he's going to kill himself, and maybe the rest of us too, if I can't find a way to stop him from these constant attacks on humans. There are so many more of them than there are of us—and they multiply so quickly. We drive them away, but others come to take their place, time and time again.

If only I could find a way to stop him—

If only I could talk to Shayana.

Then she sat up straight. *Why not? Why not go to her? I could say—I could tell Rellah that I need some herbs that don't grow around here. Snakeroot, say. Or bitterweed, or oilberry. It wouldn't be a lie, either.*

She stood up abruptly, so quickly that the cub's chin fell off her ankle and hit the ground, and he yelped in surprise.

She bent briefly, patted his head absently, then straightened, her mind still mostly on her plans. *And I'll do it now, before the hunters return, and Two-Spear is there to stop me.*

She ran back up the trail toward the camp, leaving Cloudchaser and the cub to stare after her.

Graywolf watched the elf-woman messing about with the cub, and his lip lifted in a snarl. *Burr-picking. Owl pellets! That's another pair she'll have on her side—the she-wolf and the cub together! And where Cloudchaser gives her favor, Mist follows. If this goes on much longer, there won't be anyone in tribe or pack willing to believe me!*

He shifted a little in his perch high above the ground, in a cleft of a huge old tree, and told himself to be patient.

When Willowgreen leaped to her feet it took him completely by surprise, and he was as perplexed as the two wolves when she ran back up the game trail to the holt, her bare feet raising little puffs of dust.

He waited for a moment, in case she should take it into her head to come back, then jumped down out of his tree, scattering bits of bark all over Moonfinder.

Hunt *now*? the wolf sent plaintively.

Not now, he sent shortly, and set off up the game trail at a saunter. It could do no harm, he reckoned, to come strolling casually into the holt, and it would be a lot easier to keep an eye on her from there.

He expected to see her somewhere about the central clearing; he was a little puzzled when she wasn't there. He sniffed the air, and his nose confirmed what his eyes and ears told him; Talen and Rellah were the only elves in the holt. The two High Ones huddled together beside Talen's grass-thatched shelter in earnest colloquy. Graywolf caught the sharp smell of fear from Rellah—faint, but *there*, enough to tell him that something was amiss. He walked a few more paces into the clearing, deliberately stepping on a twig to make it snap.

Two heads swiveled in his direction; two sets of large blue eyes peered across the sunlit clearing to where he stood, waiting for them to make a move, in tree-dappled shadow.

Rellah rose then, casting her long golden waterfall of hair over one shoulder, and came to *him*. The smell of fear was stronger on her—as if she feared—what?

Him?

Surely not—

"Graywolf," she said quietly, pausing just within the cool shadow of the tree.

He ducked his head; it was hard for him to meet those unblinking blue eyes, with all the force of Rellah's mind implicit in her gaze. "Rellah," he said, keeping his mind carefully blank, calculatedly cool. He would not send to the High Ones, and would not willingly bear *their* sendings. "I had thought Willowgreen was here."

Fool! he cursed himself as the High One's expression flickered. *Quickly, an excuse—*

"Moonfinder has a plague of fleas; Rockarm said she has something that drives fleas away." A lame reason, but better than none. He bared his teeth in what he hoped would pass as a smile.

The High One's eyes narrowed, and she moved a pace nearer. **Wolf-boy,** she sent, her mindforce hard and bitter. **Wolf-boy, do you care more for your chief's good than your own petty quarrels and foolish jealousies?**

He blinked, taken aback by the question, and a bit dazed by the power of her thoughts. "H-h-how—" he stammered.

Rellah's mind held him firmly, as her weak and fragile hands could not have. **Willowgreen is gone, wolf-boy,** the elf sent, each thought a cold blast of wintry chill. **She said she needed herbs that grow elsewhere and would not heed me, nor would she wait for a hunter to return and be her guard.**

Gone? The images carried with the thoughts told him where: downriver. Country unknown.

Where she went when the river swept her away—he realized, throttling down his excitement, lest it betray him. *And where she returned to the tribe from. She's going back! Could it be she's slipping off to meet with Skyfire? It would be easy enough for that one to slip away from the hunt without causing a stir. She hunts alone often enough.*

Quickly he blanked his thoughts, and stared submissively at Rellah's narrow, bare feet. He could feel her eyes on his bent head, her gaze as iceshard-cold as her thoughts. Finally, another sending. **Can I trust you to follow her and keep her safe from harm, wolf-boy? Knowing how dearly Two-Spear holds her?** *Knowing* **that if any keeps him sane, it is she?**

Or me, he thought, bare whisp of rebellious thought. *Or me.*

"I'll follow," he said quietly, taking care that none of his exultation showed in his voice. "I'll follow."

Now he looked up at the High One, his yellow eyes meeting hers. She nodded after a moment, her flood of spun-sunlight hair rippling with the movement. "Go, then," she said over her shoulder, turning away imperiously. "When the chief comes back from the hunt, if you haven't returned, I'll tell him where you've gone."

He howled for Moonfinder then, his heart wild with joy and fierce triumph—the wolf burst into the clearing at a run and skidded to a stop beside him.

The trail I want to take, and she gifts *me with it!* he exulted, pulling himself onto Moonfinder's back, fingers and toes taking familiar holds in the thick fur.

Hunt *now*? the wolf asked.

Yes, fur-brother, he grinned. **We hunt now.**

Oh, my feet hurt. Willowgreen slumped on a clump of willow roots beside the river, and dropped her legs into the lukewarm water with a sigh. *It feels like I've been walking forever. Two days and a night, and* still *nothing looks familiar. I can't see how I could have gone past the place—*

But I don't know how far I came the first time, either. The river at flood was a lot faster than it is now, and when I walked back—

She flushed a little, and giggled at herself, brushing strands of sweat-dampened hair back out of her face with both hands. *When I came back to the holt I was full of Shayana's mushroom, and I was not exactly paying attention to the passing of time* or *landmarks!*

She felt behind her for the tree trunk, and leaned into it, closing her eyes and listening to the soft gurgle of the river among the stones and tangle of roots at her feet. Her mind fogged with drowsiness. *So quiet,* she thought vaguely. *So peaceful . . .*

She hadn't meant to fall asleep, but sleep stole up on her and took her before she knew it.

Yellow eyes, sun-eyes, eyes white-hot with rage, eyes bitter with sorrow, eyes that never quite hid the pain that was always behind them.

Eyes of one who felt too much, knew too much, cared too much. Eyes too aware of mortality, within, and without.

Yellow eyes . . .

Wolf eyes, with a deeper soul showing through.

Willowgreen could not look away from those eyes, even though they glared hatred at her. *Let me be your friend*, she pleaded, silently. *Please.* The eyes did not answer—but was there a lessening of the hate?

Yellow eyes . . . she reached—and touched something past the eyes. An ache; a terrible loneliness. A certainty of inadequacy, incompletion.

A name.

Pain!

She fell from one dream into another, with a shock that made her choke and struggle for breath.

Hot pain, agony in her side, under the hand pressed there, hot blood trickling between her fingers as she ran—

She tripped, fell, tumbled against a tree trunk, the bark tearing skin from her shoulder. The fall woke new lances of fire to arc across her body from the red-agony of the wound in her side. She pushed off from the tree to stumble onward, and knew escape was hopelessly out of reach. She could hear them shouting on the path behind her, and the halloo as Gort spotted her. But she was too stubborn to give up, even now. Desperation forced her legs to keep moving; anger and fear gave her strength to replace that which was trickling down her leg in a warm, red stream. She knew this forest, as her pursuers did not.

If she could only reach the river—

Then she heard the snap of a bowstring, and tried to fling herself out of the way, and knew at the last second that she had not moved quickly enough to evade the arrow this time—

Then a blow to her back that flung her facedown on the path—gritty dirt in her mouth, the lesser pain of a broken tooth—taste of blood—

—anguish, red-hot, unbearable—

—fading—regret—

—swift-falling dark—

Pain threw Willowgreen out of dreaming with a scream clawing its way out of her throat.

She clung to the roots of the willow, dazed, disoriented, her heart pounding, her eyes unfocused.

Her mouth was dry, and her head spun. She panted, and focused on the smooth bark of the tree under her palms, trying to orient herself.

She schooled her breathing; forced her heart to slow. Shook her mind out of paralysis and back into thought—

And knew, fingernails digging into the bark of the willow, why the nightmare of running and pain had come to her. That it was no nightmare, that the mind she had touched had been one she had touched many times before.

"Shayana!"

She scrambled to her feet, leaping the tangled willow roots, speeding along the path beside the riverbank, following the fading—oh, swiftly fading!—tendril of Shayana-ness.

Shayana!

—regret—

She sobbed as she ran, but dashed the tears from her eyes and ran on, seeing through blurred vision the familiar bend of a weeping birch, a well-known cluster of rocks, reaching as she ran for the mind of her friend—

It slipped away from her, eluded her, then escaped her altogether—

Shayana—wait—

—farewell—

Near sunset she finally stumbled into the clearing where Shayana had fallen. She was half blind with tears and weariness, and her heart went cold when she saw a dark, sprawling *something* half hidden by rank weeds beside the deer trail that crossed this clearing.

No! She had not wanted to believe—

She forced her weary legs into a semblance of a run, then went heavily to her knees in the grass beside the pathetic, motionless huddle that had been her friend.

No—

She reached out to touch one outflung hand, senselessly hoping even yet that her mind had betrayed her and a hint of life still remained—

But the hand was cold.

No—oh, no—

Grief shook her and she threw back her head and howled her sorrow and loss to the darkening sky.

"*Ayoooo—*"

The wordless howl rose from her throat, terrible with anguish. Birds that had been singing in the trees about her fell silent at her cry.

"*Ayoooo—*"

She cried again when she had breath, her voice quavering as she sobbed. She gathered breath and howled again. This time another voice joined hers, another grief-stricken heart crying out beside her.

She knew, without knowing how she knew, what wolf it was that had raised his voice to mourn for their friend. *Their* friend, for the human healer Shayana had been friend to four-footed creatures as she had not been to her own kind—and most especially to this one. And he, too, had not been able to reach this friend in time to save her. Willowgreen reached out blindly, her hands encountering coarse fur, and a stub that was all that was left of an ear, and she buried her face in One-Ear's shaggy ruff and wept, while he howled for both of them.

The sun declined in the west, and bathed the river in red. Willowgreen's trail was fresh enough—

But something very odd had happened here.

Graywolf knelt beside the willow-tangle by the riverside,

frowning, puzzled.

She sat here for a long time. She probably fell asleep, because she didn't move around much—then—this is very strange.

He studied the peculiar marks in the bark of the willow, sniffed at them carefully, and frowned again. *Those look like nail marks, and they have her scent on them. Why would she scratch at the bark?*

The river burbled mindlessly behind them, giving no answers. Moonfinder sniffed at the cradle of willow roots and growled, the hackles on the back of his neck rising. **Fear,** he sent. **Willowgreen-fear.**

"Stupid fool probably fell asleep, then got scared awake by a ravvit jumping on her," Graywolf growled aloud. "Probably fell into the river—"

But no—the signs were clear to read.

She scratched at the bark; she was afraid, and she scratched at the bark. Then she jumped up.

He stood, and followed the line of her tracks, walking carefully on the unmarked grass beside them.

She went running off down the trail. But why?

There were no signs of enemies, predators—and even Willowgreen wasn't stupid enough to be frightened into running off for *no* good reason.

He knelt in the dust again; puffs of it rose as he studied the signs; he sneezed and rubbed at his nose with the back of his hand. He was more perplexed by this trail than by any he had ever read.

Fear, Moonfinder said, insistently nudging his back with a cold nose. **Ride! Willowgreen fears!**

Graywolf sighed—but his gut was going cold, and the hair on the back of *his* neck was up, now.

She could be in trouble. I—I don't want her hurt. Not really. I wanted her out of the way but I don't want her hurt! I just—I don't know what I want.

Memory came, unbidden, of Willowgreen saving *his* wolf-friends, *his* Goldeye, and then Moonfinder, and *himself* as

well, with her barks and messes. Of her patience in the face
of his insults. Of how she had never, to his certain knowledge, tried to turn Two-Spear against him. Of how he had
driven her into tears so many times before, and now—now
how he drove her into bewildered and unhappy resignation.

Knowledge came, unwanted, of his own cruelty. And what
made him cruel.

He didn't much care for himself at that moment.

He mounted swiftly then, and took hold with hands and
toes, and his wolf broke into a loping run, nose to the
ground.

Willowgreen let go of One-Ear reluctantly, afraid that he
was going to leave her. But the tall, dark wolf only wedged
his nose under her chin, forcing her to look up, then licked
the sticky-salt tears from her face as gently as if she had been
his cub. She sat back on her heels a little, sniffling into the
back of her hand and met his warm, pale-silver eyes, shining
in the twilight with intelligence and caring.

He's gotten so big! *I don't remember him being this big
before. Was he only half-grown when I saw him the first time,
with Shayana? Why, he's taller than any wolf in the pack—tall
enough he could even carry me—*

The first rays of Mother moon picked out his eyes clearly.
Blue eyes—she thought, startled that she had never noticed
the color of his eyes before. *Only Timmain's wolf-children
have blue eyes—*

Something stirred in the depths of her mind, reaching—
touching—

One-Ear sighed, and met her gaze as feral full wolves could
not. **No cub-thing now,** he sent. **—Tyrr—now.**

She froze. Her soulname. How—he knew her soulname!

And a name came to her. Not One-Ear, no.
Windwalker? she replied, tentatively, holding out her
hand. The wolf lowered his massive head and nuzzled her
palm.

She swallowed, and slid her free hand across his single flattened ear, scratching the base of it, hardly daring to believe what had happened.

I know his name—I know his name—and he knows mine.

This—this was her wolf, now—*her* wolf—her bonded soul-friend—

She had *never*, after so many years, dreamed of this—or of the rightness of it.

Suddenly his head came up, his one good ear pricked forward, his nose sniffing at the breeze. He growled, and the hackles on the back of his neck bristled.

What? she sent, fear reawakening in her.

Killers, he sent, anger coloring the thought crimson with the memory of the spilled blood of their mutual friend. **Human-killers come back.**

She scrambled to her feet and gathered herself to flee into the protection of the forest, but Windwalker flowed like liquid night to stand between her and the trees.

No, he sent, imperatively. **They come fast, with far-strikers. Tyrr ride.** And when she hesitated, he growled as he would have at a recalcitrant cub. **Ride!** he insisted.

She pulled herself onto his back, awkward, fumbling in her haste. He bore with it patiently, until she had set her hands in his ruff and her feet ahead of his haunches as she had seen the others do.

Then he leaped forward, threading his way through the tangle of trees and underbrush. She was so caught in the excitement and wonder of her first ride, that she didn't realize he was running straight for the humans until *after* he was among them.

She swallowed a shriek of fear, and clung to his back, the rank, sour smell of them thick in her nostrils. Windwalker howled and snapped to clear them from his path—the humans screamed and scattered and he darted into the shadows under the trees—

Then they were past, and too deeply into the brush for any

weapons to be of use.

Willowgreen set her fingers deeply into his ruff and laid her head along his neck, her heart rising even under the weight of grief at the speed, the play of muscles under his skin—at the magic of being, at last, a Wolfrider.

Graywolf's fingers tightened in Moonfinder's ruff, as the first quavers of a howl rose in the distance—a grief-howl. A *death*-howl.

High and anguished and full of heart-pain it rose; a howl too high, and with the wrong harmonics, to have come from a wolf's throat.

And the only other elf in this forest—that Graywolf *knew* of—was Willowgreen. He had seen signs of no other, and given his suspicions about Skyfire, he had been looking for them.

Moonfinder whined deep in his chest, gathered himself beneath his rider, and pushed his pace. The howl rose again—

But the third time, as the tone began to fail, the elf-voice was joined by a new one. And *this* voice, raised in the same, throbbing tones of mourning, was a wolf's.

What?

Now Moonfinder slowed, stopped.

The wolf's howl rose into the night sky alone, telling of sorrow too deep, loss too profound for tears.

Graywolf shivered, chill creeping along his back, and felt Moonfinder shivering beneath him.

Death. An elf and a wolf—and a death that both mourn. But who are they? And whom do they mourn?

The howl faded, and although both Graywolf and Moonfinder stilled their breathing and strained to catch the faintest sound, no other hint of elf *or* wolf came to their ears. They waited; watched—until stars filled the sky above them. Nothing. Graywolf couldn't bear the suspense any longer.

Go! he urged Moonfinder, taking handholds in his fur and bracing himself for the sudden leap forward. **Go! It *might* be Willowgreen—she might be in trouble—**

The wolf needed no further urging than that; he launched himself forward into the night in the direction of the howls, Graywolf clinging grimly to him. The last of the sun faded, vanished, and they raced on into the twilight, the dark.

Whether or not it's Willowgreen, it's an elf, a wolf, and a death—

Graywolf bent low over his wolf's neck; too low to see where they were going, too low to notice that what little wind there was came from behind them, so that Moonfinder was running scent-blind. Mother moon could not penetrate the thick dark beneath these trees; it was hard to see a clear path to run—shadows were too thick to guess where the trees might end. This was *not* Wolfrider land—Graywolf could only try and help his wolf pick out a path through this unfamiliar forest; he had no time to spare for guesses about what might lie ahead.

They only had the warning of a savage howl ahead of them—and shrieks that did *not* come from an elfin throat— to alert them to danger close by. *Too* close; too near to stop in time.

Graywolf's grip loosened a little in surprise just as Moonfinder plunged into an unexpected clearing—

—filled with humans.

Their scent was hot and rank in his nose, and they were practically on top of him. He gasped, caught without a plan, without a defense.

That little loosening of his grip was enough. Enough that when Moonfinder yelped and doubled back on his track like a weasel—his rider didn't.

He flew through the air, saw the ground coming up to meet him, and tried to tumble in midair to land on his feet—

But he couldn't twist himself enough, and landed heavily, driving his breath from his lungs and sending stars across his vision. He tried to scramble to his feet, but he was too dizzy;

he slipped and fell, and the club that crashed into the side of his head ensured that he would not rise from *this* fall.

Are we safe? Willowgreen sent, tentatively, after what seemed like an eternity of clinging to Windwalker's back. The wolf slowed to a trot, then a walk, then finally paused, head up, testing the breeze following them. She waited, trying to make out *anything* through the thick brush and the thicker darkness. She sniffed in imitation of Windwalker, but couldn't make out any scents but the sharp smell of clawed dirt, the green smell of growing leaves.

Safe, he said; then sniffed again. He whined a little, anxious puzzlement threading his thoughts.

She slid from his back, and went to her knees on the bracken when her shaky legs wouldn't hold her up. **What's wrong?** she asked.

Scent. Strange-scent. Wolf-scent, like Windwalker. Strange-scent, like Tyrr.

Strange-scent? she thought, biting her lip, trying to make out what he was trying to say. *Like me?*

Then it hit her—and cold fear stilled her heart. She clutched her hands in Windwalker's pelt, shaking.

Timmorn's Blood! Oh no—what if Rellah sent someone after me? I told her I wanted to go alone—but she does what she wants, and the others listen to her. Mist was still at the holt—Rockarm—Graywolf—

No, it couldn't be Graywolf. If I were drowning, he'd poke sticks at me to keep me off the bank—

Windwalker, what of the strange-scent-one? she asked, frantic to know the worst.

He sniffed deeply, and a growl rumbled in his chest. **With killers. Killers have. Blood-smell. Hurt-smell.**

Both? she cried.

No. Not wolf. Strange one only.

She hauled herself to her feet, and pulled herself onto his back again, her arms and legs trembling with fatigue.

Howl for the other wolf, she commanded. **Howl! Bring the other to us. We must know who it is—**

Obediently Windwalker filled his lungs, pointed his nose to the sky, and filled the night with a summoning cry. After a moment he was answered. After far too long, Willowgreen heard something approaching them. Heard the panting of a wolf pressed past exhaustion, the rustle of leaves as a beast too weary to pay heed to his feet misstepped.

But the muzzle that broke through a screen of leaves was *not* Mist's Cloudchaser, nor Rockarm's bond-friend.

It was Moonfinder.

Willowgreen shuddered, but could not look away. Humans, horrible, foul-smelling humans, danced and capered wildly in the light of a great bonfire. At the edge of their clearing, beyond the huddle of ugly little huts, Willowgreen crouched in the shelter of a bramble bush, Moonfinder beside her, watching them.

I must be mad, she thought, trembling in every limb, heart pounding, holding terror away with all her strength. *I can't be meaning to try this. I must truly be mad. One elf, two wolves—against them?*

Beside the bonfire a huddled something stirred, something scarcely half the size of one of the towering creatures that danced about it and the fire. One of the humans kicked it savagely, and it gave a weak cry of pain. Moonfinder growled, tensed to leap—

No! she shrieked at him, and the wolf subsided with a whimper. **Wait,** she said.

Hurt! he objected. **They hurt Graywolf!**

Wait. Wait for Windwalker. *Then* we go.

The huge wolf was somewhere on the other side of the human place—this was an open place, unbounded, not like the one hemmed in by dead trees. Not like the place that had held the humans that had killed Two-Spear's first wolf, Blackmane.

And what did that mean? That they were ignorant? Or confident enough of their strength that they could afford *not* to depend on barriers?

Windwalker was to make a distraction among the humans; she and Moonfinder would run into the camp and try to free Graywolf. That had been *her* plan—poor as it was, Windwalker had agreed, but had elaborated on it. Now she had no idea what it was he was going to do. He was frighteningly intelligent; and had clever thoughts like no other wolf in her limited experience. But she trusted him, as Shayana had trusted him; she *had* to trust him. She had no hope, otherwise. And now—she gritted her teeth and told herself that she *would* be able to fulfill her side of the plan.

Whatever it was that Windwalker was doing, it was taking *much* longer than she had thought it would. While she waited, aching with impatience, the humans tormented their captive with cruel glee. Willowgreen tried to ignore Graywolf's cries, stifled her own sobs, and kept Moonfinder from flinging himself into hopeless battle by only the narrowest of margins. She could feel *him* shaking with the effort of keeping himself quiet and hidden, and she wasn't certain how much longer she could bear to lie there and not *do* anything—

A distant rumble made Moonfinder's ear flick sideways for a moment.

She glanced at the sky. *Was that thunder? Timmorn's Blood—a storm could be as fine a distraction as anything Windwalker could do—a great storm, with lightning. The humans are afraid of storms, and rain and dark would hide us.*

But there were no clouds, no scent of rain on the air, no sudden breath of cool, no feeling of falling pressure or tingle of weather-sense warning.

The rumbling continued—grew louder—

—or was it nearer?

The ground beneath her trembled, quivered, and Moonfinder stared off to sun's-rising, both ears pricked forward, astonishment in the widening of his eyes. Dim memory stirred in the back of her mind of a time when she was a tiny cub, and the tribe had hunted—

Branch-horn? No—

The ground was not quivering, it was *shaking*, and the rumbling had grown until it rose even above the pounding of the humans' drums and brutal triumph cries. Now even *their* dull ears could hear it; and the dancing stopped. They froze, staring to sun's-rising, faces blank and incredulous, firelight making masks of red and yellow over their features.

Willowgreen scented dust—and scented something else, a scent she had only tasted once in her long life, strong and musky and wild with a power that made her blood sing and pulled her out from under the bush and up to her feet before she knew what she was doing.

And the humans, the stupid, dumbstruck humans, didn't even notice her there.

"*Ayoooo*—!" she howled, and a howl answered hers from beyond the rumbling, as the edge of the forest came alive and mighty trees crowning young mountains plunged toward the human place. Heads as long as Willowgreen's arm tossed wicked, multibranched tines as tall as she, and the pounding of their hooves was rivaled by the bellowing and snorting. Eights and eights and eights of them, a rushing wave, a river of horns and heads—fist-sized eyes flashing white moonlight, red firelight; froth flying from muzzles—

Not branch-horns, no. Not even the clickdeer of the cold plains could match these giants.

*Tree*horns, the great, black-coated elk of the marshlands. Lands where elves seldom went, for where the treehorns were, there were also snakes, swamp-lions, and blackwater fevers. Nothing frightened these great beasts—nothing could make them stampede rather than turning and fighting.

Nothing—except a pack of wolves.

Or one very large wolf who had cleverly convinced a herd of half-asleep beasts that *he* was a pack.

Ayoooo!

The howl sent them surging forward, straight for the humans, and *nothing* could stand against a herd of treehorns in full flight.

The humans recognized their danger—barely in time. Willowgreen was already among them, ignored in their panicked scramble for safety, when they began to flee. The lead elk blundered into the first of the wooden huts with a splintering crash as she reached Graywolf's side. Half a heartbeat later, the rest of the herd thundered into the shelters, smashing through walls, bellowing with pain as ragged bits of wood stabbed at them. But they did not swerve from their course; they stumbled, then recovered, forced onward by the press of bodies behind them.

Graywolf was unconscious and bound tightly, with ropes tying hands and feet together. Bruises mottled his face and body, and a thin trickle of blood at the corner of his mouth warned Willowgreen that something might be broken inside him.

A rib in his lung—let it be no more than that—

She dared not wait nor handle him gently; the herd was almost upon her. She cut the ropes on his feet with the flint knife Rellah had pressed upon her, and cast his bound arms around Moonfinder's neck, boosting him onto the wolf's back as best she could.

Go! she urged, and quick as a leaf in the wind, he was gone.

She looked up to see wild, mad eyes, red-rimmed, reflecting firelight, looming bright above her, and the terrible hooves of the lead elk slashing down at her—

And a great gray shadow streaked from beneath those hooves.

Tyrr!

She leaped blindly, making a snatch for the furry shoulder that rammed into her; scrambled somehow onto Windwalker's back with hooves flashing above the two of them, so near that one scraped her shoulder—

—and they were away, running out into the darkness, the freedom, the night. Behind them, fire, fear, and madness.

Everything was as it had been—except, Shayana's cave seemed woefully empty without her in it. Everything else was in its place; the bundles of herbs, the wooden bowls, the hollowed-out gourds, the flaked-flint implements. It even smelled the same; sharp, dusty scents of dried herbs, deep aroma of leather, rich hint of last night's meal, and under it all, the damp-rock smell that said "cave." It all looked as if she had left it only moments before. But Shayana would not be returning this night or any other—and the life was gone from this place she had called home.

There were no hurt animals in the niches, at least— Willowgreen was glad of that, because she did not think she would have been able to bear the sight of them, looking at her, wondering where their peculiar, half-mad tender had gone.

She eased Graywolf down off Moonfinder's back, and cut the ropes binding his swollen wrists together, then looked about for bedding, coverings. *He's unconscious; I have to get something to keep him warm while I heal him—*

There was no sign of the three-legged ferret Whist, either, nor the lizard Green—but there were three smaller lizards prowling through the cave, snatching at the insects Willowgreen disturbed as she made up a pallet for Graywolf, and those three bore a striking resemblance to Green.

The halfling was still unconscious when she was ready to move him; greenish pallor beneath his sunburned skin, breathing with shudders that spoke of chest injuries such as the broken rib she feared—

She eased him over onto the bed she had made, then worked with Shayana's firebow until she had lit a small fire to see by; Windwalker surveyed her while she worked, then curled up in his accustomed corner once the fire was going.

He watched her with proprietary care, nose on outstretched paws, eyes reflecting greenish backlights as they caught the firelight. As she knelt next to Graywolf's pallet, Moonfinder shied uneasily away from the fire, then hovered beside her, whining anxiously, not *quite* getting in her way.

As Blackmane hovered, whenever Two-Spear was hurt. Though he was "Swift-Spear," then. She smoothed back blood-matted hair, and winced at the pulpy bruise just above Graywolf's right temple. *Oh my love—this is your friend, your dearest friend, your only friend with Blackmane gone. I swear, I will save him for you, or die. No matter what he has done to me.*

Moonfinder whined again, and pawed delicately at the ragged hem of her leather tunic. **Hurt,** he sent, urgently. **Stop hurt!**

She soothed the wolf as best she could, but her own fear was hard to conquer. *I have to. I have to, that's all.*

She took a careful inventory of Graywolf's injuries—the visible ones, at least. She straightened the battered limbs of the injured elf, realigning all the broken bones—then realized that she was only trying to delay things.

Rellah isn't here, and neither is Talen—but I knew one day they wouldn't *be at my side. I am the healer. I have the strength to do this, and I will.*

She took a deep breath, closed her eyes, and placed one hand on his forehead, one above his heart, and sank her awareness into Graywolf's mistreated body.

And met with stubborn barriers, and rejection. He was strong, but confused with pain, and at first he could not tell what she was or even *who* she was. Then he knew her—and resisted her. He fought her even as she strove to knit broken bones, torn flesh, fleeing her, fleeing what was strange in her, fearing her strangeness.

No, she said/sent. **No.** And she tracked him, where he hid in the darkest lairs of his mind, blocking her out and keeping her from her healing; tracked him and saw what he would far rather have kept hidden, even from himself.

Especially from himself.

It was not what was in her that he feared, it was what she would make him see in himself.

Jealousy and cruelty, and a wish to *hurt*.

What he was. *Not* an elf. A beast, a wild, feral creature that the High Ones feared, that was flawed, that could not plan, calculate, understand, or find a direction on his own. Follower. Halfling. Wolf-boy.

Animal.

Oh yes, she agreed, as he cringed. **All of that. But look—**

Beside the jealousy, love for his elf-friend and wolf-friend that had made him push himself past his last strengths, time and time again; that made him support his friend even when he didn't agree with him. Beside the cruelty, the reason *why* he had learned that cruelty—the rejection, time after time, of those who looked upon him and thought, *More wolf than elf*. Beside the wish to hurt—all the hurts he had borne, silently, suffering and showing a mask of indifference, keeping his deepest thoughts, his ever-present doubts secret.

Half-creature? Yes. **But look—** she sent, and opened her memory to him, showing him the life-web she had seen in her vision-quest. The weave of life that made up this world, that *was* this world.

And how the High Ones, the true elves, *did not fit inside that web*.

How they were destined to fall, one by one, because they could not, would not.

The barriers wavered, as his revulsion weakened, caught by that vision.

Who is flawed? You? Or those who cannot change to suit this world? she asked, aching for them, the beautiful, the shining, the doomed. **Who is the fool? The one who knows there must be pack-leader and pack-second, and knows he has no gift for leading? Or the one who looks at yellow eyes and will not look beyond them to loyalty and one who holds the welfare of tribe and pack higher than his own good?**

She opened herself to him recklessly, aware that his body was weakening, his strength fading. Knowing that she must convince him to let her by to do her work—or else force him, and maybe damage him further. If she *could* force him. She was not certain that she could, even now, weak as he was.

I, at least, know what I am, she said acerbically. **I am a fool, but I am a healer too.** Her mind-voice softened. **Let me heal—because the pack, the Way, and Two-Spear all need you.**

He could not withstand that last. With a whimper, he dropped his barriers and let her within—

She flung herself into her healing-magic, and spent herself recklessly, wildly, passionately. Because all that she had told him was the truth. The pack needed him. The Way needed him, because his instincts were the surest, he heard the wolfsong the clearest. And Two-Spear needed him, because other than herself, Graywolf was the only other elf he could trust completely.

She knitted up wounded flesh, bound up broken bones— and because the spirit was sorely and deeply wounded, moved to touch it too—

And found what she did not expect.

A name.

A name that shook her to her bones and washed her away in a flood of sweet sorrow, and left her gasping and bewildered on a strange and alien shore—

Vrenn—Vrenn—

She opened her eyes, dazed, and met yellow eyes, sun eyes, eyes reflecting glints of dying firelight back at her. He touched her face with a hand that trembled, and whispered, mind and voice—

A name.

Her name.

Tyrr.

She looked into those yellow eyes, and saw herself, strange and magical and incomprehensible—

Then looked beyond reflection, and saw *him*, brave in spite of fear, loyal to death and beyond it. And *now* comprehended, all of him.

He did not understand gentleness, never having known it. He did not understand love, and did not recognize it in himself.

She reached to touch his face, then pulled back—

No! It wasn't *Graywolf* she should be Recognizing—it was Two-Spear! Two-Spear, her lifemate, her lovemate.

She bit her knuckle and stared into those eyes—those eyes—

This couldn't be happening—not with Graywolf—not with her lover's best friend—

It was Two-Spear's soulname she had sought for so long—

I love Two-Spear, not him—

But even as the thought arose, she knew it was a lie. She *knew* Vrenn now—and though she *still* loved Two-Spear— she loved Graywolf with equal passion. And more reason.

And all the force of Recognition.

She sobbed once, and fell into his eyes, into his arms, surrendering to a fate that was stronger than either of them.

I said I was going after herbs; I might as well bring them back, she thought, deliberately keeping her mind on small things, inconsequential things.

She stared at the supplies Shayana had amassed. Bunches of herbs bound with grass and hung on the wall, bowls and sealed gourds of berries, bark bits, crushed leaves, dried roots. There were carry-bags for anything she wished to take—and there was her own wolf to help carry things. Not that dried herbs were very heavy, but—

A dull thud behind her made her pivot, hands reaching for her flint knife.

Graywolf sprawled ungracefully on the stone beside his pallet, trying unsuccessfully to get to his feet.

"What are you *doing*?" she exclaimed, thinking only that he was still vulnerable, still weak, and should not have tried to walk without help.

"I—" He looked up at her, just for a moment, then pain and guilt shadowed his gaze, and he turned his eyes away. "I have to go. Away. Far away." He stared stolidly at the stone floor of the cave, and pushed himself slowly to a kneeling position.

"Where?" she asked, her voice going sharp and thin.

"I—don't know. Anywhere. I can't—we can't—"

He finally *looked* at her, his eyes wide with anguish. "I *can't* go back, don't you see? He'll *know*!"

"You aren't going anywhere right now," she pointed out; no need to guess who "he" was. "You can't ride for at least a hand-of-days. And how will you live outside the tribe? Who will keep Two-Spear safe from his sister if you don't? She won't listen to me. She thinks I'm nothing."

Her matter-of-fact words gave the lie to the ache in her heart. *What am I going to do? What am I going to tell Two-Spear?*

He blinked at her, rejecting Skyfire's assessment. **Nothing. You—nothing? Is she blind?**

The sending was an invitation, and she took it. **Willful,** she replied, sitting beside him on the chill cave floor. **She sees only what she wants to see. She cannot see that sometimes Two-Spear is right, and sometimes he is wrong; she sees only that he fails sometimes, and that he must therefore fail always. She cannot imagine a chief that is not always right—because that is the kind of chief she thinks she will be, if leadership passes to her.**

He snorted, and moved carefully back to his bed. **As if all wisdom comes when you tie your hair in the chief's knot. That kind of chieftess could get us killed.**

So now he is thinking "us" again. She sighed with relief. *No more words of vanishing into the forest forever.*

There are many who listen to her, she sent hesitantly, wishing she had kept the fire going. It was hard to see him clearly in the dusk of the cave. **And there are some things she says that are sensible.**

"And more that are not." He looked into her eyes, and the ache in her heart was echoed in his face. "I cannot leave the tribe."

"You *must not* leave the tribe," she said. "Better that *I* should leave, than you."

"Better neither. He needs us. Both." He laughed, a dry, humorless cough of a laugh. "It was easier when we hated each other."

She hung her head, not denying his words. "What do we tell him?" she asked softly.

"Nothing."

Her head came up, and she stared at him incredulously. "*Nothing*? How? How can we tell him nothing? How—"

"How did you keep this place secret?" he countered darkly. "How did you manage to hide where you had been from Two-Spear? *How are you managing to keep your secrets from me even now?*"

She pulled back, and evaded his eyes. "There was a healer," she said, choosing her words with extreme care. "She lived here. When I washed up on the riverbank, she pulled me out. She was very strange, and a little mad, I think. She lived alone here, and healed only animals. Windwalker was hers."

She could see the image forming in his mind—a High One, like Rellah, only crazed and solitary. "Was that who— died?"

"You heard us?"

He nodded.

A knot of tears choked her throat. "Yes. The humans—" The tears that had been threatening now fell, and she sobbed into her hands. "They hated her. They tried to kill her before

I met her. I don't know why she was where they could catch her, or why Windwalker wasn't with her—her only magic was with animals, and it couldn't save her—"

The words came brokenly, all of them true, and all of them weaving a web of deception between Graywolf and the *whole* truth. Because the whole truth was something she did not dare to confide to anyone.

"Magic" and "human" were concepts no elf would ever put together.

She dried her eyes on the back of her hands, and looked up at him, sniffling, wondering if he believed her.

He was watching her warily, as if he didn't quite dare touch her. "I'm sorry—" he said awkwardly. "It must have been hard for her here, all alone. Why didn't you bring her back to the tribe?"

"I couldn't—" She had to let him draw his own conclusions. She dared not lie, or he might sense it.

"She wouldn't leave?" He shook his head. "I think she was more than a *little* mad. To stay here, so close to humans—"

"Sometimes I thought so, too," she whispered, sniffing.

One corner of his mouth quirked as she sniffed. "You know—I *am* sorry—but this is the first time I have ever seen you cry for anyone but yourself."

That *hurt*.

She glared at him, offended. Silence parted them for a moment—for one moment the bond between them trembled under sudden strain.

But this time it was *he* who gave in. "I—I am a fool," he said unhappily. "I say the thing that hurts the worst. I should—"

She touched his shoulder, accepting the half-spoken apology. "You should tell me how we are going to hide Recognition."

There. It was out in the open.

"It has been done—"

"But not well—everyone guessed Wreath and Prey-Pacer —and—"

"Whom do we *need* to hide it from?" he asked abruptly.
"Only one."

He pulled himself to his feet with the aid of the rough cave
wall. "Only one—who is just like his sister. Who sees what
he *wants* to see."

Graywolf shook with the effort of holding himself upright;
after a moment, Willowgreen gave up and rose. He obviously
wanted to deal with this on his feet.

"But—he'll see—"

"What he *wants* to see," Graywolf insisted. "He will see
just what he has always seen. His friend and his—
lovemate—" His voice trembled on the last word, and he
continued with an effort. "We will change nothing. Not even
our fighting."

"And when Recognition calls again?" she asked softly.

"We will find a way to satisfy it."

She sighed, acquiescing, and he slid back down the wall to
land with a thud on his pallet. "Thank you," he said. "I was
not certain—"

"That I would have sense?" It was her turn for a bitter
smile. "You were probably right to doubt it. But—"

"But—"

She could not help it. **Vrenn—I love you.**

He buried his face in his arms, and was silent for a very
long time.

She had turned away and gone back to packing up herbs
when his response finally came.

And I love you.

The High Ones stood at the edge of the crowd, and for
once Rellah was glad of the uneasiness that made the
Wolfriders give them a wide berth. Their view was
unobstructed—

A most astonishing view.

Graywolf, pale and battered and sullen—plainly much the
worse for wear. Plainly recovering from serious mistreat-
ment. Beside him, Willowgreen, also pale with the pallor

that came when she had overextended her powers, laden with crude bags—

Riding the tallest wolf Rellah had ever seen.

It would have *to be tall,* she told herself dazedly. *She is the tallest of the halflings. Her legs would drag the ground, else.*

The hunters had returned only that morning, heavily laden; Two-Spear had been angry when he had learned that Willowgreen had gone off—but Talen had managed to mollify him by telling him that Graywolf was with her. He had been saner than usual, which made Talen's task easier.

But then—just as the feast of return was nearly ready—this. The two of them, riding side by side into the holt. Two-Spear had been ecstatic that his lifemate was now a *real* Wolfrider; he was so caught up in greeting her that he wasn't asking questions—yet—

Like where the beast came from, and why Graywolf clings to Moonfinder's fur as if he might fall over at any moment. And I cannot imagine what will happen when No-Name—

As if her thought had conjured him, the great black wolf *appeared* out of nowhere, and slunk into the central clearing of the holt, then took a stance with all four legs braced and hackles raised, growling challenge at the newcomer. Wolfriders quickly cleared the area—

If these two clashed in a real challenge-fight, it could get very dangerous.

But the stranger simply looked at No-Name, sneezed, and yawned.

No-Name's growl deepened, then faded, as the stranger continued to do nothing. Nothing whatsoever. No challenge, no submission.

No-Name's growl faded and the wolf's hackles lowered, slowly. The pack-leader stalked, stiff-legged, head erect, to where the newcomer waited.

They sniffed noses. The new wolf yawned once again; flashed his throat briefly. Token submission.

It was enough. Satisfied, No-Name backed off, and slunk

away to wherever it was he laired by day.

It seemed that the entire holt breathed a sigh of relief, Rellah included.

Two-Spear is unstable enough. I would not care to think what having this new wolf challenge No-Name would do to him.

But Graywolf could not maintain his hold on Moonfinder's shoulder, and he slid to the ground as his legs refused to hold him anymore. *Now* Two-Spear took note of his friend's poor condition, and demanded angrily to know the cause.

"Humans," the halfling said, panting. "Humans. They caught me; Willowgreen healed me when I was freed. They are some two days from the holt."

Rellah compressed her lips and shut her mind against the clamor that arose over *that* bit of news.

The debate waxed hot and heavy, with Skyfire all for packing up and moving them all to land of her choosing, and Two-Spear urging that the tribe deliver an unmistakable lesson.

"You all know what will happen!" he shouted aloud. "You *know* what happens whenever the humans move near. They have killed one elf already—they nearly killed Graywolf—will you wait for them to come to us and kill again?"

Rellah moved forward then, as Willowgreen paled and gripped her wolf's shoulder. "That is no answer," she replied angrily. "You have tried this before, and always the result is the same! First you kill, then the humans go—then *more* come to take their place! This is *no* place for elves! Let us find another!"

"Yes!" Skyfire echoed. "Let us go! Now! Before they come for *us*! Enough have died already in this madness!"

"We have tried your way," Rellah pressed, as others in the crowd muttered. "And always the humans have returned. Always! Kill one, and twenty rise in its place. Let us be gone from here, before they learn of us!"

Two-Spear looked from face to face, and read his answer

there. There would be no human-hunt this time. The tribe was not with him in this.

"Will you run, like frightened suntails?" he spat. "Will you let them drive us before them until there is no place left to us?"

Silence.

"If you let them drive us, we will have *nothing!*" he cried. "We will be like animals, owning nothing, building nothing —spending all of our lives in staying one step ahead of them! We will *never* find the way back to the stars!" There were tears in his eyes, but a terrible passion in his voice that moved even Rellah. But not enough. Not this time.

"Then I will go *alone!*" He snatched up the two spears of his name, and brandished them. "I will go alone, and—"

"*No!*"

Now Willowgreen moved, blocking his path with her frail body. "No!" she cried angrily, anguished. "*There have been enough deaths!* Will you go off to die, and leave your cub with no father to guide her, protect her?"

The spears fell from Two-Spear's loosened fingers with a clatter.

"Cub?" he asked numbly. "There—you—a cub?"

She nodded, slowly. He gathered her in his arms, all thought of bloodshed forgotten. The rest of the elves gathered about them to offer their own congratulations—and, perhaps, to share relief that this crisis of madness had been so narrowly averted.

All but two—

Skyfire, whose sour face bespoke ambition betrayed once again. For if Two-Spear *had* gone against the humans, she would have had the chiefship, and without a challenge.

And Graywolf.

Graywolf—who had looked, for one fleeting moment, as if *he* were the proud father. And who now looked as stricken as if Two-Spear had taken the thing he loved best in the world.

Perhaps he has, Rellah mused. *A cub means one more*

creature to share Two-Spear's love. One more creature stand-ing between himself and his friend. And yet—and yet—that does not feel quite right. There is a mystery here.

She watched Graywolf take himself off into the forest without fanfare, without a farewell.

There is a mystery here. And I think—I think I shall solve it.

Season of Sorrows

by Heather Gladney and Janny Wurts

The rain lashed through the leaves, drenching a springtime forest that was not green, but silver-gray with mist and puddles. Skyfire huddled in sodden furs, her head rested on her forearms. The red hair which dripped down her temples was the only color not leached neutral by the storm. But to the chieftess, the bleakness of the surrounding landscape was appropriate. The tribe had not returned to this part of the forest since her Dreamsinger's death seven summers past; that the weather itself seemed to weep here seemed appropriate. For Skyfire this place would never be less than haunted; and now, for the rest of a divided and struggling tribe, the place held tragedy as well.

A cry sounded through the drumroll of falling water. Skyfire raised her head, glanced toward the skin hangings which covered the mouth of the lair where Goldwing lay in childbirth. *Let this one be born living*, the chieftess thought fervently. *The tribe cannot stand another loss*. Against her preference, the tribe had returned to this holt with its memories of death and sorrow. That it was a place well suited to the raising of young could not be disputed, and with many of the tribe's females carrying cubs, old memories of necessity must be endured. But only for the good of the tribe, and only until the young were strong enough to travel. Skyfire's lips twitched into the echo of a snarl. The luck had not turned in this place. Despite the joyous fortune of seven conceptions, not one of the young delivered in these lairs had survived. Only Goldwing's cub remained, and another gotten between Skimmer and Briarleaf whose time for birthing was yet to come.

Another moan issued from the lair. Skyfire shifted uneasily, for Goldwing's labor had extended far too long. By now she would be suffering from exhaustion as well as pain, and the reason for her difficulty could not be a natural one.

A chill nose prodded Skyfire's elbow. She reached out and stroked the spiky tips of Song's guardhair. The wolf sensed her troubled mind. Closer to him than she had ever been to Woodbiter, the chieftess understood that his distress was echoed by the pack; none of the cub litters had been born living among the wolf-brothers, either. No young tussled and snarled in play among the springing new grass. This, in a year when the winter had been mild. The newborns came out glossy and full fleshed, but limp and unbreathing and lifeless.

Why? Skyfire hammered her fist into her thigh and snarled aloud in frustration. Why should the young be dying in the womb, when bellies were lean but not starved, and the tribe enjoyed robust health.

The tap of the rain on the leather curtain that fronted the lair changed timbre; Skyfire turned on reflex, and saw Rellah at the entry. The older elf was bloody to the elbow, and weariness lent a sharper edge to her customary haughty bearing. "You had better come in."

Skyfire sucked in a distressed breath. **Not another,** she sent. **By the moons, not Goldwing's, too.**

Rellah offered no reply, but spun back through the curtain.

Pained by chilled and stiffened muscles, Skyfire rose. She touched Song, bade him wait, and set aside the arrows she had been too worried to repair. As if new fletching could be done in a downpour, anyway, she thought in disgusted despair.

Behind the dripping curtain, the lair was stiflingly close.

Skyfire fought to breathe the clammy air, fought through sickness of spirit to take stock of the pitiful bundle of flesh that should have been a healthy male cub for Goldwing, but whose limbs sprawled wet and still; lips and skin were blue-gray and icy as the puddles outside. Goldwing lay with her face turned into a tangle of tawny hair. Her face was hollowed with exhaustion, her eyes closed in unconscious sleep.

"I gave her an herb brew," Rellah said, her tone just shy of challenge. She would face snarls from the pack for this night's work. Though she had done nothing but try to save lives, grief now threatened to replace reason among Wolfrider and beast alike. They rejected the true elf's healing efforts as unworldly, useless, fur-scalding pranks. Time and again, Skyfire had been forced to intervene, to confront killing wolfish rages with the slender hope that by melding elvish wisdom with the strength of wolf-pack toughness, they might go on surviving. But where the others backed down, submissive to her will, Rellah harbored grudges. "Goldwing rests, and should not be disturbed for several hours. She will know soon enough her cub was stillborn, but if she hears before she has regained some strength, the shock and sorrow might kill her."

Skyfire frowned. Always, Rellah interpreted as if the Wolfriders were prone to frailties like the High Ones. "Goldwing is a hunter," the chieftess snapped. "Tough as a branch with the sap running under the bark. She would not fade from grief." But the tragedy would set fire to troubles already building. Skyfire might use her dream of a better future to avert bloody challenges; but words and hopes could not assuage the anguish building in the holt like thunderclouds. Too many mothers grieved this season. Their distress threaded through the unity of the pack like a hard, contorted knot. They sent bereavement through their dreams, and weeping through their underthoughts, and the result of them calling out repeatedly and futilely for young who were cold meat brought a brooding edge to all the pack did.

They came to the healers now with sullenness. They bristled over allowing any clumsy, flinching true elf near a wolf's whelping; and the old, worn arguments resurfaced, that it tampered with the Way to alter what lived and what died, let alone invade the dens of nervous, solitary hunters struggling in throes of failed childbirth. Skyfire took healers with her, forced her way into the dens by reason, by sheer force of will, and by the threat of violence inherent in a body thinned by more and harder hunting than any other.

And the pack showed its suffering indirectly. The hunts grew more wild, more violent, and the kills, more risky and savage. Terrifying, to watch elves act like this, to see the very young learn a wolfsong that held more than its measure of dark pain.

Skyfire knelt by Goldwing's dead cub, and felt the hopes she had forged during her union with the Dreamsinger slipping helplessly away. The greater the true-elf strain in the mother, the harsher the stillbirth seemed to strike her. Some died; others went catatonic, or mad, or turned weeping into themselves. Only the most wolfish crossbreeds came through alert enough to nurse others, to forage, to grow angry enough to fight and to live. Goldwing was one of these. Skyfire clenched her fists over the tiny, cold body on the cave floor. Her heart felt pressed down by a weight of despair. Where once she would have examined the dead thing's limbs for herself, now she took Rellah's word that the little body held no blemish, nor any other natural reason why its spirit should have fled before it breathed.

Almost, it seemed as though some curse overhung the forest in the place where the Dreamsinger had died.

Firmly, Skyfire reined in her need to howl in grief. From somewhere she must find the resource to face the tribe with this news, to turn aside another round of challenges, if frustrated rage led to that. She turned away from Goldwing, and Rellah, and the dead cub, and stepped out into the morning.

The rain had stopped. Blue sky gleamed through drifts of

rising mist, a promise of sunshine to come. But Huntress
Skyfire took little joy from the change to brighter weather.
That moment, the sending of her own young cub slashed
across her mind, then burst just as painfully strong as any
elder true elf could send.

Mother? Come and look! Flowers!

Skyfire could not avoid knowing that Nightstar was—
besides clutching a mass of flowers—skylarking about on a
low-hanging branch, bouncing up and down and trying to
stretch, on every bounce, for a tree-gnarl overhead. Her
daughter's images always included the sort of peripheral bits
most likely to jerk an adult elf to alertness—in this case, the
vague child-swirl of consciousness that meant great height
beneath the youngster's toes.

Owl pellets! Skyfire thought. The cub born of Dreamsinger's mating owned her father's talents in full measure,
sparked to early experimentation by Skyfire's own inherited
willfulness. Star could disrupt her mother's mind from
enormous distance, send nearly as well to tribemates, flatten
her more wolfish peers, even startle the elder elves in their
own heads. When she had a nightmare, Star could bring
every pack member in the area staggering up to stop her
distress. And always, her timing was terrible. Now was no
exception. For the pack distrusted all things that were not
understood at this time. Nightstar's gifts were regarded with
suspicion, and though no one had gone so far as to claim that
the taint that killed cubs had been of her magic's making,
scrapping became more frequent among the young, and
even seasoned elders pressed their grievances. Young Star
found herself ducking aggression however frantically she
turned up her chin to expose her throat.

Nightstar, Skyfire sent in reprimand. **Climb down
from that tree. I'll see your flowers later.**

Why later? Like a spate of childish prattle, Star
followed up with image, the bright beauty of scarlet petals,
and then the thrill of challenging the treetops to touch them.

Impatience barbed with parental concern tinged Skyfire's

reply. **Because Goldwing's cub has been born dead, and the tribe needs to be told.**

Tell them for you, Star supplied, her offer colored with the hues of other flowers she had gathered, white thorn blooms, scented beetlecups, blue-eyes and purples, and something yellow and beginning to wilt that Skyfire recognized from the swamps. To have those, busy little Star had to have been in mud up to her eyebrows, and with her several taller elder cousins each one of whom knew better than to play in a place declared off limits.

Star cheerfully burst in on her mother's irritation with a rather unfocused image of the very culprits involved.

Skyfire winced, stung by the strength of the sending. Only with difficulty could she grope past her daughter's intrusive happiness to remembrance of Goldwing's loss, to the need to inform a tribe still keening from sorrow for other stillborn young.

Star, she sent firmly. **Return to the holt. Now.**

Skyfire shut out Star's burst of protest, though the effort cost her pain. Not for the first time, she wondered whether the Dreamsinger himself had been such an intrusive presence when he had been a cub; and as always when this thought occurred, she shut away the possible consequence, that such wildly precocious talent might lead to death or expulsion from the tribe. Skyfire wished fiercely to protect her child's legacy of magic for the tribe's future; if the Wolfriders were ever to grow into a life that could survive the irregular luck of each day's catch—past suffering the lean seasons with no more resource than birds, snails, frogs, or even trees—Skyfire understood the victory must come through group strength. But the Way must not be compromised. If Nightstar could not learn to defend herself, to run and survive with the hunt, if she did not learn to answer pack challenges with the instincts inherited from the wolf, no parental protection could keep her alive until she grew into the strength of maturity.

Skyfire drew upon her memory of the Dreamsinger, who

had survived as an outcast despite madness; surely the cubling he had left her would grow into the same tenacious hardiness. Hoping fervently that this would be the case, the chieftess loped through the growing light of morning to the great tree by the clearing, where the tribe gathered to hear news of Goldwing's cub.

The rain had left everything wet. Motley and draggled as their wolf-friends, the tribe stood on muddy ground and shook out soaked garments, here basking in the warmth of new sunlight, and there tugging out knots in soaked lacing. At Skyfire's appearance, all grew still, from grizzled elder wolves and riders who were briar-scratched from the night's hunt, to last year's cubs clinging large-eyed to their mother's hands. Of this season's cubs, there were none. Skyfire sighed heavily and spoke the words that needed to be said. The impact of her news spread a pall of silence over the clearing; somewhere in the press, a wolf whined. Skyfire dug her fingers into Song's silver ruff. She had no counsel to offer beyond the same vague stirrings of instinct that had prompted her to shun this place to begin with. "This holt is not safe for our kind," she tried again. "Death stalks our young here, and I say the pack should journey far away and seek another lair for the birthing of young."

The predictable voice arose in dissent; Talen's this time, and filled with the scorn that came most readily to the High Ones. "What, are we driven to run from superstition? There is nothing evil here, but only dry caves, and good hunting, and a place far from the camps of the five fingers. I say the Dreamsinger's death has turned the wits of our chieftess, that grief rules her and urges us to folly."

Skyfire bristled at this. "Am I the only one who has known loss in this place?" She gestured at the bereaved mothers among them, her lips drawn back in a wolfish snarl of disdain. "Ask Goldwing, or Red Deer, or Rain what they feel. Their cubs never lived to feel damp, or know danger. Ask Skimmer if he wishes his firstborn dead, or alive to risk the hazards of the trail. There are too few pregnancies among our kind to allow another childbirth to go wrong."

A muttering arose at her words, cut again by Talen's loud derision. "Who are you to claim these births did not end as nature intended? Might not the wolf-blood that Timmain introduced be the factor that weakens our stock? Perhaps it is so, that elves and beasts should never have intermixed at all!"

Muttering deepened to growls, as the more wolfish members of the tribe raised hackles. Skyfire gathered herself to intervene, to avert a senseless fight that had its seeds in the frustrations and unhappiness that undermined the unity of them all.

That moment, Nightstar's sending slashed shrilly into her mind. **Mother, look, flowers!**

Huntress Skyfire was not alone in being tormented. Star's enthusiasm pierced every mind in the clearing with near-to-unbearable clarity. This was not the first such intrusion; Star could and did frolick through elvish hereditary memories with the irrepressible energy of a cub sharing a dreamberry vision. She stamped all over the prideful dignity of High Ones and wolflings alike with her impatient questions, and this time, with the loss of Goldwing's cub so recent, the intrusion became too much. Resentment against the Dreamsinger's inherited magic raised hackles, and a muted growl of outrage stirred through the pack.

Skyfire trembled on the edge of indecision. Even as chieftess she could not intervene; the Way must not be compromised, must not be set aside, even for safety's sake. Dreamsinger's wild-talented half-outsider child must win her own place in the tribe's hierarchy. This law stood for survival itself, and must never, ever be changed.

Star, be careful. Skyfire sent. **Your flowers bring the others no happiness at this time. They grieve for Goldwing's cub.**

Yes. This with impatience from Star. **Trying to figure out how—**And repeated, with some force, the colorful image of flowers.

The rest of the tribe met this offering with offense; except Skyfire, whose eyes opened wide as she realized something far more jolting.

Amid the posies Star had gathered lay a flower never seen within the forest. Poisonous green, and veined with black, its heavy, down-curved petals stood out from the innocent colors of the other blooms. Skyfire squinted, trying to pull more detail from her daughter's sending. The closer the chieftess examined that blossom, the more alarmed she grew. The shape, the color, the sheer unlikely size of it held a wrongness that made her skin creep.

Shown an unmistakable presence of danger, Skyfire acted. The malcontented growls of the tribe became an intrusion she no longer might tolerate. "Quiet!"

Resentful the tribe might be of her intrusive little daughter-cub, but the Huntress unequivocally still ruled. The pack stilled, and even Talen quelled his surly outburst while the chieftess sent warning back to Star.

Those flowers are not natural, little one. Let them lie where they grew, and beware. Come back to the holt.

Faintly, very faintly, came the preoccupied answer. **Yes. I just told you—impatience—trying to figure out how—**

No! Skyfire started up into a run, her hunting bow banging across her shoulders. **Avoid that place—warning—**

Too late; Skyfire landed jolting from her next startled stride. She did not hear Star's singing echoing through her head anymore. The silence chilled. Gently, carefully, as she might have stalked an alerted buck, she sent to the black-haired cub that was all her lost Dreamsinger had left her. **Where did you find that flower, Nightstar?**

No answer came back to her. None at all.

Skyfire felt suddenly directionless without the background buzz of prattling she had known through six turns of seasons. Vaguely aware of the tribemates who gathered, jostling around her, she cleared her mind and listened. Silence; except for the thought patterns of other Wolfriders. More than one among them had the effrontery to reflect how much less troublesome things were when Star's stray magic, fizzing off in all directions like lime-water from a spring, was out of their limited range.

Out of range! Skyfire thought angrily. Nightstar had never been out of range, not even in her sleep! As if aware of her worry, Song shoved his nose in the Huntress's palm. The wolf's restlessness spurred her to action.

Skyfire shared with him the image of her cub, dark-haired and silver-eyed and slender-boned as her Dreamsinger father. **Find!**

Song snapped his jaws beside her knee in breathless signal. The Huntress shed her bow and bounded onto his back. His heavy, silver-tipped shoulders bunched under her knees, and he surged ahead in leaping strides. Wolfriders and elders exploded out of his path. Skyfire barely noticed the friends who tugged at her sleeve, vainly trying to stay her rush until an armed party could gather to accompany her search. "Follow," she called back over her shoulder as her wolf-friend plunged into the woods. She would not wait for the pack. Alarmed beyond caution, the chieftess and Song bore through brambles and whipping branches in the direction of Nightstar's last sending.

The cub's scent-trail at first was easy to follow, a track that led from the holt in meandering fashion, here showing signs of pausing to dig for roots, and there, the imprinted dents of childish knees as Star paused to chase beetles with a stick. Nothing untoward showed here, but only a young one's curiosity, exploring the woods after rain. Song sniffed impatiently and surged ahead, his lope skirting the edges of the swamplands and a train of muddy footprints leading deeper into the hummocks and still pools. Oaktree's, Skyfire identified by the inturned toes, and White-Pebble's, and certainly Sprig's, whose laces were never tied, and whose occasional stumble showed plainly in the damp soil. In a few more strides, the culprits themselves became visible, muddy and wide-eyed, and no little bit mollified by the sight of chieftess and wolf exploding upon them at full charge.

"Get back to the holt, all of you, now!" shouted Skyfire. Her tone held fiercest command. The cubs dropped their forbidden posies and fled. As their chieftess passed them by, she had time to notice that Oaktree was not among them; he would still be with Star, then, and endangered as well, and for that Talen would bring more accusations.

The trail led deeper into the swamp. Song was forced to double back and spring from one firm foothold to another. There was no path. Just meshes of swamp reeds, and treacherous hummocks, and the occasional spread roots of a willow. Splashed with mud, and laboring now, Song floundered through a pool. Skyfire snarled in sympathy and suggested climbing down, which earned her a ringing snap that stopped just shy of severing toes. Song preferred to bear her on, and in some of his moods, the chieftess had learned emphatically not to cross him. The wolf held Star in high esteem, and her danger urged him forward.

Past the muddy bank where Nightstar had first intruded upon her mother's attention, the signs left by herself and her companion led clearly. Here, the swamp narrowed, and the pools showed frown-wrinkles of current. The outlet brook flowed away through rocks, then joined the wider stream which coursed in white-water snags to tumble and echo through the ravine. Skyfire shivered with a chill shared by the wolf under her knees.

That deep cleft in the rocks was a place she avoided above any other. Yet the trail of Nightstar and Oaktree led that way, two pairs of tracks moving side by side with no thought for memories or the perils that might lie ahead. Chieftess and wolf pressed on. Yet in the end, neither the nose of a wolf, nor Wolfrider cunning, nor grim elvish hunting experience solved the cubs' disappearance. The scent-trail led straight to an unseasonably fruiting bramble that glowed fall-ripe in the middle of spring. Song paused between strides, stiff-legged and uncertain; and Skyfire regarded the swelling purple berries with a gut-deep suspicion that these were none of her daughter's making. The magic that moved here was not of the Dreamsinger's line, but other, more cold and twisted and poisoned than Wolfrider senses might encompass. Instinctively, Skyfire knew not to touch the fruit, temptingly placed though it was in the midst of a gloomy and unpleasant clearing. Her flesh crawled, and her gut cramped, and for an inexplicable reason she felt dizzy.

"On, Song," she whispered, and added a nudge of her knees. It had been a long winter, and though wider hunting range under Skyfire's leadership had yielded an easier spring, the morale of the Wolfriders had been low. They did not pursue the game with their usual enthusiasm, and those tribe members who did not hunt were hungrier than usual, the more so with the choicer morsels from the kills going to females weakened by dangerous childbirths. One wandering cub who lacked fear might well have accepted the bait of those unnatural berries; and another, older one, might have abandoned better sense by her example. Pressed by foreboding, consumed with worry for Oaktree and Star, Skyfire urged Song ahead.

Beyond that unnatural briar, the trail vanished even to the most persistent and determined nose. Song cast right, left, and circled in frustration, silver eyes turned to his elf-friend. He whined in puzzlement. Oaktree's wandering tracks seemed to step into the void by the outcrop of rock topping the ridge that overlooked a stepped descent to the streambed.

Skyfire slid off Song's back. She repeated the wolf's cast about the clearing, and knelt beside a broken fern fiddleneck, almost hidden in a crevice of stone. Half of the fern was bursting bright green, almost too tender for even the slenderer hands of a true elf gathering potgreens. But no one was going to use these plants for eating: divided by an unnatural centerline, the other half of the shoot was sere and withered as if touched by the frosts before snowfall. Again Skyfire felt the stir of impending danger, as if she stalked the trail of something evil. The magic of the Dreamsinger had been mad, often beautiful, sometimes cruel in an edged and tragic way. But never dark, or lurking, or sinister, as the emanations she sensed from whatever force had distorted this growing fern. The precocious experimentations of Nightstar were filled always with joy and blind innocence; never lurking in crannies like traps. Sure of this, but less sure of herself than she had felt since her duel with Two-Spear, Skyfire rose slowly to her feet. She had no choice but to trust instinct, and believe what should not be possible. The magic that moved here was not of her loved one's making; and with the tribe distrustful of Dreamsinger's influence, and Nightstar's too tangible inheritance, she dared not wait for the support of the hunting pack. This trail she must follow alone, lest uncertainties meld into fear, and turn pack sentiment against the cub she had fought and killed to see raised. At stake was the dream-vision that might better the future of the tribe.

Skyfire leaped onto the comfort of Song's furred back. Together wolf and elf-friend left the clearing in pursuit of the utter unknown. The trail of warped plantlife led downward toward the stream. Sunlight had not reached here; mist clung thickly between trees still dripping with rain. But the eerie half-gloom could not hide the wrongness, a confused, patched spoor of scorched and frost-seared earth that continued in the direction of the ravine.

Such marks had not been here last time Wolfriders had come this way. The woods had suffered terribly, as if ball lightning had ricocheted among the trees and seared black swaths through the foliage; but no thunderstorms had happened for many eights-of-days. Skyfire checked in a moment of wrenching hesitation. Given any option, she would not choose this path. Ahead, between cliffs of knife-sharp rocks, lay the place where her Dreamsinger had fallen to his death. For the Huntress, the screaming remembered in her mind—the fall brought about by murder—clouded the sound of the water below. For the silver-eyed wolf who carried her, the site called back scent-memories that confused; Song had wandered the forests as a loner with Dreamsinger before settling with Skyfire and pack-life. The wolf whined his uneasiness. The stink of burned things, and worse, put a strange, wild note in his cry.

Skyfire drew an unsteady breath. "Easy, Song," she urged, though her voice shook. "We must go forward."

Ahead, a great promise had been destroyed and a vision had nearly been lost: mad or not, the Dreamsinger's magic had revived Timmain's vision of unity between Wolfrider and true elf on the world of two moons. Now, a dead mate's legacy to Skyfire, to all the tribe, came down to a little lost cub and her kindly but sometimes ravvit-brained elder friend, Oaktree, vanished somewhere among unnatural signs.

Song shivered and paced ahead. He moved like a wraith through lingering curls of mist and the dripping undergrowth.

Neither warmth nor morning sunlight had reached the ravine. As Song and Skyfire stepped through a cleft of dark rock like a doorway, they moved through the gray on gray of a landscape choked in mist. Rainwater glistened on the outcrops, and the rush and splash of waterfalls echoed and reverberated in endless discourse. Skyfire narrowed her eyes at the tumbled rocks, and at water-silvered mosses where stones punched through the brook and were lost in submersion again. Even here the wrongness made itself evident. Brightbird nestlings choked the current, a sodden little jam of unfletched wings and gaping beaks. The flock that had hatched them had abandoned the site; the mud nests chinked between the cliff walls were empty, and the air bereft of scolding chatter. With pang of pity for any bereft parent, Skyfire thought of Goldwing. These bird cubs had fared no better than hers.

All wasted, came a sending into Skyfire's mind. Faint and sad, so faint; but the voice was Star's.

Where are you? Skyfire demanded, forcefully as any leadership challenge.

The reply came back, loud enough that the chieftess doubled over in pain. It seemed as if Star's sending had been gathered up and magnified by *something:* **Just outside a funny hollow place. Magic called me, and I didn't trust it because I saw flowers turned into something nasty—fear— all kinds of strange things are happening—**

WHERE? Skyfire sent, frantic with parental concern. **Are you safe, Nightstar? Is Oaktree with you?**

Childish impatience answered, clear as brook-water laughing. **I'm safe. Waiting, with Oaktree. Waiting for you to unwind the killer magic.** And the sending ended with the clear impression of a presence that lurked in the ravine, a presence that through the spring had stalked the pack, but was now grown strong enough to threaten more . . .

Frustrated to bared teeth, Skyfire clenched a hand on her belt-knife. She was a huntress, quick of reflex and deadly with weapons, and courageous enough to attack anything that might threaten her tribe or cubling. But the workings of magic were beyond her.

Nightstar sent back, as if aware of her mother's confusion. **No. You bear the blood of Timmain, and she shape-changed to a wolf to make our kind. The magic runs in you. Seek it.**

Skyfire cursed. She tried to reach her cub, tell her that her childish wanderings through elvish and tribal memories held no more promise than dreams. But Star seemed preoccupied by the presence of someone else, not Oaktree but an adult. Skyfire received an indistinct impression as her endangered cub tumbled over and made faces between her knees at an eerie image of an elf who had a strangely familiar face, but not one readily identifiable through such fleeting and blurred contact.

Where? Skyfire sent again. **Nightstar, who is with you?**

A cool, elvish touch flowed like river currents beneath Star's awareness, elaborated and clarified youngling thoughts into a strange, almost dual sending. **Down here, in the rocks.** Skyfire had never had such a peculiar sensation, nor ever heard of its like. She saw plainly as if the cub were pointing her hand. **The evil is here, where the other magic died.**

Amid rocks, threaded round by the white and tumbled currents of the stream; the same stones that had shattered the Dreamsinger's body when he fell. Skyfire shuddered at more than memory. Nightstar's meddling may have found the source of the contagion, but her vague references to Timmain had shown no way to unwind it. And now Star had endangered more than Oaktree and her mother: through her, all others in the pack and the holt were now threatened —for magic responded to magic.

Whatever blighting force had twisted and licked through the forest to strike the plantlife to unnatural growth, now built to a palpable presence. Skyfire felt her hair stir in the charged air. Something was alerted, down there in the ravine. Star's widely cast sending had roused a danger that should never have been disturbed to find consciousness. Beside the chieftess, Song wrinkled his muzzle in a soundless snarl as his gray-tipped guard hairs prickled erect.

The wolf listened as tensely as his elf-friend for any sound, for something he could not quite smell, but only feel stirring in his pelt. In his confused, wolf-limited senses, Song was right to tense for an attack. A sound like the boom of thunder rumbled away sullenly in a sky that could not logically produce such noises; for there was no storm. A few tail-brushes of cloud fluttered across the sun, dappling the trees beyond the ravine. That was all.

There— Star's picture pointed clearly at the root of evil.

Skyfire stared at the deepest, most mist-filled hollow in the rocks below. The ravine contained too many equally evil memories, but its tumbled shadows looked also as if it might once have been a lairing site, or might be once again, for a pack like their own. Skyfire could almost see; but the magic confused all senses, including that of time. Where wolf instincts could not lead, and elvish ones went mad, *there*, the problem stirred and gathered. Through Nightstar's wyrd-sighted presence in her mind, Skyfire almost *knew* the coiled thing laughing down there in the dark beneath the rocks. Star's perception gave the thing the same structure as the ball-shaped horrors that bounced through the woods to chase and terrify, and murder the hapless wildlife. Years upon years of woods experience blurred in the wolfsong of the hunt told the chieftess how violently wrong this presence was. Skyfire's hair floated now, bristled erect as the fur of the wolf at her side.

Song's lips shivered back soundlessly from his teeth as he stared into the ravine where his former elf-friend had died. **Disease—insanity—taint,** his beast-mind roared in hers. **Destroy it.**

For the wolf knew a thing. Packmates had lost cubs to the scentless creature that stirred in this place. Now, sensing the same killer in the mist, Song was as inflexibly pitched to attack as Star was with her half-playful, childish magic. The madness boiling in the wolf and the danger posed to the cubs combined to a drive like madness.

Destroy, the chieftess agreed, gritting her teeth. **Caution.**

Through Nightstar's affinity for magic, or perhaps through herself, Skyfire felt energy surge from the ravine's silence, coiling up eagerly in answer to Song's agitation. The wolf understood only a whirling, scentless, unfocused, choking sense of danger poised to envelop him. He shivered against his elf-friend's restraining hand, unaware that his hatred, his very fear, flared like a beacon to that gathering presence—and how hate called to hate and shaped answer.

It gathers to any discord, Star sent in warning.

Quiet! Skyfire sent sharply, and forced her will even over the wolf's raw turmoil. The Huntress fought back her own rage; with all her pack-leading strength, she forced reason on the beast and herself. And though the mind behind the wolf's silver eyes whined horribly, his body went rigidly still.

Skyfire unclenched one aching hand, but left the other fisted to the haft of her belt-knife. Star promised she was safe; the chieftess had no choice but to gamble that this was true—not a safe premise, with a child-genius and another cub who often as not had a mind full of owl pellets for woodcraft. And Skyfire herself was too much the wolf to be trusting in elf-memories of Timmain, however strong the third and benevolent presence she had sensed in her cubling's sendings. If she stalked this hateful magic-trap, she must risk that Star's intuitions were correct, that a Wolfrider such as herself could survive and destroy what her mind had no means to understand. And if all went wrong, if she died in the attempt, she had to hope that Nightstar or Oaktree would have sense and strength left to send and urge the rest of the tribe to flee.

It gathers, Star sent, and shattered every other thought in Skyfire's mind.

The mist that billowed and thickened in the ravine, then welled over jagged edges of rock, was not physically *there*. Skyfire's eyes made out only a vague shimmering—a phenomenon peculiar enough to make Song back away, seek the highest promontory he could find to avoid its uncanny touch. Skyfire held her ground. She did not move or speak as the cold substance flowed over her. The presence of *something* rolled across her mind with the fog. Its touch was many-layered, distinctly cold, and then hot with a volcanic fury worse than any wolf the chieftess had soothed out of rage-born grief. This *thing* could send, and did, blanketing everything in its path. Horrible, mechanical, man-village, metal-death images fleeted past: violent twistings of hunts, of killing the helpless that kicked inside the womb, or crushing wolf-throats turned up in pack submission. Through the madness, Skyfire seized upon one thing above the rest: images of infants yet unborn sucked dry of all life.

That moment, as her wolf had before her, she identified the enemy that had driven tribe and packmates to sorrows too deep for expression.

This presence was a relic, not a living being; bits stuck together from warring extremes of elvish magic and insane bloodlust. The two deaths in this place had made it, Skyfire understood as it washed over her form like cold waters. For through the evil, deadly coils of the thing, she sensed melodies twisted to discord, notes that once had fallen clean and clear and called up flowers out of season. This was the Dreamsinger's song itself, but warped, fermented to a dissonance that nonetheless tore her raw. Skyfire heard, and recognized, and knew. This thing had been made when the Dreamsinger's magic was rent away in violent death. A current had been left, shaped of pain and confusion and betrayal, and that spark had attached to a murderer's vengeance-bent madness, the essence of Stonethrower's hate.

Skyfire sank back against gritty stone. *I made this thing*, she realized with a chill that all but undid her. She had released this fell magic, unknowing, when she had called in desperation, and Stonethrower had died with Song's jaws crushing his throat. The mad, outcast disciple of Two-Spear's cadre had died, and set this ugliness free. And it had fed monstrously large. Skyfire forced her head up. Now she understood the trap's circular strength: as with Song's rage, the tribe's growing, collective anger only swelled the warped magic that stalked them. Star with her half-formed instincts was right to attempt to unmake it—Skyfire understood with the intense clarity of pain under the fog's charged and seeking touch. Like a vicious circle, this presence went on gathering and holding and twisting emotion-wrought energies until the weakest links of its structure must eventually give way like worn-out leather thongs. Very soon its distorted, malign currents would explode in every direction, flinging cold, raging hatred everywhere.

Skyfire had to fight past her own guilt and grief for

thoughts of her own. She flung a desperate sending to her daughter. **How must I unmake this thing?**

And she felt the magic react, turning and centering ponderously upon Song, upon her. Star was doing something peculiar, far away. Almost, Skyfire could follow her daughter's whirling thoughts. Then something seemed to click in the chieftess's mind. She lost all sensation of chill and fire that the creeping fog had loosed across her awareness, and she knew only that due to Nightstar's intervention it turned and flowed on.

Run, Mother. As it passes, follow! Star's sending seemed weaker now, dangerously faint.

"To me!" Skyfire shouted. Song launched from the clifftop in a lunge and came down on straining legs beside his elf-friend. She sprawled onto his back, gripped his thick mane. His warmth enveloped her hands, her mind; blessed, silver-tipped fur, blessedly sane wolf-mind.

"Go!" she urged her wolf-friend, and the muscles of the beast under her knees sprang and hardened into a run.

But the woods offered no haven for flight. Visions of dying infants clouded Skyfire's mind, blocked her sight of trees and thickets. She shook her head violently, and when that failed, blindly trusted Song's guidance, gripping the wolf's ruff so hard that on other days he would have snapped and yelped. This time his quarters just drove his hindpaws harder into the ground. Or perhaps Skyfire only felt her wolf's driving momentum in her mind as he struggled to leap free of that airless shimmer of magic.

There— Star's brilliant sending burst like a beacon through the storm in Skyfire's head. **That way, down that hollow.**

Yes, there— came a dispassionate new voice: Oaktree's touch mingled with Star's sending as easily as if they had been practicing and working on the strange new melding for a hundred years. This, the first proof that Skyfire's hopes could become reality. But time could not be taken to appreciate; Oaktree called for help with all of the urgency he could summon. **Save the tribe.**

The sending felt like an icicle driven squarely through the center of the chieftess's fears. She did not feel up to this. If, as Star suggested and Oaktree experienced, Timmain's magic flowed within her, she had never felt it. This evil, born of the things she most wished to eradicate from tribe life, and also of the love and the dreams she cherished, became for her the most diabolical of all torments, worse than starving, worse than pain, worse than the ultimate shame of pack rejection. And yet she could not turn away this challenge. She was perhaps the only one, Wolfrider or elf, who could unravel this magic trap. She was chieftess by main force of will, strongest, and the only logical choice. Her own cub, and all the other unborn young of pack and holt depended upon her efforts. For the thing combined from Dreamsinger's dying magic and Stonethrower's obsessive hatred had grown strong enough to track, now. Wherever the tribe fled, this horror would follow, seeding destruction and death throughout the forest.

We will steady your mind when your need comes, came Oaktree's encouragement, mingled with Star's warmer eagerness, and that peculiar, river-current undertone that formed the strange, third presence from elf-memory that Skyfire had sensed earlier. **Remember you are not alone.**

Grim with a resolve that was anything but firm, Skyfire forced her eyes open. She and Song had penetrated deep into the ravine. Ahead, the creek flowed out of a narrow aperture between boulders and fanned wide through a sandy wash. Pooled in the shallows were the draggled corpses of small animals, fish, and frogs, and the pitiful wet body of a dapple-deer fawn. Skyfire felt Song check under her, and a glance at the dead things showed why. All of the creatures were deformed, grown wrong in some way that threw the natural progression of their development out of phase. The deer showed the antlers and hooves of an adult, grotesque on a body barely past the age for birth. The more horrible were frogs and songbird chicks caught between transformations, here a head sleeked with veins like an embryo, and there, a polliwog's body on a fully formed pair of back legs.

Skyfire choked back a wave of nausea, and under her hands, Song lifted his head and howled. **Wrongness!**

The chieftess sent to him sadly. **Yes. This, and our own cubs twisted out of life before they grew to whelping-time.**

Magic grown into a life-bane, Star agreed distantly. **You must pursue.**

Skyfire glanced about swiftly, but did not see either her cub or Oaktree anywhere about the pool with its wretched jam of corpses. Heartened at least by that, she wheeled Song on past the hollow—and into a barrier so intangible neither one of them sensed it. Something picked up rider and wolf and hurled them forward and down with a wrench that drew a yowl of disorientation from Song. Skyfire almost lost her grip as he twisted under her, then slammed to a four-footed landing that jolted her off balance. She slipped sideways, confusion augmented by eyesight that insisted no fall had occurred, but only a step across innocent ground.

Only Song's reflexes spared her. His accepting wolf's mind took the anomaly in stride, and one shoulder shrugged mightily under her, tossing her safely onto a spine that flexed to power a hard, all-out run. **Go!** the wolf's sending sang to her. **Hunt and fight to kill.**

They had crossed the boundaries of the magic's evil influence. There could be no turning back now. And yet within a stride, this chase became like no other. Song passed through the cleft in the rock, his claws clicking and splashing through the creek; and Skyfire's mind reeled in and out of memories. Once again she sat, not on a running wolf's back but in a rain-dark thicket outside the lair where Goldwing lay in labor. Except now the night and the mist were not natural, but caught and twisted into streaming nightmare shapes, of distorted cubs, and faces of tribemates warped to unrecognizably vicious expressions. Skyfire blinked, tried to call back the reality of danger and the ravine. For a moment, harsh, silver-tipped fur bristled around her wrists, rolling with the thrust of Song's stride. Then the sensation vanished, left her adrift in a dream-song braided into knots of malevolence.

Keep following, Star's voice echoed from a seemingly impossible distance. *Oaktree and I, and our spirit-guide will lend you what strength we can.*

Skyfire found herself back inside the lair, standing once more over the pathetic, bloody bundle that had been Goldwing's cub. Only this time, the creature was not dead. It writhed, distorted, malformed, a hideous eyeless parody of a newborn. Skyfire was conscious of Rellah's disgust, of her own gorge rising at the sight of a thing that was not and could never be the result of a natural breeding. She drew breath to declare the thing condemned, to beg that it be torn limb from limb by the pack before whatever contagion had spawned it might spread.

But Goldwing cried out piteously and begged that the creature be spared; and her voice blended with other voices, Sun's, and Oaktree's, and the spirit-memory of an ancestress. **Skyfire no! Do not succumb to the trap's evil dreams.**

"You aren't going to be soft, and let that malformed child live on and suffer," Rellah said coldly. "By the tenets of your Way it is not fit to survive. Will you bring it up to know pain, and perhaps feed it nourishment that might leave other bearing mothers deprived?"

Skyfire closed her eyes, but the sight of the thing that was not a cub stayed with her. Still she saw the hands and feet of an adult stuck onto a faceless body that had no eyes. She swallowed against an overwhelming spasm of sickness and gasped out, "The law of the pack does not condone murder. No elf must die."

Aware of an overwhelming weight of loneliness, Skyfire longed for the support of the pack and the tribe. Yet when she reached out and sought companionship, she found no solace. Slanting, wolfish eyes shone feral reflections back at her, and white teeth bared in aggression that was more beast than elf. Nothing of intelligence, of kindness, showed in the mad faces of her tribemates. The trap had touched them with its killing coils, and the hearts of too many grieving pairs lent it foothold.

Skyfire became aware of movement around her, of other minds pressuring hers toward a course that could only bring oblivion. She had, she realized dimly, called the pack and the tribe to her; or the trap had, of itself, lured them in. For a confusing instant she rode Song in painful, racing strides against a tightening fog that Star and Oaktree lent distant strength to counter. But the support of the cubs was dwindling, and their combined force of magic had now grown intermittent. Head bent close to Song's silver ears, Skyfire strained to use every slender resource she had in her.

Her efforts were not enough. Hideous things in the mist dragged at her, sapping her.

Nightstar! she sent, desperate in her need, and knowing she would bring death to the tribe and her daughter-cub if her will failed.

A surge answered, Star's touch like a warm, grubby hand in hers. Still astride Song's back, Skyfire took a queer mental step around a corner, and suddenly found herself shielded. She dared not think of the cost to her loved one, who had arranged this reprieve from cold terrors. Granted clear space for thought, the chieftess found herself racing through the ravine's deepest chasm, ever closer to the site of the Dreamsinger's death. In her mind, she felt the sendings of tribe and pack, alive and vicious with pain. The mental presence of so many grieving adults together at once was intolerable. The feelings emanated, built, braided into a note of wild terror that stood rooted in every pair struck fertile who had lost young.

All but consumed by the ache of communal loss, Skyfire raised her will, as she had each time in the past. She reached out with all of a chieftess's stubborn command to turn the insanity away. Except now the thing had swelled too strong

for one single mind to control. Skyfire saw this. Before cries
and growls of rage could deepen into surly notes of challenge, she understood that individual force had been precisely the wrong response to crisis. For the nature of the trap
was to separate, to play upon dissatisfactions and breed
disharmony, until tribal unity was scattered into crosscur-
rents of hatred and dissent. Scattered, alone, the Wolfriders
would embrace the miserable lives of outcasts, and the first
harsh winter, the first failing brought on by injury, disease,
or weather, would kill them.

Skyfire tightened her grip in Song's thick coat. She was not
going to allow it, not going to suffer the sight of Stonethrower's death wish upon them lent impetus by the ghost of
her Dreamsinger's talents. She would not value her own life
above a bitter return to scattered, twig-chewing barbarism,
and the destruction of Timmain's brave dream. Although
contemplation of the alternative left Skyfire feeling weak,
she knew that Nightstar's headlong instinct to unwind this
creeping, malign attack before it grew too large and devoured them was the right one. The tragedy lay in the fact
that the cub was far too young, her gifts too undeveloped,
and her sense of her own self-preservation as yet untem-
pered by experience.

Skyfire fought against an impulse to falter in her purpose;
scary to think how much the tribe's survival depended upon
the strengths of two immature cubs.

Yet this battle had no space for fears. **Come!** Skyfire
sent across the Wolfriders' collective anguish. She touched
the minds of grieving mothers, and wolves maddened to a
slashing desire to kill. She embraced the thoughts of
dissidents, and others half abandoned to the seductive currents of the wolfsong. As chieftess, Skyfire called, and
gathered her following to her. The tribe, or the fog, or maybe
the very air resisted her efforts. Underneath her, Song
dodged and flexed and forged ahead as if he struggled
against unseen currents. She felt him call into play the odd
link between him and the raging madness which underneath

hatred yet held the buried essence of an outcast's solitary drives. The wolf, once outcast himself, seemed at times to anticipate how the magic would strike them, and where it was blind to their movements. For his pack, and his pups, and the elf-friend who sharpened his memories of the Dreamsinger, Song would use his outcast's bond of madness to claw his way along the ravine until the fog stopped his breath, or he got close enough to battle it to oblivion.

The pair made progress slowly, stiff-bristled with the tension of battle joined, chieftess and trembling wolf. With her mind wheeling between the riding wolfback in the ravine, and the twisted, hideous images of stillborn cubs, Skyfire strove to instill unity over the wailing disharmony that divided the tribe. She sent, desperately; sometimes she spoke aloud as if she raved in the grip of high fever. Yet against the madness that tore like storms through her being, she offered up explanation of the trap's voracious appetite, and its origins given life through murder.

The minds of the others fought her. Dark thoughts came to her, edged with reddish flickers and the snap and click of jaws, as if minds more than half wolf already reverted to something more primitive and bloodthirsty. Over and over amid the confusion, one clear thought struck through. **Other stillbirths after this.** And linked, the resentful notion that the Dreamsinger had brought in this taint, and perpetuated its existence through Nightstar.

"No!" Skyfire protested. "Only if we abandon pack unity." Then, aware she had spoken and not sent, she pressed her emphatic denial on the minds of wolf-friends and riders. **Beware, packmates. What stalks and kills is not true magic, but hatred lent awareness to seek destruction. The drained-off energies of our dead cubs fed it, swelled its evil nature until it gained strength to hunt on its own. Our isolation guides it, and our grief nourishes it still. Had Nightstar not gone in and uncovered its true nature, we all would have died of its poison.**

But the clamor did not recede, and sanity did not return to

buoy Skyfire's efforts in support. The drag of the next steps became agony. Song trembled under her now, and Nightstar's support seemed reduced to an echo, a dream, a sunrise overcome by primal darkness and a sky sucked dry of stars or moons.

And the next step carried wolf and rider both, into nothingness: the vortex of the magic-warp itself. Skyfire felt the shock of final contact ripple into her being, and through her, like the shiver of a bug in a web, the collective minds of the tribe. Even now the others did not sense the danger; still they clamored for Nightstar's death.

Sadly, Skyfire gathered the shreds of her concentration. **This may kill you too, my wolf-friend,** she sent to Song. Her chin fell forward, rested on her companion's furry skull. It took all her strength to hold her eyes open and behold the sharp jumble of rocks that had macerated the life from the Dreamsinger's body. Beneath her, she felt the wolf trembling, too. He stood with his nose almost touching the mist-coiled pools, though his instincts cried out for him to run.

Then, into that moment that was the nadir of all hope, Nightstar's sending came clearly. **Help you now.**

Song took a shuddering last step, and the outlines of ravine and stream melted away into mist. Skyfire looked ahead, saw the figure of an elf take form in the fog. He had dark hair, and silver eyes, and a form that tore at her heart. Here, in the center of all evil, the chieftess of the Wolfriders beheld the image of her mate.

"Dreamsinger?" she said aloud, while Song snarled and shivered in abject terror under her knees. She dismounted, bemused, and as if from the other side of a dream, Nightstar's sending reached her.

Not the Dreamsinger, Mother. What you see is the ghost of his magic. It wears his form to make you forget the hatred that Stonethrower left to drive it.

Skyfire stared white-lipped at the face of her beloved. "Dreamsinger," she repeated. Her voice shook. And again

Star's sending broke her advance.

Mother, you must save the tribe. Shatter the false illusion.

Skyfire's eyes stung with tears. As if her cub had sent no warning, she spoke to the silver-eyed apparition who sat, as he had often sat in life, with his swinging feet dangling over a rock. "Dreamsinger, I acted in error. I see that now. If I had not tried to force change upon the tribe, you would still be alive weaving magic."

The image regarded her sadly. He did not seem part of any taint, but sorrow itself personified, tragedy and tears and a cold like a frost come in springtime. Skyfire clenched her fingers in Song's rough coat. Aware, but only dimly, of Nightstar's voice ringing in the back of her mind, the chieftess drew a deep and difficult breath. "I see more clearly now," she said haltingly. "The tribe must wait for your gifts until wiser times. Magic is too dangerous a blessing for us now, when, like Stonethrower, we are still preoccupied with dissent."

Skyfire bent her head. Without pause to take stock of the cost, thinking only of her tribe's survival, she accepted defeat. She let go of the dream that had driven her since the morning she had wakened in the warmth of the Dreamsinger's arms, and the air had been heady with cherry blossoms. "Go in peace," she whispered.

Dimly she felt Star's efforts reach through her; distantly, like echoes, she felt her daughter-cub's sendings shape into a melancholy farewell. The image of the elf on the rocks began to dissipate. It grew fainter, sparkled like cobwebs in starlight, and then faded altogether, leaving wet stone, and chill earth, and the throaty chuckle of stream water. Skyfire, blinking away tears, beheld sunlight that held no flash of magic. She sat, leaning heavily on the flank of her panting wolf-friend.

"He's gone," she said softly. "The hate and the beauty have left us."

That instant, she noticed the silence in her mind. Panic

snapped her to her feet. **Nightstar! Oaktree!** Frantically, Skyfire cast outward with her senses, seeking the strange guardian drawn from elf-memory that for a time had augmented the efforts of the cubs. But her inner mind picked up nothing, no trace of childish chatter, nor even the smallest echo of Oaktree's merry laugh.

"Song!" cried Skyfire. As the wolf bounded to his feet, she scrambled astride. Aching in every joint, and too worried to acknowledge the pressure of inquiries from the pack and the tribe who converged upon the ravine in concern, the chieftess of the Wolfriders turned once more downstream, toward the place from which Nightstar's last sending had issued.

She found both cubs on a grassy verge, throwing pebbles into a pool of still water. There seemed to be nothing wrong with them. Oaktree's red hair was tousled as ever, if dampened with streaks of swamp muck. His clothing was a disgrace. Nightstar was no less filthy. Her black hair had come unbraided and fell in snarls over her shoulders, and her huge, silver-gray eyes looked up in greeting as her mother bounded into view on Song's back.

And yet for all that, something profound had changed. Skyfire felt it the instant she met her daughter's gaze and touched the mind behind. All of the Dreamsinger's legacy of magic was vanished, mute; it had gone, been undone by the unbinding, back in the darkness of the ravine. There remained only wolfsong behind the depths of Nightstar's eyes. Only that moment did the chieftess recognize what her cub had sacrificed to destroy the trap's vortex. Timmain's dream would sing in Star's spirit no more.

"The tribe was not ready for her," the chieftess whispered to her wolf; the words stung, without comfort. "Maybe one day, after many dances of moons, and many hunts, that will change."

Song whined, licked her hand in consolation for concepts he did not understand. **Hungry. Hunt soon,** he sent in wolfish eagerness.

Skyfire nodded, accepting that life must go on for herself and her tribe. Skimmer's cub might now be born alive. There was that small victory. But the sorrow would never fade, that the cub and the father who would pass on the hope of a better life to their offspring should have sacrificed their talents to that end.

Firstborn

by Allen L. Wold

It was that time of year when the sun was still hot but the air, the wind especially, was decidedly chilly so that, depending on where you were and what you were doing, you could be both warm and cool at the same time. That was the way Freefoot felt now, both inside and out.

He stood, alone, on the prairie far north of the holt, on a low rise of ground barely three times as tall as an elf, but broad, and so gentle in slope that, had he not known it was there, he would not have noticed its ascent as he walked to the top. It was the only undulation of its size in all the vast green and gold grassland, as far as he could see in any direction. And the prairie was so flat that, even from this minute elevation, he could see very far indeed.

Away to the south and somewhat east were the silhouetted figures of two Wolfriders, their bodies up to their chests concealed by the ripening grasses, their wolf-mounts completely hidden. The sun would march two, maybe three handspans across the sky before they came to where Freefoot was. It was enough time. Beside him, his wolf Shag settled down to doze.

The crest of the low rise was marked not so much by a change in slope as by a change in the texture of the ground. Elsewhere on the prairie the soil between the roots of the grasses was smooth and fine, thickly covered with the thatch of dead grass from countless seasons gone. Here there was

gravel—bits of white quartz, gray flint, even some redstone
and black slate. Most of it was small, the size of Freefoot's
thumb, but occasional pieces were larger, some as big as his
two fists pressed together. Many of these larger pieces had,
ages ago, been brought together in a long, low, narrow pile
in the middle of the area. Freefoot glanced at the pile, then
up and away, across the prairie toward the west.

The sun, still rising behind him, warmed his back, the
back of his head and arms, his neck. A soft but steady wind
from the north blew cold across his face, his chest, through
his hair. Thus it was, here, at this time of year, as it had been
the few times he had been here before.

Away in the west he could see shadows moving across the
prairie, going against the wind. There were no clouds in the
sky, the darkness on the long grass was a herd of antelope,
the kind with horns like long, curved bows, to judge by their
movements. The prong-horns did not travel in so great a
number, and the heavier hump-shoulders stayed close together and did not scatter around the edges as this herd was
doing.

Freefoot had seen several such herds, and herds of other
antelopes, during the two and a half days he'd traveled since
leaving the forest, as well as many solitary animals or smaller
groups. Indeed, he had feasted this morning on a striped
long-leg which he and Shag had brought down just at sunup.
It was a fat year, the first such in many. It made him sad to
think that he and his people were going to have to leave it
behind.

He could smell other meat on the wind which came down
from the cold-lands to the north. With no trees, no hills to
disturb the breeze, a good scent could travel farther than the
eye could see. The scents were mixed, of course, and thinned
by the smell of grasses, a stream too far away to be seen, and
all the expanse of air, but among the scents Freefoot could
detect the peculiar pungency of a nosehorn, a bit of carrion,
and the musky aroma of a longtooth cat.

Rich hunting, now, after four or five eights-of-seasons of

poor fare. It had been a longer lean time than usual, and the returning bounty promised to be greater than usual too, but Freefoot and his people could not stay to enjoy it. Humans were too close, too many in number, too determined to take the land. Freefoot would have to lead his people away, south, deeper into the forest. He hoped that the hunting there would be as good as it was here.

He had hoped, nearly a seven of eights-of-years ago, when the humans had first come, that they would move on, or that they could be driven away, or would not pose the same threat they had in his mother's time. But that had been just wishful thinking. The Wolfriders had been hated and feared by the humans from the start. Though humans lived only a few seasons, five or six of eights, little more than some animals, they had long memories, and told stories, and in this way remembered the time when their ancestors had known elves, and so attacked the Wolfriders whenever they saw them. The Wolfriders had had to go back to hunting at dusk and dawn, even at night, which was not the way of wolves. They'd had to watch, and move, and even abandon their holt in Halfhill when it was found by a human hunting party. The elves had lived there in peace for almost seven hundred years. It hurt them now, especially the elves who had been among the first born there, to have to move away.

Freefoot looked back to the east. The sun was still rising, though near the top of its climb, and the rippling of the grasses in the north wind shimmered like water. The sun felt good on his face, though it made him squint. At his feet, Shag moaned. Freefoot looked down at his wolf-friend, who stretched his legs into a more comfortable position. His head lay just a handbreadth from the long, low, narrow pile of rocks.

The mound had been there a long time. The gaps and crevices between the lumps of quartz and flint and slate and redstone had been partially filled in by windblown dust, and even a few grass blades now grew among the rocks. The grass was less dense a cover on the rest of the rise anyway, where the gravel and wind-hardened soil provided little purchase for the roots. The mound of rocks was all but bare.

A shadow passed across the mound, and Freefoot looked up to see one of the great prairie hawks banking high overhead. It must have seen Shag lying there, and thought the wolf dead and hence an easy meal, in spite of the elf's presence. Freefoot spoke to Shag, who raised his head. Above, black and white and russet against the blue sky, the hawk wheeled again. It had seen Shag's movement and was no longer interested. A living antelope, one of the half-grown, would be easier prey. The bird soared off, in no great hurry for its lunch. Shag put his head down again and went back to sleep.

Freefoot turned back to the south. He was surprised to see how much closer the two Wolfriders had come. Now, with the sun higher up in the sky, they were no longer silhouettes, but were still too far away for him to make out their features. Not that he had any need to.

The situation had been reversed the last time he'd been out there to the rise. That had been a long time ago, though the memory of the visit was clear and sharp in his mind—if he chose to remember. He had not thought about those events very often during the last two hundred years or so, and when the memories had intruded, he had carefully put them out of his mind. Except when he had decided that Starflower, his lifemate, and their two older sons, Fangslayer and Longoak, should know. He had told that story just one time. It had been painful. It was painful to think about now. But then, that was why he had come back here, to think about it, to remember. With the coming of the humans, the elves would move away, and he might never see this place again.

Once again he slowly scanned the horizon, pausing at each shadow, each hint of movement, each sign of life. From here the world looked so big. In the forest, one could never see the horizon, even if one climbed a tree as high as one dared before the branches gave way. Here, with nothing to impede the view, the edge of the world was all too apparent.

It was one of the things that drew Freefoot out here, rather than down deeper into the woods. Of course, south of the holt one could climb high ridges, higher plateaus, and far away many eights-of-days even mountains. From those elevations, clear of the horizon-concealing trees, one could see much of the world indeed. But it was not the same as here on the prairie.

Besides, there were other reasons.

The last time he had been here it had been another who had stood on the rise, watching, and it had been Freefoot who rode his wolf out of the south. He and—Bent-Tail it had been then—had left the woods two days before, and on the morning of the third day had risen early, caught one of the tiny springer antelopes, and continued northward. He was traveling alone, except for his wolf-friend, as he liked to do when he could. The burdens of being chief, even in a peaceful and eventless time such as his, wore him down, tired him out, made him eager to get away, to wander aimlessly in the way that had given him his name.

As he rode northward the small rise became visible in the distance, an imperceptible elevation on the otherwise perfectly flat horizon. The prairie was huge, and in his various wanderings Freefoot had by no means seen all of it, but such irregularities as this were rare, and Freefoot had a memory of once having seen one like it, a long time ago. He rode toward it, there being no reason why he should not. After all, he had nothing better to do.

Around him the tall grass rustled gently. The wind blew steadily down out of the north, bringing with it scents of distant antelope herds, a stinker, and—an elf? Yes, at least one, and the pungent tang of the rare prairie goat.

How far away was the source of the scent? He looked straight into the wind, though of course it shifted a bit from moment to moment, so its present direction could give him only an indication of its origin. Still, it was the rise from which the scent seemed to be coming. Bent-Tail could smell it, too. He'd had experience with prairie goats, and though still hungry after their meager breakfast, was not eager to challenge the true master of the grasslands.

Freefoot kept his eyes on the rise as he rode toward it. The scent got gradually stronger as he neared, though sometimes it vanished for long moments as the wind shifted slightly. It was not a scent he recognized—any of his own people he would have known by their smell even from this distance— so he guessed the elf to be one of that small band which wandered the grasslands far to the north of the holt. That being the case, he had to assume that whoever was up there was probably watching, advantaged by even that little elevation, concealed by the grasses turning golden with the coming of winter.

Three times before in his life Freefoot had met strange elves, and each time it had been difficult. Two of those times it had been prairie elves, and the third time it had been a forest elf but one who was not a Wolfrider and who had no wolf-blood. Those experiences had been frightening, and exciting, and not without danger. He had been with other Wolfriders each of those three times, but Freefoot was alone now, and thought he would be wise to be cautious.

Even so, he did not slow or change his course, and some while later he heard a tiny sound coming from the now not-so-distant rise. Unless there were antelope near, there were few things on the prairie that could make noise, except for the wind, which susurrated through the grass with a constancy like, though a sound different from, the noise that a quiet stream makes. Freefoot had seen no signs of antelope in this direction, and such scents of them that came to him were from a long way off, so the noise had to have been made by the goat—not, of course, the as-yet-unseen elf. Prairie goats were a little taller than wolves, so this animal's head would be just below the tops of the grasses at this season. Elsewhere on the prairie their hooves would make no sound on the soil and grass-thatch, but on the rise would be rocks, resistant of the relentless weathering processes that turned the prairie flat, and what Freefoot had heard was the clunk of a hoof striking stone.

The unseen elf must have realized that Freefoot could hear even that small sound, because a moment later he stood up, just head and shoulders above the grass, staring straight in his direction. Freefoot stopped then, and stared back. The other elf was still too far away for him to make out his features, but Freefoot did not have to see the other's face to know that he was one of the prairie folk. On his head he wore a helmet decorated with prong-horns—something no forest elf would have done, for fear of it getting caught in tree branches or undergrowth.

Neither elf raised a hand, neither elf called out, and after a moment Freefoot started forward again. Though the smell of goat got stronger, Bent-Tail did not become excited. Freefoot kept his eyes on the other elf's face, and though he felt some apprehension, he kept his outward self calm. He had not seen this elf before, but he knew his people, and knew that there was no danger—unless the descendants of banished Two-Spear and his few companions had changed a lot, as they well could have.

And they had, if this elf was any example. Though partially of Wolfrider blood, all traces of wolf and forest life were long gone. Instead of a jacket he wore a loose cloak of leather made soft by chewing. The elf's skin, where it was exposed on chest, face, and arms, was burned a dark tan by exposure to the sun, instead of being the ivory of a shadowed forest dweller. His posture and demeanor were different too, upright and defiant, without the habit of stealth. His face, as Freefoot drew near enough to see it, was expressionless, though there was much behind the eyes that was not being let out. These elves had indeed changed, and though they were Freefoot's cousins not that many times removed, they were as different from the forest dwellers as elves still with wolf-blood could be.

Freefoot rode, relaxed in spite of his inner tension, casual about his glances though he watched the other almost constantly, with only an occasional sweeping search of the horizon, first one side, then the other. The other elf stood motionless, steady, and did not once look away. Even in this small way they showed their differences.

At last the ground began to rise under Bent-Tail's paws. As the wolf brought his rider to the top of the rise, Freefoot was able to see, a few paces behind the other elf, the prairie goat that served him as his steed.

It was an eminently suitable animal for an elf to ride. It was a little taller at the shoulder than a wolf, but weighed quite a bit more, with a deep chest and broad shoulders. Its legs were sturdy, ending in sharp, cloven hooves. Prairie goats had the habit, if they knocked an adversary down, of rearing back on their hind legs, then jumping forward to land with all their weight concentrated on the two front hooves, held closely together. The blow was enough to crush a rib cage, break a spine, or crack a skull.

But a goat's primary attack and defense were its head and horns, the great ribbed horns that curved up and back and out from above its eyes and that, in this case, spiraled full around three times, extending out to the sides a forearm's length from its head. The thickest part of the horns projected forward from the top of the goat's head, and it was with this double curve that the goat, springing forward on strong hind legs, butted its rivals, opponents, and enemies. If pressed closely it could swing its head from side to side on its strong neck, ripping and tearing with the sharp points of its horns. Faced with a predator, it did not just butt, but gored, slashed, feinted, a violent and furious attack that only a swordfoot or a huge and solitary longtooth cat could overcome. Even the huge hump-shoulders stayed well clear of a prairie goat.

Bent-Tail stood and watched the goat warily. The goat, head partly lowered, hind legs flexed, watched the wolf in turn. And as warily, Freefoot and the stranger elf watched each other.

They were a different people now, even more than they had been the other times that Freefoot had met them. Life on the prairie posed different threats and problems, required different solutions, exacted a different price in order to survive. In manner, dress, expectations, these two elves were truly strangers, alien to each other. And yet they were kin, both with wolf-blood, though the prairie elves had less and rode different mounts now.

Freefoot was not afraid of this elf, younger than he by quite a bit if he could judge. But he was cautious. Freefoot had no taste for fighting, for confrontation, for a contest of wills. He preferred to let his people do what they wanted, in their own way, and those times when he had to exercise his authority as chief were never pleasant for him. So he sat now, watching the other, knowing that the prairie elves were proud, and cautious too, and unfamiliar with his ways, and suspected that this other might in fact be a bit afraid of him, though his deeply tanned face showed no expression. After all, in spite of Freefoot's preferences, he was in many ways very much like his mount, and so might be perceived as a predator.

The moment of mutual regard was not as long as it seemed, but it was long enough. Freefoot, still firmly gripping the thick fur of Bent-Tail's neck with both hands, swung his leg back and over the wolf's hindquarters and dismounted. Bent-Tail, responding to Freefoot's silent sending, sat, then crouched down on the gravelly soil. As he did so, the goat behind the other elf visibly relaxed.

"Good hunting," Freefoot said.

"Good hunting to you," the other answered. "What brings a Wolfrider so far out into the tall grass?"

"Nothing important," Freefoot said. "I just wanted to get away from my cares for a while. I like to wander alone when I have the chance."

"As do I," the other said, "though I am not able to do so often."

"This is a most unusual spot," Freefoot said, seeking some topic on which they could converse.

"It is," the other answered. "There is none like it else except where the edge of the prairie can be seen."

It was not a Wolfrider's habit to stare too long into another's eyes, and Freefoot felt uncomfortable under the stranger's unbroken gaze. He did not wish to challenge this other, so he glanced around at the prairie, vastly more of which was visible from even this small rise. When he looked back the stranger was still looking at him. The goat, too, had not moved, its large brown eyes staring fixedly at Bent-Tail. This steady gaze was just their habit, and not, as it would have been among wolves, a sign of aggression. And it would appear that the stranger did not take Freefoot's wandering eyes as a sign of cowardice. He had recognized Freefoot as a Wolfrider, and so must have met them or heard of them before. Freefoot thought of Stride, who also liked to get away, alone by herself from time to time, and whom he frequently envied because she was far more free than he to be able to do so. Perhaps she had met this elf or some of his people some time in the past.

Down on the flat of the prairie, even from wolfback, it was not possible to see far when the grass was as tall as it was now. But from the rise the horizon extended far into the distance, and Freefoot could see, toward the east, a disturbance in the grass that he was sure was made by a small herd of antelope, perhaps the small but solid hook-horns. The stranger noted Freefoot's attention, and turned to look the same way.

"Shall we hunt together?" Freefoot asked.

"Yes," the other said, and went to his mount.

It was an act of friendliness, and a test at the same time. Freefoot climbed up onto Bent-Tail's back, and the two elves rode, side by side, down from the small rise into the thicker grass. For this one hunt they would trust each other, while observing each other, to see what each was made of, how they worked, whether they could cooperate, who would dominate and who would follow. When the hunt was over they would have a better idea of who they were, and how they would relate to each other. If all went well they would share mutual respect. But if either showed great weakness, or cowardice, or ignorance, then the other would establish dominance at once, and there could be no friendship. This was as true of goatrider as of Wolfrider.

At the bottom of the gentle slope Freefoot could no longer see where the hook-horns were, but the goatrider, far more familiar with the prairie, seemed to know his way, so for the moment Freefoot let him have his lead. They did not speak as they rode at an easy canter, but Freefoot watched the goatrider, and the goatrider watched him.

Freefoot had to trust that the other knew where they were going, though he thought the antelopes had been more to the east and not so much to the south. As it turned out the goatrider was circling around so as to come at the antelopes more from downwind. A Wolfrider would have done the same, but in a different fashion.

The antelopes were indeed hook-horns, bodies thick, legs sturdy, their heavy heads just below the top of the waving grass. Hook-horns moved in small herds of two or three of eights, with one dominant male, several nonbreeding or off-males, four to eight females, and as many young and yearlings as might be. The best of these to take would be one of the off-males, an animal least likely to be missed by the rest of the herd.

Freefoot and the stranger slowed their mounts as they approached, still some hundreds of paces away, and looked over the animals upwind of them. There were three off-males to choose from. One was very large, and would most likely take over leadership of the herd when the current bull grew too old or lost a fight. Another was rather small, not much more than a yearling. The third was of middle size, a bit larger than a cow, and not likely ever to breed. Freefoot and the other elf looked at each other, without speaking saw that they agreed on their prey and, at the goatrider's signal, started their attack.

As they urged their mounts into a run the two elves separated, so that when the herd finally noticed them and started to flee they came at the animals as much from the sides as from the rear, the middle-sized off-male that was their target at the center of their charge. A wolf can run fast, though burdened as Bent-Tail was he was hard-pressed to gain on the antelopes, and the prairie goat, too, did little more than keep up, and hook-horns, though slow to start and slow to gain speed, did indeed gain speed, and gradually went faster and faster until it would appear that there would be no chance for the two elves to catch even the slowest of them.

But though Freefoot's favorite weapon was an axe, he also carried a bow, and even as he pursued his quarry, he strung it and fitted an arrow to it. When the hook-horn began to pull away from him he drew his bow, but movement off to one side made him hesitate. He looked and saw the goatrider, swinging something around and around his head, like stones tied to the end of a long cord. This was something new, and Freefoot held his fire to see just what this strange weapon could do.

The goatrider swung the weighted cord around and around until their chosen prey chanced to lurch aside and was for a moment separated from the nearest of the rest of the herd. Then the goatrider let loose his weapon, which spun through the air in a flat arc toward the hook-horn's legs. When it hit, the thongs wrapped around the animal's legs, drawn tight by the weighted ends, and the hook-horn crashed to the ground.

The antelope's halt was so sudden that Freefoot and the other elf were past it before they could slow their mounts. The other antelopes sped on their way, unheeded. The goatrider looked at Freefoot, expression on his face for the first time, a grin of triumph. Freefoot grinned back and gave a short, barking howl.

Which perhaps was a mistake, because either the sound, like that of a wolf, or the moment's pause gave the downed hook-horn a chance to recover. It leaped, struggling, to its feet, disentangling itself from the weighted cord as it did so, and started to run away. And Freefoot and the other elf were at a dead stop. By the time they got up to speed, even though it would take only moments, the hook-horn would have had a chance to regain its own speed, and they would never catch it.

So now it was Freefoot's turn. Even as he observed what was happening, he urged Bent-Tail, not directly after the hook-horn but in an angle. He drew his bow, and as the angle between him and the antelope presented the animal's side, let fire one arrow. It sang through the air, aimed just beyond the antelope's nose, and the hook-horn ran into it so that it penetrated just below and behind the shoulder. It ran five or six paces more, and then crashed to the ground. Freefoot glanced at the goatrider long enough to note the other elf's look of admiration, then rode Bent-Tail to the fallen prey.

The two elves arrived at the dead animal at the same time and dismounted. They looked at each other with mutual respect and admiration. "Let me retrieve my tangler," the goatrider said, and turned to walk back to the place where the hook-horn had first fallen. Freefoot knelt and carefully drew his arrow from the antelope's body. The flint head would have to be retied, but the arrow was otherwise sound. He put it away in the quiver at his belt, and waited for the goatrider to return.

They butchered the animal there, Freefoot using his flint knife, the goatrider using a strange knife, as long as his forearm, made from sharpened antelope horn, which every now and then he stroked with a piece of sandstone. When freshly honed this horn knife was almost as sharp as flint, but it lost its edge quickly. The advantage was that it had a cutting edge as long as itself, not just a few finger-widths as with a flint knife.

When they were through Freefoot gave Bent-Tail part of the liver, a kidney, the heart, and a slab of leg-meat. The goatrider, who had been ready to pack the meat up, stopped and waited with Freefoot until the wolf was finished with this small reward. The goat, meanwhile, was munching grass. When Bent-Tail was done they remounted their animals, carrying half the hook-horn each and, with unspoken consent, rode back to the rise.

In the middle of the highest part of the ground they cleared away the rocks and sat down to eat. But this time it was Freefoot's turn to wait. The goatrider collected dead grass, dried clumps of grass roots, and still-standing near-hay, and with a bit of flint and a piece of shiny yellowish stone the like of which Freefoot had never seen before, struck a spark and started a small fire. He gestured to Freefoot to select his meat, and as Freefoot did so built his fire larger. Then he took several slender sticks, partly darkened by fire but carefully cleaned of bark, from a bundle at his back, under his cloak. He cut some chunks of meat for himself, and skewered these on the sticks, which he then set into the ground so that the meat was held over the fire. He added more dried roots and the half-golden hay to the fire, so that it burned hot and smoky.

Freefoot watched with amazement. "Did you learn this from humans?" he asked.

"No," the goatrider said. "Do humans smoke their food too?"

"They call it cooking," Freefoot said, "though I've never seen it done. Haven't seen a human in, oh, five hundred seasons or so."

"I've never seen one," the other said, "though I've heard of them from the elders." He turned his meat, so that the bloody raw uppersides could be browned by the smoke and flames, which he had to continually attend.

After a bit the meat was burned to his satisfaction and he took the skewers from the fire which he now let die. Then as he bit gingerly at the hot meal, Freefoot gnawed hungrily on his own. Each of them watched the other eating, half fascinated, half disgusted, until they both, and Bent-Tail too, whom Freefoot fed some more, were satisfied.

By this time the sun had started its fall down the far side of the sky. Freefoot and his companion were tired, satiated, and beginning to feel comfortable with each other. As it was now becoming a little chilly the goatrider put more roots and twisted grasses on the dwindling fire. Then he looked up at Freefoot and said, "My name is Hawkcatcher. I am called this because I can take a hawk from the sky, with a tangler such as this," he touched the now coiled, weighted cords at his waist, "though one more lightly made."

"I'm pleased to meet you," Freefoot said. "My name is Freefoot. My people call me that because I'd rather wander around than be their chief." He smiled as he spoke, but as he spoke he saw Hawkcatcher's face once again become immobile and expressionless. He could not imagine how, but his words had offended the goatrider.

"Tell me," Hawkcatcher said, "are there other Wolfriders who bear the same name?"

"No," Freefoot said. Why should his name be so important to this strange elf? For it was that, apparently, which had made him so suddenly go stiff and formal. "I am the only one."

"Your father, perhaps, or another who no longer lives?"

"No, I am the only one." He watched the other's expressionless face, and for the first time saw that there was something about the shape of the brow, the set of the mouth, that was somehow familiar to him. "I seem to know you," he said. "Are you sure we have not met?"

"We have not," Hawkcatcher said. "I would have remembered it if we had. After all, you are my father."

The wind, at that time of year, blew down steadily from the

north, bringing with it the promise of white-cold to come. As it blew it hissed through the tall grass now turning gold with the change of season. Aside from this constant and unchanging susurration, and the single click as the goat shifted a foot and lightly struck a stone, and the sound of Bent-Tail's gentle panting, and the pounding of his own blood in his ears, Freefoot found the whole world to be in utter silence.

"You are Two Shadows's child, then," he said at last. Remarkable, he thought, how loud his voice was in all this emptiness, how swallowed up it was by the grass and the wind and the sky.

"I am," Hawkcatcher said. And now, in the light of the lowering sun, Freefoot could see something of Two Shadows's face in this other's, and something of his own as well. And yet Hawkcatcher was so different from Fang-Slayer, Freefoot's eldest son—second eldest, by at least a hundred years—or from Feather, who was still a child. Not only, of course, did Hawkcatcher have a different mother, but his whole life was different, and his way of looking at the world.

"Is your mother well?" Freefoot asked. It had been more than three hundred years since he'd seen her—here, he now realized with a rush of memory that threatened to overcome him, here in this very place. Memories that he'd forgotten, pushed aside, hidden away, now came stumbling back.

There had been four of them that time, riding their wolves across the prairie, which stretched as far as they could see in all directions. Freefoot was pleased enough to be away from the holt, little though his responsibilities taxed him, although he rather wished he had been able to come alone. But his companions had insisted that they needed the recreation too, and he had to admit that the hunt had been fun so far.

Beside Freefoot rode Grazer, tallest of elves, on huge Slobber, who was equally large but was a rather gentle animal for all that. Beyond Grazer rode Sunset, ornamented with brightly colored feathers and beads, her clothing elaborately dyed red and blue and bright yellow. Behind the three rode old Springwillow, who had been Skyfire's friend and who was Freefoot's now, a plain elf and a competent one.

They were hunting antelope, of which there were a wide variety and a large number out here on the prairie. They had followed a herd of prong-horns across the long grass, taking the less fit as opportunity arose, gorging as they went, hunting as much for sport as for necessity although, of course, they wasted nothing and took no game in vain. Soon they would tire of this aimless hunt, but by then they would have identified the big animals that the herd could best do without, the eldest bucks and does. When they were ready, they would take out five or six of these and carry them back to the holt to share with the rest of the tribe.

At least, that was the plan, and that afternoon seemed like a good time to put it into action. The herd of antelope, moving steadily through the tall grass, now turning golden with the change of seasons, was beginning to get restless. Another kill, or too hard a push, or too long a pursuit, and they would flee, and the prong-horns could easily outrun the wolves, burdened as they were with their elf-friend riders. The sun was hot but the cool wind blowing down out of the north brought the scent of longtooth cats, and that made the antelopes nervous. If the four Wolfriders were going to take their chosen prey—four for the tribe and one or two for themselves and their wolves to share on the trip back—they would be wise to do it now.

They studied the movements of the herd as the prong-horns began to ascend a gentle rise, the only such elevation on the whole prairie. The slope wasn't very steep and the elves would not have noticed it if the leading antelopes didn't visibly rise up above those following. But it was enough of a slope to slow the prong-horns just a bit, and it gave the Wolfriders just the degree of advantage they wanted. They charged in among the antelopes, taking them by surprise, and so were able to get near to their chosen prey.

The leading edge of the herd came to the top of the rise and then suddenly broke to the sides, as if frightened by something they had found on the other side, and started to flee in two groups, to right and left. The Wolfriders were confused and surprised by this sudden change of motion, but they continued their attack on the selected antelopes, which were still in the main body of the herd and still climbing toward the top of the rise. In spite of the gentleness of the slope, the antelopes couldn't get up to full speed, and were further hampered by the milling of their leaders caused by the as-yet-unseen obstacle, so the elves were easily able to close.

Grazer, with his long lance, charged first and took his chosen antelope just behind the shoulder. It was a clean kill, but as the prong-horn fell it dragged the point of the lance down with it, and Grazer was forced to let it go lest the shaft break.

Meanwhile Sunset had thrown two darts into the antelope which was her target. These light weapons did not kill it, but made it stumble and turn so that Springwillow, who was riding with her, could finish it with her spear.

Freefoot, a bit apart from the others, had his bow drawn and rode with an extra arrow clenched in his teeth. He shot at his antelope, a good shot that hit the animal well back of the shoulder, but it was not fatal. The prong-horn did not break stride. Freefoot's movements were almost automatic and without hesitation as he nocked the second arrow and shot again with a longer lead. This time he hit the prong-horn through the thick part of the neck, which would also have been a nonfatal blow but, combined with the first, was enough to bring the animal down.

By this time Grazer had circled around and recovered his lance and was now racing past Freefoot. There were still two or three antelopes to kill if they wanted this hunt to be successful. Sunset, swinging her throwing axe, was right behind Grazer, but Springwillow had dismounted Snap-Weed, the better to pull her spear from where it had gotten jammed in the spine of the prong-horn.

Freefoot stopped his wolf, Bearbiter, long enough to make sure that his antelope was truly dead, then joined the others just as Springwillow rode past him. He caught up with her quickly, and they came over the top of the rise almost together, and stopped short when they saw what had made the herd act so strangely. On the far side of the rise, riding big-horned goats instead of wolves, were other elves, not of the holt, who were also culling the herd, and who had brought down several of the strongest and best. These strangers saw the Wolfriders at about the same time, and everything—except the antelopes—came to a sudden halt. Around them the herd of prong-horns scattered. The Wolfriders, at the crest of the rise, stared down the gentle slope at the five goatriders who, at the bottom of the slope, stared back.

It was rare to meet strangers of any kind, and except for Springwillow none of Freefoot's companions had had much experience with it. And from the way that the elves on the other side looked up at the Wolfriders and fidgeted, it would seem that they were equally inexperienced. They all sat on their mounts for a long time, scattered as they were, while the antelopes ran away and out of sight.

After a bit the five goatriders came together into a group. Two of them were male and three were female, and together they had brought down six prong-horns, which lay in the now-trampled grass nearby.

"What do we do now?" Grazer whispered to Freefoot.

"Maybe we should just back off," Sunset suggested. The goatriders were conferring too.

"Just stand a minute," Freefoot said quietly. Then he slowly walked Bearbiter a little way toward the other group.

With the prong-horns gone, the smell of the goats was now quite pronounced, and all the wolves were a little nervous, and so too were the goats, and all the elves had to work to keep their mounts under control. Freefoot did not go far but halted Bearbiter just three eights-of-paces from his companions, and then one of the stranger elves, a tall female with a great mane of golden hair, rode toward him an equal distance and stopped. It was enough to bring them within speaking distance, but just barely.

What does one say to a stranger? Freefoot had never met a strange elf before. Every time he started to speak he thought that the other elf wouldn't understand him and stopped short. Judging by the other's expression, she was having the same difficulty. But at last Freefoot took a deep breath and said loudly, "I hope you have had good hunting."

"We have," the other answered. She glanced around at the antelope bodies lying on the grass. "And yourselves?"

"We have three, on the other side of the rise. We hoped to get two or three more before returning home."

"We cannot carry all we have," the other elf said. "We could let you have one."

"That is very kind of you," Freefoot said. Then he dismounted, and the other elf did the same. The elves behind her hesitated a moment before following suit. Then Freefoot felt a brief, wordless sending from Grazer, and knew that his own companions had gotten off their wolves.

On foot, then, the two hunting parties joined their leaders. The goatriders were all young though mature, slender, and darkly tanned. Their clothing, though similar in some ways to that which the Wolfriders wore, was distinctly different in other ways, being looser, softer, and, especially when compared with Sunset, far less colorful.

Grazer came up beside Freefoot. He was nervous, had to clear his throat twice, then he said, "Greetings. I am Grazer, the leader of the hunt, and this is my chief, Freefoot."

"Greetings," said the golden-haired elf. "I am Goldmane" —she shook her hair—"and leader of my hunt. My chief, Graywolf, could not be with us."

The name of Graywolf was well known to Freefoot and Springwillow, of course, and gave them the knowledge to surmise who these elves must be. "Is Two-Spear no longer your chief, then?" Freefoot asked.

"Two-Spear is dead," Goldmane answered, "an eight of eights-of-years and three ago. How do you know of him?"

"He was once chief of our people," Springwillow explained, "though that was a very long time ago. I knew him then, but I did not know him well."

"Then we are kin," a dark-haired goatrider said hesitantly, as if she were afraid of how the Wolfriders might respond to that.

"If you are of Two-Spear's lineage," Freefoot said. Two-Spear's departure from the tribe had not been amicable, and Freefoot was somewhat fearful lest the goatriders hate him and his companions for having driven their ancestor away. But even as he thought this he could see that the goatriders were equally apprehensive, and for a moment it seemed as if both sides would be so cautious that nothing further could happen between them.

Then Grazer broke the impasse. "We can find more game to carry back to our holt," he said. "Let's share what meat we have now, and become friends if we can."

Goldmane and another goatrider, a heavily built male, exchanged glances, then Goldmane said, "We would be honored."

They quickly decided to bring all the game to the center of the rise, and each group went off to recover its own kill. There was some small trouble when first the wolves and goats came together, but this was quickly resolved by the animals themselves, with only a little help from the elves, as both goat and wolf decided that the other was too dangerous to fight and not really a threat and not worth the effort anyway.

There were nine antelopes altogether, more than they could eat, of course, but the elves butchered them all so that they would keep better when both parties, after the feast, went out again to find other herds so that they could bring sufficient game back to their homes. When the butchery was done the wolves were fed, and the best parts handed out among the elves. There was little conversation while they ate, but as they became satiated they became more sociable.

"Where do you live?" Sunset asked Goldmane.

"Here," Goldmane answered, "in the tall grass."

"Surely there are more than five of you," Grazer said.

"Indeed there are," the stocky elf, Stonefist, answered. "Our tribe numbers some three of eights, including kids. How about you?"

"There are five of eight and four of us," Freefoot said. "We live south, in the forest. Where are the rest of your people?"

"North and east of here," the other male, Buckmaster, said. "At least for the most part, at this time of year. We travel the great prairie all year long and, unlike you, have no permanent home."

"How will you find each other," Freefoot asked, "when you want to meet again?"

Two Shadows, a slender and wild-looking female, looked at him, and her expression indicated some confusion. "We always know where we are," she said, "don't you?"

This started a discussion, which took quite some while, made difficult as it was by both caution and unfamiliarity with each other's terms. But at last each group was able to make clear to the other how their respective mental abilities worked.

It turned out that the goatriders could no longer communicate silently as Wolfriders did, sending words and thoughts and messages directly from mind to mind, but had instead acquired the ability to always know where others of their kind were, regardless of whatever distance which might separate them. Goldmane and her companions, though they were at the southernmost reach of their hunting area, could "feel" the rest of their people, who were several eights-of-days' ride away to the north and, at this time of year, to the east.

"How many then," Springwillow asked, "of Two-Spear's eight companions still live, besides Graywolf?"

"None besides he," Evensong, the dark-haired goatrider, said, "and no one understands him at all."

"Your ancestors must have been very prolific before they died," Springwillow went on.

"The Wolfriders are not alone in the world," Goldmane told her. "Some seasons after leaving the tribe, Two-Spear and his fellow outcasts came on another group of elves, who had wandered down from the far north, and who had no wolf-blood in them at all. The two groups joined company, and we have since been joined by a few more elves who came from far to the west, beyond where even Wolfriders once lived. Most of our ancestors are now dead, but yes, for a while many kids—or cublings as you would call them— were born, both in Recognition and out, especially when the parents were from different tribes. That did not last long, however, and few are born these days, barely e- nough to make up for those we lose to accident and dis- ease. Our numbers have not changed in many eights-of- years."

"And yet Graywolf is still your chief," Freefoot said.

"He is," Two Shadows said, "but that is more by courtesy, since he is more wolf than elf in some ways and has no taste for leadership, only dominance. He is far more different from us than you are."

Then the prairie elves told how they had come to ride goats. The wolves that Two-Spear and his fellow outcasts had brought away with them had not prospered on the prairie, and no other wolves had been found to breed with them, and they had died out long since. But the goats were tougher animals than many, and these that the prairie elves rode had been bred up for size, strength, aggression, and ridability.

The Wolfriders had no concept of breeding animals for

desirable features, and it took the prairie elves some time to explain what they meant. The Wolfriders didn't like the idea much. The goatriders did this with no other animals, however, and had learned this skill from the relatives of their northern ancestors, who lived in the land of constant snow.

The nomadic life of the goatriders was very strange to Freefoot and his companions, and the Wolfriders found the ideas hard to grasp. They, in their turn, told the elves of the prairie something about the holt at Halfhill—which their cousins still knew of but which was not where they had heard of it being when Two-Spear was banished from the tribe—about forests, mountains far to the south, and how this hunt was different from their usual hunts. Freefoot explained how they had come away from the places of men a long time ago and had been free of them ever since. The goatriders, too, had kept clear of men, whom they remembered with great bitterness as being not only the enemies of their ancestors but the indirect cause of their banishment.

By now it was getting late in the afternoon. The long conversation at last came to an end. The elves ate some more, and then Stonefist, who had been silent most of the time as if trying to work up courage to say something, finally said what was on his mind. "How is Huntress Skyfire?" he asked.

"She died some two hundred years ago," Freefoot said, "and I became chief in her place. I am her son."

"Are there many who remember Two-Spear?" Stonefist asked. "He was my father."

"There are a few," Springwillow said. "I, for one, knew him when I was very young and called Sapling."

"So much has changed," dark Evensong said. "I know these names from stories, though they died before I was born. We are strangers to each other, but we are cousins after all, and we share a common past. We are both hunting people, but this rise is the only place where we might meet by chance, and so we are not in competition. We might as well be friends."

"Indeed we might," Freefoot said, and all the elves agreed.

They ate more then, and became more relaxed in each other's company, and though both sides remained a bit cautious about the other, they enjoyed being with each other, and decided, as the sun began to go down at the edge of the world and the sky above became a great cloudless flame, that they would not make two separate camps but spend the night together. The goatriders built a fire, using dry grass, matted thatch, and clumps of thick grass roots which they dug up from the south slope of the rise where the ground was drier. It was a small fire but a welcome one, and more than the Wolfriders would have known how to make out here away from the plentiful wood of the forest.

They sat together, and spoke of themselves to their new friends, and after a bit Sunset brought out a bag of dreamberries which she passed around. The goatriders had heard of these but had never tasted any, they being a fruit of the forest, and found the effects of the berries quite overwhelming. There was an awful lot of giggling and staring into space for a while.

Then the goatriders in turn—those who could still stand —went to their animals and brought back skins of what they called wheatberry wine, made from the fruit of certain of the grasses which grew elsewhere on the prairie. Now it was their turn to laugh as the Wolfriders, who were unfamiliar with this form of intoxicant, found it most potent and exhilarating.

Still they were cautious with each other, and though there was much light conversation the two groups of elves each stayed to their side of the fire. The party continued as the two moons rose high in the sky, and when they nearly touched, a glancing kiss, the wolves set up a howl. This surprised and upset the goats, and once again there was some little danger of the animals attacking each other. But the forest elves fed their wolves again, the prairie elves calmed their goats, and now, since all the elves were daypeople after all, they made up their camp for the night.

They were not yet so trusting of each other that they failed to set a watch. Sunset and Buckmaster drew first for each side. They sat more or less together, opposite each other across the tiny bed of coals that was all that was left of the fire, and talked quietly together, as did their reliefs when their turns came.

The night passed uneventfully and the next morning, after a substantial breakfast, they counted up what meat they had left and, given what they would have to eat on the way home, it wasn't enough to bother bringing back.

Both sides agreed that they had to start back home at once, and each invited the other to come with them, at least partway, to share in further hunting. But prairie elf and forest elf alike were far beyond the extreme edges of their normal hunting ranges, and so neither felt they could accept the other's offer and thus travel even farther from their homes. Each group was minded to head back to their own people and catch what they could along the way. And so they agreed, reluctantly, that the best thing to do was part company, with the hope that maybe they or other parties would meet again.

But even as they were saying their good-byes Goldmane turned away and looked off into the distance, away to the west. "We may be able to hunt together after all," she said and pointed. The others looked too, and sure enough, it was a herd of some kind, hump-shoulders as far as the prairie elves could tell, and they were coming toward the rise.

"There are enough of us," old Springwillow said. The hump-shoulders were huge animals, and the forest elves had hunted them only on occasion, when a herd came far south to within a half a day's ride of the forest.

"Two of them," wild Two Shadows said, "would provide us with plenty of meat for ourselves and our people back home."

The other elves were equally enthusiastic, so they worked out a plan, then mounted their wolves and goats and set off.

The nine elves split into four groups and circled around to either side of the approaching herd. Tall Grazer was teamed with Goldmane, and Sunset with Buckmaster, while Springwillow rode with stocky Stonefist, and Freefoot went with Evensong and Two Shadows.

The hump-shoulders did not pay them much heed—indeed seldom paid anything other than longteeth much heed—and the hunters had plenty of time to pick out several promising animals. The four elves on one side chose a large young bull, and the five on the other side of the herd selected another which was slightly older and slightly heavier.

The hump-shoulders did not naturally fear elves, were among the few prairie animals that did not fear the goats, and did not know what wolves were, so the two hunting parties were able to maneuver in quite closely to their chosen prey. But both groups of hunters would have to strike at the same time for, once hit, the hump-shoulders would stampede, and there would be no second chance.

On a signal from Goldmane, they struck, each team bracketing its chosen target. And though Wolfrider and goatrider had not hunted together before, and could not share a sending, they worked well together, did not get in each other's way, took advantage each of their own special weapons, and the two teams brought down their selected prey within moments of each other, leaving the rest of the herd to panic and race off toward the rise.

The two hump-shoulders, separated by some five of eights-of-paces, lay heavy and huge on the now trampled grass. The elves of both tribes got off their panting mounts. It had been a very short hunt, but a strenuous one, and all the elves were, if truth be known, somewhat surprised at its rather sudden and rapid success. The hump-shoulders were not very far from the rise, but they were far too heavy to move, so the elves began the job of butchery where they were.

First the animals were skinned. Each party would take one of the skins home. But as he worked next to Two Shadows Freefoot felt an odd confusion come over him, so that his movements were clumsy, his attention wandered, and once or twice he nearly cut himself.

Then each of the hump-shoulders was gutted, and the best of the innards were taken out and eaten on the spot, with the wolves getting their fair share. Still Freefoot felt strange, and had he not been so self-conscious over his inability to concentrate he might have noticed that Two Shadows, too, seemed to be having some difficulty.

When they had eaten all they could of the rich, inner meat, the rest of the carcasses were cut up. It was not the way for elves to leave anything edible behind from a hunt, but they still had plenty of antelope left over, and their mounts would be heavily burdened so that the elves would have to walk. The only thing to do was to make up bundles, as large as they could, of what was best, and abandon what was left to the carrion birds.

There was still too much to carry, so they decided to spend a quiet afternoon and evening resting where they were so that they could eat as much as they could, and then leave for their respective homelands early the next morning. But rather than take everything to the top of the rise they prepared a new camp on the flat of the prairie, just a bit removed from what remained of the hump-shoulder carcasses.

When a wolf or an elf is stuffed full of meat there is no problem with just sitting back for several hours, or longer if need be, attending to nothing more important than digestion. And so it was now, with little talk and all of it comfortable, a modest sharing of dreamberries and wheatberry wine, and plenty of dozing under the hot sun, sheltered from the cool breeze by the tall grass which rustled over their heads where they lay. Goats, of course, could munch away contentedly forever.

But the situation between Freefoot and Two Shadows was becoming impossible. Freefoot couldn't keep his eyes from the other elf, nor she from him, though they both strove to put the rest of the elves between them. After all, though they were closely related and still shared much culture, they had different places to go, different obligations to meet, and had no time for foolishness such as this. But somehow, try though they might, they always managed to find themselves together again, and though they strove to keep their unwanted fascination to themselves, it was impossible to conceal their attraction for each other from the other elves. Goldmane, Sunset, Buckmaster, Grazer, and Evensong watched Freefoot and Two Shadows with expressions of mixed amusement and concern. Conversation gradually died, and soon the two elves found themselves the center of the unwelcome attention of all their fellows. The other elves did not say the obvious, but watched and waited for Two Shadows or Freefoot to be the first to admit the problem, and shared, with them, their mixed feelings about what it meant.

Then Springwillow, eldest of the Wolfriders, put her hand on Stonefist's arm. He was eldest of the goatriders. They exchanged glances, then stood up and went off into the tall grass to confer. Freefoot knew what they were talking about, and Two Shadows did too, as did all the others, but nobody said anything. Freefoot once again tried to move away from Two Shadows, but found when he sat down that he had somehow gotten even nearer to her.

The other elves were not finding it easy either. That which was happening between Freefoot and Two Shadows was usually a cause for rejoicing, but they were strangers to each other, had obligations to other people, and there could be no easy solution to the problems that the consequences of their condition were sure to bring.

The two elder elves did not confer long. When they came back they stood before Freefoot and Two Shadows, who at last got to their feet.

"You are my chief," Springwillow said to Freefoot, "but I

am your elder. You know what has happened, and what you must do."

Freefoot looked at Two Shadows as Springwillow spoke. If he let himself admit it, he could think of nothing better to look at.

"It is Recognition," Stonefist said to Two Shadows, who seemed to pay no heed but instead found something of immense interest in Freefoot's eyes. "Our tribes are different, but what of that? You must do what you must, as you truly wish if you let yourselves admit it. As for what happens afterward, that is another thing."

It was what would happen afterward which was of greatest concern to both afflicted elves. Other affectionate attachments would pose no problem, of course, either past, present, or future. But elves who Recognize each other not only yearn to mate and produce a child, but also to share that child with each other during its growing years, and to share more of their own lives as they are able.

But they were from different tribes, who lived far from each other. Neither elf could leave their own people to live with the other. Freefoot, after all, was chief of the forest elves, and Two Shadows, as it turned out, was the prairie elves' best night tracker. Neither could be spared.

Recognition was a difficult experience enough, but these two had special problems that none of their companions here or at home could help with. No one knew what to do when two elves from different tribes Recognized each other. They could not stay together, nor could they separate. Freefoot didn't want Two Shadows to bear his cub somewhere out of his reach, and Two Shadows didn't want to be alone when her kid was born. But what could they do?

The other elves recognized the difficulty all too well, and discreetly gave them room and left them out of their conversation. Freefoot and Two Shadows struggled alone together for a while longer, neither speaking to the other, indeed not really having to, and at last, as the sun began to fall down toward the edge of the world and the sky began to grow dark, they saw that there was no hope for it. The need of their Recognition was painful, so they left the others and climbed, uncertain and anxious, to the top of the rise.

The two moons were nearly full, low in the sky but rising as it grew dark, the Daughter above, the Mother below. Freefoot and Two Shadows stood together in the sparser grass on top of the rise and watched as the two moons came together, kissed and passed, so that now the Daughter was below and the Mother above. But this was one of those rare moments when, instead of separating, the two moons moved together again, kissed and passed again. It was an omen.

"We will meet again," Freefoot said.

"It still isn't fair," Two Shadows told him. "Why do we have to be from different tribes?"

There was no answer for that, none that the elves could comprehend had they been told. Recognition was a fact of life, sometimes hard, though usually a source of great happiness. It happened, and there was no recourse.

They spoke together for a while, trying in a few short moments to learn something about each other, so that they wouldn't feel so much like strangers. Freefoot found himself liking this wild prairie elf, and that almost made it worse. He couldn't be sure but he felt that perhaps Two Shadows liked him too, just a little bit.

Behind them the camp of the elves was quiet. They were as alone as they would ever be. The two moons moved slowly across the sky, drawing farther and farther apart now, but Freefoot and Two Shadows grew closer and closer together.

They were wakened once, when it was still dark, when companions, they didn't know who, drew a warm skin over them to protect them from the chill and damp. Half asleep, they cuddled together, and the two moons went their separate ways down toward the horizon.

At dawn Springwillow and Stonefist came up the hill together, talking loudly to announce their approach. Freefoot sat up and stretched. He ached. He was not used to sleeping on the hard ground, and this ground had rocks in it.

"It's time to go," old Springwillow said. Two Shadows rolled over and dragged the skin up over her face, thereby exposing her feet and legs.

"We must get the meat back to our people," solid Stonefist said. "Come as quickly as you can."

The two elder elves left them then. For a moment Freefoot and Two Shadows clung to each other. Freefoot sought for something to say, but there were no words that were adequate. He could tell, deep within his body, that the purpose of the Recognition had been accomplished, and still he found himself drawn to this stranger. And now they would have to part, and he didn't know if he could keep his regret, his sorrow, his grief under control.

"Is there no way we can stay together?" Two Shadows asked.

"I would go with you if I could," Freefoot said. "I think the life of a nomad would suit me very well indeed. But I am the chief of my tribe, and I can't just walk away from them. I must go back. You are not a chief, you're more free than I. Can you come with me?"

"I see in the night the way none other of my people can," she said. "I should be with my tribe even now, instead of here on this hunt, and with the darkness of winter my eyes will become even more needed. I would go with you if I could, but I too must return home."

The sun rose above the edge of the world, and they knew that their friends would be waiting for them. They threw off the skin that covered them and began to dress. They spoke more, quietly, wistfully, but they both knew there was no hope. Freefoot could not live without his wolves, his violent hunting life, and could never be happy in the stoic, formal society of the goatriders, however much he might enjoy their constant wandering. And Two Shadows could never be comfortable with the violent Wolfriders, nor long endure staying in the forest holt, and could not live without the structured society that her people shared. The two tribes might meet now and then without friction, but for either of the elves to go with the other tribe would be a great hardship indeed and, in their cases, a hardship for others besides themselves.

At last they could excuse no more delay. They could hear the sounds of voices coming from the common camp, so they walked, slowly, down the gentle slope of the rise to rejoin their friends. They found them eating a light breakfast, tactful but curious about what the two had decided.

"It would be better, of course," Goldmane said, "if you could stay together. Perhaps, Freefoot, you could come and live with us for a while."

"No," Springwillow and Grazer said together, and Sunset just shook her head.

"Freefoot is our chief," Grazer went on. "While he lives, no one else would take his place, and if he went with you it would leave us leaderless."

"Perhaps Two Shadows could come live with us for a while," Sunset suggested.

"No," Stonefist said.

"We couldn't spare her," Goldmane said at the same time.

"Two Shadows is too important to us," Buckmaster went on, and told how her night vision served the whole tribe.

"And besides," Evensong said, "our birth rate is now too low, and we know too well the value of a child born in Recognition, especially one with more wolf-blood, since our wolf-blood is growing thin. This child must be born among us."

These arguments were too similar to those which Freefoot and Two Shadows had already answered between themselves, and both were angered and saddened by the repeat. "Enough of this," Freefoot said. "Two Shadows and I have already talked this out, and we can see no solution. We each must go back to our own people." The other elves fell silent.

Freefoot and Two Shadows stood together, with their arms

around each other, and paid no attention to the others, who eventually went on about the business of packing up their mounts and getting ready to leave. Though the activity went on around them, it was almost as if they were alone.

"I will come and see you," Freefoot said, "as soon as I can."

"It's a long way," Two Shadows said. "How will you find us?"

"I don't know. When are you farthest south?"

"During the winter, but then we are far east of here. This is the best time of year if you can come."

"It's hard to get away. I try, but I seldom have much time."

"Please come, next year if you can."

"I will try," Freefoot said. "I want to see you again, and see our cubling, our kidling."

"Promise me you will come."

"I promise."

"She is dead," Hawkcatcher said, "a three of eights and three seasons past, trampled by hump-shoulders on a hunt."

Freefoot could not answer for a moment then, "I am sorry," he said, and he was, truly. He could still remember Two Shadows's face, narrow and tan, though he had known her for so short a time so long ago. He could remember the way she walked in the moonlight, the sound of her low voice, the flash of her hands.

"Why should you be sorry?" Hawkcatcher asked. "You never came back." He stood and turned, then knelt, picked up a fist-sized chunk of quartz, white but streaked with red the color of blood, and flung it away into the tall grass beyond the rise. It was a good throw, farther than Freefoot could have thrown it. Hawkcatcher stood staring after it, long after it fell to earth, his back to Freefoot. "You promised you would come for her," he said.

"I tried," Freefoot said, "many times," and it was not easy for him to keep his voice even, "but I was unable to leave my people."

"You promised my mother you would come for her," Hawkcatcher said as he turned to face Freefoot again. His voice, his body, betrayed no anger, though his words hinted at a very great anger indeed.

"I am the chief of my people," Freefoot said, "I cannot just go off as I wish."

"You promised," Hawkcatcher repeated.

"I know, and I'm sorry. But my people were more than five of eights then, against only two of you, however much I cared. It was not a choice I wanted to make."

"Are you sure? Perhaps you were glad to never see my mother again—"

"We were Recognized!" Freefoot said as an anger of his own began to heat up in him, pushing aside the shock and wonder and regret. "Neither of us asked for that," he went on. "But it happened."

And had not happened again. Starflower, his lifemate, had borne him two cubs, but they had never Recognized each other. Their fondness for each other could hardly be more than it was, nor their lifelong commitment any more profound. But they were not Recognized—and Freefoot and Two Shadows *had* been . . .

Hawkcatcher was staring at him. "I didn't know that." Hawkcatcher's eyes flickered as if he were confused.

"She didn't tell you?" Freefoot asked, astounded.

"No. Though I should have known. A few children are born out of Recognition, but not many."

"About half our children come into the world that way," Freefoot said. "All are equally precious to us."

"But not me," Hawkcatcher said, and now the bitter tone in his voice, the anger, the hatred, could not be denied. "If you Recognized my mother," he said, and his eyes glittered with ill-concealed emotion, "then you knew a child would be born of that mating. But you didn't care enough to come back and see me."

"I tried," Freefoot said again. "I wanted to come. But I am

not as free to leave my holt as I would like to be."

"And yet you are here now."

"Yes, I am here now."

It had been a long time since he'd tried to find Two Shadows. Though he dared not admit it, he had all but forgotten about that one meeting, and the promise. The first year he had tried desperately to break away from his duties, but that had been the year of the sickness. Seven elves had died, and the few who had not caught the fever had all they could do keeping the others alive. The next year he had been on a big hunt far to the south, and by the time they had returned it was full winter, and the chance for all travel that far north had passed.

And so it had been, season after season. There had been times, later, when he'd been free to wander, and he *had* come out, but it would seem that he had not come far enough. This small rise was on the far borders of the goatriders' territory, and was visited by them, if at all, only at certain times of the year. Had he gone farther—as in fact he knew how to do—he might have found her, with her people, somewhere, to the far north. But he had not done so.

And the seasons had rolled, and his duties, as minor as they were, had intervened, until at last he stopped trying. And this time, though he dared not admit it, he had come not to find her, but just to get away from the holt for a while, to escape.

"And it is too late now," Hawkcatcher said. "Two Shadows is dead. But I am glad," he said, though he did not sound glad, "to meet you at last."

"I am glad too," Freefoot said, and he truly was, though the emotions inside him were far from comprehensible. That Two Shadows would bear him a cub was the inevitable result of Recognition. It was that which had tormented Freefoot most, during those first seasons, when he had been unable to take the time to find Two Shadows, as he had promised. Two elves who Recognized each other usually mated for life, but not always. Indeed, it was possible, though rare, for Recognized elves to not like each other at all. Freefoot had liked Two Shadows well enough and more, but it was the cub he had never met which, then, had drawn his thoughts back to this low rise on the prairie.

Perhaps he should have tried harder. Hawkcatcher was a cub any Wolfrider could be proud of. His strength and grace were evident in every movement, his competence proved by his health and presence here, his intelligence obvious in his speech, his wisdom in his bearing and his manner . . . except for that distance which he kept between himself and his father, compounded of strangeness, suspicion, and anger.

"Come back with me to the holt," Freefoot said to his son.

"I will not go anywhere with you," Hawkcatcher said. "I am sorry now that I hunted with you, that I shared meat with you."

The words were like a blow. "But why?" Freefoot asked. He found it hard to breathe.

"Because you are an oathbreaker. You knew my mother would bear a kid, and you were afraid to assume your responsibility. You mated with my mother but you never cared for her, and you certainly never cared for me. You abandoned us—"

"That's not true," Freefoot tried to say.

"And you are a liar," Hawkcatcher said. He stepped up closer to his father so that his face was just a handspan away. "And you are a coward." He pressed forward, and Freefoot was forced to step back. "You dare not fight me," Hawkcatcher said, almost softly, an almost smile on his face.

"I *will* not fight you," Freefoot said. "You are my son. I wouldn't do anything to hurt you."

"You cannot hurt me. You are a weakling. If it would not shame me, I would strike you down now."

Freefoot backed away. "You don't need to hate me like this. I *did* come looking for you, many times, but I never found your people. The prairie is large, and it took me four days just to get here. I did not know where to look for you, but look for you I did."

"You did not look very far nor very hard." Slowly, Hawkcatcher drew his long knife. "You just make excuses. My mother tried to make excuses for you too, but I saw her pain, her loneliness, year after year." He took a step toward Freefoot, holding the long horn knife, edge up, out to the side. "She suffered until she died. Now it is your turn. Stand and fight me."

"I will not," Freefoot said. He held his arms away from his body. He had put down his bow and quiver when they had prepared to eat, but his axe still hung from his belt. "I never meant to hurt you, I will not hurt you now."

"You are afraid to try." Hawkcatcher suddenly lunged, slashing across the air with his knife. The movement caught Freefoot by surprise, and the blade of antelope horn sliced through the front of his jacket, and through the skin underneath. Freefoot staggered backward, not so much hurt as shocked.

Hawkcatcher held his long knife out in front of him, waving the point at his father's face. "You will fight me, or I will kill you." Freefoot shook his head and backed away again. "Or run like the coward you are," Hawkcatcher taunted.

And this time Freefoot stood his ground. He knew, he thought he knew, that Hawkcatcher was just trying to provoke him, but an accusation of cowardice is not easy for a Wolfrider to bear, and this was the fourth such in as many moments and Freefoot could not pass it off.

"You are mistaken," he said softly, "about this and about many things." Maybe, if he talked to him long enough, the first rush of anger would pass, the shamed surprise at discovering with whom he had shared a hunt and meat would leave Hawkcatcher, and the two could talk more rationally. It hurt Freefoot to think that he could never win his son as a friend, but if he could talk him out of his rage—convince him that, unlike the goatriders, Freefoot had not the ability to find any other member of his tribe, however far away they might be—at least they could part company without violence—and Freefoot *would* come looking for his son again, with his people's approval or not.

And so thinking he was again taken by surprise when Hawkcatcher lunged at him, the point of his knife aimed at Freefoot's heart. Only Freefoot's wolflike reflexes saved him, making him leap back before he knew what was happening. He realized the seriousness of the assault only when he saw his own red blood dripping from the point of the horn blade.

Perhaps Hawkcatcher was a bit surprised by his own success, for he hesitated just a fraction of a heartbeat before lunging again, and this time Freefoot was able to easily dance out of the way of the stabbing knife. But this only angered the younger elf, who now pressed his attack with vigor. Freefoot was forced back, and back, and tripped on a rock and fell. At once Hawkcatcher was at him, and Freefoot was barely able to roll away in time.

He came to his feet in a crouch, and plucked the flint-headed axe from his belt. Hawkcatcher lunged again, and Freefoot tried to block the blow with the axe, perhaps to break the horn weapon, but Hawkcatcher was too fast, knew too well the fragility of his knife, and pulled his attack so that Freefoot's axe merely whistled through the air.

It was a clumsy if deadly fight. Freefoot was larger, heavier, stronger, but his axe was a heavy weapon, and his swings were therefore slower, and he had to recover after each. Hawkcatcher was quicker, faster, lighter on his feet, and his weapon weighed little and struck quickly, but he dared not let even one blow from the axe strike it or it would shatter. And so they fought, Freefoot trying to keep out of Hawkcatcher's way and trying to disarm him if he could, while Hawkcatcher tried to catch his father and at the same time avoid the heavy-headed axe that was not aimed at him but only at his weapon.

Freefoot kept his head, and fought purely defensively. In time they would both tire, and then the fight would end perforce. Hawkcatcher, on the other hand, got more and more angry, more and more enraged, but instead of losing control, his attacks became stronger, his lunges longer, his strikes more accurate, until at last he was pricking Freefoot every third time.

If Freefoot was going to survive this fight, he would have to do more than just defend himself. He would have to counterattack, either to wound or to kill.

But he couldn't bring himself to do it. "I would rather die than kill you," he called, panting, to his son.

Hawkcatcher stopped then, suddenly, breathing heavily, his head slightly tilted to one side, his eyes, brilliant and mad, staring as if into Freefoot's soul. "Would you indeed," he said.

"I would." Freefoot lowered his axe. "You are my child after all."

"You have no other children?"

"I do."

Hawkcatcher smiled, in a strange way. "You would leave them fatherless."

"Rather that than kill you."

"You cannot kill me. You cannot even touch me. And your arm is beginning to tire. Soon I will kill you, whether you yield to me or not. And then your mate will be alone, your children will be orphans, and your people will have no chief." His grin grew broader, and more insane. "It's the easy way out, isn't it?"

Freefoot had never thought of himself as much of a leader, but Hawkcatcher's words stung. He felt guilty about not seeking out his cub before, though his claim of pressing responsibilities had been true. He had said, before, that the needs of the many overrode the needs of the few and his own desire to find Two Shadows and her cubling. How could he now yield to his distaste for what he must do? Suretrail, the tribe's second in command, was more than capable of leading the elves of the holt, as he had demonstrated many times in Freefoot's absence, but the tribe would be thrown into turmoil during the transition, and if he didn't come back they would come looking for him, and that could only result in more hardship.

Hawkcatcher struck, and Freefoot barely turned aside. He swung his axe backhanded, at Hawkcatcher's shoulder. Maybe he could wound his son so badly that he would have to stop fighting. But Hawkcatcher was even more agile than before, and the blow never struck. Again the younger elf attacked, again the older elf barely avoided death as he sought to disable his opponent, and again he failed.

Then Hawkcatcher feinted at Freefoot's face, and struck instead low down at his belly, not a fatal wound, but a painful one, a long wound, between skin and muscle, a wound that bled copiously.

Freefoot almost didn't feel it. But he knew that the next time, Hawkcatcher would kill him. He knew that there was no way he could disarm his son, no way he could simply wound him. The pain of that knowledge hurt far more than the jagged tear along his side. It was almost more than he could bear.

He was not aware of how long his thoughts wandered. It was not so much an indulgence in memory as a literal return, in his mind at least, to events past. And it was not that, *per se*, which obscured the passage of time so much as the nature of wolf-time, in which there was only "now," no past or future, only a present, whether of objective reality or subjective memory or fantasy. In wolf-time there was no time. Whatever one's attention was directed to, that was all of reality, outside in the world or inside in one's thoughts.

And so, though he had not expected to hear the other two Wolfriders approach so soon, he was not surprised when they did so since, after all, one moment was the same as another, and just because the sun had moved another handspan across and now down the sky, and the shadows of grass and wolf and himself had turned around from west to east, that was no cause for alarm. This moment— as he looked down the gentlest of slopes toward the two Wolfriders now only a few moments away—and the previous moment two hundred seasons before, and the one before that when it had all begun, and the one before that when he had thought that there was still time enough to remember—all were the same moment after all, and as he thought about them now the moments could not be separated or distinguished, indeed they could not even be ordered.

But as he watched his lifemate and his third and youngest son approach, the threads of time sorted themselves out again. After all, he was not just wolf, but elf too, and the greater part, and as such he had past and future as well as present—especially future.

He couldn't help, as young Oakroot drew near, but search his face, his features, for some resemblance to that other son. But all he could see was himself reflected, and Starflower, a little bit of each in a face that was for the most part Oakroot's own.

Shag sniffed, sat up, sniffed again, recognized the approaching scents, and waited beside his elf-friend. A moment or two later Starflower, riding Snapper, and young Oakroot on Grimjaw—only his third wolf—came to the top of the rise and dismounted. Neither spoke, though Starflower did send a wordless thought of comfort.

Freefoot stepped aside as they neared so that they could stand beside him by the long, low mound of stones. Shag got up and out of the way, and went over to greet the other two wolves on his own terms.

Both Starflower and Oakroot knew the story of course, though, like Fangslayer and Longoak, they had never been here—and now Fangslayer and Longoak would never get the chance. Freefoot's lifemate and youngest child—nearly full grown, Freefoot thought, just three eights-of-seasons more —stood quietly, looking at the mound.

At last Oakroot spoke. "Have you visited this place often?"

"Not since the stones were laid," Freefoot said. "And we won't come here again. The humans are too many and too close. And too dangerous."

"What about his people?" Oakroot asked.

"I cannot believe," Freefoot said, "that the humans would have befriended our prairie cousins, and they almost certainly would have met by now, so Hawkcatcher's people must have been—driven away, at best, or killed, more likely. If they were still alive, I would have expected them to come to us long before now. We are kin, after all, and they knew where we were, even if we have forgotten them. I'm afraid they have been destroyed."

"We don't know that," Starflower said.

"No, and we never shall. If they escaped alive, the humans are between us and them, and we'll never have the chance to meet them."

"It's strange to think," Oakroot said, "that we lived so near each other, but never visited each other."

"We were too different," Freefoot said. "Even that first time, even then we had become too unlike each other to have easily become friends—and the last time we were all but strangers. They smoked their meat and did not eat it raw. And they put their dead on the ground." He gazed down at the mound.

"Why did you cover him up?" Oakroot asked.

"He asked me to, before he died. It was the only thing I ever did for him."

Though it was just shortly past midday, the wind from the north began to grow noticeably cooler. Far off on the northern horizon, barely visible, was the first of the huge storm clouds that brought with them the cold weather and the snow. It was the first sign that the season had truly turned, though they would not feel it for some eights-of-days yet back at the holt.

Except that there was no more holt. The humans who had found it had ravaged the dens, and the elves now lived with their wolf-friends in the woods. And they would all be going farther south, away from the coming cold as well as from the humans.

Freefoot didn't want to go. Since the humans had come, his responsibilities as chief had multiplied. He had more and more often had to exercise his authority, make decisions, assume command—lead. It took more and more of his time, until he was hardly ever able to get away by himself. As it was, of the whole tribe, only his lifemate and his sons had not been angry with him for taking the eight-of-days it needed to make the trip here and back—but then, only his lifemate and sons knew the whole story, and none was alive now save he who had actually met the cousins of the long grass so long ago.

And with the journey southward, up to the highlands and whatever lay beyond, Freefoot's responsibilities would grow only greater. He wished he could escape all that, go looking for the prairie elves, as he should have done so long ago, far away to the north and east now, to see if they had by some chance escaped the encroaching humans. How long would that take, if they were there at all—not just an eight-of-days or two—a season? an eight-of-seasons?

The wind blew, cool now, and the scent of carrion was gone. Far away were antelopes, moving south from the vast northern prairie, to escape the worst of the cold, some of them to graze right at the edge of the forest. The hissing of the grass grew louder as the wind grew stronger, and a new note crept in as the grass began to move more vigorously, a sound not so much like a stream as like the waves on the lake just north of the forest.

Far off to the west a herd of bow-horns made a darkness in the grass. To the east was nothing. North were the storm clouds, a dark irregular line on the horizon. To the south, invisible, was the forest where Freefoot's people waited for him to return and lead them away. Overhead, a hawk cast its shadow on the mound of stones, and then was gone. And a moment later Freefoot too, with Starflower and Oakroot, were gone, riding their wolves back, to do what they had to do.

Howl for Eldolil

by Nancy Springer

Though Oakroot had long since achieved the age by which most young elves had settled into a role in the tribe, he felt no such sense of purpose. In fact, he felt quite useless to the Wolfriders. He had a gift, that of bonding with animals, but of what use was it? Aside from their wolf-friends (of which Oakroot had one, Shadowpaw), Wolfriders needed to eat animals, not bond with them. He had a puzzled preoccupation with a small brown pool in the Everwood, but of what use was that? None, so far as he could tell.

Of course Oakroot knew his soulname, and therefore himself, what he was: a dutiful but reluctant warrior, a so-so hunter, at best a fair tracker. Very well. He should have been just another runner with the pack, a brown-haired, brown-eyed elf of no special distinction. All of his mediocrity would have been all right, in his eyes and in the eyes of his tribemates, if it were not for one thing: he was Freefoot's son.

Someday the tribe would look to Oakroot for leadership, and how was he to provide it? Almost any other Wolfrider would make a better chieftain than he. In fact, very likely some of them would challenge him, and how he would answer a challenge, he had no idea. Whether to concede, or stand and fight and be beaten and exiled . . . Being the chief's son, that was what made it hard.

Harder yet, when he could not do so simple a thing as track a limping old elf across stony ground.

For what felt like the fortieth time in as many moments Oakroot slipped off Shadowpaw, knelt and studied the half-frozen surface of the steppes. What had possessed old Eldolil to leave the Everwood and take off in such an inhospitable direction, and just at the threatening time of year?

Still on wolfback, a four of somewhat younger Wolfriders watched, waiting without much patience for Oakroot to lead on. They had been out of the sheltering Everwood for some days on this errand, and were cold and apprehensive and impatient. "Just let him go, I say," one of them, Thrust, burst out. "Two-Spear was right. Full elves are nothing but trouble and a burden on the rest of us."

"Eldolil was the very last," Oakroot said softly, speaking more to the hard ground than to Thrust. With his own words he realized he was thinking of the immensely aged elf as already dead.

"Took himself off, probably, because he knew what you and the others like you thought of him," flared Rivermist at Thrust. A pert youngster, scarcely more than a cub, she always took what she considered to be Oakroot's side—whether because he was the chief's son or because she liked him, Oakroot did not know. Or care. He had no interest in lovemates. Too many other thoughts lay heavy on his mind.

"Of course he knew!" Thrust retorted at Rivermist. "How could he help knowing he was a nuisance? He was never of any use."

"Flowers are of no use either!"

"Yes, and they wither and die at a touch."

Oakroot was not listening to the quarrel. "The very last of the High Ones," he repeated numbly, still staring at a trail gone cold as the chill late-year air, the rising wind.

"Weather coming," said Blueshale curtly to Oakroot, putting a stop to the bickering; the other elves awaited Oakroot's response.

Oakroot knew there was weather coming. He did not have to be told. Any Wolfrider could smell the storm in the wind, see the bruise-colored clouds gathering on the horizon. He had to make a decision whether to risk his followers and go on, or abandon Eldolil and turn back toward the Everwood. Puckernuts! Why had his father assigned him to head this search party, anyway? Probably because he did not want to spare any of his better trackers. There had been considerable doubt as to whether to follow Eldolil at all. When an elf, and especially a full elf well knowing his own mind, walks away from the tribe, it is often best to let him go.

It would have been the sensible thing to turn back. No one would particularly miss silent, angry old Eldolil. But Oakroot felt something stubborn tugging, calling inside him, much as a pool of brown water sometimes called him. And what was there for him to go back to? Just the gentle mockery of those strangers who called themselves his tribemates . . .His decision snapped into place in his mind.

"Turn back," he told the four on wolfback.

"At last!" Coming from hasty young Thrust, the words were a jeer. Four wolves swung round in unison. Only Oakroot's Shadowpaw stood still, awaiting him. But Oakroot did not mount.

"Dewberry," he called to the oldest of the four Wolfriders, "you're in charge of getting the search party back to Halfhill."

They all swiveled and gawked at him. Then Dewberry shut her mouth and nodded. But Rivermist protested. "Oakroot! What about you?"

"Ride," he ordered, "before the storm catches you."

Dewberry echoed his command, and the four shot away at their fastest pace, with Rivermist trailing.

Oakroot mounted Shadowpaw and rode in the opposite direction, no longer attempting to follow the cold trail.

"What about me, indeed?" he grumbled. "I'm a bow with no string, that's what. I'm smoke but no fire. I'm no better for the tribe than old Eldolil."

Silent, Shadowpaw padded on.

* * *

Oakroot sheltered from the storm in a rock cleft at the foothills of some nameless mountain beyond the steppes. It was a fearsome storm, by far the worst Oakroot had seen in his some-few-hundred years. Sleet rained down, ice balls the size of sling stones pelted the world of two moons. Late day turned to a night eerie with thunder and green skyfire. In the midst of that storm Oakroot felt a heart-wrenching portent, of what he did not know . . .With Shadowpaw curled beside him, he survived. He was not cozy, he did not enjoy himself, but he survived.

When it was over and day had dawned he looked out at a world gone slate gray, sky and ground. From out of the vastness floated a mournful, tuneless piping, as if a cub destined to be a songshaper was coaxing a plaint from a willow twig. Oakroot looked up. A skein of southering gray swans was passing over, scudding darker and faster than the clouds.

Frustration had made Oakroot strong. He focused thoughts and eyes on the flock leader and sent forth the force of his will. At first the line of swans faltered but surged on, like a spear thrown into the wind. But then the great cob who led the flock stalled in mid-flight and plummeted downward. The flock veered to follow him, then swirled in confusion and scattered. Only when the mountaintops began rushing by did the falling swan beat his mighty wings (their spread twice as wide as Oakroot was tall, their strength enough to break his bones) and guide himself to a landing on the boulder where Oakroot awaited him.

Oakroot stared into eyes yellow and hard as antler horn. **My apologies, sky brother,** he told the great bird. **I have need of you.**

He tried to mesh his thoughts with the blunt, flat images in the mind of the waterfowl. It was hard. The cob's wash of mind was wet, power-hungry, fish-hungry, lecherous, waddling, gray-dark as its webbed feet and restless as the surface of Muchcold Water.

Daring the hard black bill and great wings, Oakroot placed

his four-fingered hands to each side of the swan's sleek gray head; it stood nearly as high as his own. Into his own mind he brought the image of Eldolil. Tall, the old elf had been much taller than he, and slender, and in his great age almost translucent, something about him as airy as the skein of wild swans sketching its way across the low sky. **This one,** he told the cob, his warm oak-brown eyes staring into the chill cloud-yellow ones. **Have you seen him? Tell me.**

At first in the bird's mind he felt only waft of night wind, white light of two moons, rush of landscape spinning past. Then he sensed—was that Eldolil? Birds saw everything differently. It was like seeing another bird, a flying thing for some reason not yet in flight, a strange, attenuated, yet supremely beautiful stork or crane striding up a mountainside. But birds did not wear furs. The thing had the great sky-colored eyes and pointed ears of a full elf.

Where? Oakroot demanded.

Old one. The swan's mind was still intent on the being it had observed.

Yes! Where?

Going to magic place.

There were no words in the swan, actually, only an awe and a flash of white mountain that meant nothing to Oakroot. He had no choice but to press. **WHERE?**

Not far. We came since coldwet. I take.

The swan would lead him. It was far more than could be expected of the wild thing, courtesy so surprising that Oakroot blinked and broke contact. "Thanks," he muttered aloud, removing his hands from the swan's smooth gray-feathered cheeks, rubbing his eyes. This sort of mind contact, with a being so different from himself, was exhausting. But there was only a little more to do. In a moment he would meet eyes with the swan again, convey to it his profound gratitude—

A hungry whuff sounded from close by Oakroot's side, and Shadowpaw sprang.

No!

It was too late. Oakroot had rested his eyes a moment too long, and the swan lay dead, its fine curved neck nearly severed by Shadowpaw's jaws. The wolf whimpered and cringed under the force of Oakroot's sending. He could not understand why his elf-friend was angry. He was hungry, and surely his elf-friend was hungry, and had his elf-friend not been clever, to summon such a large bird for them to feast on?

Oakroot took a deep, trembling breath.

Never mind, Shadowpaw. It's all right. He should have instructed the wolf beforehand. So accustomed was he to the gray deadly shadow padding beneath him or by his side, he had forgotten the wolf was close at hand, with its own instincts to heed. **Go ahead. Eat and be strong. I don't want any.** He was very hungry, but he could not have eaten the swan, not after speaking with it mind to mind. Bonding with animals, as he had told himself earlier, was of small use to a Wolfrider.

Let Shadowpaw feast. All was not lost. Oakroot had seen the direction from which the swans had flown.

Up the foothills (the ice melted, sullen, in the tepid light of a gray sun) and onto the mountainside. Within the day the terrain grew too steep for Oakroot to ride. He scrambled along the jumbled slopes while Shadowpaw hunted small furry rock-dwellers nearby. From time to time he paused. His pricked ears swiveled to catch the least sound. Nothing but the soughing of wind. His sensitive nostrils sniffed the air. No sign.

As he walked he began to send.

Eldolil?

No answer.

Eldolil!

Nothing.

With a flash of hungry temper he wondered what insane impulse had sent him after the old elf on his own. Eldolil seldom spoke to him, any more than he did to any of the others. Aside from pointed ears and four-fingered hands, Oakroot had nothing in common with Eldolil.

The very last of the full elves . . .

With more of pity and less of vexation Oakroot thought what it must have been like for Eldolil, a great-grandson of the High Ones . . . hard to think of that withered old stick as a scion of the High Ones! Yet when he was a cub—or not a cub; a youngling—Eldolil must have seen the High Ones face to face, perhaps even spoken with them. And then spent the rest of his long, lingering days among Wolfriders—

Oakroot growled deep in his throat. He did not like to think of himself, a Wolfrider, as seen through Eldolil's eyes. Yet he could not deny that Eldolil must despise him because the wolf-blood in his ancestry made him small, stocky, tough, adaptable, a barbarian who bonded with wolves and ate raw meat—and had made him forget much. Like the other Wolfriders, he slipped readily into wolf-time while the peaceful days strung themselves together. Like the others, he could not clearly remember . . .

Who were the High Ones? Whence had they come?

Where was the magic place?

What did it mean to be an elf?

The Way of the Wolfriders . . . but there had been elves before there was a Way. Eldolil had lived through terror, that much Oakroot remembered. There had been a time in the chieftaincy of Two-Spear when Eldolil might have lost his immortal life at the hands of other elves. So deep had the misunderstanding between full elves and their part-wolf comrades grown that Two-Spear could propose to kill all the remaining full elves. Only Skyfire's challenge, and her establishment of the Way, had saved Eldolil and some few others.

The Way: that no elf must die.

When he sent again, Oakroot's sending was quieter yet more clear, more carrying, and full of respectful tenderness. **Eldolil. It is I, an elf like you, searching for you. Answer me.**

And back came the dry, dispassionate answer. **Oakroot. I might have known it would be you.**

Some distance upslope Eldolil lay in the lee of a great crag.

"Freefoot is wise, to send you," he remarked in the same sere tone as Oakroot scrambled up to him. "I would have answered no one else."

"What? I—" Oakroot panted as much from bewilderment as from the steepness of his climb. Eldolil's pale, thin face did not move, but Oakroot sensed his amused scorn.

"Tsk. Do you not yet know yourself, chief's son? You are a misfit, like me. Too much of the High Ones left in you. Though not," Eldolil added sourly, "nearly enough of their power."

Oakroot did not answer. He was feeling Eldolil's white, four-fingered hands—as icy cold as the sleet of the storm that had battered the old elf—and noting the passive, nearly fleshless, nearly bloodless look of Eldolil's limbs; though the full elf was twice his height, it seemed to Oakroot that he could have lifted Eldolil in one hand, that Eldolil had turned somehow nearly weightless, like a great bird, that Eldolil might float away on the first puff of air, like a dry leaf or a feather. **Shadowpaw!** Oakroot called in a panic to his wolf-friend. **Bring food! A ravvit, whatever you can find! Anything!**

"By the High Ones, I want never to eat slimy raw meat again!" burst out Eldolil, who had intercepted the thought. But then his voice gentled to a whisper. "Trying to save me, Oakroot? For what? Another few years of scratching fleas in the woods? I have had my fill of that. I meant to make my way back to where I began, but now I think I will just let go. After some few thousand years I have had enough of living; I am done."

Oakroot tried to warm the old elf's hand in both his own and could not speak. It was true; though all his instincts cried out against giving way to death, his mind knew truth when he saw it. Eldolil was leaving like a puff-flower seed on the wind.

Shadowpaw, he instructed when the wolf brought meat, **lie beside Eldolil to warm him.** There was no fuel on these barren slopes for a fire.

"Oakroot," remarked the old elf with amusement sharp as a wolf's fang, "do you think I invited you here to comfort my dying moments? I have no such need."

"There must be something—I can do . . ."

"There is. You can go back to be a worthy leader for your people."

"I!" And Oakroot nearly laughed; suddenly his voice held the same dry bite as Eldolil's. "Of what use am I likely to be to the Wolfriders?"

"Think of yourself less as Wolfrider and more as elf." No sharp teeth in Eldolil's voice any longer; it came out of his frail body calm, hushed, and sure. "And look into my eyes, Oakroot, so that I can show you what it means to be an elf. Come. You are a bonder, and I am the strange creature with whom you must speak mind to mind."

Those great eyes deep as sky, all the colors of cloud and midnight and azure day and sunset . . . Oakroot gulped and met them with his own of humble woodland brown.

And at once felt himself lost. Perhaps because he was himself nearly as starved as Eldolil, he passed quickly into vision. Or perhaps Eldolil's power as a bonder was even greater than his own.

Back, he was going back in deep time to a time beyond Timmorn, beyond Wolfriders, almost beyond Timmain . . . Oakroot saw elves as he had never imagined elves, full elves who were not ravaged, dessicated old sticks like the Eldolil he knew, but erect and fire-eyed and full of passion and—oh, their slim, wild bodies, their faces, so beautiful he could scarcely bear to look . . . Was he seeing the High Ones? He could not be sure, the images were confused, blurred by time perhaps—these were old, old memories—or perhaps Eldolil's mind was already slipping into death . . . It was all a whirl of dance and stride and magiclight and the swirl of noble colors in cloaks and capes and tunics . . . And then the light went out. Oakroot found himself back in a cold, bitter world, shivering in harsh smoke-cured furs. Eldolil lay very still. And in the smooth, ice-white contours of that silent face, those lidded eyes, Oakroot saw for the first time what Eldolil must have been when he was young.

He lifted his head and raised the howl for Eldolil.

Oakroot stayed beside Eldolil's body for what remained of that day. He ate the food Shadowpaw brought him, and rested, and thought.

When the two moons rose he lifted his voice again in a howl, a different sort of howl, summoning the strange long-legged wild wolves of the mountaintops to come and tend to the body of Eldolil. For the full elf, though he had not ridden wolves or bonded with them, though no blood of wolves ran in his veins, was a Wolfrider still. Oakroot could not leave his body to be picked by crows.

When the first stone-colored shadows began to move in the night, Oakroot left that place.

His hand on his wolf-friend's neck for support, he skittered down the steep talus-littered slopes. By daybreak he had reached the foothills, where he mounted Shadowpaw and at full speed ran back toward the Everwood and the Wolfrider tribe. For something of a full elf's arcane power had come to him from the ancient, magic place with the passing of Eldolil's spirit thither, and he now understood the meaning of the portent he had sensed in the storm.

It was not only for Eldolil that he had howled.

"Oakroot!" Rivermist met him at the edge of the Everwood, her eyes huge. He did not slow pace to speak with her; instead she and her wolf-friend swung alongside him and matched pace with Shadowpaw. "I have been watching and waiting for you," Rivermist stammered. "Something—something has happened."

"I know," Oakroot said.

"How can you know? I—I don't know how to tell you."

Therefore he said it for her. "My father is dead."

"Freefoot has died," she said at the same time, her eyes misting. Then they widened. "Oakroot! Who has told you?"

"Eldolil." This was in a sense true.

Oakroot rode at top speed, facing straight forward into the wind, unwilling to talk, unwilling to look at Rivermist. She was young, and very pretty, and it was obvious now that she liked him and not merely Freefoot's son; the son of Freefoot was likely to be challenged for the chieftaincy soon enough. Those who did not care to accept the leadership of Oakroot the Mediocre had had plenty of time in his absence to arrange their opposition. In all likelihood he would be exiled, and his followers (if he had any) with him. Therefore Rivermist was risking much by riding at his side. He wondered briefly why he did not care to take her as his lovemate, then dismissed the thought. There were other things to be thought of.

He said, "How did my father die? Was it of the skyfire?"

"The fearsome green skyfire, yes." Rivermist shuddered and told the tale as she had heard it when she had returned to a mourning tribe along with Dewberry and Thrust and Blueshale.

Busy with many tasks, the tribe had paid little attention to the approaching storm. Of course some of the Wolfriders had noticed the rising wind, the darkening sky, but what of that? Wind and rain were nothing to hide from, and if it got worse, the dens were close at hand. Treetops blocked sight of the eerie skyfire approaching and of the enormity of the storm.

"It hit like a club. It knocked down those in the open. It stunned some. Everyone was addled, bewildered, thrown into a panic. Even the oldest say they couldn't think for a moment. Those near the dens ran for the dens, and some of the others crawled to rocks or fallen logs or huddled on the ground. But a few of the youngest cubs ran for trees."

Of course. From their earliest days the cubs were taught to climb trees in case of danger. Up a tree they would be safe

from bears, rutting stags, runaway hunts, humans. But a tree
was the worst place of all to be in a skyfire storm.

"Freefoot found them there." Of course. He would have
been making his way around from den to den, bent and
slashed by the storm, checking on everyone. He would have
gone looking for the missing cubs. "They were too dazed or
scared to climb down when he called them, or even when he
sent. The trees were whipping in the wind, and it was as if the
cubs were frozen to them by the sleet; they couldn't seem to
let loose long enough to move. So Freefoot went up after
them."

"Yes," said Oakroot in a low voice. He had halted
Shadowpaw to let the wolf pant; he looked at Rivermist now.
"Are the cubs all right?"

"Fine, every one of them. By the time Freefoot had pried
loose little Redbush her parents had come, and he just tossed
her down. Faster than climbing. And the same for Mouse,
and Sweetleaf—he hurried to them through the treetops,
and dropped them down. And just after he got
Sweetleaf . . ." Rivermist's voice faltered away.

"Yes," said Oakroot, and he sent Shadowpaw forward
again. He knew what skyfire did to trees. He had seen the
splintered branches, the wide gashes spiraling down the
trunk to the ground, the bright yellow bleeding wood
showing through the wound. He did not need to know what
skyfire had done to his father.

Without looking at her he spoke to Rivermist. "You have
befriended me. Even now that I am likely to be exiled you
continue to befriend me. Why?"

She snorted like a treehorn. "Oakroot, you are going to
have to be wiser than that if you are to be our chieftain! I like
you, that is all. Why should I not?"

He felt that he owed her truth. "I cannot be your
lovemate," he told her awkwardly. "Something in the
way . . . I am not sure what—"

"I have not asked you to be my lovemate! You have always

been intent on everything else but that. Be my friend, that is all."

Still riding fast, he reached out to her with one four-fingered hand, and felt her touch that sealed the bond.

They rode on in silence for a while, and it was as if some shadow of Freefoot's death rode with them. Rivermist dispelled it.

"He went quickly," she told Oakroot. "They say he did not even cry out. They say he was dead before he fell."

It was far better than being killed by humans. Some small comfort in that. Nevertheless, dead was dead.

Freefoot was dead, and Oakroot would be chieftain—perhaps.

Almost the entire tribe was out on the common between Halfhill and the river when Oakroot came riding in. But it was not to greet him that they were assembled there. The Wolfriders' eyes were on Fangslayer and Suretrail—eminent elves, both, and both at least twice as old as Oakroot.

". . . because I am the war leader!" Suretrail was saying. As indeed he was, an excellent warrior and trainer of warriors. Oakroot had known his training, though seldom his approval.

"The war leader!" Fangslayer rebutted. "And when was the last time we went to war?" It had been a long time. The Everwood was vast, and the humans were timid and stayed near its fringes. But, Fangslayer implied, meat was a daily necessity. "The tribe's hunt leader is he who should be chieftain. And that is I, Fangslayer!" Quite so; he had been hunt leader since Oakroot could remember.

Uneasily, trying to avoid an actual challenge, the tribe was taking sides, some Wolfriders edging toward Fangslayer's sector of the common, some toward Suretrail's. If most of the Wolfriders could agree on one leader, perhaps the other could be persuaded to concede . . . but it was not happening. The tribe had split in half, and friends glowered unhappily at each other from opposing sides, and a rift opened up between the two groups.

Up this rift as if up an aisle Oakroot rode at the stately wolf-walk, and all eyes turned to him and stared. Except for Rivermist, few had observed his approach until then.

Up to silent, gawking Suretrail and Fangslayer he rode, and then he dismounted, and Shadowpaw stayed by him like a comrade in battle. Oakroot ignored Fangslayer, but stood erect before Suretrail, the oldest surviving member of the tribe. To him he offered a simple leather thong. "War-master," he said with steady eyes, "would you do me the honor of placing the chief's lock in my hair?"

Suretrail, dumbfounded, seemed not to know how to respond. But before he needed to do so uproar broke out. All of the elves were impressed by Oakroot's sheer temerity, and many were delighted. Behind him (he did not look around, but stood with his gaze on Suretrail) Oakroot heard exclamations, quarreling, laughter, and a few cheers. Fangslayer, however, was incensed.

"You, our chief!" he bellowed in his blunt way. "In Timmorn's name, why?"

"I will tell you all why." Oakroot turned around, and the tribe fell silent to hear him.

"Three reasons," he told them, laconic; it was the first time he had stood up before the entire tribe and addressed them. Unlike that old wind-mouth Fangslayer, Oakroot was not one given to much puff and talk. "One: I see the tribe tearing apart as I watch. These two have you split in half. But on me you will all be able to agree. You know what I am: one who wishes no quarrel with any of you. You can have me as your chieftain and still have a bold wolf of a war leader"— Oakroot glanced briefly at Suretrail—"and a sly wolf of a hunt leader." Oakroot nodded at Fangslayer.

"Two: If either Suretrail or Fangslayer becomes your chieftain, he will want to lead you in all things. You are not much accustomed to that." Oakroot chanced a smile at his tribemates, and saw the wry answering smiles in their eyes.

They knew he spoke truth, both about the bossiness of the challengers and their own unwillingness to be bossed. "But I would be a chieftain like my father Freefoot, who trusted his tribemates to judge wisely in all they did both for their own sakes and the sake of the tribe; who seldom chose to lead."

Oakroot took breath. The tribe awaited him in utter silence, even old Suretrail, who stood with a rawhide thong dangling from one hand, even crusty Fangslayer. And the Wolfriders had gathered together to hear Oakroot. No longer did a rift divide their midst.

"And the third reason is this: I have had a vision. The last of the full elves, while he lay dying, has showed me a vision of what an elf should be."

These elves had small use for Eldolil. But before they could mutter and turn away, Oakroot spread his hands and sent, a sending that included them all, filling their minds with the visions Eldolil had given him, of the tall elves, those who might have been the High Ones, vehement and beautiful in their bright clothing: but then the vision changed. It was not only Eldolil's memory any longer, but also Oakroot's dream, and he showed the Wolfriders themselves as elves, as they appeared to him: beautiful. Dewberry, lithe as a young wolf before she carries her first litter, slipping through the Everwood. Thrust, his face as ardent as his name. Catcher, Dreamsnake, far older than he yet still fair as moonlight. Starflower, his mother, aging like a great beech tree, lovely. Suretrail and Fangslayer, courageous, straight-backed, stalwart. All of them, all, beautiful in their differing and changing ways . . . and Freefoot, bearded and wise, his spirit beautiful still, joining the great pool of the spirits of their ancestors, Wolfriders and half-elves and full elves and High Ones . . .

And Oakroot himself, as he knew himself now. Sending, he showed himself to his tribemates, offered all his thoughts and dreams, all but his soulname for their inspection. Once he had thought himself alone, a stranger in the midst of his tribe, a misfit, as Eldolil had called him, but no longer. He had ceased to think and think of himself, like a mother wolf worrying over a pup; instead, his thoughts were on his people, and he would cherish them, his Wolfriders. Knowing himself, he now knew them. He was a scion of Timmain, he kept the Wolfriders' Way, but beyond that: he was elf. He held one of his four fingers to the power and magic and majesty of the High Ones.

When the sending was over, the Wolfriders stood in deepest silence, and blinked, and felt no need to speak to each other. The choice was obvious, as obvious to Suretrail as to any of the others. He blinked, then came forward to place the chief's lock in the oak-brown hair of his young chief, and Oakroot bowed his head and accepted it.

Looking up, Oakroot faced his tribe. His Wolfriders. They were truly his people now.

He met Rivermist's eyes first, seeing something of his own victory reflected there . . . She was very beautiful, this friend of his, with hair that floated like cloud wisp or autumn mist, eyes the shining gray of running water. Someday, he hoped or knew, he would dress her in finest soft doeskins colored that same shining gray, instead of the coarse, stiff, and heavy hides she wore. He would array all his people with clothing more befitting their beauty, in supple leathers of sunset crimson and ash-leaf gold and windflower blue and indigo.

For though he did not claim the name for himself, he knew that the Wolfriders would come to call him Tanner. That, and one further gift of knowledge had come to him from Eldolil's dying eyes: knowledge of the meaning of a foul-smelling brown pool. Knowledge elves had once possessed and wandering Wolfriders had forgotten, of the ways to tan fine leathers.

Silence still, until it was ended by the voice of a joyous young elf. "We have howled for Freefoot's passing," Rivermist cried. "Now let us howl a different howl for a new chieftain! Let us howl for Oakroot!"

Heads tilted skyward, voices lifted in riotous chorus. As if some disaster had passed them by, a calamity far worse than storm of sleet and green lightning, many of the Wolfriders hugged each other. Some of the cubs, feeling though not understanding the relief of their elders, started a dance. Oakroot went to find his mother, who stood still very much cloaked in grief, and held her.

"Listen," he said, not loudly, and his tribe quieted and listened to him. "Listen, my tribemates. This is my first command to you as your chieftain: gather on the hilltop at the rising of two moons. Tonight's howl will be for Eldolil."

The Changeling

by Diana L. Paxson

Goodtree set her palm on the smooth trunk of the beech tree, allowing her awareness to quest inward, seeking the flow of life that moved from soil to sky. The winter that had followed the great drought had been a bad one; dry, but bitterly cold. Even last week, the forest had been somnolent, but today, the energy of the tree pulsed strongly.

She stared up at the interlace of branches that netted the sky. Was the pale blue hazed with green? She could not be sure if it was the tips of new buds or the life energy of the tree she was seeing, but there was certainly something there, valiantly striving toward the sun. She sighed, visualizing starchy roots swelling beneath the melting snow, of tender inner bark, sweet sap rising in the wood. The starving times were nearly over. Only the meat the Wolfriders had smoked after the fall hunt had gotten them through the winter. Even so, both elves and wolves were gaunt; it was getting hard for any of them to think of anything except food.

Certainly it was hard for Goodtree to think about anything else these days. The curious thing was that although she could see how thin her wrists and ankle bones had gotten, her breasts were, if anything, fuller, and her belly was flat, not concave as it should have been this time of year. Could some of the stored meat have gone bad? She did not feel ill—only odd, as if she had just been sick, or she was about to be. She wanted sunshine! She wanted the feel of the sun's heat, warmer than a wolf's flank, on her back. She wanted tender new grass to lie on, and the green smell of spring.

She tested the air hopefully. Surely there was a softness to the breeze that stroked her hair that had not been there yesterday. There was moisture in that air, the scent of melting ice, of thawing soil. It was not spring, not yet, but the promise of it, oh yes! Goodtree arched her back and stretched, enjoying the feel of her own body again after so many months when living in flesh was simply something to be endured.

Then, in the thicket behind her, something coughed. Goodtree became motionless, rigid as the tree trunk. Wolf-senses extended carefully. The sound came again. Something was certainly in there. Goodtree's nostrils flared as a breath of wind touched her cheek. *Bear* . . .

Very slowly, Goodtree turned. Branches quivered as something large and heavy moved in the thicket. She heard snuffling, and then a plaintive squeal which was answered by another coughing growl. The breeze was blowing more strongly now, and she could identify odors. The rank, musky scent of a mature female came clearly, and with it something fresher, milkier.

A cub! No, there were two of them, she realized as a branch cracked a little farther away. The trunk of the beech tree was too broad for climbing, but a nearby oak offered welcoming branches. Goodtree leaped, and as the blunt snout of the bear poked through the thicket, she scrambled upward.

Her nose had not deceived her. They were brown bears, the female's coat winter-ragged and rumpled, the cubs dark and glossy. The she-bear would be hungry, thought Goodtree, and ill-tempered from her long fast. But the cubs were round balls of fur. The mother's stored fat had gone to nourish them. Bright-eyed with wonder, they followed their dam into this strange new world.

The female half rose, paws dangling, sniffing the wind. Goodtree could see her swollen dugs, and her own breasts tingled faintly in sympathy. She took a sudden breath and forgot to let it go.

Milk for a cub . . . Could she herself be carrying young? Still clutching the tree branch, Goodtree let the senses that had touched the life in the beech tree probe inward. Surely there was something—a spark of life like the first gleam of sunlight on a winter's dawn. It was still tiny, but it was there!

And why was she so surprised? Conception was, after all, the purpose of Recognition. She should have expected this. It must have happened in that first, ecstatic reunion with Lionleaper into which Acorn had forced them, or soon after, before the winter closed in. It would be a year from next autumn, then, before the cub could be born.

I'm not ready, she thought, and then, in the next breath, *how can I wait so long?*

The she-bear, unable to identify the scent that for a moment had tantalized her, dropped to all fours again and began to nose at the base of the tree. A swipe of her paw sent the last dirty snow flying. Some of it caught one cub on the snout, and the baby whuffed in surprise.

Goodtree stifled a snort of laughter. The bears' ears twitched; for a moment, one of the cubs stared directly at her. But it did not understand what it was seeing, and its mother was calling. It turned, tripped over a projecting root, and tumbled after its sibling. The mother made a sound of exasperation deep in her throat, and Goodtree grinned.

Sister, I am not laughing at you, she thought as the bear's haunches disappeared into the tangle of branches. *But at myself!* Cautiously, she slid down the trunk, hung for a moment from the branch, then let herself drop lightly to the ground. Keeping carefully downwind, she followed the bears' trail. The mother had found nothing worth eating in this clearing, but her nose was better than an elf's for locating edible roots, and her great paws more powerful for digging them out than slender, four-fingered hands. But they were not as skillful—there should be good gleanings when bear-mother was done.

The trail was clear enough, and the babies had not yet learned to be silent. Soon Goodtree heard wood being wrenched, the hollow *thunk* as a log fell, the smashing of smaller branches. Something must have pricked the she-bear, for Goodtree heard a snarl. It sounded as if the wood were dry. Was the bear after some edible fungus growing from a dead tree? She hurried a little, and peered between the slim stems of a leafless sapling.

It was dead wood. But not an old tree—Goodtree's eyes widened. Unmistakably, the interlace of brush and branches that the bear was tearing apart had once been a dwelling of men. And not so long ago. Her nose was picking up the man-scent clearly at the same time as her eyes noted the ashes of a dead fire. The earth around the hut was well trodden, and there was no loose wood on the ground nearby. She picked up the odors of several individuals. The humans must have been here for some time.

The remains of the hut collapsed and the she-bear began to paw among the ruins. Goodtree wondered what she had found. Surely by now the human camps must be as bare of food as the holt was. Then the bear's snout dropped, the massive head jerked, and the bear came up with a human arm in her jaws.

Goodtree stepped back, her stomach churning. It could not have been there long, for bears were not by preference eaters of carrion. It was the arm of a starved oldster, and the part she could see had barely enough flesh on it to cover the bones. She wondered why she was reacting so strongly. After such a winter, the human might have been glad to give up the struggle to live. The Wolfriders gave their own dead to the pack, after all. But that was part of a reciprocal cycle to which both parties had agreed. She shivered and turned away, knowing that she would scavenge nothing here.

And then she heard from within the tangle of branches a cry. It was only a faint mewling; the sound that a cub makes when it wakes alone in the den. But Goodtree felt something within her twist painfully. The she-bear had heard it, too. She half rose, her great head swinging as she sought sound or scent to reveal her prey.

Goodtree tugged a stone from the half-frozen soil and flung it at the nearest of the cubs. The baby squeaked, more in surprise than pain, and the mother's head came round. Goodtree's fingers were already closing on another stone; she threw, and the second cub squealed. As the she-bear's great bulk flowed into motion Goodtree was already slipping through the tangle of birches. She wanted to stay downwind as long as possible, but in a moment the bear would wind her. Scent clung too well in this damp air. She grabbed another rock and threw it at the first cub, then darted for the wreckage, nostrils flaring.

The bear cubs had never been hurt before, and both of them were complaining. But Goodtree's pricked ears caught another sound. Rough bark scraped her arm as she reached. A blur of brown seen sideways told her that the bear was turning, but Goodtree's fingers brushed something warm. She gripped it and leaped away, yelling, as the she-bear started toward her. For a moment the sound confused the beast, but the breeze brought the scent of live meat, elf and human mingled. With a roar, the she-bear charged.

Goodtree ran. Bare branches offered openings for an elf to slip through. But the bear crashed through such puny obstacles. She needed a tree. The small creature clasped beneath her arm was wailing thinly. Still running, Goodtree tugged open the front of her tunic, and tried to wedge the creature inside. Thank goodness it was too weak to squirm free. Behind her, wood shrieked as the bear burst through.

She knew, in some part of her mind that stood separate from the Goodtree who was scrambling so desperately over the tumble of rocks beyond the birchwood, that all she had to do to save herself was to drop the child. That was all, and then to watch from some place of safety while the bear's jaws closed. The she-bear needed food to make milk to nourish her cubs—the young of one creature would feed that of another. In the world of two moons, that was the way life was. That was what her mind said, but Goodtree's body, which now cradled young of its own, glimpsed a rush of icy water below the rocks and leaped for the log that spanned the stream.

It was only a fallen sapling uprooted by the last storm, no thicker than her arm, and slippery with spray. But for agile elf-feet it was a highroad. Goodtree danced over it and darted up the far bank. Her ears were cocked to catch any sound behind her, but it was not until a stout tree branch was within reach that she dared to pause, to turn, to see the she-bear reared up on the far bank, frustration glittering in her small eyes.

From one of the rocks above lifted a small furry head. Goodtree saw the cub's mouth open, though the rush of the stream was too loud for her to hear any sound. But the she-bear, with one last baleful look at her vanished prey, turned, and began to clamber upward. Goodtree sighed, released the branch, and started for the holt. Snug against her skin, the human child ceased its whimpering.

"The human cub is still burning with fever. Perhaps it will die—" Acorn said softly. Lionleaper took a swift step toward the entrance to the den, then turned to face him again.

"Then I wish it would happen soon! Goodtree's been wearing herself out nursing the wretched thing. Doesn't she know that we need her too?"

Acorn sighed. "She cares for it, Lionleaper—remember, she has nursed wolf cubs the same way. If she had been capable of leaving this little one to the bears, she would not be Goodtree . . ."

"Oh—I know! But she does have other responsibilities. It's not as if the cub were one of our own. In a few years it will die anyway, no matter what we do!"

Acorn began to smile. With tawny hair ruffled and arms akimbo, the other elf looked like a cub himself.

"Go chase something, Lionleaper. You need the exercise! I'll try to talk to her."

His lifemate looked up and grinned. For a moment, the two clasped arms, then Lionleaper's lithe stride carried him out of sight among the trees. Acorn's nostrils twitched as he moved toward the dark entrance to the den. He willed himself to ignore the sweet stink of sickness as he went in.

Elf eyes widened to see in the dimness inside as Acorn crawled through the passage. The chief's den had been hollowed out beneath the roots of the largest of the holt's beech trees. There had been room to spare for him and Lionleaper and Goodtree, until she brought home the child. She sat back as he eased past her, and he reached out to touch the cub's forehead. Dry heat pulsed against his palm as if a fire burned within, but the little one did not stir.

"He is worse, isn't he—" Acorn said softly.

Goodtree glared at him. "Why should you care? I heard you, you and Lionleaper. Would you have talked that way if it had been our own cub burning here?" She shut her lips on whatever else she was going to say. The baby mewed a little then and Goodtree dipped the leather teat into the bowl of broth and dribbled liquid into his mouth. For a moment he smacked and sucked, then he slid into sleep again.

"Shall I see if Brightlance and Grayplume are here?" Acorn asked softly. Outside, the Everwood was bursting into glorious bloom. With starvation behind them, the Wolfriders could afford to share. Grayplume had pupped recently, and she was willing to let the child nurse from her dugs from time to time.

Goodtree clasped the thin body to her full breasts. Worn with anxiety as she was, with her bright hair lank from lack of sun, still she had a radiance that he had never noticed before. Did it come from the intensity of her love for this scrawny thing?

"Bearling, my little cub, listen to me! You have to wake up and eat, you have to fight to live!" She rocked the cub, and Acorn could see that he had lost weight in the week since she had brought him back to the holt. His throat tightened with sorrow, for the child, or for her?

"Goodtree—" Acorn tried again. "Let me stay with him for a while. You can't do the cub any good if you don't get some food and fresh air—"

"He has lost one mother already. I can't leave him alone—" She cradled the child protectively. "I remember what it's like when your mother is always too busy to take care of you!"

He felt as if she had struck him. He had been younger than Goodtree when Tanner's lifemate had died, but he remembered how the tribe had talked. Strange, that he had never thought to wonder how Stormlight's rejection of motherhood might have hurt her child.

"It will do the cub no good if you fall ill because you are kept from the sun and the air!" he said stubbornly. "If the only way I can take care of you is to watch him, then I will. Goodtree, do you think I would hurt the poor thing?"

After a long moment she shook her head. Then, carefully, she laid the baby back down in his nest of sweet-smelling grasses and scraps of soft hide. "I don't know what I think. I only know that I can't abandon him."

"Why? Wolfriders can't afford to feed useless mouths. In the past you've never shirked hard decisions. This cub is not even one of our own!"

"And if it were?" she snapped back at him. "If we had a cub, and it got lost and a band of humans found it, what would you want them to do?"

"Give it back to the forest or kill it mercifully . . ." he began. Then he felt his cheeks begin to stretch in a foolish grin as the reasons behind everything he had been noticing became clear. "A cub . . . Are you going to have a cub, Goodtree? Is that why you feel so protective now?"

As she looked up, he saw confirmation in her eyes, and for a moment he could not breathe. His spirit swung free on a tide of remembered music. It was his song that had brought her and Lionleaper together. He had been linked to them at the moment of this cub's making. The new life that was growing inside her was part of him, too.

"I shouldn't have told you," Goodtree said sadly. "Now everyone will be watching me, and whispering."

"Goodtree—" he began helplessly, trying to understand. Then she smiled, and suddenly everything was all right again.

"Does Lionleaper know? No, of course not—he would have turned the holt upside down!" Acorn found himself focusing on her body again. Now he could see the glow clearly. She had never been so beautiful.

You'll have to tell him, Neme, he said in the speech of the heart. **He has gone hunting. Follow him. I will watch over the child. You know it will come to no harm with me . . .**

When soul touched soul, she believed him. As she got to her feet, Acorn was drawing the wooden flute from his belt. Its joyous song followed her as she moved toward the brilliant day.

Perhaps Acorn's music had brought healing, or perhaps the strength that had enabled the human child to survive starvation got him through the crisis. Whatever the cause, from that day on, the baby began to thrive, and Goodtree was too glad to enjoy her own happiness without guilt to question anything. She called the child Bearling, because of the way she had found him, and because, as he began to grow, the sturdiness of his brown-skinned body gave him a bear's bulk beside the grace of the Wolfrider young.

Goodtree had thought him an infant, but malnutrition had slowed his development. With regular feeding, Bearling grew at a rate astonishing to those accustomed to the long childhood of the elves. Her own pregnancy was still barely visible, but she was constantly aware of the new life taking shape within her, and the child she had adopted flourished in the reflection of that joy.

"He is an animal," a Wolfrider would say, watching Bearling pull himself up by a handy branch, or take a few, tottering steps clinging to Leafchaser's rough fur. "So are we," one in whom the wolf-blood of the tribe showed more clearly might answer. "He is not animal enough. How can he ever understand the wolfsong!"

But the murmurings were muted. Acorn and Lionleaper were united in their determination to protect Goodtree from anything that might cause her pain, and that year, the Everwood flourished as if rejoicing in her fertility, while the branch-horns grew fat on grass that sprang luxuriantly from the fire-cleared plain. How could anyone complain in the midst of such abundance? For once, the Wolfriders ate their fill, and no one envied Goodtree her happiness.

By the end of the summer, they had as much meat as they could preserve, and though that winter was as cold as the one before it, the Wolfriders lay snug in well-stocked dens until the snow was gone. By the time it was warm enough for Goodtree to come out for more than necessities, her belly was visibly rounding, and she could begin to believe that before winter came again her cub would be born.

Goodtree stood with her hand on the rough bark of the beech tree, but her attention was only half on the life she could feel pulsing sunward within.

"Bearling—don't go too far—" she called as the dark head disappeared through the budding hazel leaves. A Wolfrider cub would have known to stay close, or at least so the others were always telling her. Was that true? The last birth in the tribe had been Silvertwig's, and in those days, raising cubs had been the farthest thing from Goodtree's mind.

I should have paid more attention, she thought ruefully. *I should have known that Recognition and bearing would be as inevitable as the chieftain's topknot for me!* For a moment she wondered why she had not resisted motherhood as strenuously as she had fought against every other responsibility. Then a wail from beyond the bushes launched her into instinctive action. *Perhaps this is the reason,* she thought as she gave the boy a quick check for injury, then swept him into her arms, cooing reassuringly. *By the time I was forced to face the inevitable, he had taught me what caring for a little one means!*

She held Bearling against her with fierce protectiveness. Through the fringe of his dark curls she could see a tumble of old wood that looked oddly familiar. Goodtree blinked, recognizing the remains of the human camp which had been destroyed by the bear. The forest had had a year to take back the clearing. By now, the bones of the child's family would be scattered and clean. Still, she did not want Bearling playing here. She started to turn away. Then she realized that something else had changed.

Beyond the old hut, freshly cut stumps showed pale against the dark wood. In the midst of them was a new-made heap of earth and stone. Bearling squirmed in her arms, but ignoring his protests, Goodtree tightened her hold. Carefully, she moved toward the mound. She had never seen such a thing. It was not natural, that was certain. Not natural . . . She stopped short, staring down at the clear outline of a human foot in the soft soil.

Leafchaser— she called silently, wanting confirmation from the she-wolf's keener senses. Branches quivered and a gray snout poked through. **Leafchaser, tell me— what has been here?**

Her wolf-friend moved slowly forward, head swinging as she quartered the area around the mound.

Men come . . . three, one female . . . two days past. Made mound. One pissed on this tree. The wolf drew back

with a snort, and glanced sideways from yellow eyes at
Goodtree.

Taking a deep breath, the Wolfrider looked at the mound
again. It had been built as carefully as the beavers constructed their lodges, but no beaver lodge was ever decorated like this one. Thrust into the top of the mound was a
pole to whose top had been tied four hunting arrows, each
pointing in a different direction. Strips of red stained leather
and tufts of raven and owl feathers fluttered from the place
where they were joined. Below them, a slab of wood was
bound to the pole. Upon its surface she saw a circle with a
dot in it which reminded her oddly of an eye, and the
imprint, colored red with ochre, of a five-fingered hand. But
not even Leafchaser could tell her what it might mean.

There was no danger here, but abruptly Goodtree felt cold.
Bearling had begun to cry again. Ignoring his wails, she
called the wolf to her side and climbed on. In a moment they
were loping toward home.

"The humans are back for certain," said Joygleam grimly.
"I've found man-sign twice now to the north and west, and
by the lake of the white stones yesterday."

"Do you think that they've come to stay?" asked Goodtree.

Acorn watched the eyes of the hunters move from
Joygleam's face to Goodtree. Her father had still been the
Wolfriders' leader the last time humans had lived in the
Everwood. One family of wandering hunters dead of starva-
tion made no difference. A permanent village in the area
would change their lives.

Light and shadow dappled Goodtree's face as a soft breeze
ruffled the tops of the trees. The holt was in full leaf now.
Somewhere above them a goldwing was serenading the sky.
It was a perfect early summer day. Why did they have to spoil
it by talking about men? Goodtree's expression gave nothing
away.

"I don't know," said the huntress, "men usually build

things when they move into a new territory, don't they?"

"True enough," Longreach answered her. "They can't just live in the forest. They have to make it different, build walls to keep the wildness away."

"Maybe these are just hunters, then," Brightlance said hopefully. "What we saw were the remains of campfires, and bones. Three males and a female—that's not enough to start a village of men."

"They have built something . . ." Goodtree spoke reluctantly. All eyes snapped back to her as she told them about the new mound. Acorn exchanged looks with Lionleaper, remembering the human child whom Leafchaser was guarding not too far away. Goodtree had said nothing to them about this discovery. He wondered why.

"I don't like it, Goodtree," said Longreach when she had done. "It's typical for them to hide the bones of their dead that way, but that pole bothers me. When men get to decorating things and waving them about, it usually means they're afraid of something. And if there's one thing that makes them more dangerous than anger, it is fear."

"Do you suppose—" It was Snowfall who asked the question for which Acorn had been trying to nerve himself. "Do you think that they've come looking for their child?"

"It was a bear that scattered those bones!" the chieftess exclaimed. "They would know that from the toothmarks. Why should they doubt that the bear carried the body of the baby back to her den? If they even knew there was a child. We don't know that this band is even related to the other one!"

Acorn stared, recognizing a note in her voice that he had last heard when the human cub was so ill. *We can't keep him*—he thought with a pang, surprised to realize that he had become fond of Bearling too. *But how can we make Goodtree see that too*?

Goodtree went back to the ruined hut several times that spring. She told no one, and she took neither Leafchaser nor the child. Once she found a bunch of newly picked flowers on the gravemound. Later, she saw that the pole now bore the newly cleaned skull and rattling claws of a bear. She shuddered, wondering if it had been the she-bear who had chased her, and if so, where her half-grown cubs were now. Longreach said that humans liked to decorate their dwellings with such trophies, whether to boast of their prowess as hunters or to frighten their enemies he did not know.

It was just another of the things that the Wolfriders did not understand about humans. Goodtree killed animals for their meat or their hides, and tipped her weapons with their bones or horns. But what use was a skull? Why couldn't the humans leave their dead alone?

The third time she visited the gravemound, she heard someone weeping. Softly she slipped forward, too silent for human hearing, even if the creature had been listening. It was a female. She could see hacked and matted hair, but it shocked her to realize that as humans counted age, this woman was still young. Was she weeping for the old one whose bones were weighted by this heap of stones and soil, or for the child?

This close, the mix of rancid grease and woodsmoke and sweat that was the man-scent made Goodtree's stomach rebel. The female was missing teeth, and her eyes were dull. Goodtree remembered how Bearling's smooth brown skin glowed in the summer sun, the fresh scent of him, the firm plumpness of the flesh beneath. She thought of the children she had glimpsed in the human village when she herself was a child, long ago. They had been thin and filthy, constantly quarreling. They grew up into men who were just the same. And this woman was already old. She would die while Bearling was still young, and leave him alone.

I can't give Bearling up to live that way—she thought, only then realizing she was answering a question that no one had yet asked.

* * *

That summer the plain was rich in game. In the tales Longreach made of that time the springers leaped from every clump of brush like grasshoppers, and the little quick-living fish glittered like stars in every evanescent waterhole. Memory of how drought had parched that plain just two summers before faded into the long dream of the wolfsong. Even Goodtree might have forgotten that time, had it not been for the cub that was growing steadily within.

That summer, Lionleaper and Acorn hunted without her. Goodtree was content to stay close to the camp, following Bearling's wanderings as he explored this new world and talking to Moss, who helped with all their birthings, about cubs and their ways. And so the golden days cycled toward autumn, when the branch-horns returned. And then everyone was too busy with the hunt to think of anything else at all.

Goodtree rested her head on Lionleaper's thigh and licked her lips with a contented sigh. The light of the westering sun shimmered in the rising smoke and edged the prairie grasses with gold. Raw meat was good, when the salt-sweet blood awakened the wolfsong. But for days the harsh smoke had been turning raw meat into tangy, tough slabs that would last the winter through, and now it seemed equally good to throw the remainder of the carefully gathered wood on those fires and smell the sizzling fat as the last of the branch-horn carcasses roasted over glowing coals.

It was also necessary. A Wolfrider could chew on rotten hides when hunger pressed belly against backbone, but meat that has hung for several days in warm weather quickly loses its allure. With the sharp taste of garlic to spice them, and starchy lily bulbs toasting among the coals below, roast meat made a memorable meal to celebrate the ending of a fall hunting rich beyond most of the tribe's memories.

And then there were Freshet's dreamberries. When the tribe returned to the Everwood, they would gather a new crop and dry enough to last them through the coming year.

These were the last of the harvest from the previous autumn, but there was no longer any reason to hoard them. Goodtree popped another berry into her mouth, and slowly, appreciatively, began to chew.

Lying this way, the hard mound of her belly rose like a hill practically beneath her nose. She lifted one foot and waggled it in the air.

"What's that for?" asked Lionleaper, tossing a gnawed bone back into the fire.

"Just wanted to make sure it was still there!" Goodtree felt laughter bubbling within her. "Belly's too big—can't see my toes!" Her body shook with merriment, no, it was just her tummy. Both of them watched in fascination as something ridged the smooth mound from within and changed its shape so that it sagged to one side.

"Getting cramped in there, umm?" Lionleaper patted her belly gently. "He's going to be a big one, a great hunter, like me!"

"*She*—" said Goodtree, with a grin.

Lionleaper looked at her, eyebrows lifting.

"I'm picking up feelings now, and it's a she-cub in there."

Lionleaper blinked, then shrugged. "A great huntress, then, and beautiful!" His hand moved to cup her round breast, and Goodtree turned so that the weight of her belly would rest on the earth, snuggling into his embrace.

She closed her eyes, feeling the familiar moment of dizziness as the power of the berries began to open the doorway to the waking dream in which all memories were Now. Goodtree could feel the presence of the cub within her like a spark, waiting to flare into full awareness when birth would propel it from the warm safety in which it floated now into the world where the senses reigned. Had it been like that for the High Ones when they chose bodies? Goodtree wondered dreamily. She sent the cub a pulse of love, and was rewarded with an answering warmth that sent her deeper into the dream.

She tried to remember if she had ever communicated with

her own mother this way, but despite that moment of forgiveness in which Goodtree had found her name, all her memories of Stormlight were full of pain.

I'll do better, little one, she sent to her cub. **I won't leave you the way my mother left me!**

And suddenly, in the eternal present of the dreamberries she was back in the clearing, feeling the warmth of Stormlight's embrace, and then the agony as the cudgel that had sought Goodtree's life crushed her mother instead.

Gasping, Goodtree fought to thrust the vision away. She only realized that her body was struggling as well when she felt herself being shaken and in a moment of clarity understood that it was Lionleaper, not her father, who was holding her down.

Neme, Neme! Come back—it's all right. You're safe. It's all over now. He helped her to sit up.

Goodtree realized that she was weeping. She could feel Acorn on her other side. She clung to their calm strength, willing the vestigial buzz from the berries away.

"Sorry—" she gasped. "It was Stormlight . . . I *remembered*." She shuddered, and rested her head against Acorn's chest.

He nodded. He had been born a few seasons before her. Of course he would remember how Stormlight had died.

"I know she loved me." She hiccoughed and shook her head. "But she didn't know how to mother me. What makes me think I'll do any better when it's my turn? I couldn't bear for my cub to be hurt that way."

"Is that why you've been practicing on Bearling?" Lionleaper laughed. Instinctively all three of them glanced over at the heap of furs where, wolf or elf, all of the tribe's cubs lay curled in sleep by the fire.

She couldn't see him. Goodtree sat up straighter, eyes narrowing. He must be hidden beneath the others. A thought roused Leafchaser, who was lying upwind, worrying at a bone.

Test the air, wolf-friend. Is the human cub there?

How slowly everything seemed to move . . . It took forever for Leafchaser to amble around the fire to nose at the tousled heads and rumpled fur. Goodtree got to her feet as if she still moved in a dream. Acorn and Lionleaper blinked stupidly up at her.

He's not there! She was not capable of words. **Leafchaser says his trail leads onto the plain. We've got to find him before darkness falls!**

Not all of the Wolfriders could be roused from the dreamberry haze, and there were wolves from the pack too full-gorged to run, but Goodtree's will drove all those who could hear her across the plain. At dusk the longtooths began their hunting. Packs of foul dogs that looked like debased cousins of their wolves hung about the waterholes or strove to steal the scavengings from stronger predators.

She clung to Leafchaser's neckfur, shuddering as she thought of the many things that could happen to one small human child! Bearling had not even the wolf-sense that was born in any child of the tribe. Older cubs might get into trouble exploring, but the little ones were born knowing they must not go out of scent of home. The eyes of elves and wolves alike expanded as the light faded. But Bearling would walk in darkness. Would he be afraid?

A yip from Fang brought them veering down a grassy slope toward a drying waterhole. A favorite place for anything that preyed on grass-eaters, thought Goodtree, straining to see.

"He came this way—" called Lionleaper. "There's a footprint here not an hour old!"

Leafchaser halted, tongue lolling, as Goodtree slid from her back. The boy's scent came clearly, with none of the sour fear-smell. If Bearling had been in danger then, he had not known. The scent-trail looped around northward then, as if the child wanted to retrace his steps, but did not know the way. She started up the far slope, bent low to catch the scent that clung to the damp grass, and felt Acorn's grip on her arm.

"Light!"

Goodtree straightened. For a moment she thought it was the sunset, but she was facing north. Her skin went cold as she realized she was looking at the light of a fire. She sensed firelight and the scent of meat roasting . . . Bearling would be certain he was heading for home. The Wolfriders paused, their pricked ears asking Goodtree for direction.

We'll go on— she sent silently. **But very carefully!**

She did not need to state the obvious. They had met no other elves within the memory of any Wolfrider now alive. If there was another fire-maker on the prairie, it could only be man.

It was Lionleaper's keen eyes that first saw him, a small silhouette against the light of the humans' fire. Bearling's posture showed his confusion. Even a three-year-old human could tell that the shapes and smells were wrong. Beyond him other shapes moved in the firelight, tall and ungainly. Hunting had been good for the humans as well. Why had it never occurred to Goodtree that hunger would also drive the humans onto the plain?

Don't move, little one, we are coming— Abruptly Goodtree remembered that his mind was closed. Awkwardly she crept forward. "Bearling—" she called, ever so softly. Could his human senses hear?

Goodtree, stop? Lionleaper's sending was sharp with alarm. Two of the humans were carving meat from the branch-horn haunch spitted above the fire. Others sat in a circle around it, old and young together, except for one woman who stayed apart from the others, head bowed. Jabbering, a big man with angular patterns scarred into his brown skin and bone ornaments knotted into his black hair pointed his spear at the meat and then at the sky, and from the others came a murmur of praise.

"Bearling!" Goodtree called again. The small shape

turned. Goodtree half rose to reach for him; glimpsed movement beside her and saw Lionleaper darting forward.

He can't see you—he can't smell you! Don't—

The Wolfrider grabbed, and Bearling let out a startled wail. Lionleaper was speeding back to them. But the figures around the fire had heard. In the momentary stillness, Goodtree could hear Lionleaper brushing through the grass. Then the baby got his breath and began to yell in earnest, and the big human with the spear roared and charged.

Goodtree felt Leafchaser's cold nose shove her palm and scrambled onto the she-wolf's back. Lionleaper had Bearling with him on Fang already, but the child was still wailing. Light and shadow danced crazily across the grass as one of the humans grabbed a burning brand from the fire and ran forward. Wolves and Wolfriders scattered in all directions. Red light flared in slanted wolf eyes. Abruptly the tone of the shouting altered. Surprised questions changed to a sickening scream of fury and fear.

Follow Fang! Goodtree's fingers clenched in the coarse fur as the she-wolf surged into motion beneath her. She felt, rather than heard, the first thrown stone go by her. A startled yelp told her that someone had been hit, but they were all still running. Looking back, she saw faces distorted beyond the normal ugliness of humanity.

They were shouting—dreamberry memory told her the meaning from a time when Wolfriders and humans had met before. "Wood demons!" that was what they cried, as if the elves were evil creatures out of their own terrified tales. But the creatures that pursued the Wolfriders were the demons here.

The intensity of the yelling diminished as the Wolfriders faded into the darkness. Bearling was still crying, but with all the noise the humans were making he could not be heard. Goodtree urged Leafchaser after Fang. They did not stop running until they came to the waterhole.

* * *

Acorn stood at the rim of the hollow, listening to the drumming that pulsed across the plain. The rest of the Wolfriders huddled below the skyline by the pool, panting after the mad dash that had brought them to this illusory security. The prairie rolled away in dim billows beneath a star-strewn sky. To the north and east, elf-sight, expanding, could make out the darker band that was the Everwood, but nothing moved but the blades of dry grass that bent before the wind.

"Goodtree—the humans may not have elf-sight, but they're not blind!" There was desperation in Lionleaper's tone. "They can track too, and come morning, they'll be hot on our trail! They're bound to find us eventually. On the open plain there's no place to hide."

"I don't deny that," came Goodtree's reply. But she was, thought Acorn. "Stop shouting. It's what *we* are going to do now that we have to decide!" Acorn heard a strangled sound from Goodtree's other mate, but it was Oakarrow, whose wolf was still licking the graze where one of the stones had winged his rider, who replied.

"That should be obvious. We trot back to camp as fast as we can go, pack up our meat, and run!"

"Laden like that, we'll go slowly—" Brightlance observed.

"Are you proposing that we leave all that good meat for the humans to find?" Snowfall sounded outraged.

"I'd rather they found the food than us! If we go fast, and we go now, they'll think we've disappeared into thin air."

There was an uncomfortable silence. They had survived winters without stored food before, and nobody wanted to do it again.

Acorn sighed. "No, they'll keep looking—" He made his way down the slope as the others turned to look at him. "Don't any of you remember Longreach's tales? They'll follow us as long as they have breath. They have seen the child!"

Heads turned until everyone was looking at Goodtree,

who sat with Bearling clasped close in her arms. He had fallen asleep with his mouth pursed like a rosebud, one chubby hand still gripping her curly hair.

"That is what we would do, if it were one of our own," said Snowfall slowly. Lionleaper and Acorn exchanged glances above Goodtree's bent head. If they had insisted on returning the baby, months ago when the humans first returned, could they have avoided this day?

"He *is* one of our own," said Goodtree, her voice rising. "Our wolves have nursed him, our cubs are his littermates, his home is our dens. What would we have done differently if I had birthed him?"

Nothing, Goodtree, Snowfall answered gently in the speech of the soul. **Elf or wolf or human, the needs of cubs are much the same. But what will we do with him when he is grown?**

He will never have a soulname, Goodtree— sent Brightlance. **He will never be able to speak like this, without words.**

He can't have a wolf-friend either, added Oakarrow. **How could he talk to it?**

He couldn't hunt with us— The silent debate continued while the Mother moon hunted her child across the sky. **Who would he mate with?** came the thought of another.

He will die as the wolves die, while we continue, Acorn knelt beside Goodtree, looking down at the child. **Humans do that, Goodtree—humans grow old!**

Though the argument was silent, Bearling must have picked up the tension. He whimpered and burrowed more deeply into Goodtree's arms.

See how he trusts me! How can I let him grow up into one of those savages? came her answer. **You saw their faces, you heard!**

Acorn sat back on his haunches. **Because they are his people. . . . And because it is for the good of the tribe!**

Goodtree straightened, staring into his eyes. **Acorn, are

you challenging me?**

All the starlight focused into twin moons that filled his
sight. Even now, he thought dimly, though the will of the
tribe was against her, he could not force the green glow of
her eyes to dim. His resistance faltered as some deeper
awareness recognized behind her eyes others, silver and
amber and sky blue, a refraction of power that went back six
generations. Facing Goodtree, he faced every chief who had
led the Wolfriders since Timmorn, sometimes by strength or
wisdom, but always by sheer uncompromising strength of
will.

*I made her accept her mating with Lionleaper two years ago
because she was physically weakened,* he understood then,
*and because, though she could not admit it, that was what she
really wanted to do.*

Acorn began to tremble. Without his will, his chin was
lifting in surrender. Then he understood another thing. It
was not only a chief's power he was facing, but the desperate
fury of a she-wolf defending her young. Suddenly he gave
way.

**Goodtree, Goodtree—we are all your cubs too! For the
sake of this one child will you abandon the whole tribe?**

Slowly, normal awareness returned. Acorn struggled to sit
up. Lionleaper was looking at him with amazement, while
silent tears drained the light from Goodtree's eyes in glittering trails like dissolving stars.

"I will take him . . ." Acorn said hoarsely. "You do not
have to go."

She shook her head. "He would be afraid. If I must give
him up, I will do it myself, with love."

The stars were fading in the eastern sky as Goodtree
slipped from Leafchaser's back in the hour between darkness and dawn. The human camp was just ahead, and the
mixed scents of woodsmoke and human bodies hung in the
moist air. Lionleaper and Fang had come to a halt beside her,

and she heard the faintest rustle of grass as Acorn left Twitchear and came toward her. She shifted Bearling's limp weight on her hip. Exhausted by exercise and emotion, he was sleeping with the boneless abandon possible only to the very young; he had scarcely stirred during the ride.

Won't you even wake to say good-bye to me? She knew that it would be better if he stayed asleep, but she felt her eyes beginning to sting with the treacherous tears once more. Her lower back ached dully; it had been some time since she had had so much exercise. Lionleaper touched her arm, offering to take the child, but she shook her head.

Dew on the long grass cooled Goodtree's feet as she moved forward, the two males close behind her. Behind them, the three wolves settled patiently to rest. A hint of human scent reached her and she stopped, nostrils flaring. It was strong here, and fresh. She tilted her head, testing it, and realized that she had smelled it before.

Look for a human female, very near—

Nodding, Acorn and Lionleaper swung out to either side. In a moment Lionleaper was gesturing.

The woman lay curled beside a patch of clumpgrass, one arm still outstretched as if in appeal. It was the woman who had put the bunch of flowers on the mound. Didn't her people care that she was alone out here, or had she refused to abandon her quest when the others returned to the safety of their fires? But Goodtree knew already that this one went her own way. The woman's hair had grown out and she looked better fed than she had been in the forest, but her face, like Goodtree's, was stained by tears.

Little one, my little bear, is this the mother who bore you? The suspicion she had buried could no longer be denied. *Then I give you back to her, but remember me in your dreams.* For a moment Goodtree clasped Bearling closer, then she kissed his forehead and his fine, strong-springing hair. Silent as a dream herself, she moved forward and laid the boy down at the woman's side. He did not wake, but even as the

Wolfriders drew away, he was turning toward the warmth of her body.

They will think he came here by magic, sent Lionleaper.

Until they notice our tracks in the dew! Acorn replied.

Lionleaper grinned suddenly. A silent call brought the three wolves loping toward them.

Run in a circle around the human until all our tracks are gone!

Goodtree leaned against Acorn. She was still aching, even though the weight of the child she had been carrying was gone. She felt as if she had eaten bad meat. She didn't want to ride back to the others. She wanted to crawl into a nice dark hole somewhere and not think about anything anymore.

Let's go! she sent to the others, grimacing. **There's no reason to stay here anymore.**

They were two thirds of the way back to camp when a wrenching sensation in Goodtree's belly made her gasp. Leafchaser halted as she slipped, panting, to the grass, then nosed at her belly.

Blood . . . good . . . cub come soon.

Goodtree's eyes flew open. The she-wolf was sitting beside her, grinning complacently. She took a quick breath, her mind beginning to work with extraordinary swiftness as she recognized the significance of the warmth she felt between her thighs. Her eyes narrowed as the two male elves turned back, their eyes widening in alarm. She grabbed Leafchaser's fur, and by the time they reached her, she had pulled herself to her feet again.

"Lionleaper, your wolf is the strongest. Go get Moss. She'll know what else to bring," she said before he could ask what was wrong. She watched with interest as the color left his face completely, then flooded back again.

"The cub—" Acorn began. "Is it now?"

"I'll walk as long as I can. Acorn can help me." She could

see their protests fade as she stared them down. She reached out to stroke Lionleaper's hair and he caught and kissed her hand.

Neme . . . Neme . . .

"Yes, I love you, and the sooner you go the sooner you'll return!" He nodded, and flung himself upon Fang's back. In moments they were disappearing across the plain.

Need a den, came Leafchaser's thought as she took a step forward.

Need a lot of things. Ask Twitchear to scout ahead, look for a hollow somewhere. Goodtree could feel Acorn's concern, but what was going on inside her body was rapidly becoming more important than anybody's feelings, including her own. She had hoped that she would be wolf enough to deliver easily, but any she-wolf would have realized what was going on long before.

"Lionleaper should be here—" muttered Acorn after a little while.

"You told me yourself . . . cubs come first!" The clenching in her belly was rapidly making it impossible to walk. All she could think of was curling up in some safe darkness. Then Twitchear was loping back to them with news of a rocky outcrop. There would be shade there. She stumbled toward it.

Goodtree lay panting, as all awareness concentrated in the muscles that were working to bring the cub into the world. Acorn had gathered sweet-scented grass to make her a bed. But then there was nothing he could do. His anxiety distracted her. She summoned up the concentration to send.

Mergin . . . sing to me . . .

For a moment there was silence, and then a soft sound began. Springtime was in Acorn's music, ice melting, sap rising strongly in trees. Goodtree felt the meaning, though she could pay no attention to the words. But she felt herself sinking into the wolfsong, one with the music and the life in the land; and tensed muscles relaxed and all the energies of her body focused on the single task.

And presently she heard her own soulname throbbing in the music, mingled with another—*Lleyn* . . . and for a moment a third sound that sang through the music until she could almost shape a name. Then she felt Lionleaper's strong grip on her right hand and fell back into her body. She reached out with her left, felt Acorn take it, and grunted, all her being gathering like a bent bow to release her cub into Moss's waiting hands.

Very gradually, Goodtree came back to ordinary awareness again. She felt sore and exhausted, but content, as she did after a successful hunt, or a good run. She opened her eyes. Lionleaper and Acorn were beside her, and beside them, Moss, crooning to something wrapped in the softest of hides.

"It's a female, as you told me," said Lionleaper. "And strong!" He and Acorn were both grinning as if they had done it all. Slowly she became aware that an awning of stretched hide supplemented the shadow of the boulders. She could smell elves and wolves all around her; the whole tribe was here!

"The humans!" She tried to raise herself, and Lionleaper pushed her back down.

"Gone!" He laughed. "Joygleam tracked them. They must have found Bearling and the woman first thing this morning, and then packed up and hightailed it back the way they came."

"Wolf-demons . . ." Acorn nodded sagely. "That's what they'll be thinking. The wolf-demons made themselves invisible and returned the child, then changed back into wolves and flew away!"

"Drink this—" Lionleaper had broth for her, salty and reviving, in a cup carved from a piece of serpent-nose horn.

If I had not given Bearling back to them, the men would have pursued us, Goodtree thought, swallowing. *They would have caught me, and maybe the others, when the cub was born.*

But she still felt his loss. She reached out, and Moss put the warm bundle that held her cub, exquisite from the tips of the whorled ears that peeked through her nimbus of golden hair to her tiny four-fingered hands, into Goodtree's empty arms.

Hero Worship

by Len Wein and Deni Loubert

It was not the most elaborate trap Mantricker had ever set, but all things considered, it would more than suffice. It had taken him only a short time to build, culled from the fallen branches of nearby trees, a loose construction of branches and briars, held together by a cunningly hidden series of vines. Anyone who chanced to walk beneath the tree to which the trap was attached would hardly notice the slight disturbance of the sprawling foliage that encroached on the side of the path or the apparent tangle of overgrowth that spilled onto the pathway itself. They would not notice, that is, until they had stepped onto the trigger branch that snapped the shrewd trap into motion, leaving the victim trapped in a basket of greenery, dangling helplessly six feet above the pathway they had so casually been walking down an instant before. (Unless the passerby was an elf, of course, in which case, Mantricker presumed, the trap would be obvious.) But Mantricker wasn't trying to catch elves here; he was hoping to snare some unsuspecting young *human* hunter, overconfident and full of himself on his way home from the kill.

As Mantricker sat crouched on that tree limb above the shadowed path, he silently surveyed the area around him. The trees were at their most lush at this time of year, their leaves an emerald-green so vivid that it almost hurt the eyes to stare directly at them. It was midday and the forest seemed atypically quiet, most of the local wildlife having found some sort of shelter to escape the summer heat. Yet here, in the deeper inner forest, the ever-present shadows were cool and inviting. A light breeze tickled the young elf's nose, giving him the momentary illusion that the nearby river was far closer than it actually was.

I can smell the water, and almost taste the small silverfins swimming lazily in the deep pool near the human village, mused Mantricker, aware of both his and Bentclaw's growing hunger. *Well, perhaps later we can wander by and see if the five-fingers have left a few silverfins for an enterprising young wolfrider and his friend to dine on.* But only after this latest trick was sprung, and the young chief-son had first dined on some hapless human's frustration and discomfort.

Now Mantricker's thoughts returned to the seasons most recently past. *How easy they had been, for a change,* he thought, *how prosperous, how unnervingly uneventful.* Game had been plentiful, bellies were full, and everyone seemed content just to enjoy their good fortune. Everyone but Mantricker, that is. Boredom and restlessness had quickly overcome his natural elvish caution.

As the long, slow, lazy weeks passed, he found himself spending more and more time spying on the tall ones' village. Sometimes entire days were spent perched upon his favorite limb, smelling the smoke from their fires, and grinning silently at their crude victory celebrations when they returned from the hunt.

Truth to tell, it was an exaggeration to even call the humans' habitat a village. It was just a small grouping of rude huts at the outermost edge of the wood, each with its own small hearth, but with a far larger communal firepit at the center of the clearing. Most of the villagers were related to one another on some level, and the community's power structure seemed, to Mantricker, to be somewhat similar to the elves' own system of chiefs.

Although his mother, Goodtree, wanted nothing more than to leave the humans to themselves and be left in peace in turn, Mantricker simply couldn't stay away from them—

with their noisy celebrations at hunt's end, their endless parade of screaming children, and their strange ceremonies at the time when the moons would both swell to their fullest. Mantricker had been warned many times to not tempt fate, and Goodtree would be furious if she knew what he was planning. But somehow, the young Wolfrider just couldn't turn away from such an opportunity for mischief.

As the days passed, he began to play little tricks on the unsuspecting humans. Sometimes he would slip into their village at night and steal their hunting bows, leaving the weapons stacked in an abstract heap in the center of the village, or by the pathway at the forest's edge. When the tall ones went out to hunt, he would follow silently, springing their game traps as soon as they had laid them down. The other elves warned him to be more cautious, but to Mantricker it was all a marvelous game. Spying on the human village, besting them with elaborate little annoyances such as the trap now set below, seemed an entertaining way to test his will against theirs. It kept him sharp, helped him develop his own hunter's instincts. After all, it wasn't as if the humans were a serious threat to the wolfriders, though he never for a moment underestimated their potential for sheer destructiveness. It was just that the five-fingers were such easy targets, and it was such fun. Certainly more fun than sitting around back at the holt, listening to Acorn and Longreach sing tales of ancient victories in the fullness of twin moonlight.

Suddenly, there was a rustle below him and Mantricker was roused from his reverie, glancing down at the trap he had laid along the humans' path to the river. *Not that they use the waters often enough to rid themselves of their stink*, he thought. *Timmorn's Eyes, but you can scent a human approaching from the other side of the forest.*

Below the elf and just a few feet farther along the pathway, Bentclaw waited with about as much patience as a wolf can have. Bentclaw had been long past his youngling stage when he came to Mantricker, before the elf had earned the name he had chosen for himself. To many, it was just one more way in which Mantricker was different from the others of the tribe. The elf and his wolf-friend were close, and Mantricker had more than a little respect for the wisdom he so often saw in Bentclaw's eyes. Although the wolf would never act in opposition to his friend, Mantricker sometimes found himself suddenly aware that he had stepped across the line from safe action into folly, the emotional link between himself and Bentclaw was that strong. At the moment, Bentclaw was weary from the midday sun and hard-pressed to understand his companion's strange new interest. *Why can't we go sit in the shade of a nearby thornbush now and check the man-trap later?* the wolf wondered. But patience had been asked for. So Bentclaw waited.

Soon, both wolf and elf were listening to the sounds of clumsy feet along the pathway. Mantricker grinned quietly to himself. Whoever approached, it was much too noisy to be a wolfrider. He settled in to watch the fun, as the unseen human neared the trap. The footsteps continued for a moment, then stopped abruptly, to be replaced by the savage snap of branches, and the whistling whoosh of vines being whipped through the air. Long before the angry shouting began, Mantricker knew his trap had been sprung.

Since these foul-smelling creatures were so clumsy, it hardly seemed fair to take much trouble with the snare. Even so, Mantricker knew that it wouldn't take the young hunter much more than a handspan of shadow-crawl to extract himself from the sinewy tangle of branches that now hung above the path and begin to look about in rage for the perpetrator of his humiliation.

Oh, and Mantricker intended to let the human know just exactly who it was who had so artfully outsmarted him.

Scurrying down from his lofty perch, Mantricker scampered along the path to confront his captive audience. The young elf approached the twisting netlike tangle cautiously, wary in case his victim might still be clutching its dagger or spear, more than eager to put them to use. The figure, half-hidden in the shadows of the trap, seemed somehow smaller than a human warrior ought to be, its body thinner, its hair longer. And, more oddly than that, it was now moaning.

So much for him, thought Mantricker with disdain. *If this sad creature cannot free himself from so simple a trap, let him rot. One so cowardly deserves no better fate.*

The young elf whirled, about to vanish back once more into the forest's comforting shadows. He rose on the ball of one foot, then paused. Something was not right here, some primal instinct told him, something was not at all as it should be.

For a moment, Mantricker stood, staring up at the writhing trap, long graceful fingers gently stroking his chin as he studied the small figure struggling above him. *It just doesn't look right, doesn't sound right, doesn't—*

That was it. The sound. It was not the low throaty growl of an incensed hunter, but rather the high-pitched wail of a child. A *female* child.

Mantricker slapped his forehead in sudden realization, then moved closer to the trap to carefully study the howling bundle within. Yes, that was it, all right. Instead of the bold young hunter he had hoped to snare, Mantricker now saw it was a young human female who struggled inside. The she-cub's limbs were thin, and yet her body was beginning to blossom into the promise of womanhood.

Mantricker leaned back against the tree, arms crossed, and watched in amusement as the female's cries of frustration mingled with the rattling of the branches. This young human struggled with an intensity that far outweighed her size, Mantricker noted. Her rage at her awkward situation continued, even as her struggles slowly became weaker and weaker, until at last she sprawled motionless in the trap, scratched and exhausted, but still clutching the tangle of branches as if demanding her freedom. Mantricker was frankly amazed that she had struggled for as long as she had. Most humans weren't the strongest of creatures and would have tired long before now, he thought.

For a moment, the woman-child simply lay in the trap, body curled in defeat. Then she peered out between the branches, and for the first time noticed Mantricker standing below her. She gazed down at him, the young elf quickly realized, not with the sheer primal fear most humans experienced when confronted with one of their ages-old enemies, but rather with a kind of innocent curiosity. She stared at him imploringly, then spoke.

"Well, don't just stand there," she said, "Free me." Fascinated by this young she-cub, Mantricker merely stood his ground, saying and doing nothing.

Again, she pleaded. Again, Mantricker ignored her. Then, slowly at first, but with growing intensity, she began to cry, a plaintive wail that carried across the forest, echoing back through the underbrush.

At this, Mantricker became annoyed. The female's cries would alert the other humans, bring the villagers running, or worse, any hunters who might happen to be near. That had not been the plan when the young elf set his trap in that long, lonely hour just before sunbreak. He might easily be able to handle one or two humans, Mantricker decided, but certainly not an entire tribe of them.

I have to find a way to silence her, thought Mantricker, *quickly. If her crying brings the whole village down on me, it will only prove to Mother that her fears were well-founded. She might forbid me ever to go near the humans again. And what fun would there be in that?*

Impatiently, Mantricker slapped the side of the trap, counting on this sudden unexpected action to frighten the female into silence. Instead, she only cried out that much louder, still pleading with him to free her. It was obvious to Mantricker that, despite her greatest efforts, the female could not free herself.

The wisest thing to do is to simply abandon her here, and watch out for myself, the young elf thought. *At the very least, it might leave the holt with one less irritating human to deal with.*

He considered the ramifications of this, as the woman-child's cries continued. It seemed to Mantricker that she had a great deal of courage for one so young, and the elf couldn't help but admire that. He had not counted on becoming this involved in something that had begun merely as a lark, but killing a helpless cub who was simply in the wrong path at the wrong time was not an act of courage, he realized, but of cowardice.

Like it or not, Mantricker decided, he would have to free this howling she-cub himself.

Cursing himself under his breath, Mantricker cautiously moved forward. The spring branch that had triggered the trap was within his reach from a convenient position in the lowest limb of a nearby tree. With that branch properly counterweighted, the whole trap was quickly and easily lowered to the ground. This accomplished, Mantricker crouched on the limb, waiting patiently for the female to clamber out of his trap. To his surprise, she did not move. Then the young elf noticed something.

Her arm, Mantricker realized. *It's tangled in a briar branch. No wonder she can't free herself.*

After lashing the spring branch to the tree, Mantricker leaped down, then reached into the trap to free her from the briar. There was no easy way to remove the branch without scratching the female's thin arm to some extent, Mantricker noted, but nonetheless the young one didn't even flinch as the vicious thorns were dragged across her tender flesh. The moment she was finally freed, Mantricker stepped away, expecting her to flee from him in terror. Instead, the female simply stood and stared at him.

"Go away, little fool," snapped Mantricker in the elfin tongue, growing impatient now, and attempting to wave her away with an irritated sweeping motion of his hand. "Run for your pitiful life."

But the young human merely stood her ground, studying Mantricker curiously, still without a trace of fear. In truth, there was something else in her dark brown eyes, something almost akin to worship.

Stepping cautiously forward, the woman-child gestured to herself. "I am Elona," she said, then pointed a slender finger at him. "And who are you?"

Mantricker hesitated. He had learned something of the guttural human tongue from his long nights studying their village and their ways. But this was an advantage to be kept secret and protected for the moment when it might someday provide a needed advantage. And yet he could think of no other way to discourage her. Furious with her for forcing him into this awkward position, Mantricker spoke.

"I am your worst nightmare," the young elf said, assuming his fiercest pose. "A demon spirit-beast who means you only harm. Flee from me, child, while you still can!"

Instead Elona smiled at him, tenderly touching the fresh scratches on her arm. "If that is so, why did you free me?" she asked gently. "Why did you help me when it would have been so much simpler to leave me to die?"

Mantricker paused, uncertain of how to reply. Then, finding no alternative, he decided to resume his fearsome pose. The young elf raised himself onto the balls of his toes, attempting to glare down upon this obstinate she-cub threateningly, and thus perhaps finally frighten her away. Instead, Mantricker discovered he and the female were precisely the same height, and so instead he found himself merely staring at her eye to eye. Realizing how silly he thus appeared, Mantricker dropped his fearsome pose and glared at Elona grimly.

"We are of two different races," the elf said impatiently, attempting to explain. "And the peace that currently exists between our people is a tentative and uneasy thing at best. Just be thankful that I let you live and begone."

Instead, Elona peered straight into his eyes, with a friendliness that was both unexpected and unnerving.

Confused by her reaction and exasperated by the whole situation, Mantricker gestured once more for her to leave. Elona did not budge, and instead cautiously reached out a slender hand to touch one of his pointed ears. Mantricker jerked his head away, and growled at her, still trying in vain to chase her off. The young elf found himself somewhat intrigued by her, and yet her stubbornness made him angry. He realized the female had obviously mistaken him for her rescuer, and for some reason this embarrassed him.

"You can say whatever you want," Elona said softly, "but I do not believe you and your people are the monsters my father has told me you are. For some reason, I think you *want* me to believe you're dangerous, but what you really are is—" She paused at the word, unable to look at the elf directly.

"—a hero."

That was about all Mantricker could stand. Bewildered by her reaction and knowing that the longer they stood in the pathway the more dangerous it was for him, the young elf suddenly grabbed the female's arm and roughly shoved her in the direction of her village. Elona merely smiled at his urgent attempts to push her down the path.

Suddenly, another sound intruded upon the scene; the frenzied thrashing of other humans quickly drawing closer, calling the female's name. It was obvious Elona's urgent shouting had had its desired effect. Mantricker turned toward the sound, the hair at the nape of his neck bristling. He glanced back at Elona angrily.

"I am sorry," she said. "I didn't mean to—"

"Meant or not, it's done," Mantricker replied. Then, he turned and melted back into the thick of the forest, leaving her alone.

She turned and headed back to her village, with a great deal of looking back over her shoulder in his direction.

My hero, she thought, staring into the underbrush as a worried group of humans finally approached her, calling her name. *A real hero, like in the tales the old ones tell at campfire.* Then, surrounded by her people, Elona turned and walked with them back along the familiar pathway that led to her home, still glancing back often over her slim shoulder as she went.

Hidden safely in the shadows, Mantricker watched her go, softly shaking his head sadly, as if trying to shake off the odd confusion now churning within him.

This female, thought Mantricker, *is going to be trouble*.

Back beyond the forest's edge, Elona's village was a flurry of activity, as the women worked to prepare for the sacred feast that was soon to come. In a mere handful of sunsets, it would be the Time-of-Two-Moons-Joining, one of the holiest of nights. All the cookfires were burning high and the children watched in fascination as the witch-woman chanted into her herb pot. Still in the company of her rescuers, Elona approached the clearing in front of her family's hut. Her father and the other men of the village would soon be back from the hunt, she knew, so for now it was mostly the women and children who scurried about, preparing the smoke-hut for the fish and meat they knew would soon be at hand, and pounding the nuts they had gathered from the forest into a soft gruel that would be buried in the ground and left to ferment for the feast.

Minutes later, Elona sat in her hut, talking to her mother about her rescue. Elona's mother, once a beautiful young woman like her daughter, now wore her long years of hard labor as a weight upon her shoulders and the pain of birth and child-rearing as a well-lined map upon her face.

"He was like a wild animal, Mother, beautiful and free," explained Elona. "He rescued me from that terrible trap, then let me go. I do not know why Father calls the forest-folk demons. He was just wonderful."

Elona's mother looked up from the nuts she had been grinding, a bowed and beaten woman with six children around her and less than thirty winters behind her.

"Do not dare to speak like that," her mother said, in a low voice filled with a lifetime of fear. "If your father hears you, he will beat you! You know how those demons have harassed him all month. No, he will not want to hear of this!" She stared at Elona with muted terror in her eyes. "You must never speak that way of the forest demons, child! If you do, you will attract them here and we will all be killed in our sleep! Just tend to your chores and keep your tongue still!"

With that, the older woman turned her weary back to Elona and returned to her grindstone. Elona reached a comforting hand toward her mother's shoulder, then paused. It would do no good to try to change her mother's mind about this, she realized. The woman was too frightened, too set in her ways.

Instead, still thrilled and excited by her morning's adventure, Elona left her mother to her work and went outside to tell her friends of what had happened. These friends ranged in age from the littlest, Lia, who had just barely learned to walk, to Rain, a gangling youth who was looking forward to his initiation into the secret rites of the tribe's hunters after this next feast. They crowded around Elona, whom they all acknowledged as their leader, especially when it came to doing those things their elders had forbidden them.

Not that they always believed her tales of what she saw in the forest, of course.

Kir, who although bigger than the others and easily old enough to be a hunter for the tribe, was resting from his newest misfortune, a foot he had caught in one of his own traps. Kir had always had his suspicions about Elona and her tales of playful forest spirits. Until lately, that is, when an inexplicable series of mishaps in the forest had finally made a believer of him. Kir swore he would go spirit-hunting as soon as his foot healed.

"We'll see how good their demon-magic is against a stout bow and arrow," Kir would brag to the others when Elona wasn't close enough to hear. He never bothered to mention, of course, that he was afraid his sharpened arrow would simply wind up in another portion of his own anatomy. Personal damage aside, Kir truly believed these unfriendly spirits needed to be rooted out of their forest. Unfortunately, Elona had this unpleasant habit of beating him up whenever he spoke of the forest spirits that way in front of her. For the most part, Kir decided silence was by far the better part of valor, at least where it concerned Elona. It was embarrassing to be beaten by one so much smaller than he was. At the moment, Kir's patience was wearing thin regarding Elona's latest exploits, and he was weighing in his mind the wisdom of doubting her word in front of the others against his anger at what he felt were such blatant lies. It was even worse that the others were listening to Elona's every word with open-mouthed wonder and excitement.

"And he was not huge at all, not a giant as Father has told us, but rather short, no taller than I am," Elona explained, describing the encounter to her circle of playmates with extravagant gestures. They listened to her tale in awe, afraid to believe a word of it, but believing it nonetheless. "And then he loosened the vines and set me free. He wasn't fierce, I tell you, but wonderfully gentle, and quite . . . beautiful!"

Suddenly, a threatening shadow fell across the giggling group and a gruff voice, like the distant growling of the gods during a rainstorm, descended upon them.

"Come with me, child," the voice ordered.

Elona glanced up in fear, to find her father, a brutish dark-tempered man, looming above her. It was obvious to Elona that he had overheard her tales and was not at all happy. "I said, come with me," he repeated. Then, roughly, he grabbed her upper arm and dragged her to her feet, pulling her away from her friends and toward their hut.

"Why must you continue to tell such lies?" her father shouted, once they were inside. Elona's mother was no-where to be seen, having fled the hut moments earlier lest she suffer some of what Elona knew was next to come.

In his rage, her father towered above her, causing Elona to back away from him until her spine was flush against the inner wall of the hut. Though frightened, she remained defiant of him. Hurt by his unreasoning anger, she wished he would once, just once, listen to her.

"But they are not lies, Father!" she replied, her voice little more than a whisper. "What I have told the others is all absolutely true."

Her father, worried that someone else might somehow hear her, pushed his daughter farther against the wall of the hut, glaring at her. "Listen to me, Daughter, for I will not say this again," Elona's father demanded. "Demons live in these woods, eager to eat foolish children like you! You must stop telling these outrageous stories or the elders will think you are crazy and order you banished!"

Elona, struggling to maintain her dignity, but beginning to feel more like a child and less the magical being who had earlier consorted with spirits, sniffled at him. "But it isn't a story, Father," Elona protested. "A forest spirit did rescue me. Perhaps they are not the vile demons you have always said they are."

"You *are* crazy," her father roared. "How can you forget what these creatures have done to us? Or have they perhaps possessed you?"

With that, he slapped Elona savagely across the face, the impact slamming her head back against the hut wall. Then he muttered something about hoping this had knocked some sense into her head, and stalked to the mouth of the hut.

For a moment, he paused in the doorway, glancing back over his shoulder. "There will be no more talk about kindly demons, do you hear me?" he warned her. Then he was gone.

Elona slid down the hut wall and sat, quietly crying. *I wish Demontricker was not off on the hunt right now*, she thought. *I know he would believe me.*

She paused, remembering the bond that had grown between herself and the bold young hunter over the last few seasons, then slowly she smiled. She alone, of all the tribe, had truly understood what had transpired when Demontricker had earned his name many seasons ago during a meeting with one of the forest demons. From this understanding had grown a friendship that virtually defied all the laws of the village. Even though Demontricker was a grown man now, with a wife and children, and Elona was only a young girl, not yet spoken for by any of the tribe's young hunters, there was a bond between them that no law of man or gods could sunder.

I will tell Demontricker all about this when he returns, she thought. *He will understand.* Elona found this thought strangely comforting. Then, with a sigh, she turned her attention to the unpleasant task of skin drying. It was one of her regular chores, and Elona knew she had best get it done if she wanted to eat with the others that night.

There will be other opportunities to see my elusive forest spirit again, she thought, *and spirit he is. I will never think him a demon, as the others have. He is a spirit, a lovely spirit, and he is* mine!

Several days passed. With the game still plentiful and the weather kind, the Father Tree had become a center for the playing of games, the retelling of tales, and the renewing of old friendships. The food seemed almost eager to throw itself onto the cookfires, and it was generally agreed that it had been a particularly splendid season for dreamberries. While many of the elves simply enjoyed their unexpected good fortune, the older residents of the holt were wise enough to know that all this bounty would not last and cautioned their younger comrades to make some preparation for the lean winter ahead. The younger elves did what little work they were inclined to do good-heartedly, almost as if they were humoring their elders. Still, everyone knew that such good fortune could not last forever.

Nonetheless, there were more lovemates joined and more Recognition than in any other summer in memory. It was almost as if nature were taking time to catch its breath, using the uncommonly good weather as a way of giving the elves a chance to heal their wounds, inner as well as outer.

Although the hunting was almost embarrassingly easy, it

still was needed from time to time to keep the tribe, which had been growing larger and healthier, furnished with fresh meat. A small group of younglings had come back from a scouting trip to report that they had spotted a large herd of black-neck deer on the far side of the dreamberry hill. It wasn't far, perhaps a half-day's journey from the holt. They happily volunteered to hunt down these black-necks and bring back food for the others.

As Mantricker had assumed, the kill was accomplished with very little trouble. The black-neck herd had grown fat and lazy from the summer's easy feeding and thus was not at all alert. It was almost as if the herd needed thinning out, the elves agreed, and they would be happy to oblige. The buck the elves decided upon was older than the others and obviously growing blind. This had made him slower than the other black-necks and the elves pulled him down with ease. They closed in for the kill, and soon were eating their fill.

As the band of elves began the process of skinning the black-neck and carving up the pieces for transport back to the holt, one of the wolves suddenly uttered a low growl that was usually reserved for the sour smell of humans approaching. As one, the elves snatched up the weapons that were never beyond an arm's reach, and rose from their kill to scan the forest's edge. Acorn and Longreach began circling around to the moss-covered side of the trees, while Far-Touch and Mantricker chose the other side of the wood to track the approaching presence. They had been fanned out in this fashion for the length of several heartbeats, when Longreach spotted a lone human female wandering through the forest. As the other elves picked up his sending, they gathered in the shadows along the edge of the trail she seemed to be following, waiting in grim anticipation of what might come next. The elves were as silent as dew on the leaves, and as watchful as black-necks in cat-country, as the young female slowly made her way to the clearing where their kill now lay, alone and untouched since the wolf's first warning.

Mantricker studied the female carefully, then touched a hand to his forehead and slowly shook his head in disbelief. The female was, of course, Elona.

Despite her father's warnings, she had ventured into the woods once more to track down her "hero" and thank him properly for rescuing her. Elona was frightened to have come so deep into the forest alone, and yet somehow confident that her elusive rescuer was still nearby, ready to protect her should the need arise.

I must be as crazy as Father thinks me to be doing this, she scolded herself. But since scolding had never stopped Elona before, no matter who it came from, it certainly wasn't about to stop her now.

Elona took two more steps, then suddenly the elves were upon her, their weapons at the ready, shouting furiously. Terrified, Elona tried to flee, turning this way and that, always finding an angry elf before her, his weapon blocking her path. Finally, with nowhere else left to run, Elona found herself backed against the wide bole of some ancient tree, the elves' spearpoints at her throat.

As the point of one blade pressed forward, slightly pricking Elona's pale flesh, a voice from the back of the pack of elves suddenly shouted, "Wait!"

Mantricker was surprised to discover the voice had been his own.

"Why are you stopping us?" asked Longreach. "The world will be a far better place with one less five-finger to concern us."

"Look at her," demanded Mantricker, gesturing toward the frightened figure. "She is only a cub, who has gotten lost in the woods. She doesn't even know where she is. Surely we have no need to kill her."

Far-Touch stepped up beside his friend now, bow in hand. "She's too close to the Father Tree," he disagreed. "She'll go back to the other humans, tell them where we are. Do you really want them to destroy the holt? You know that's what they'll do given half a chance."

Mantricker stared into his companion's dark eyes in silence. Then he stepped forward purposefully and gently lowered the other elves' spears from Elona's throat.

"All right, I agree that finding her here is dangerous, but killing her will only make the other humans more angry," argued Mantricker. "Once they find her body, they'll come out in full force to find us."

"And what is our alternative?" asked Far-Touch grimly.

"Let me lead her out of here, and leave her somewhere beyond the wood," said Mantricker. "I doubt she will ever be able to find her way back."

The other elves snorted in disgust, some even turning their backs on Mantricker to peer at each other with unspoken questions in their eyes. Nearby, the wolves paced nervously, their noses in the air. Finally, Acorn turned to Mantricker, and spoke.

"What's happening to you?" asked Acorn, with some concern. "Have you been rolling in dreamberries or have you suddenly decided to adopt this she-cub? You know the humans do not protect their girl-children. I doubt they would even notice were she to disappear entirely. So why do you—"

"Just let me handle this," interrupted Mantricker impatiently. "I will see she is returned to her village and that will be the end of it."

"But she is dangerous," said Acorn.

"She is a cub," replied Mantricker, who obviously did not agree. "Besides, her death, even if it is not avenged, will bring the precarious peace we have kept with the humans to an end."

Longreach plucked a stem of grass to chew on as he watched the angry exchange between his two friends. He was thoughtful, as a plan of sorts formed in his mind. Finally, he sent it out for all the elves to hear. **We can kill her quietly, you know, without the humans ever being aware it was our doing. If we were to throw her into the river to drown, for example, the tall ones will think it an accident.

Then we will not only be rid of her, but there will be no disturbing the precarious peace.**

But Mantricker would not budge from his previous position. "There is no need to go that far," he insisted.

When Acorn continued to argue that her death was necessary to protect the holt, Mantricker finally lost his patience. He stepped up to Acorn, his nose within inches of the other's face, so close his presence was almost a physical force, pushing against Acorn until he took a step back. The challenge in Mantricker's eyes was clear.

"Are we no better than the humans, then?" he asked of the others as much as of Acorn. "Must our answer to everything be violence and death? Surely we are smart enough to find some other way!"

Finally, Acorn and then the others relented. "Fair enough," said Longreach. "If you say you can rid us of this human without her giving away the location of the Father Tree, then do it. But it is your responsibility, and the outcome is on your head. Goodtree will know who brought the humans to the holt if that is the result of this."

Still, in the end, Mantricker had his way, and Elona gazed up at him with pure adoration shining in her eyes. Although she could not understand what her hero and the others had said, she could still read the tone of their voices and the intent of their expressions enough to understand what had happened. *He has saved me again*, she thought. *He truly is my hero.*

Mantricker glared at Elona with great ferocity, but the effort was wasted on her. He pushed her roughly in the direction of her distant village, and she started to walk away, although halting every few steps to see if he was still following her. Finally, Elona began to understand that he would not, could not, openly go with her, so she began the long journey down the forest trail to her village alone. Mantricker shadowed her from the side of the trail, to make certain she returned unharmed.

As she walked, Elona's mind was alive with images of her

friends' astonished faces as they would look when she
returned to tell them her newest adventure. *How astounded
they will all be*, she mused. *Even Father will finally have to
admit that I am right and that the spirit-man is my protector.*

Now her head began to fill with visions of herself and her
spirit-man in the seasons to come, living together as the wise
leaders of her people, sitting around the feast fires, teaching
her people new ways to live in peace. Young Kir would
finally look up to her, no longer able to scorn her dreams,
and even the witch-woman would come to her for advice.
Yes, she thought, as she hurried down the pathway at a faster
pace. *They will come to me seeking wisdom. Let's see my father
beat me then.* She smiled shyly to herself, not really seeing
the forest before her at all.

With that irritating young female finally gone, Mantricker
returned to the tree to find a group of very curious and angry
elves awaiting him. What did he think he was doing, they
demanded, allowing a human to walk away like that? Had
Mantricker forgotten who and what the tall ones truly were?

As Mantricker attempted to explain, he quickly began to
realize that he wasn't even certain himself why he was being
so easy on this foolish human female. He told the other elves
of the trap he had set and of her struggles to escape it. He
told them of how he had set her loose and of how she never
seemed afraid of him the way the other humans always were.
As he spoke, Mantricker began to realize he felt a certain
admiration for the she-cub's courage, as well as some
strange sort of responsibility to her.

Finally, Far-Touch interrupted Mantricker's tale. "And
what of her newfound knowledge of us?" he asked. "What of
the fact that she may come searching for you again, and this
time perhaps find the holt as well? It's all very fine for you to
admire her courage, but it's that same courage which will
bring her back to these woods again and again. Your saving
her from us today will only serve to make her feelings for you

that much stronger. And what will you do if, the next time she comes, she does not come alone?"

Now, almost to his own surprise, Acorn found himself challenging Mantricker. "I am sorry, my friend, but we cannot allow her to lead others to the holt," he said sadly. "It is not a decision to be taken lightly, but it is one that cannot be avoided. We have no choice but to hunt her down and kill her."

For a moment, Mantricker merely glared at his companions, then he bent to pick up his bow. "You are right," he agreed, "something must be done to prevent the child from returning, but death is not the only solution. In the name of our friendship, I ask you to give me a chance to try another way."

The other elves glanced at each other in disagreement. Then Acorn spoke up. As always, he was the first to see Mantricker's point of view.

"If anyone can outtrick a human, it is Mantricker," said Acorn. "Surely outtricking a cub should not be too difficult. I say we let him try." Acorn glared at the others and, reluctantly, they finally agreed.

Mantricker spent the next few days in the company of his wolf-friend, trying to come up with a plan. Truth to tell, Bentclaw didn't understand Mantricker's constant pacing or the lack of any real hunting being done. Normally, his elf-friend was the best of company, always willing to chase anything tasty that chanced to cross their path. Bentclaw began to wonder if perhaps he should just go away for a while, leave his friend to his own devices, but Mantricker seemed to need him around. In the evening, Mantricker would go for long walks, attempting to touch some thought that was always just out of reach. *What is it that she-cub wants from me?* he mused. But the answer to that was an elusive quest, for Mantricker soon realized he had very little knowledge of what it was humans really wanted.

At sunset the next day, Mantricker sat and watched the Wolfrider cubs at play, some taking the role of the heroic hunter, others busily creating make-believe tools from whatever was at hand. It was another hot evening and many of the elves had gone to the river's edge to cool off in the welcoming waters. Walking down to the river, Mantricker simply paced along the side of the bank, trying to worry the thought that bothered him as his wolf-brother would worry a particularly tough piece of meat. As he watched the younglings' antics, something in their heroic playacting made Mantricker think of Elona and her vision of him as some sort of hero. She was really still little more than a child, Mantricker realized, even if he sometimes felt he could clearly see the woman in her. Unfortunately, the child in her was looking for a hero, and for some unfathomable reason, she had decided upon him. Mantricker knew the clue to solving his problem lay in that single scrap of knowledge, but how to best put it to use was still beyond him.

So long as she sees me as her hero, he thought, *she'll just keep on coming back*. How then to turn her from the forest without taking from her that which she so obviously shared with all children, her idealism? Mantricker shook his head as the weight of that thought pressed down upon him. *What am I thinking?* the elf demanded of himself. *The plan is to get her out of the forest, not more into it. Perhaps Acorn is right and I have been too much into the dreamberries of late. But how to persuade her that I am not what she believes me to be? Perhaps, instead, I can make use of what she thinks I am . . .?*

And that was the beginning of the Great Idea.

Two evenings later, after more aimless wandering through the forest with his preoccupied elf-friend, Bentclaw, in boredom and desperation, suddenly broke from Mantricker's side and chased a tasty-looking thumper into the underbrush. He followed it through the thickening forest, across a grassy field, and toward the nearby river. At the riverbank, the terrified thumper, no fool he, made a sharp right turn into a convenient burrow and the wolf, unable to stop his enthusiastic charge, plunged headlong into the water.

After a second or two of thrashing about in shock and confusion, Bentclaw came up for air, covered with water-weeds and panting in delight at the coolness of the water. The long green strands that dripped from his head made him look for all the world like some ancient monster from the old tales told round the campfire. Mantricker laughed at his old friend's antics, and then suddenly grew pensive. He stared at Bentclaw for what seemed an eternity, then a triumphant smile spread across his face.

And, with that, the Great Idea was complete.

Mantricker spent the following day at the holt, digging through his burrow for some old items he had thought long lost and all but forgotten. Old scraps of hide and broken thongs were tossed aside in haste as he searched through the odds and ends collected over his lifetime for a particular hide he had abandoned just this past winter when his mother had presented him with a newer, larger one.

Later, the younglings crowded around the holt as they watched Mantricker and Bentclaw engage in some new battle games. They were unlike any games the cubs had ever seen before, and even Bentclaw himself was a bit puzzled by them. He couldn't see how these wrestling matches would help to bring them new food but, glad to have his good friend back to normal at last, Bentclaw indulged him, learning the new tricks he was shown.

The next evening, after the great fireball had finally dropped below the earth's rim and the twin moons had completed about an eighth of their night's journey, Mantricker stole softly through the forest. Silently, he crept along the same pathway where he had first seen Elona. The forest was alive with the rustling of the night creatures going about the business of survival. The young elf listened to this with only half an ear, the largest part of his attention focused on the business at hand, and the role he would play tonight.

Soon, Mantricker was standing just outside the village. All was quiet. The young elf noticed that many of the humans were already in their sleeping skins, and happily snoring away. *The tall ones are weak fools who toil in the heat of the day*, he thought. *Little wonder they have already retired to their huts*.

Mantricker walked boldly through the village, past the small plain huts of the younger couples and the larger, more elaborate huts with woven designs on the roofs that belonged to the elder hunters and their families. The cooking fire at the center of the circle of huts was already cold, Mantricker discovered, as he touched it when he passed, thus confirming his suspicion that there would be no insomniac stargazers around to unwittingly witness his entrance. Even he was astonished by his boldness, as he crept right into Elona's family hut and tapped her gently on the shoulder. As she wakened in terror and confusion, Mantricker's hand closed across her mouth to quiet her inadvertant cries. Recognizing the intruder, Elona ceased her struggling and grew quiet. Calmly, she reached up and removed the elf's hand from her mouth. Then, rising silently, Mantricker motioned for her to follow him. He looked nervously around at her slumbering family, but they slept on as if dead, totally unaware of his presence.

Elona was pleased, though not completely surprised, that her rescuer had finally come for her. *He is, after all, a hero*, she thought, *and a forest spirit at that. I knew it was only a matter of time before he had to come back for me, to show me his world, to share it. But how like him to be so bold as to steal into my parents' hut in the middle of the night.*

Now, she thought, *I will have tales to astonish even my father when I return.* With that, Elona gathered up her cloak and followed her hero out into the wood, leaving the village behind her without so much as a backward glance.

Once in the forest, Elona found her surroundings dark and more than a bit forbidding. All around her, the foliage seemed to produce strange sounds, noises which stopped abruptly as she drew near to their source. Elona was keenly aware of the shadows that enveloped her and felt her breath catch in her throat as all the chilling tales of shadow-demons who devoured wayward children whole suddenly came back to her, unbidden. She knew the half-glimpsed motion at the corner of her eye was only the product of her imagination. At least, she hoped it was only her imagination. All around her, Elona saw shapes that might merely be branches, or perhaps something more. And those bulky shadows to the side of the pathway were only bushes, weren't they? Well, weren't they? Perhaps. Then again, perhaps not. After all, the forest was not a place where even her father would venture after the sun had set, let alone in the fullness of the night.

Elona glanced over at Mantricker, studying his lean muscular body, his pointed spirit-ears so keenly able to hear the truth of the forest's mutterings, and she felt reassured.

He would know if there was any danger here, she thought, *and he would boldly chase it off with a wave of his spear*.

Mantricker turned to Elona and pointed farther down the pathway. Her mind was still crowded with visions of horrific demon-beasts, but she brushed them away impatiently.

He is a hero, my spirit-man, she thought. *Others might find the forest at night a dangerous place, but I have* him *here to protect me. This is his special place, and he would never let anything harm me here.* And, her own courage thus restored, she walked beside him with confidence.

Time passed as the two walked closely together through the darkness, the silence between them strangely comforting. They were far from the village now, and well into the forest. Finally, Mantricker pulled Elona from the pathway and into the underbrush. He turned to her and explained in his halting human-tongue, "We must go this way now, or your people will find us too quickly. There are many things I need to tell you, but not here."

Mantricker turned, expecting her to follow him into the heart of the pathless forest, as he picked his way past the brambles that blocked their way. Soon they were past the brambles and into a part of the benighted wood that Elona had never seen before. It was majestic, crowned with tall branches high overhead. The forest floor was scattered with wildflowers and sprawling creepers. As they walked side by side, Mantricker began to speak once more, weaving tales of the many adventures that he'd had before he'd met her, consciously acting out the role of the romantic figure Elona had dreamed of.

"I remember clearly all the sunrises I have watched alone over the turn of the seasons in the many faraway lands I have seen," said Mantricker. "I have watched the black-necks travel in herds as boundless as the sky and swum in rivers of bottomless green beside silverfins the size of trees. Many would be frightened by such things, but I knew you would not be one of them."

Mantricker knew that Elona saw him, not as he truly was, but as she needed him to be. Thus he continued to expand upon his tales, making them even more sweeping in scope.

"I spend most of my days protecting my people, and in that time I have had no one with whom to share all this. I have longed to find another like myself who might understand me, but my people are a timid lot, afraid to explore the wondrous bounties of life with me. I knew you were different when I first saw you. Your bravery told me you would be unafraid to taste of all I have to share."

Mantricker turned to look at her, and Elona felt something stir within her. *By the gods, he is lonely*, she thought with surprise. *With all that he has done, all that he has seen, he still has no one with whom to share the world's beauty.* She felt honored that he had chosen her to tell of his particular loneliness. *He is a chief without equals. Yet for all his power as a spirit-man, he still cannot command someone to understand him.* She gazed at him with new admiration, as she began to speculate what bright miracle had made him choose her above all others.

We are so alike, he and I, she thought. *He knew this even before I did. As no one in the village understands me, so too do none of his fellow spirits understand him.* She considered carefully what he was telling her, as she thought about the accident of chance that had first brought them together. *I know that I can grow to see the forest as he does, that his love of it can be my love of it. Together we can bring both our peoples closer together. We can conquer our differences by understanding one another. Our people can live side by side. We will become legends to our children and they will sing of our triumphs at the feast fires for generations to come.* Elona smiled as Mantricker continued talking of the many adventures they would soon share.

"We will explore new places where no one else has ever been," said Mantricker. "I want to share the sunset with you as it glints on the high mountains, and watch the boundless black-neck graze in the endless valleys to the south. There are hills where the caves are filled with their own inner light and plains beyond that which even I have never seen. And I want to discover them all with you."

"But where will we go first?" Elona asked in awe. "And how will we get there?"

Her hero only looked at her and smiled. "We do not need to concern ourselves with such matters now," he answered, "for we are above such petty things. We will have the whole of the world to travel and explore, and we will share these adventures together, my brave one."

Elona listened to him, and suddenly wasn't so sure if she was really his "brave one" at all, as she began to realize that she might never see her family or friends or anything else she knew, ever again.

But is that so bad a thing? she wondered. *Father has never believed me, and Mother never really supports me. I doubt they'll even notice that I'm gone. But when I return, perhaps they'll see me in a different light.* She paused for a moment. Mantricker was watching her.

Well, she thought, *that is,* if *I return.*

Now Elona began to remember the times she would play with her little brother, and the prayer-songs she was still learning from the old wise woman in the village. She would miss those.

"Couldn't we travel for just a little while, and then come back?" she asked Mantricker, as he glanced at her from the corner of his eye. She was beginning to have her doubts now, that much he could see. But he showed her no such doubts in return. Instead he merely took her hand and sat her down on a fallen tree above the riverbank. He stared deep into her trusting eyes, a twinge of regret for what he was about to put her through being impatiently pushed aside as he set the final scene.

"We must go now, little one, or we will have no time to spare before your people discover you gone," he said. "I know they must value you as much as I do, so we must leave this area immediately."

Mantricker pulled Elona to her feet once more, then paused. Even as he did, Elona suddenly heard a terrifying roar rising from the darkness. Before either of them could move, a huge shaggy beast came crashing out of the underbrush toward them. Though it ran on four legs, like any other beast of the forest, this behemoth was like no forest beast that Elona had ever before seen. Its fur was shaggy, and seemed to be at least six or seven different shades of brown and gray, all at the same time. Her eyes widened as the creature rushed toward her, and she could have sworn she saw two heads where only one should have been. The beast stank of dampness and of foul things left long in the back of old caves, a rank odor that was accentuated by the deep angry growling that seemed to come from both its throats.

The hideous creature hurled itself at Elona, but suddenly Mantricker stood between them. He thrust Elona aside at the last possible instant and caught the brunt of the monster's onslaught full in the chest, the impact knocking him back off his feet. The beast was upon him in an instant, and Mantricker struggled with it valiantly, his efforts obviously aimed at pulling the creature away from the terrified Elona, as she watched in dumbstruck silence, frozen by her fear.

As Elona stood rooted to the spot, the elf and the monster wrestled back and forth across the ground, rolling over the surrounding bushes and spilling out into the riverbank itself. Sometimes it seemed as if the behemoth's grip on Mantricker's shoulder would ultimately reach around to his throat, but each time Mantricker somehow managed to evade those deadly fangs.

As the battle continued, Mantricker put his hands around the beast's throat and strained to turn its gigantic misshapen body around. Instead, they both lost their footing and tumbled slowly down the riverbank into the azure waters, where they splashed and struggled for a few minutes more.

Shaking herself from her terrified trance, Elona shouted her savior's name. Mantricker turned once in the water to look at her, then suddenly the beast was upon him once more, its sheer weight plunging them both beneath the surface. Mantricker's arm rose from the roiling flow one last time, almost as if waving at Elona, then he and his attacker both sank below the surface, and disappeared from sight.

Elona screamed.

The minutes felt like hours as she scanned the rushing river, praying in vain for some small sign of her spirit-hero. But not even a stray bubble broke the water's surface to indicate his survival. Elona stood on the riverbank fearfully, crying in silence, her hopes slowly dying as she waited for her spirit-man to surface.

But, of course, he never did.

Finally, heartbroken, Elona turned from the river's edge.

She had long since shed all the tears she had in her, and their tracks stained her face as she headed back toward the path to her village. Her hero had sacrificed his life to save hers, but somehow she didn't feel honored as she thought one would when she'd heard of such things in the tales. All she felt was loss. A terrible sense of irreplaceable loss and fear, now that she was walking through the darkness alone and unprotected. Sorrowfully, Elona hurried along the pathway, back toward the safety of her village and her family hut. Suddenly she did not feel herself to be the stuff of which legends are made, but rather a fearful little girl lost alone in the forest.

From the hidden shelter of the thick reeds on the opposite bank of the river, a dripping Mantricker silently observed Elona's tearful departure. For an instant, as he watched her go, the young elf wondered if perhaps they could really have gone and found those distant sunrises he had spoken of so eloquently.

But no, he quickly realized, those were merely stories he had told to persuade the weeping woman-child. Or were they? As Mantricker pondered, Bentclaw licked his face happily, then tried to shake the last of the river's water from his hide. The ugly old pelt the wolf had worn when he attacked his elf-friend now lay by the river's edge, having served its purpose in the creation of the "monster."

For a moment, Mantricker wondered if perhaps this had been too easy. But now, watching the she-cub leave, he knew he had done the right thing. His gaze followed her, as she looked fearfully around her, then headed back along the familiar pathway. She would think twice, the young elf knew, before venturing into this monster-laden forest again. And that should satisfy the other Wolfriders, he thought.

At last, when he was certain the girl was gone, Mantricker rose from the reeds and sat on the riverbank, scratching Bentclaw absentmindedly behind one ear and promising him countless ravvit hunts as a reward for his part in this adventure. The young chief-son found himself wondering how he had ever stumbled into playing the role of hero in the first place. He had done nothing but torment the she-cub from the beginning, and yet she persisted in seeing him as anything other than what he truly was.

Perhaps someday, Mantricker thought, *I will make sense of these humans.*

THE MIGHTY ADVENTURES OF CONAN

☐ ☐	55210-5	CONAN THE BOLD *John Maddox Roberts*	$3.95 Canada $4.95
☐ ☐	50094-6	CONAN THE CHAMPION *John Maddox Roberts*	$3.95 Canada $4.95
☐ ☐	51394-0	CONAN THE DEFENDER *Robert Jordan*	$3.95 Canada $4.95
☐ ☐	54264-9	CONAN THE DEFIANT *Steve Perry*	$6.95 Canada $8.95
☐ ☐	50096-2	CONAN THE FEARLESS *Steve Perry*	$3.95 Canada $4.95
☐ ☐	50998-6	CONAN THE FORMIDABLE *Steve Perry*	$7.95 Canada $9.50
☐ ☐	50690-1	CONAN THE FREE LANCE *Steve Perry*	$3.95 Canada $4.95
☐ ☐	50714-2	CONAN THE GREAT *Leonard Carpenter*	$3.95 Canada $4.95
☐ ☐	50961-7	CONAN THE GUARDIAN *Roland Green*	$3.95 Canada $4.95
☐ ☐	50860-2	CONAN THE INDOMITABLE *Steve Perry*	$3.95 Canada $4.95
☐ ☐	50997-8	CONAN THE INVINCIBLE *Robert Jordan*	$3.95 Canada $4.95

Buy them at your local bookstore or use this handy coupon:
Clip and mail this page with your order.

Publishers Book and Audio Mailing Service
P.O. Box 120159, Staten Island, NY 10312-0004

Please send me the book(s) I have checked above. I am enclosing $ _____
(please add $1.25 for the first book, and $.25 for each additional book to cover postage and handling.
Send check or money order only—no CODs).

Name _____
Address _____
City _____ State/Zip _____
Please allow six weeks for delivery. Prices subject to change without notice.